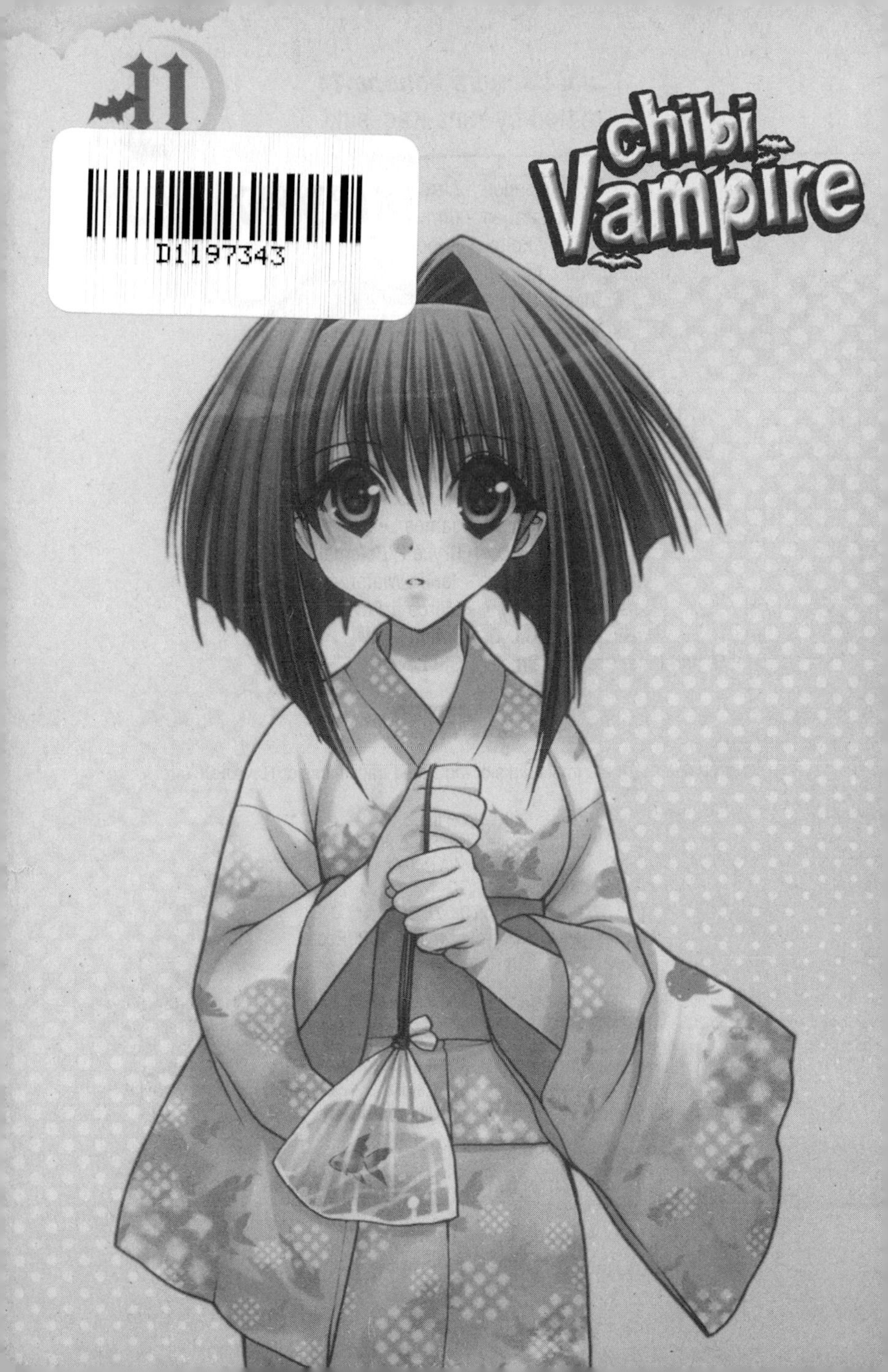
11
chibi Vampire

Chibi Vampire Volume 11
Created by Yuna Kagesaki

Translation - Alexis Kirsch
English Adaptation - Christine Boylan
Copy Editor - Hope Donovan
Retouch and Lettering - Star Print Brokers
Production Artist - Vince Rivera
Graphic Designer - Colin Graham

Editor - Alexis Kirsch
Pre-Production Supervisor - Vicente Rivera, Jr.
Pre-Production Specialist - Lucas Rivera
Managing Editor - Vy Nguyen
Senior Designer - Louis Csontos
Senior Designer - James Lee
Senior Editor - Bryce P. Coleman
Senior Editor - Jenna Winterberg
Associate Publisher - Marco F. Pavia
President and C.O.O. - John Parker
C.E.O. and Chief Creative Officer - Stu Levy

A **TOKYOPOP** Manga

TOKYOPOP and are trademarks or registered trademarks of TOKYOPOP Inc.

TOKYOPOP Inc.
5900 Wilshire Blvd. Suite 2000
Los Angeles, CA 90036

E-mail: info@TOKYOPOP.com
Come visit us online at www.TOKYOPOP.com

KARIN Volume 11 © 2007 YUNA KAGESAKI.
First published in Japan in 2007 by FUJIMISHOBO CO., LTD.,
Tokyo. English translation rights arranged with KADOKAWA
SHOTEN PUBLISHING CO., LTD., Tokyo through TUTTLE-MORI
AGENCY, INC., Tokyo.
English text copyright © 2008 TOKYOPOP Inc.

ISBN: 978-1-4278-0825-7

First TOKYOPOP printing: November 2008
10 9 8 7 6 5 4 3 2
Printed in the USA

Chibi Vampire

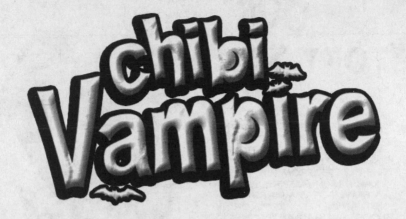

Volume 11

Created by
Yuna Kagesaki

TOKYOPOP®

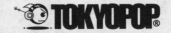

HAMBURG // LONDON // LOS ANGELES // TOKYO

OUR STORY SO FAR...

KARIN MAAKA ISN'T LIKE OTHER GIRLS. ONCE A MONTH, SHE EXPERIENCES PAIN, FATIGUE, HUNGER, IRRITABILITY—AND THEN SHE BLEEDS. FROM HER NOSE. KARIN IS A VAMPIRE, FROM A FAMILY OF VAMPIRES, BUT INSTEAD OF NEEDING TO DRINK BLOOD, SHE HAS AN EXCESS OF BLOOD THAT SHE MUST GIVE TO HER VICTIMS. IF DONE RIGHT, GIVING THIS BLOOD TO HER VICTIM CAN BE AN EXTREMELY POSITIVE THING. THE PROBLEM WITH THIS IS THAT KARIN NEVER SEEMS TO DO THINGS RIGHT...

KARIN IS HAVING A BIT OF BOY TROUBLE. KENTA USUI—THE HANDSOME NEW STUDENT AT HER SCHOOL AND WORK—IS A NICE ENOUGH GUY, BUT HE EXACERBATES KARIN'S PROBLEM. KARIN'S BLOOD PROBLEM, YOU SEE, BECOMES WORSE WHEN SHE'S AROUND PEOPLE WHO HAVE SUFFERED MISFORTUNE, AND KENTA HAS SUFFERED PLENTY OF IT. MAKING THINGS EVEN MORE COMPLICATED, IT'S BECOME CLEAR TO KARIN THAT SHE'S IN LOVE WITH KENTA... AND THIS BECOMES PAINFUL TO KARIN AS SHE SOON DISCOVERS THAT LOVE BETWEEN HUMANS AND VAMPIRES IS FROWNED UPON BECAUSE CHILDREN BETWEEN THE TWO SPECIES LACK REPRODUCTIVE ABILITIES. AS KARIN STRUGGLES WITH FEELING THAT SHE AND KENTA AREN'T MEANT TO BE TOGETHER BECAUSE OF THE DEFECTS WITH HER BODY, CHANGES SEEM TO BE HAPPENING TO HER LITTLE SISTER, ANJU...

THE MAAKA FAMILY

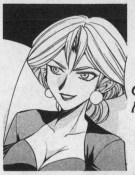

CALERA MARKER

Karin's overbearing mother. While Calera resents that Karin wasn't born a normal vampire, she does love her daughter in her own obnoxious way. Calera has chosen to keep her European last name.

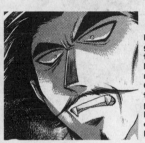

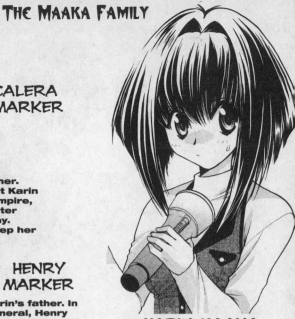

KARIN MAAKA

Our little heroine. Karin is a vampire living in Japan, but instead of sucking blood from her victims, she actually GIVES them some of her blood. She's a vampire in reverse!

HENRY MARKER

Karin's father. In general, Henry treats Karin a lot better than her mother does, but Calera wears the pants in this particular family. Henry has also chosen to keep his European last name.

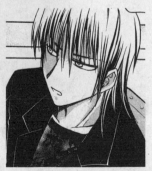

REN MAAKA

Karin's older brother. Ren milks the "sexy creature of the night" thing for all it's worth and spends his nights in the arms (and beds) of attractive young women.

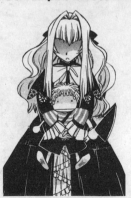

ANJU MAAKA

Karin's little sister. Anju has not yet awoken as a full vampire, but she can control bats and is usually the one who cleans up after Karin's messes. Rarely seen without her "talking" doll, Boogie.

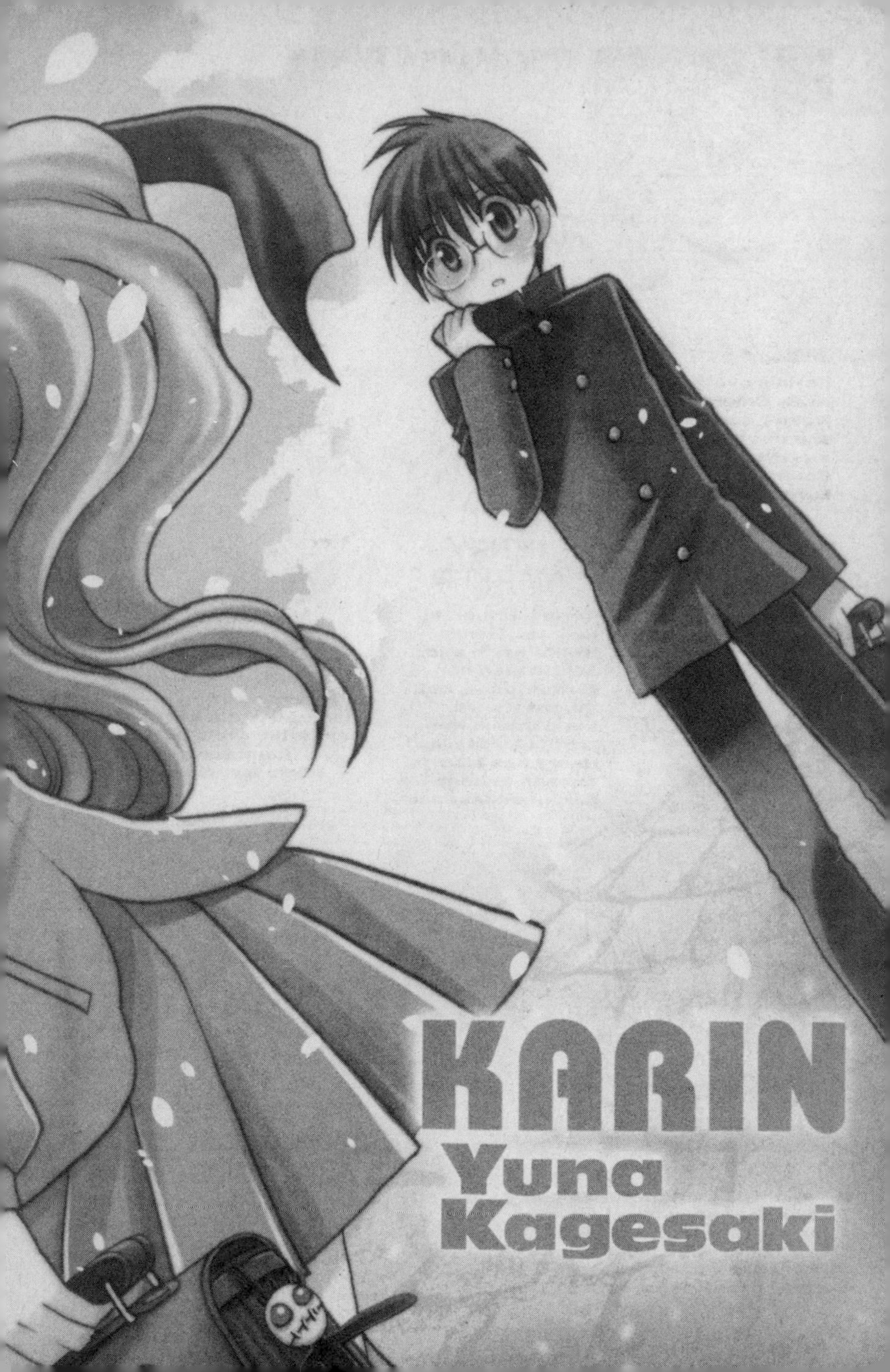
KARIN
Yuna
Kagesaki

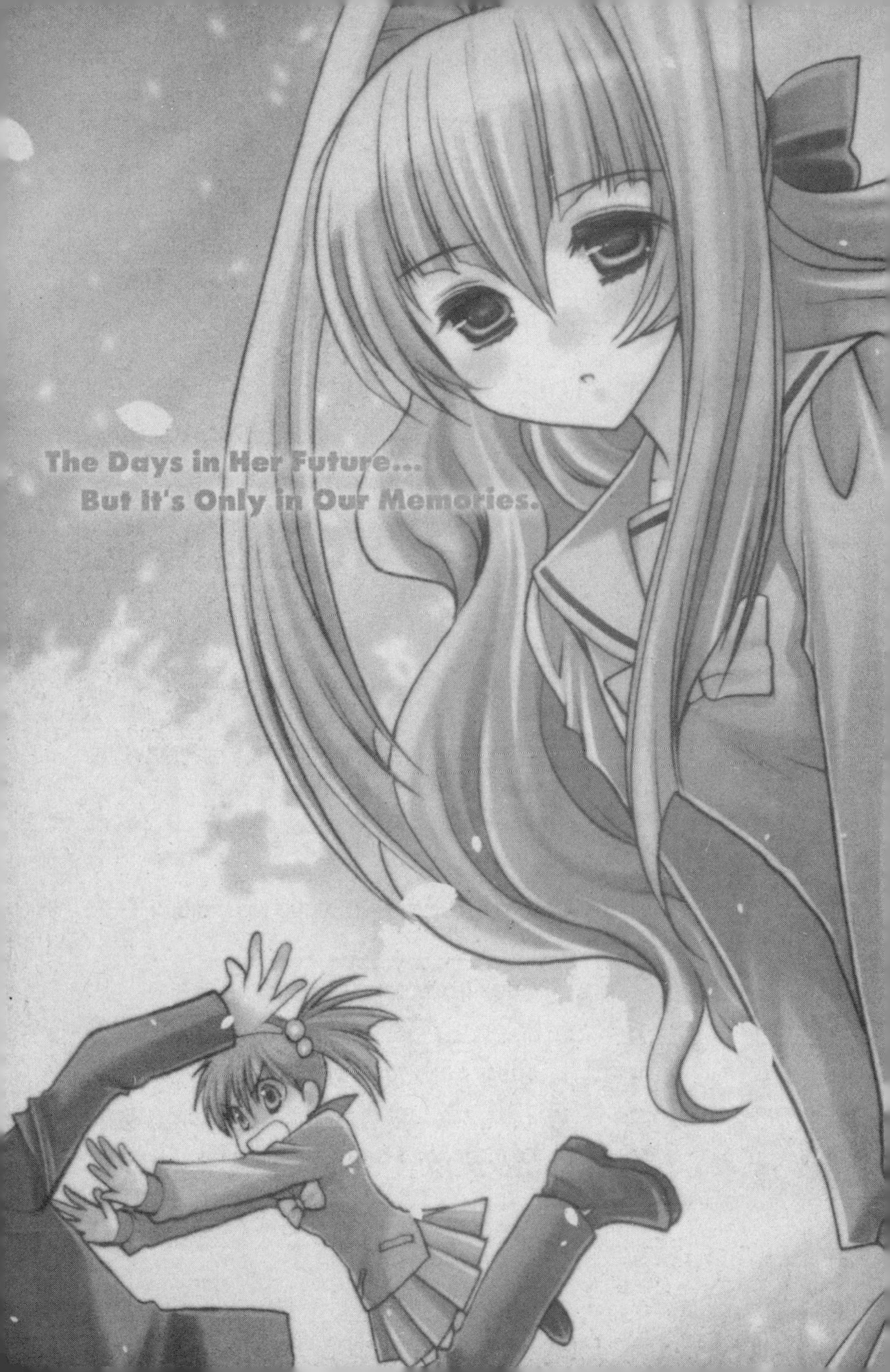
The Days in Her Future...
But It's Only in Our Memories.

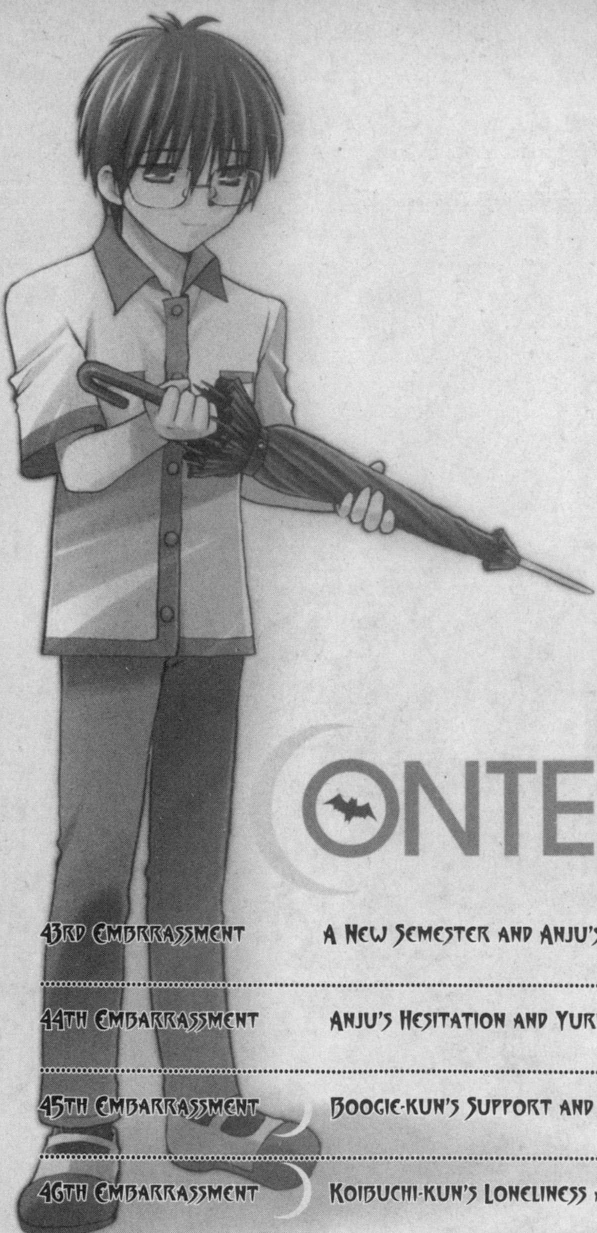

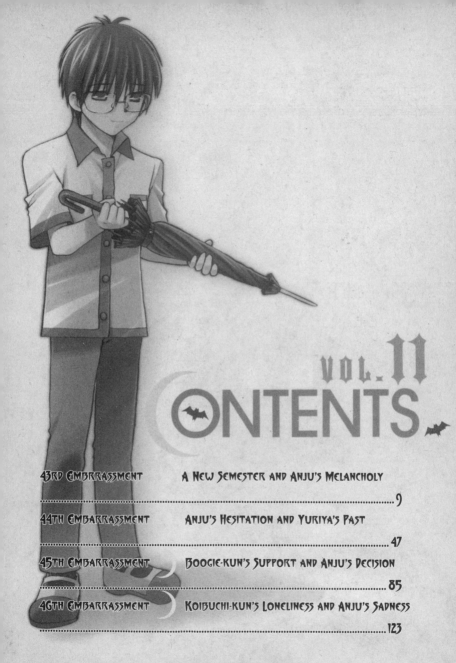

VOL. 11

CONTENTS

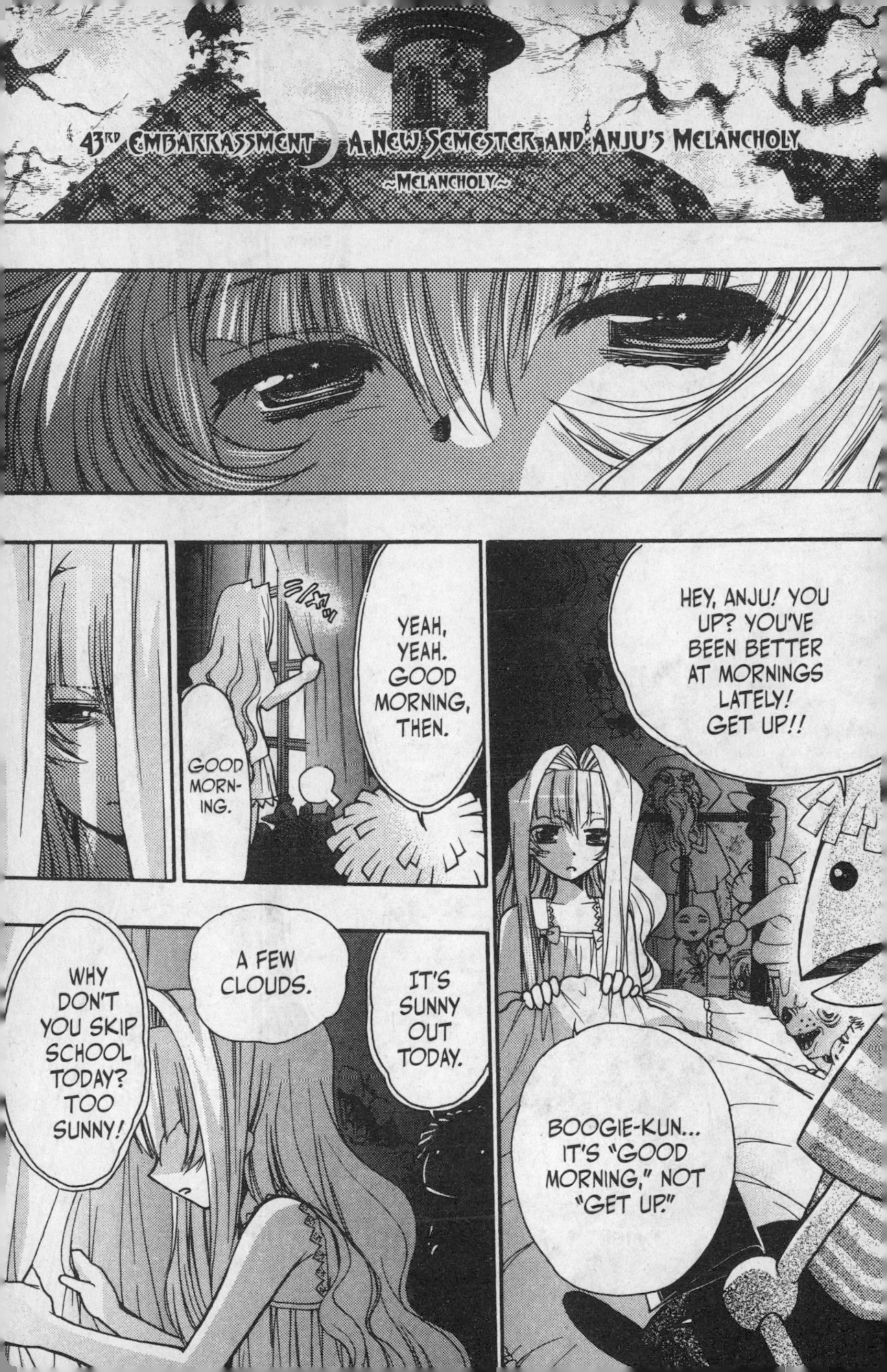
43RD EMBARRASSMENT A NEW SEMESTER AND ANJU'S MELANCHOLY
~MELANCHOLY~
HEY, ANJU! YOU UP? YOU'VE BEEN BETTER AT MORNINGS LATELY! GET UP!!
BOOGIE-KUN... IT'S "GOOD MORNING," NOT "GET UP."
YEAH, YEAH. GOOD MORNING, THEN.
GOOD MORNING.
IT'S SUNNY OUT TODAY.
A FEW CLOUDS.
WHY DON'T YOU SKIP SCHOOL TODAY? TOO SUNNY!

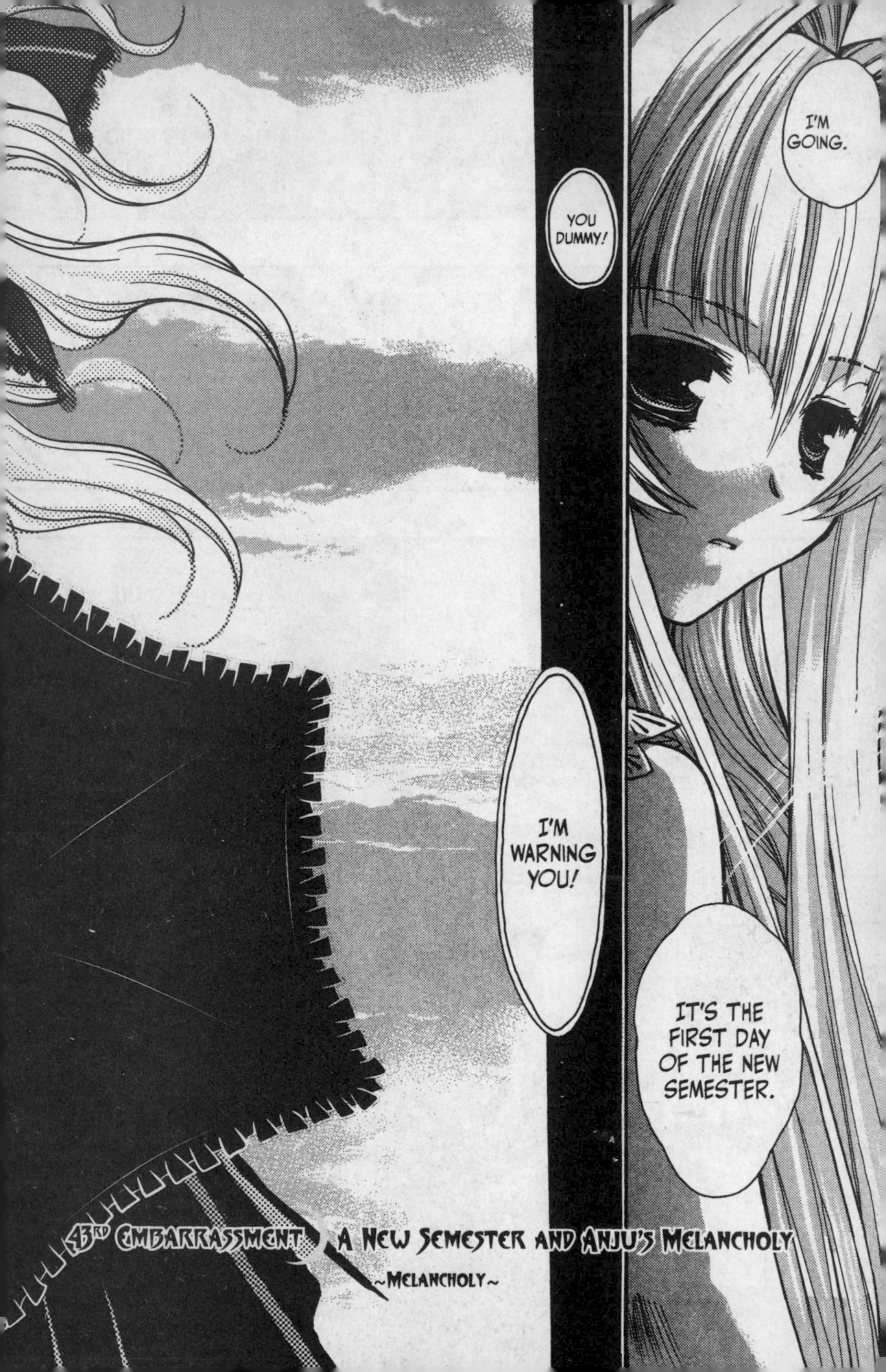
I'M GOING.
IT'S THE FIRST DAY OF THE NEW SEMESTER.
YOU DUMMY!
I'M WARNING YOU!
43rd Embarrassment A New Semester and Anju's Melancholy
~Melancholy~

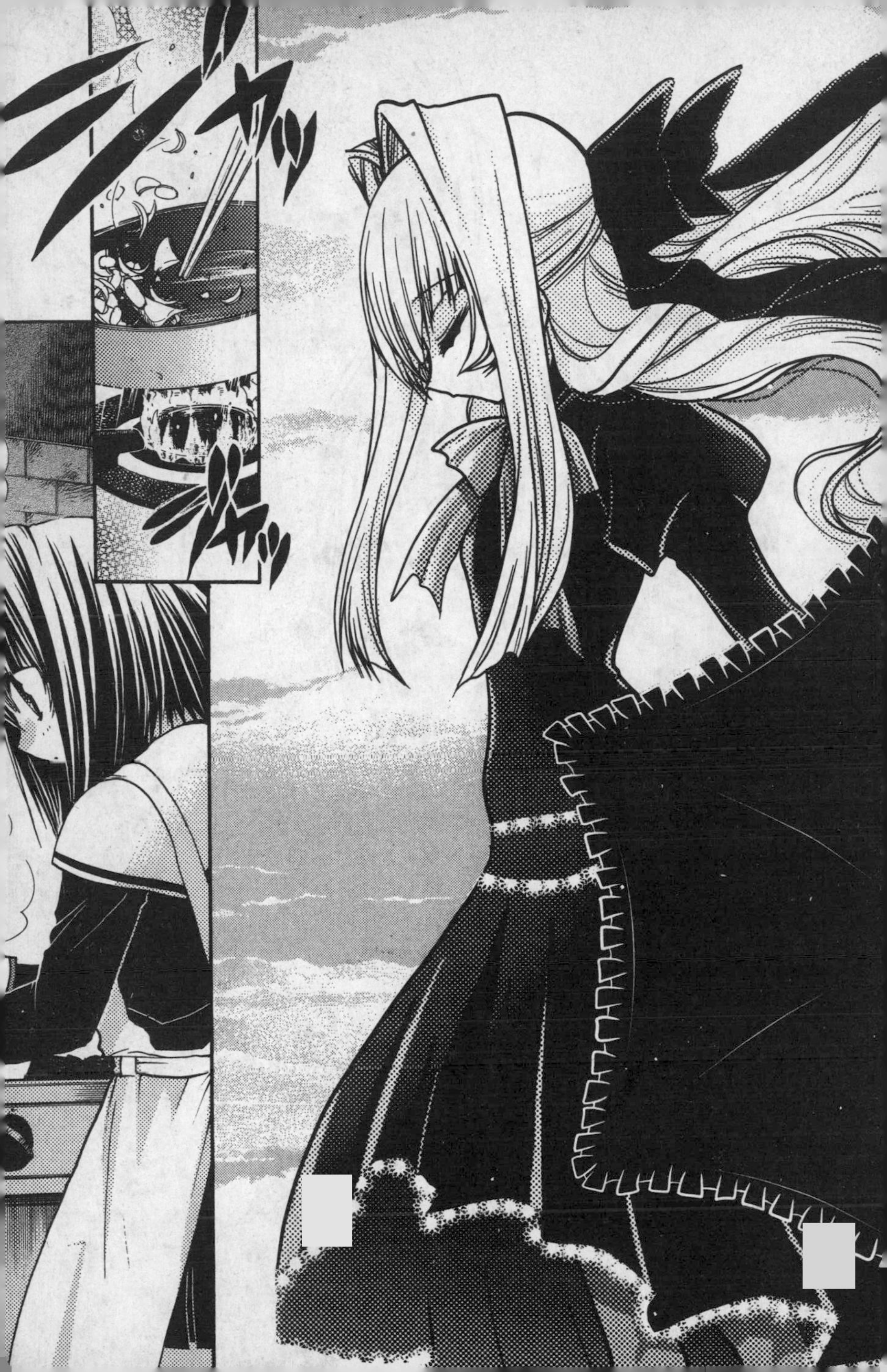

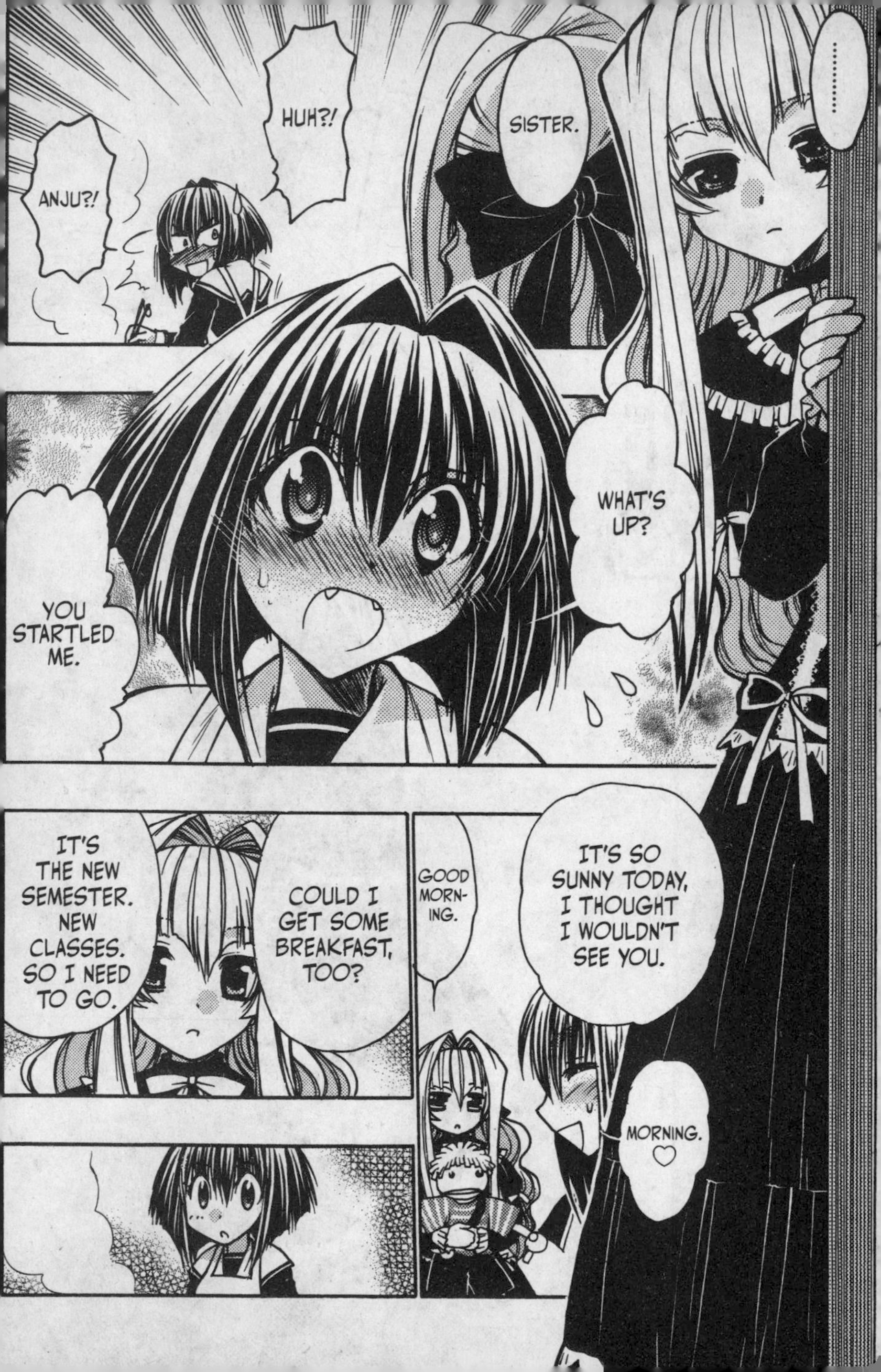
......
SISTER.
HUH?!
ANJU?!
WHAT'S UP?
YOU STARTLED ME.
IT'S SO SUNNY TODAY, I THOUGHT I WOULDN'T SEE YOU.
GOOD MORN-ING.
MORNING. ♡
COULD I GET SOME BREAKFAST, TOO?
IT'S THE NEW SEMESTER. NEW CLASSES. SO I NEED TO GO.

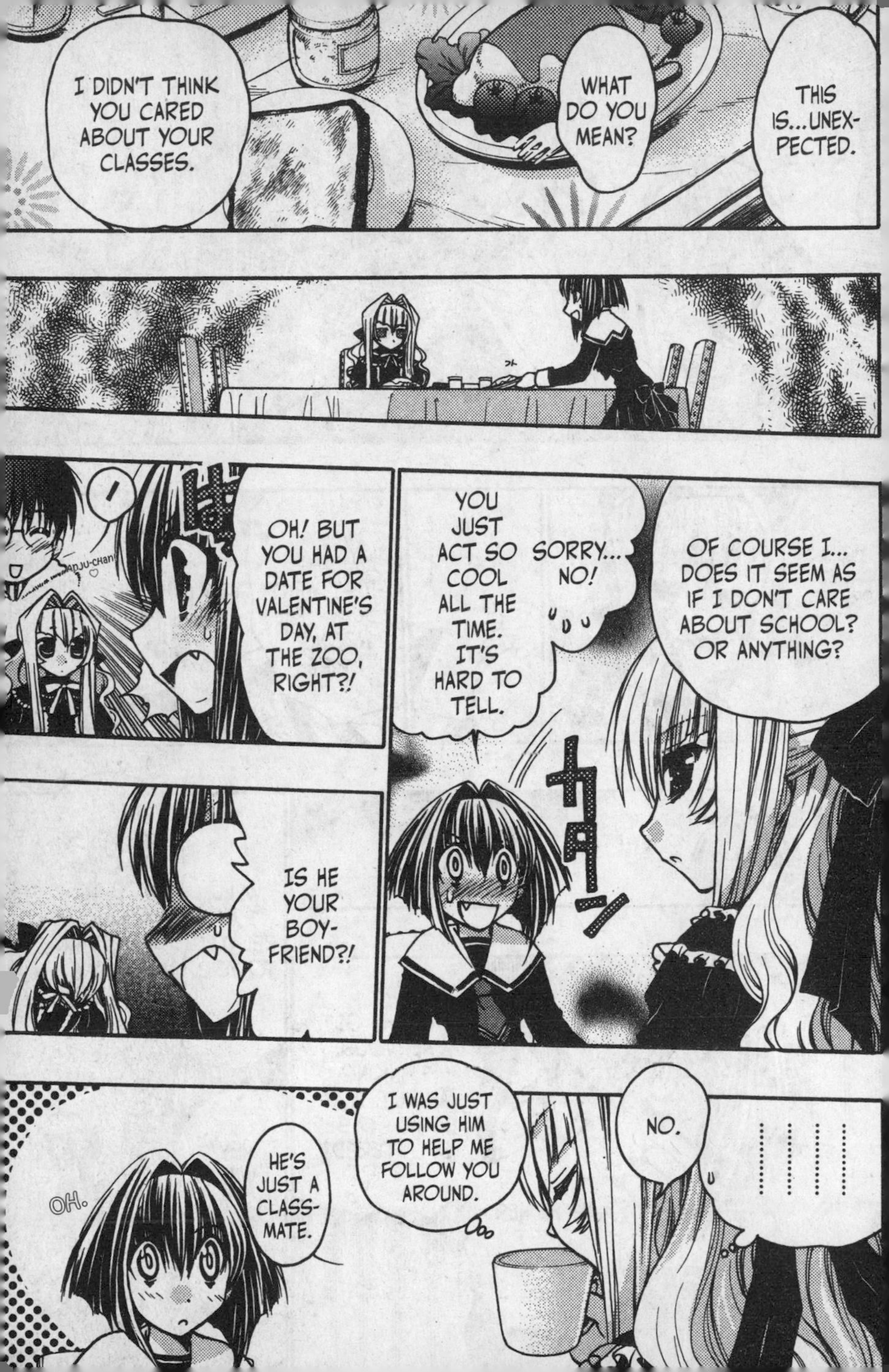
THIS IS...UNEXPECTED.
WHAT DO YOU MEAN?
I DIDN'T THINK YOU CARED ABOUT YOUR CLASSES.
OF COURSE I... DOES IT SEEM AS IF I DON'T CARE ABOUT SCHOOL? OR ANYTHING?
SORRY... NO!
YOU JUST ACT SO COOL ALL THE TIME. IT'S HARD TO TELL.
OH! BUT YOU HAD A DATE FOR VALENTINE'S DAY, AT THE ZOO, RIGHT?!
ANJU-CHAN! ♡
IS HE YOUR BOY-FRIEND?!
......
NO.
I WAS JUST USING HIM TO HELP ME FOLLOW YOU AROUND.
HE'S JUST A CLASSMATE.
OH.

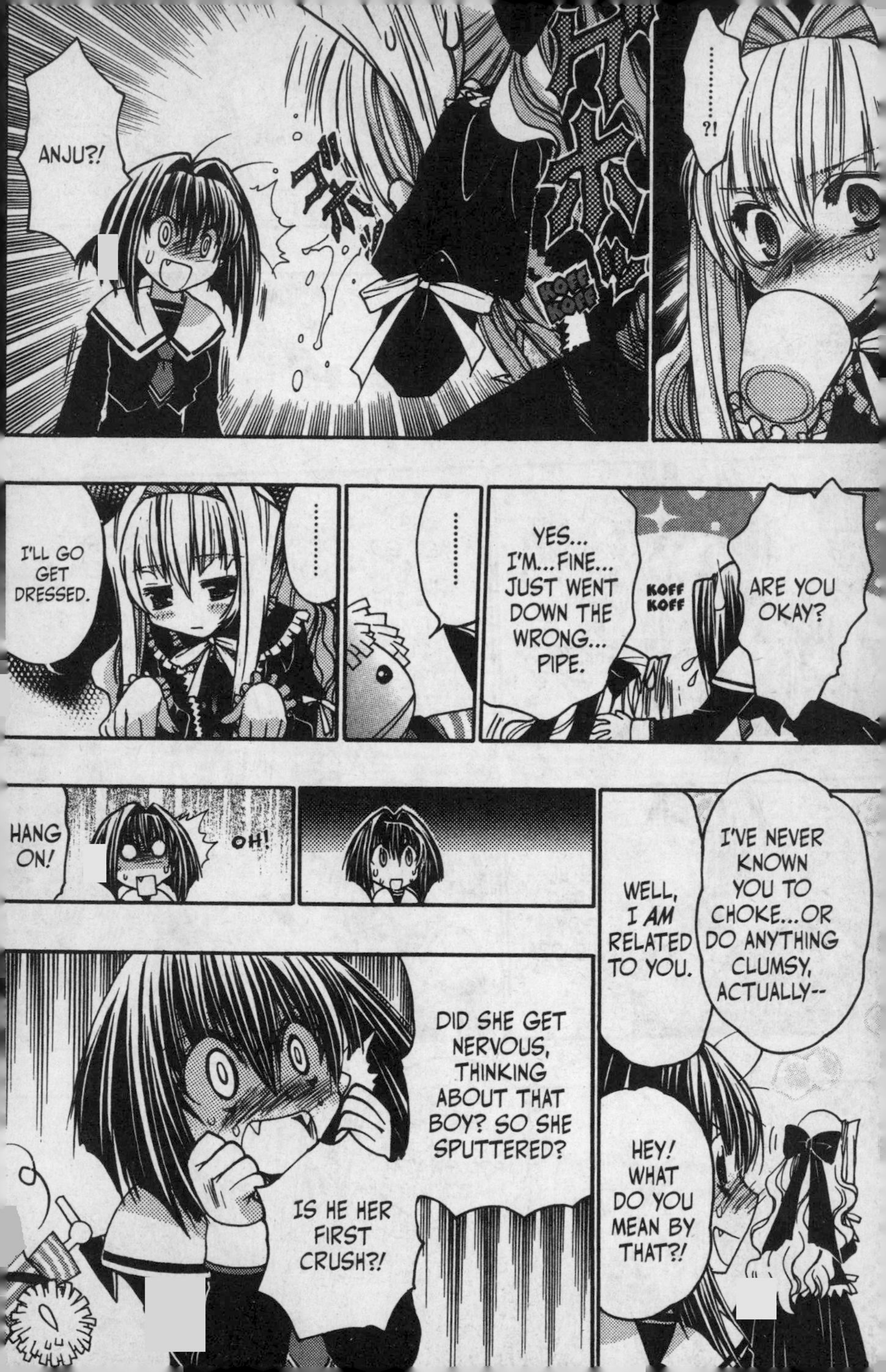
......?!
KOFF KOFF
ANJU?!
ARE YOU OKAY?
KOFF KOFF
YES... I'M...FINE... JUST WENT DOWN THE WRONG... PIPE.
....
I'LL GO GET DRESSED.
I'VE NEVER KNOWN YOU TO CHOKE...OR DO ANYTHING CLUMSY, ACTUALLY--
WELL, I *AM* RELATED TO YOU.
HEY! WHAT DO YOU MEAN BY THAT?!
OH!
HANG ON!
DID SHE GET NERVOUS, THINKING ABOUT THAT BOY? SO SHE SPUTTERED?
IS HE HER FIRST CRUSH?!

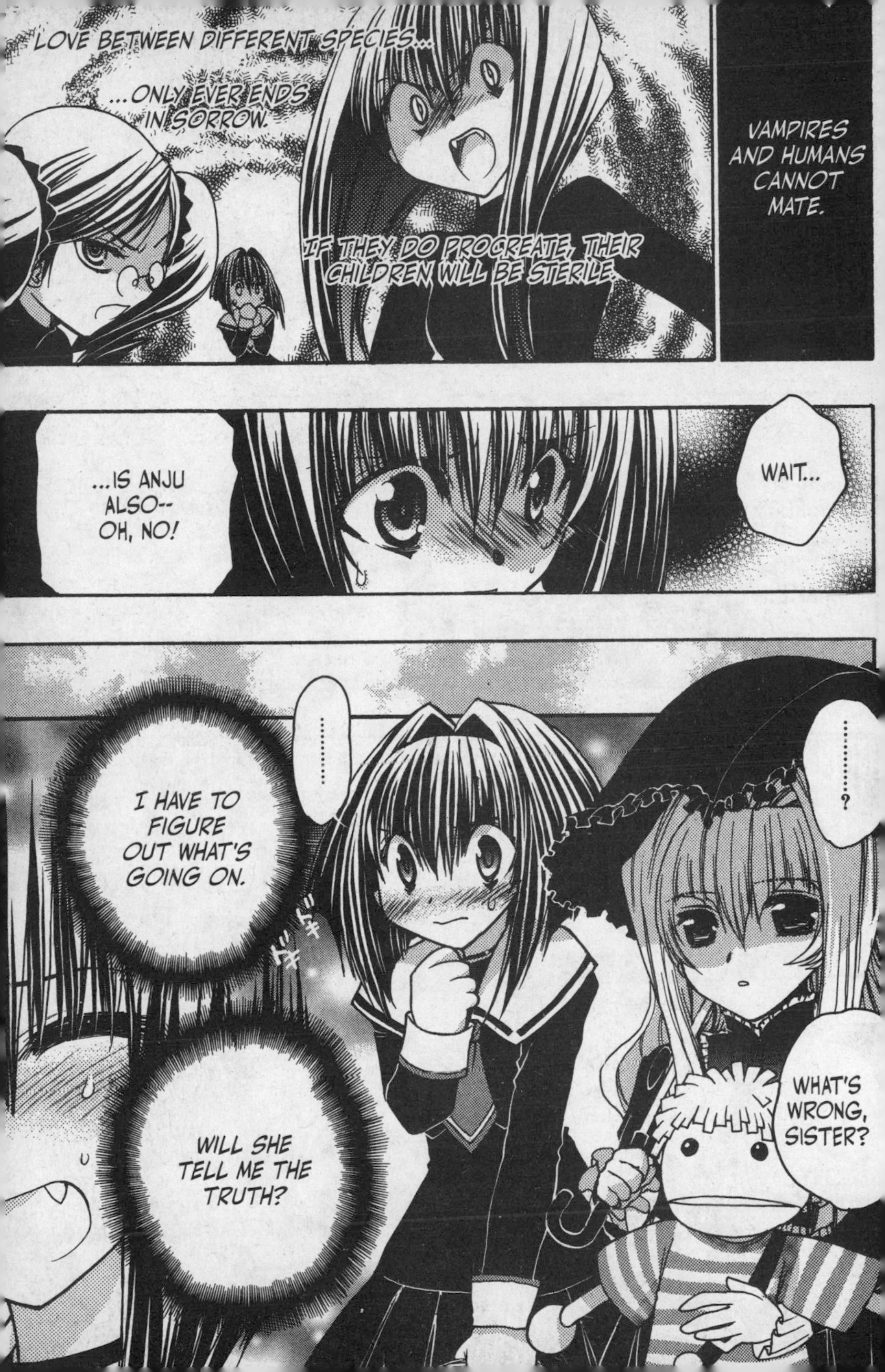
VAMPIRES AND HUMANS CANNOT MATE.
LOVE BETWEEN DIFFERENT SPECIES...
...ONLY EVER ENDS IN SORROW.
IF THEY DO PROCREATE, THEIR CHILDREN WILL BE STERILE.
WAIT...
...IS ANJU ALSO-- OH, NO!
......?
WHAT'S WRONG, SISTER?
......
I HAVE TO FIGURE OUT WHAT'S GOING ON.
WILL SHE TELL ME THE TRUTH?

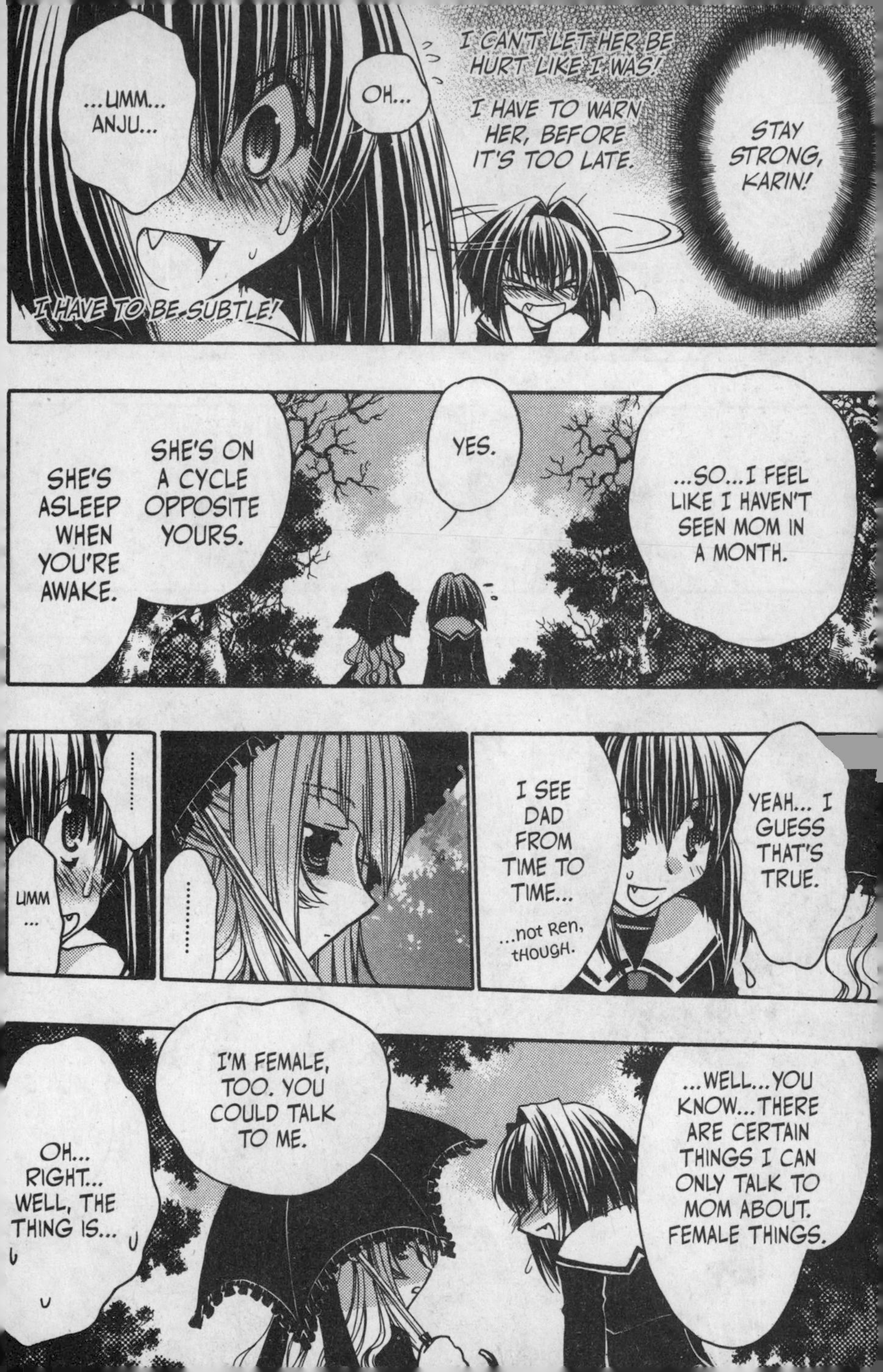
STAY STRONG, KARIN!
I CAN'T LET HER BE HURT LIKE I WAS!
I HAVE TO WARN HER, BEFORE IT'S TOO LATE.
OH...
...UMM... ANJU...
I HAVE TO BE SUBTLE!
...SO...I FEEL LIKE I HAVEN'T SEEN MOM IN A MONTH.
YES.
SHE'S ON A CYCLE OPPOSITE YOURS.
SHE'S ASLEEP WHEN YOU'RE AWAKE.
YEAH... I GUESS THAT'S TRUE.
I SEE DAD FROM TIME TO TIME...
...not Ren, tHOUGH.
....
....
UMM ...
...WELL...YOU KNOW...THERE ARE CERTAIN THINGS I CAN ONLY TALK TO MOM ABOUT. FEMALE THINGS.
I'M FEMALE, TOO. YOU COULD TALK TO ME.
OH... RIGHT... WELL, THE THING IS...

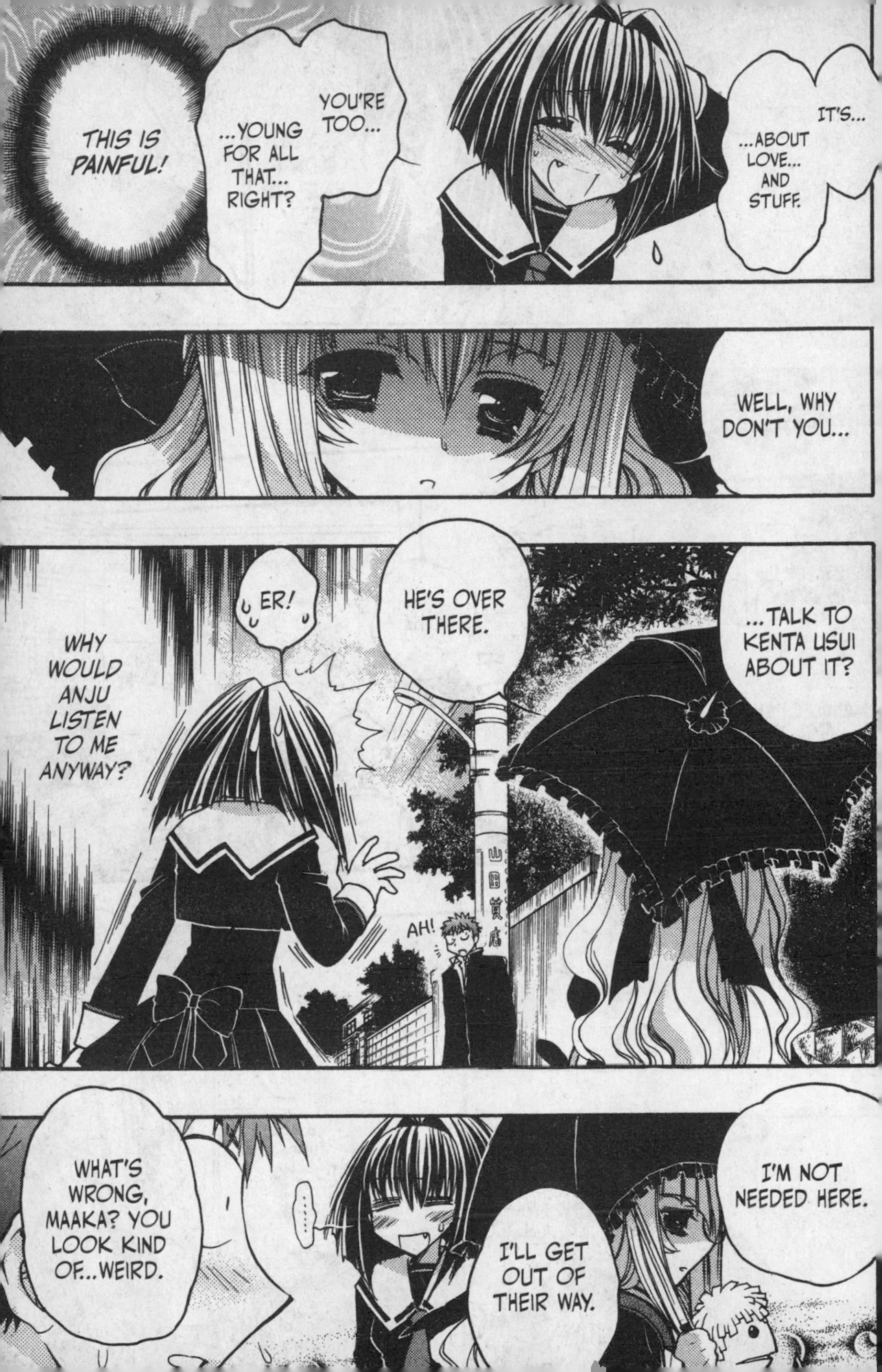
IT'S...
...ABOUT LOVE... AND STUFF.
YOU'RE TOO...
...YOUNG FOR ALL THAT... RIGHT?
THIS IS PAINFUL!
WELL, WHY DON'T YOU...
...TALK TO KENTA USUI ABOUT IT?
HE'S OVER THERE.
ER!
AH!
WHY WOULD ANJU LISTEN TO ME ANYWAY?
I'M NOT NEEDED HERE.
I'LL GET OUT OF THEIR WAY.
......
WHAT'S WRONG, MAAKA? YOU LOOK KIND OF...WEIRD.

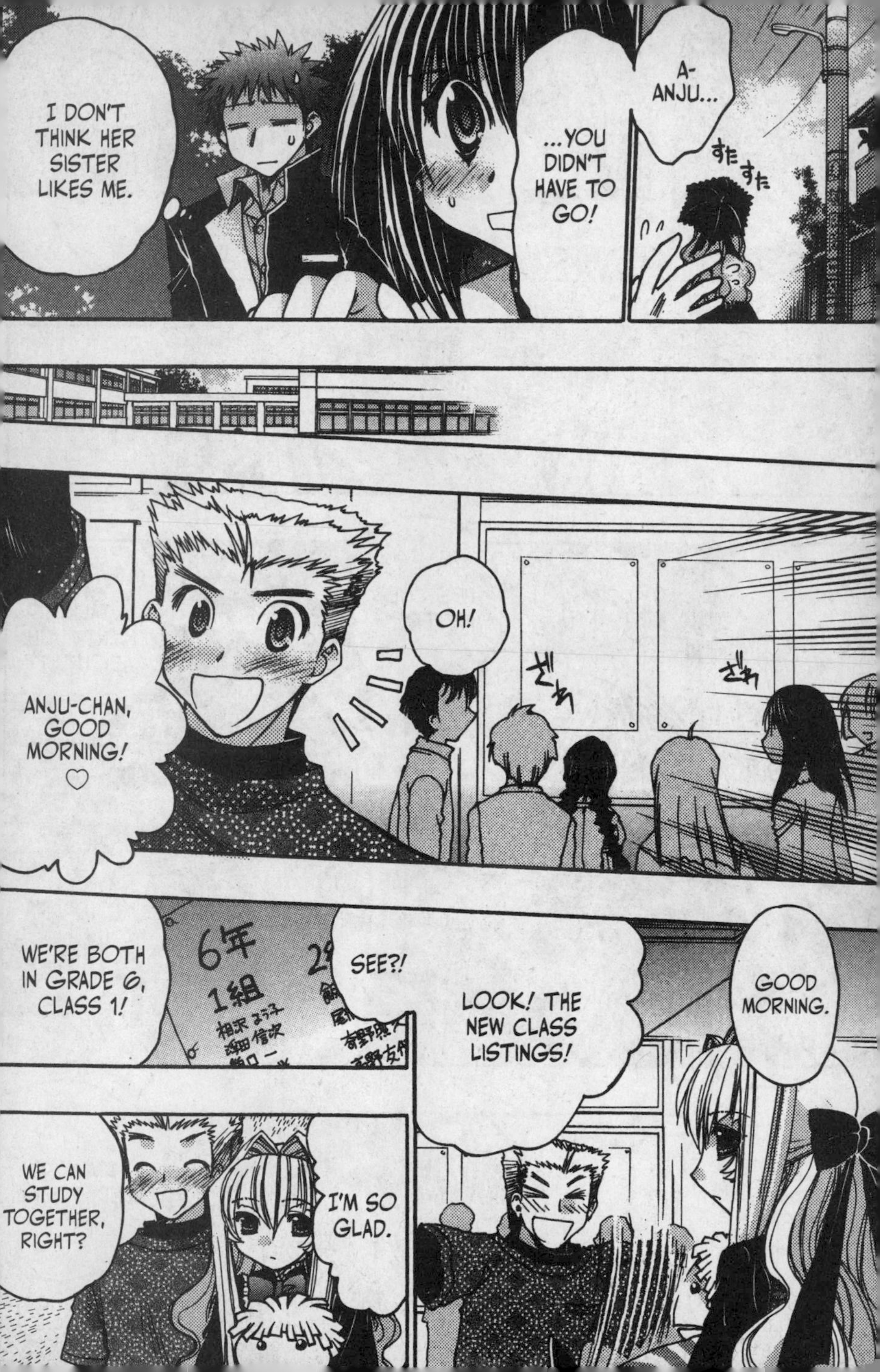
A- ANJU...
...YOU DIDN'T HAVE TO GO!
すたすた
I DON'T THINK HER SISTER LIKES ME.
OH!
ざわ
ざわ
ANJU-CHAN, GOOD MORNING! ♡
GOOD MORNING.
LOOK! THE NEW CLASS LISTINGS!
SEE?!
6年
1組
WE'RE BOTH IN GRADE 6, CLASS 1!
I'M SO GLAD.
WE CAN STUDY TOGETHER, RIGHT?

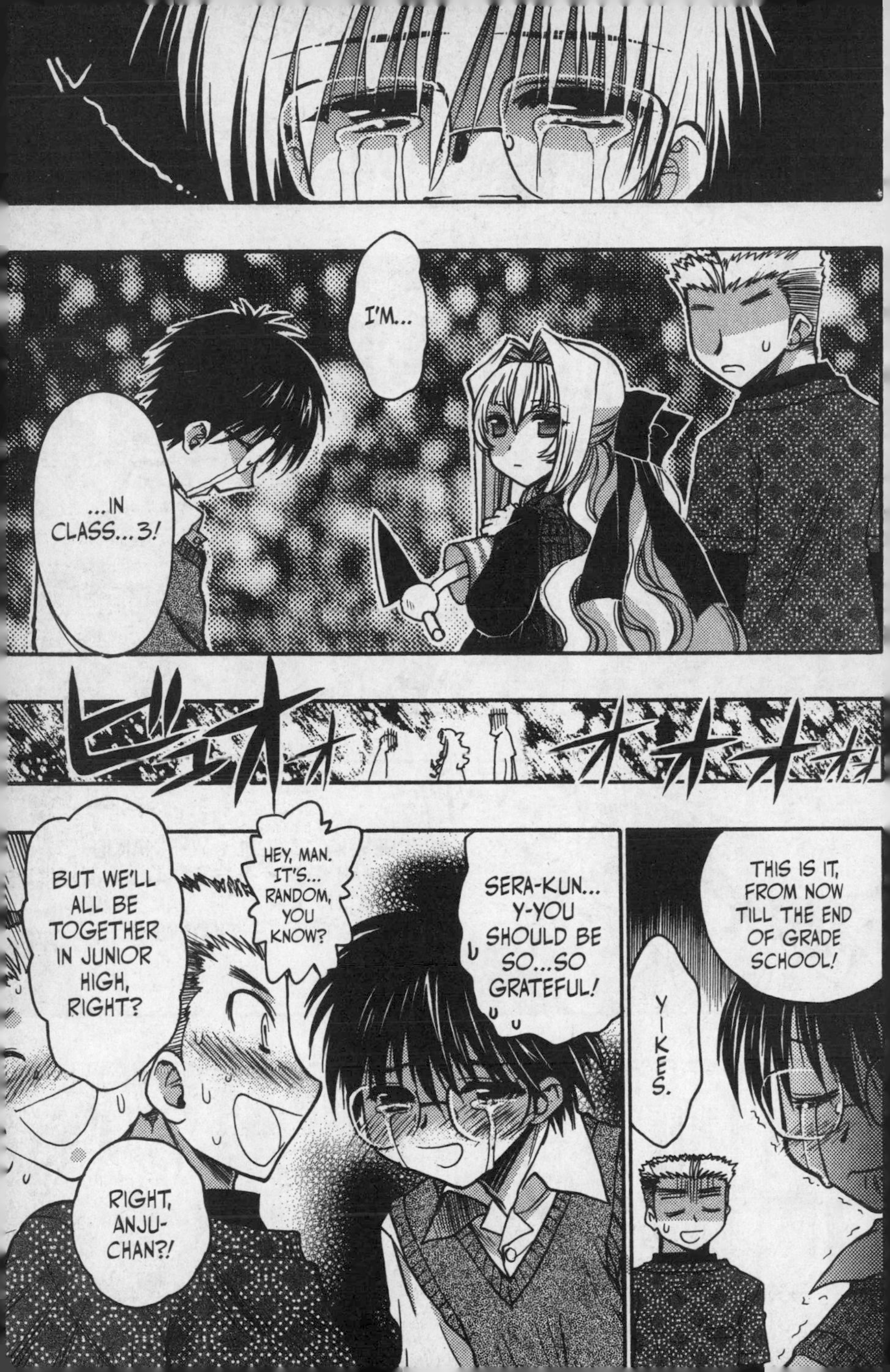
I'M...
...IN CLASS...3!
THIS IS IT, FROM NOW TILL THE END OF GRADE SCHOOL!
YIKES.
SERA-KUN... Y-YOU SHOULD BE SO...SO GRATEFUL!
HEY, MAN. IT'S... RANDOM, YOU KNOW?
BUT WE'LL ALL BE TOGETHER IN JUNIOR HIGH, RIGHT?
RIGHT, ANJU-CHAN?!

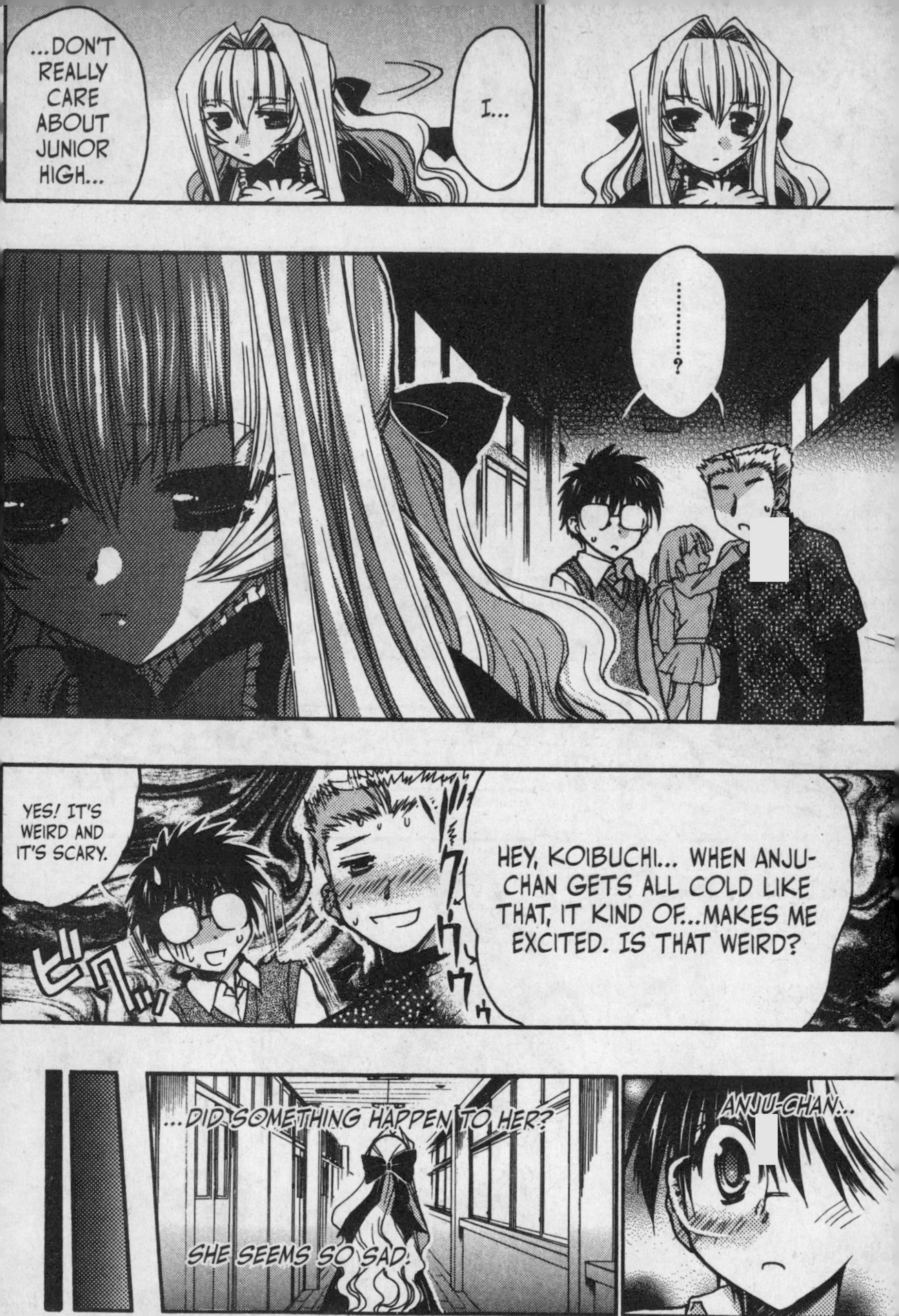
I...
...DON'T REALLY CARE ABOUT JUNIOR HIGH...
......?
HEY, KOIBUCHI... WHEN ANJU-CHAN GETS ALL COLD LIKE THAT, IT KIND OF...MAKES ME EXCITED. IS THAT WEIRD?
YES! IT'S WEIRD AND IT'S SCARY.
ANJU-CHAN...
...DID SOMETHING HAPPEN TO HER?
SHE SEEMS SO SAD.

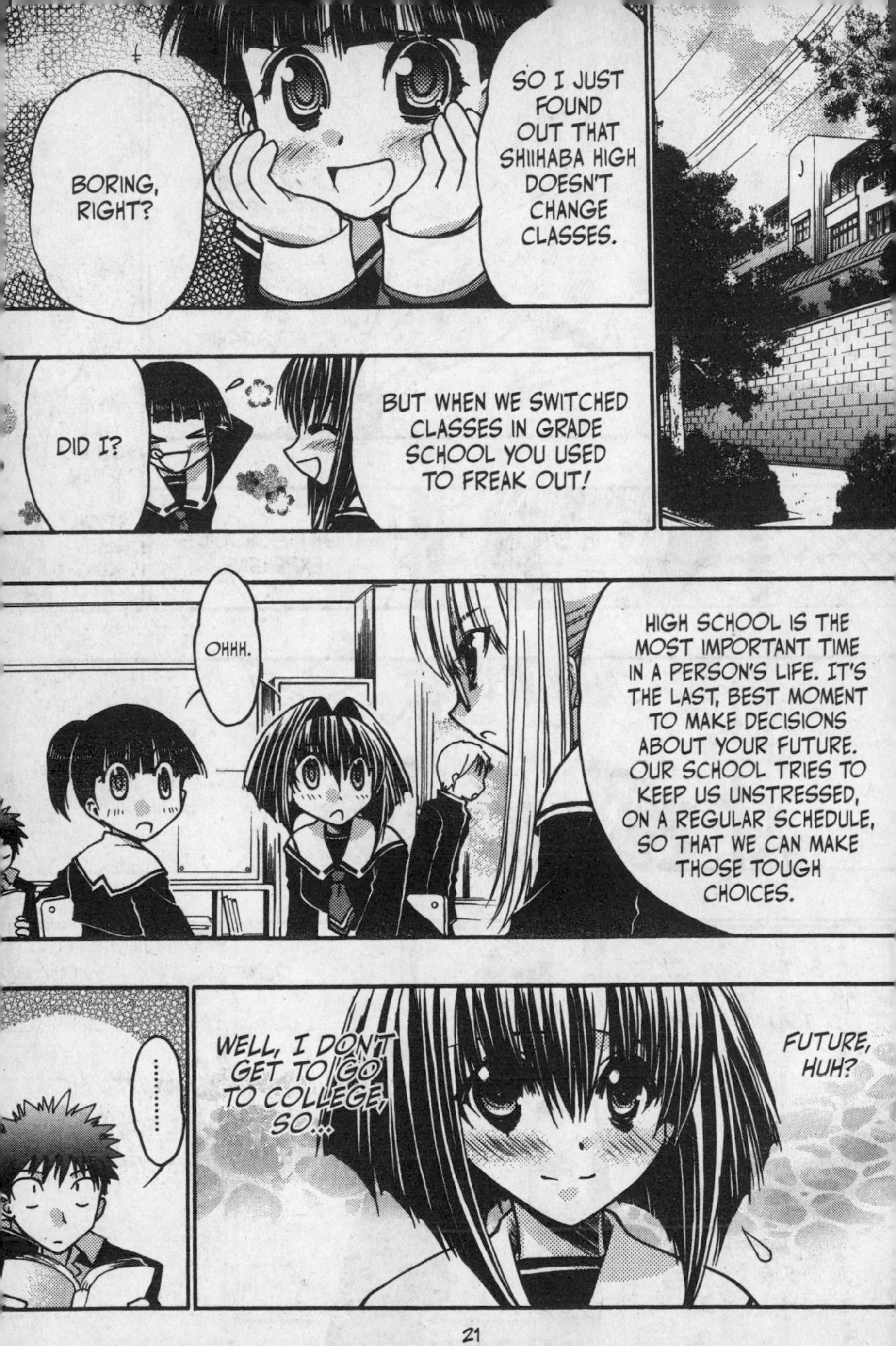
SO I JUST FOUND OUT THAT SHIIHABA HIGH DOESN'T CHANGE CLASSES.
BORING, RIGHT?
BUT WHEN WE SWITCHED CLASSES IN GRADE SCHOOL YOU USED TO FREAK OUT!
DID I?
HIGH SCHOOL IS THE MOST IMPORTANT TIME IN A PERSON'S LIFE. IT'S THE LAST, BEST MOMENT TO MAKE DECISIONS ABOUT YOUR FUTURE. OUR SCHOOL TRIES TO KEEP US UNSTRESSED, ON A REGULAR SCHEDULE, SO THAT WE CAN MAKE THOSE TOUGH CHOICES.
OHHH.
FUTURE, HUH?
WELL, I DON'T GET TO GO TO COLLEGE, SO...
....

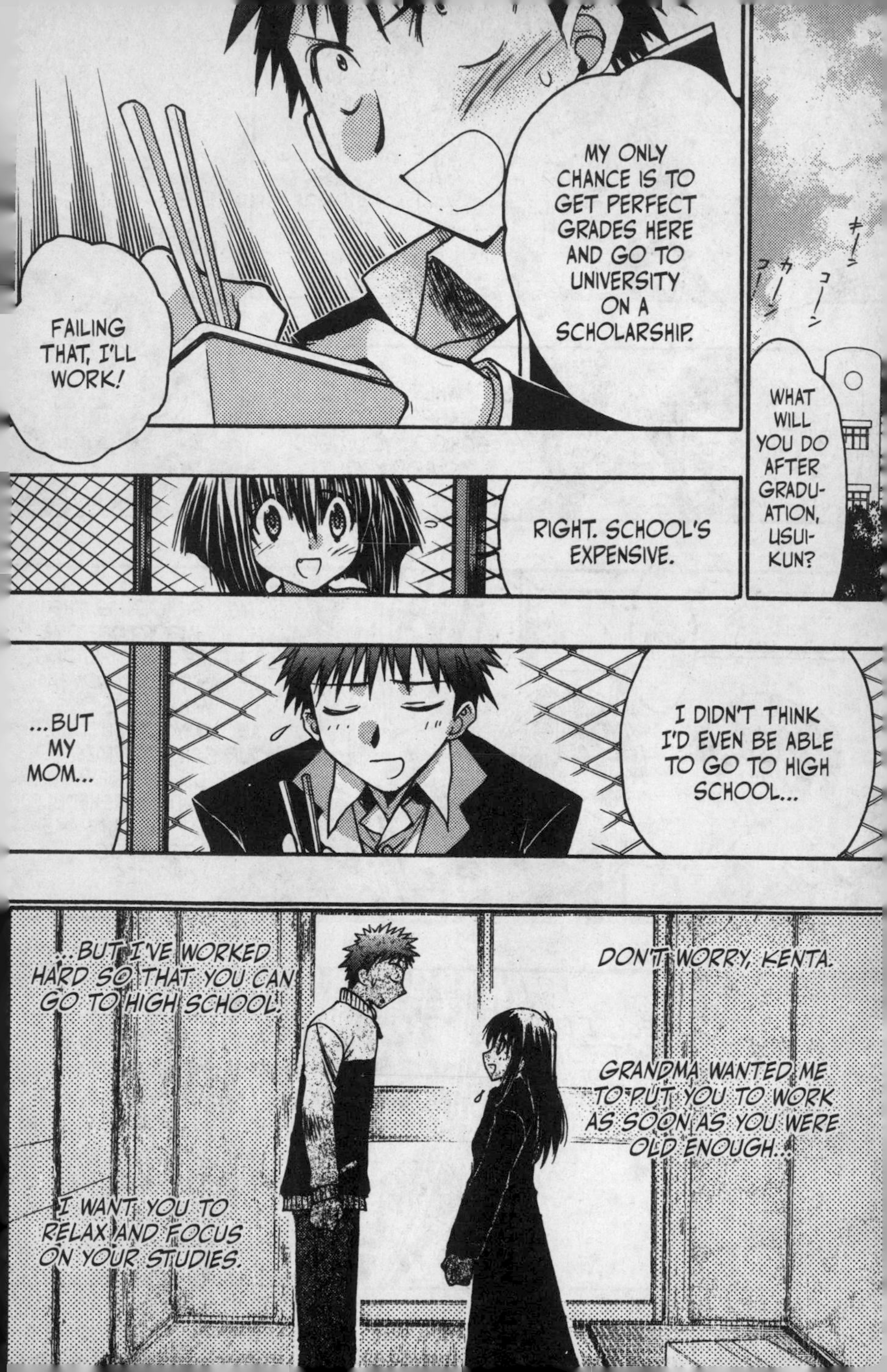

キーンコーン
カーンコーン
WHAT WILL YOU DO AFTER GRADUATION, USUI-KUN?
MY ONLY CHANCE IS TO GET PERFECT GRADES HERE AND GO TO UNIVERSITY ON A SCHOLARSHIP.
FAILING THAT, I'LL WORK!
RIGHT. SCHOOL'S EXPENSIVE.
I DIDN'T THINK I'D EVEN BE ABLE TO GO TO HIGH SCHOOL...
...BUT MY MOM...
DON'T WORRY, KENTA.
GRANDMA WANTED ME TO PUT YOU TO WORK AS SOON AS YOU WERE OLD ENOUGH...
...BUT I'VE WORKED HARD SO THAT YOU CAN GO TO HIGH SCHOOL.
I WANT YOU TO RELAX AND FOCUS ON YOUR STUDIES.

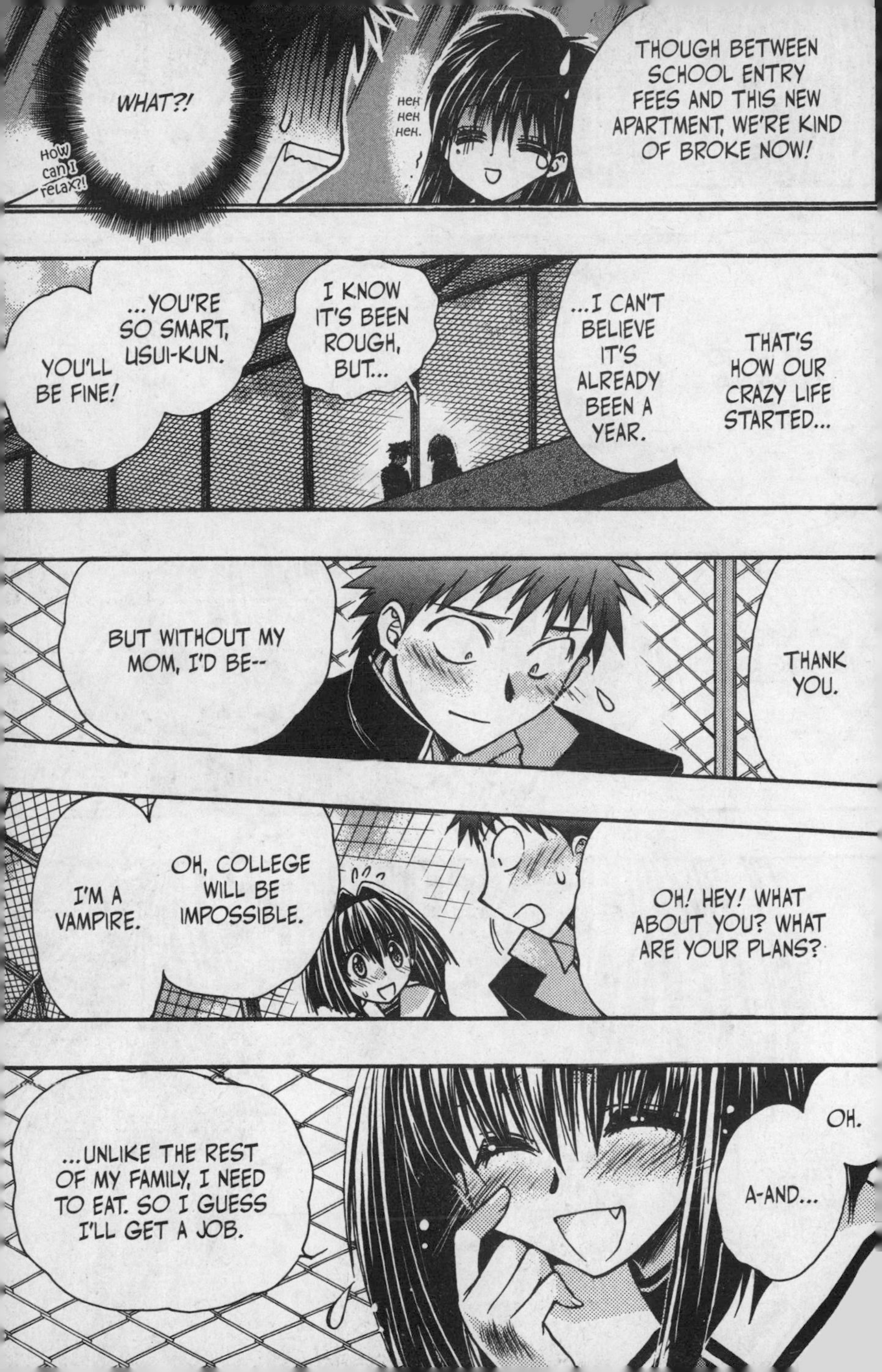

THOUGH BETWEEN SCHOOL ENTRY FEES AND THIS NEW APARTMENT, WE'RE KIND OF BROKE NOW!
HEH HEH HEH.
WHAT?!
HOW CAN I RELAX?!
THAT'S HOW OUR CRAZY LIFE STARTED...
...I CAN'T BELIEVE IT'S ALREADY BEEN A YEAR.
I KNOW IT'S BEEN ROUGH, BUT...
...YOU'RE SO SMART, USUI-KUN.
YOU'LL BE FINE!
THANK YOU.
BUT WITHOUT MY MOM, I'D BE--
OH! HEY! WHAT ABOUT YOU? WHAT ARE YOUR PLANS?
OH, COLLEGE WILL BE IMPOSSIBLE.
I'M A VAMPIRE.
OH.
A-AND...
...UNLIKE THE REST OF MY FAMILY, I NEED TO EAT. SO I GUESS I'LL GET A JOB.

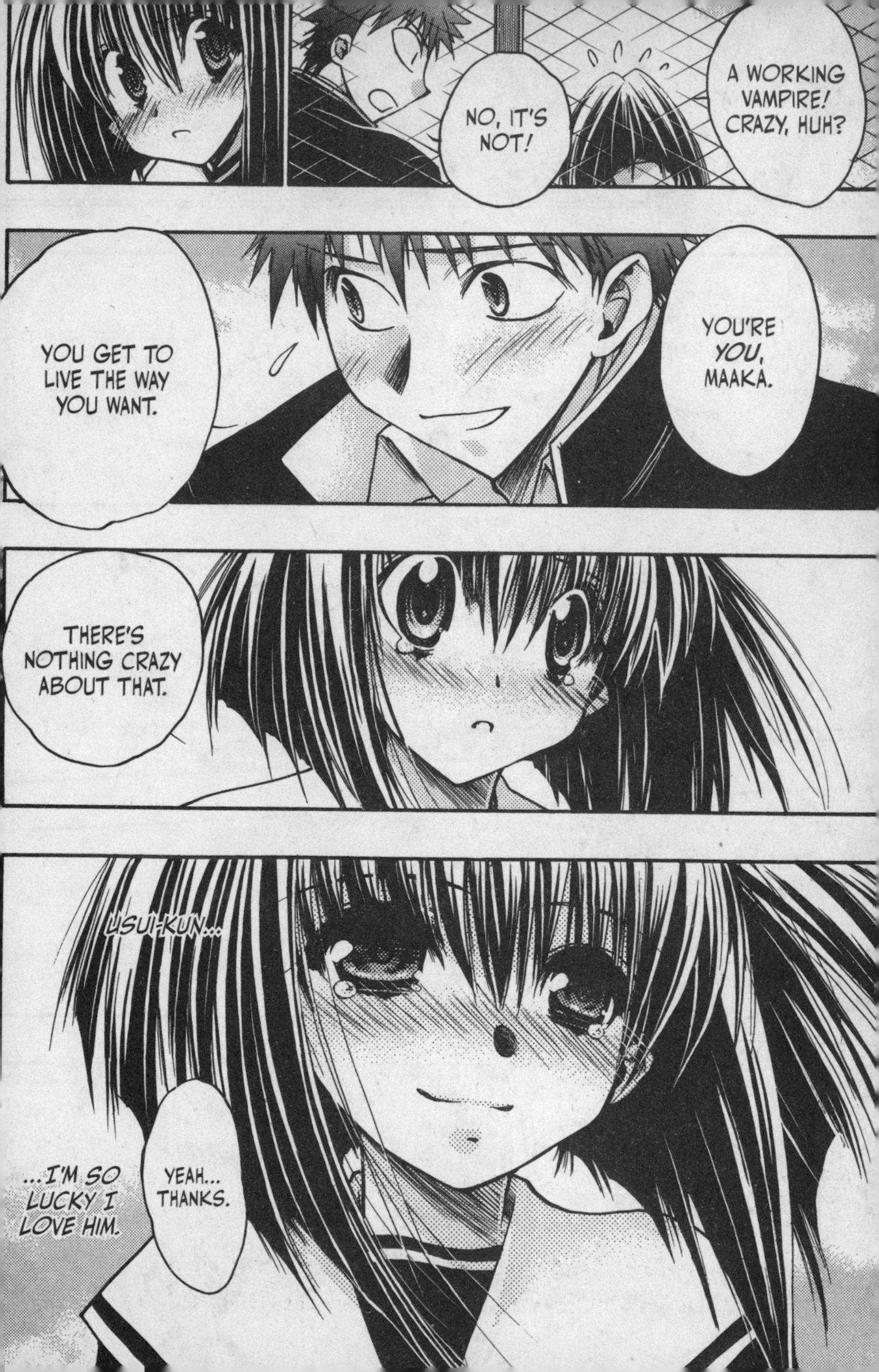
A WORKING VAMPIRE! CRAZY, HUH?
NO, IT'S NOT!
YOU'RE *YOU*, MAAKA.
YOU GET TO LIVE THE WAY YOU WANT.
THERE'S NOTHING CRAZY ABOUT THAT.
USUI-KUN...
YEAH... THANKS.
...I'M SO LUCKY I LOVE HIM.

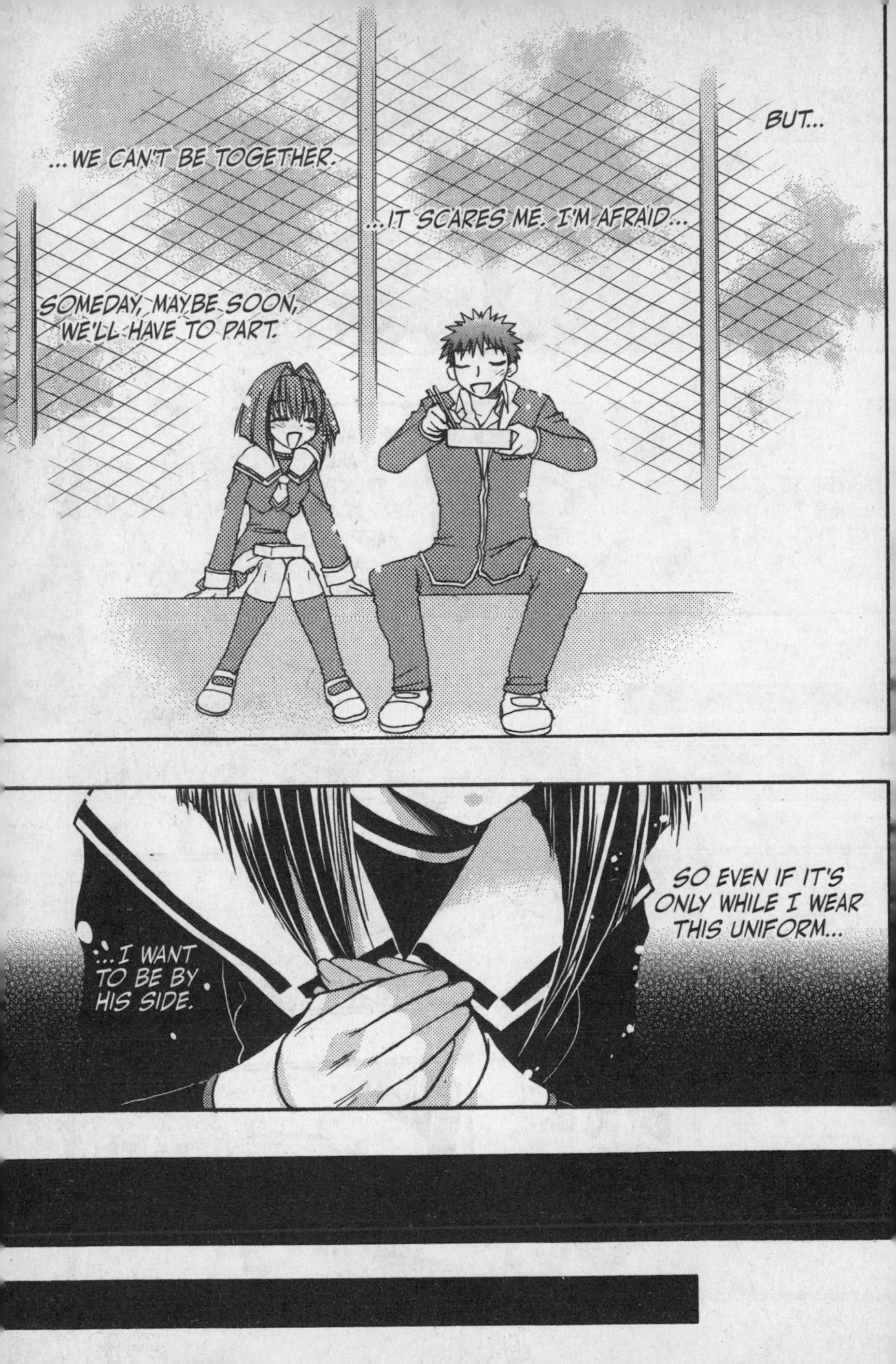
BUT...
...IT SCARES ME. I'M AFRAID...
...WE CAN'T BE TOGETHER.
SOMEDAY, MAYBE SOON, WE'LL HAVE TO PART.
SO EVEN IF IT'S ONLY WHILE I WEAR THIS UNIFORM...
...I WANT TO BE BY HIS SIDE.

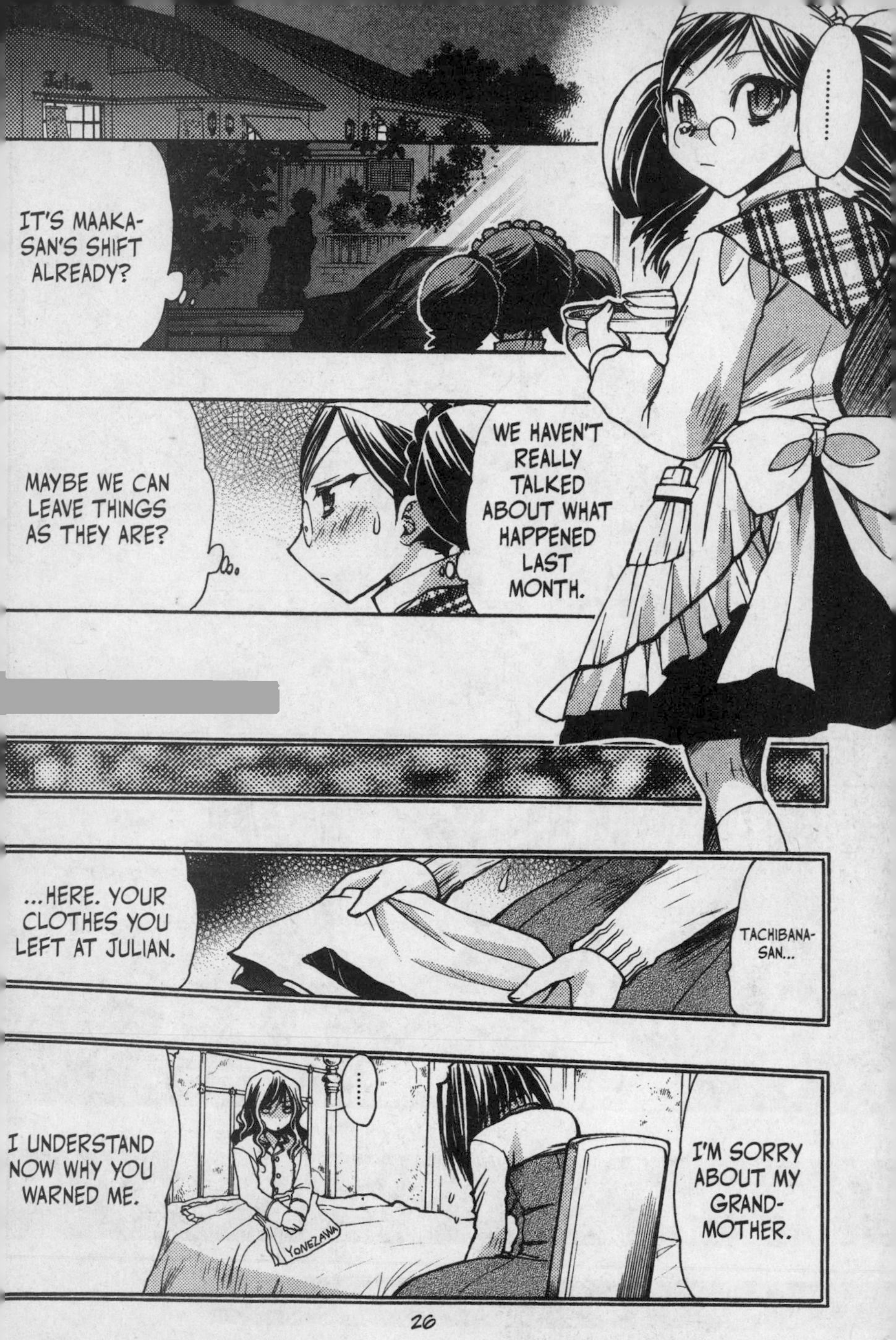
......
IT'S MAAKA-SAN'S SHIFT ALREADY?
WE HAVEN'T REALLY TALKED ABOUT WHAT HAPPENED LAST MONTH.
MAYBE WE CAN LEAVE THINGS AS THEY ARE?
TACHIBANA-SAN...
...HERE. YOUR CLOTHES YOU LEFT AT JULIAN.
I'M SORRY ABOUT MY GRANDMOTHER.
......
YONEZAWA
I UNDERSTAND NOW WHY YOU WARNED ME.

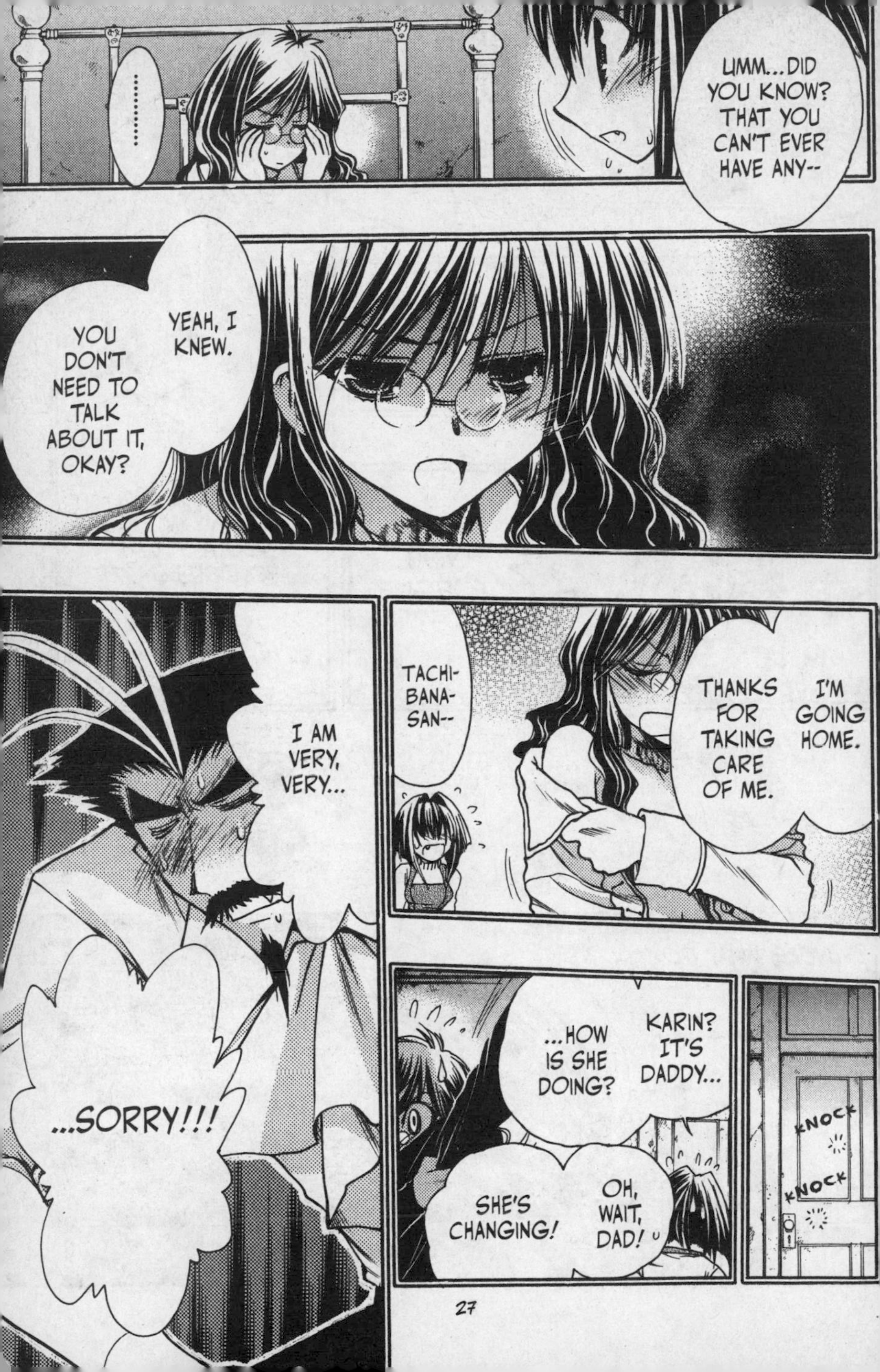

UMM...DID YOU KNOW? THAT YOU CAN'T EVER HAVE ANY--
....
YEAH, I KNEW.
YOU DON'T NEED TO TALK ABOUT IT, OKAY?
I'M GOING HOME.
THANKS FOR TAKING CARE OF ME.
TACHI-BANA-SAN--
KNOCK
KNOCK
KARIN? IT'S DADDY...
...HOW IS SHE DOING?
OH, WAIT, DAD!
SHE'S CHANGING!
I AM VERY, VERY...
...SORRY!!!

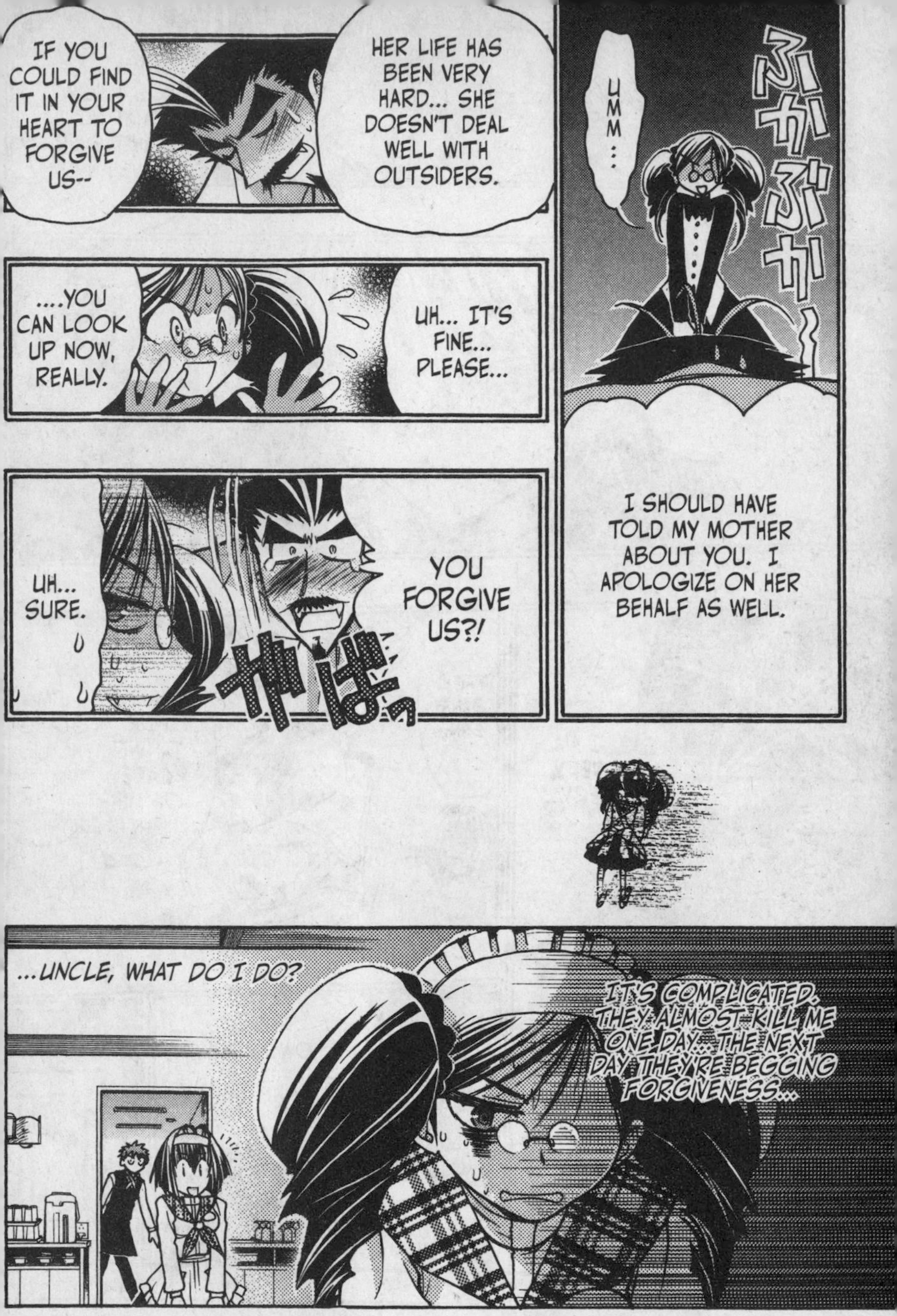
ふかぶか〜
UMM...
I SHOULD HAVE TOLD MY MOTHER ABOUT YOU. I APOLOGIZE ON HER BEHALF AS WELL.
HER LIFE HAS BEEN VERY HARD... SHE DOESN'T DEAL WELL WITH OUTSIDERS.
IF YOU COULD FIND IT IN YOUR HEART TO FORGIVE US--
UH... IT'S FINE... PLEASE...
....YOU CAN LOOK UP NOW, REALLY.
YOU FORGIVE US?!
がばっ
UH... SURE.
IT'S COMPLICATED. THEY ALMOST KILL ME ONE DAY... THE NEXT DAY THEY'RE BEGGING FORGIVENESS...
...UNCLE, WHAT DO I DO?

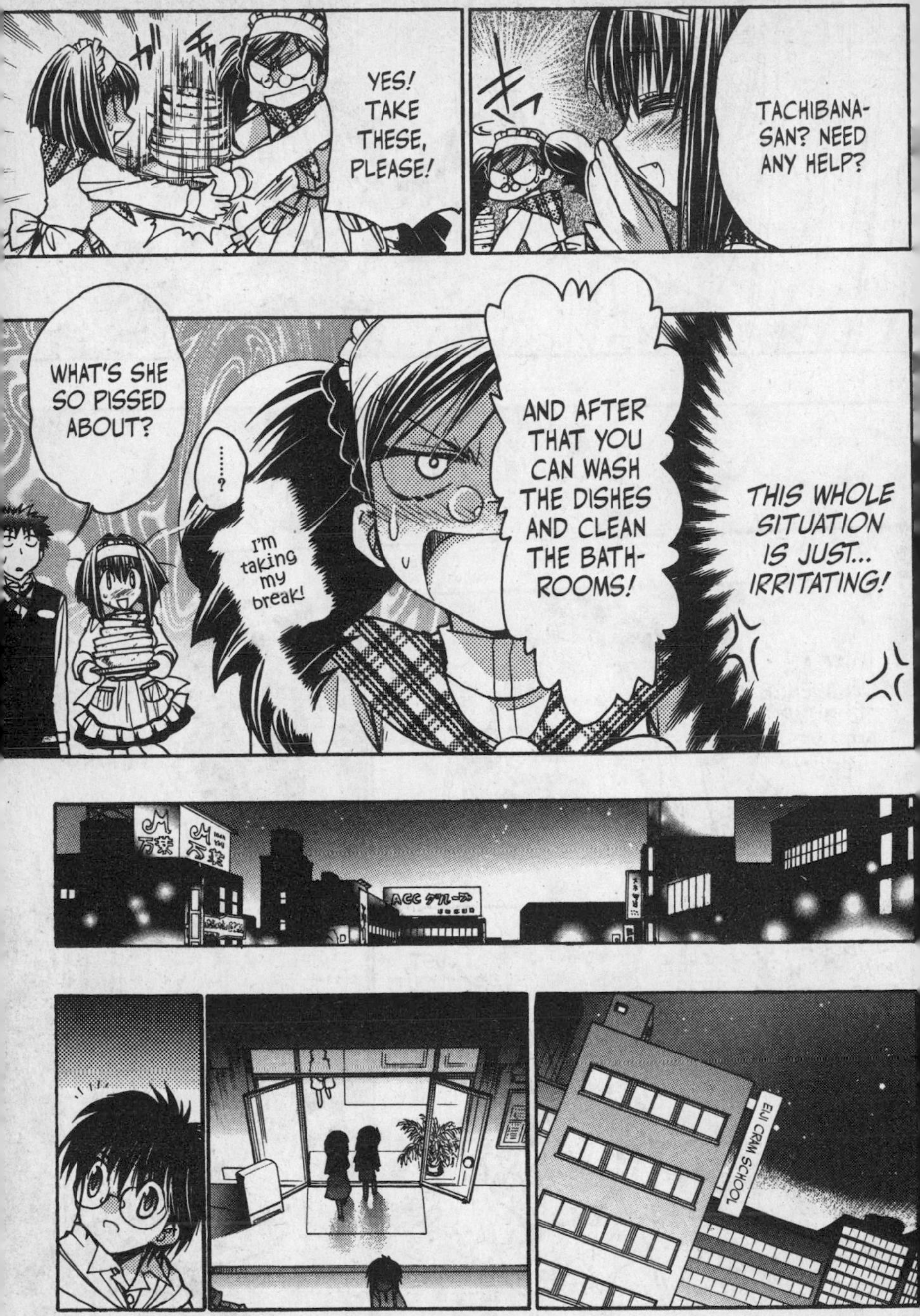

TACHIBANA-SAN? NEED ANY HELP?
YES! TAKE THESE, PLEASE!
THIS WHOLE SITUATION IS JUST... IRRITATING!
AND AFTER THAT YOU CAN WASH THE DISHES AND CLEAN THE BATH-ROOMS!
I'm taking my break!
......?
WHAT'S SHE SO PISSED ABOUT?
EIJI CRAM SCHOOL

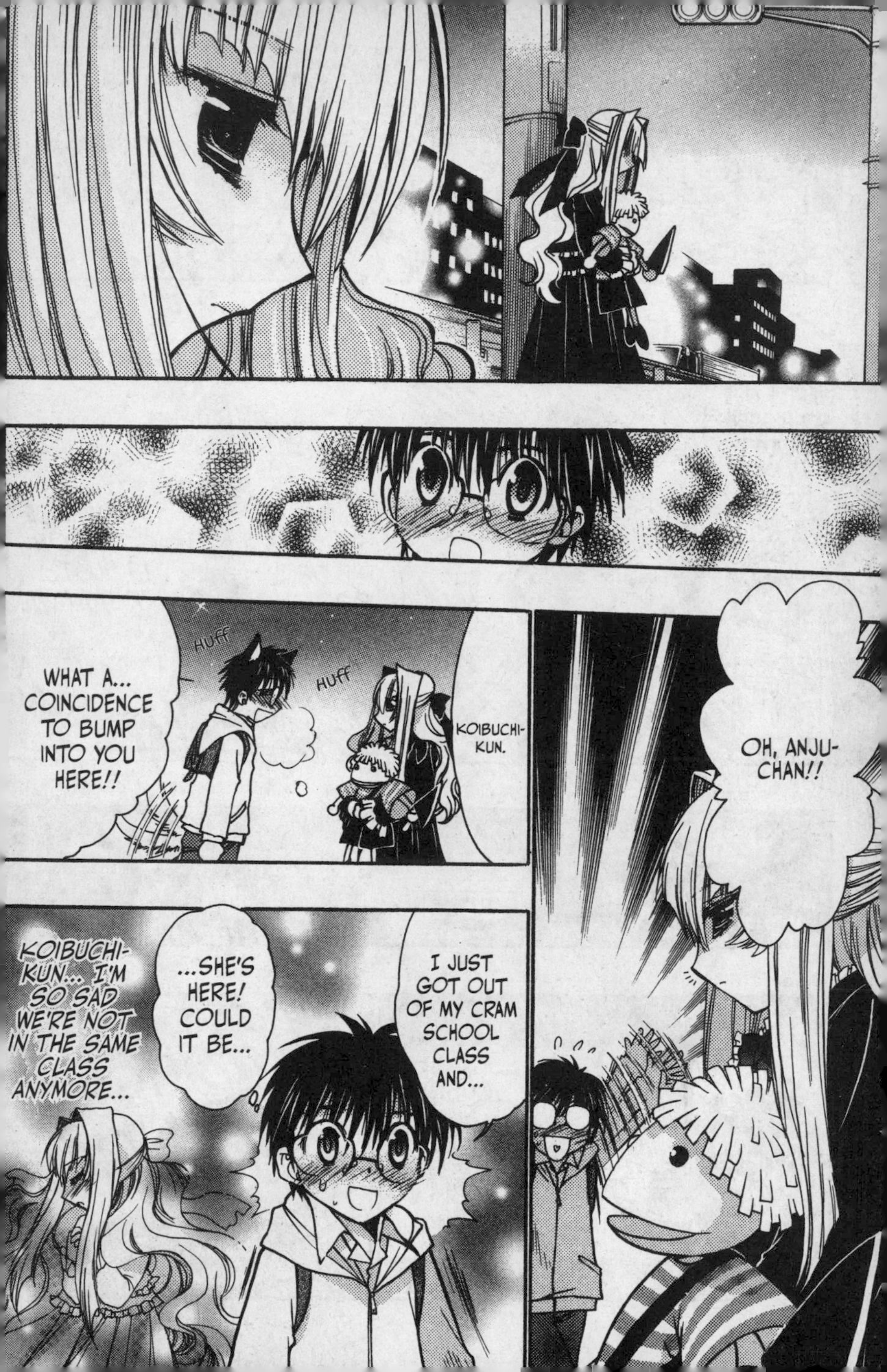
OH, ANJU-CHAN!!
KOIBUCHI-KUN.
HUFF
HUFF
WHAT A... COINCIDENCE TO BUMP INTO YOU HERE!!
I JUST GOT OUT OF MY CRAM SCHOOL CLASS AND...
...SHE'S HERE! COULD IT BE...
KOIBUCHI-KUN... I'M SO SAD WE'RE NOT IN THE SAME CLASS ANYMORE...

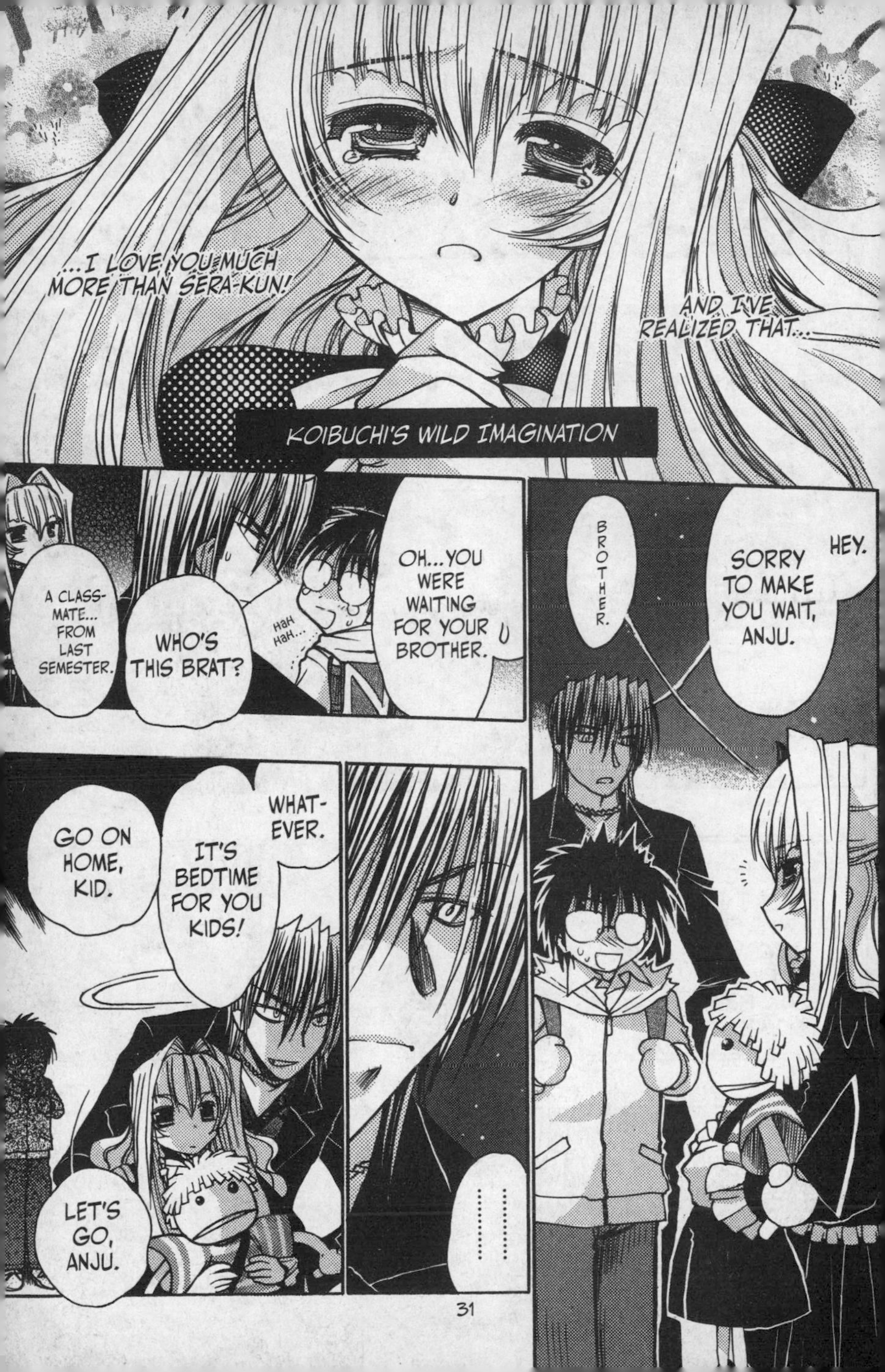
AND I'VE REALIZED THAT...
...I LOVE YOU MUCH MORE THAN SERA-KUN!
KOIBUCHI'S WILD IMAGINATION
HEY.
SORRY TO MAKE YOU WAIT, ANJU.
BROTHER.
OH...YOU WERE WAITING FOR YOUR BROTHER.
HAH HAH...
WHO'S THIS BRAT?
A CLASSMATE... FROM LAST SEMESTER.
WHATEVER.
......
IT'S BEDTIME FOR YOU KIDS!
GO ON HOME, KID.
LET'S GO, ANJU.

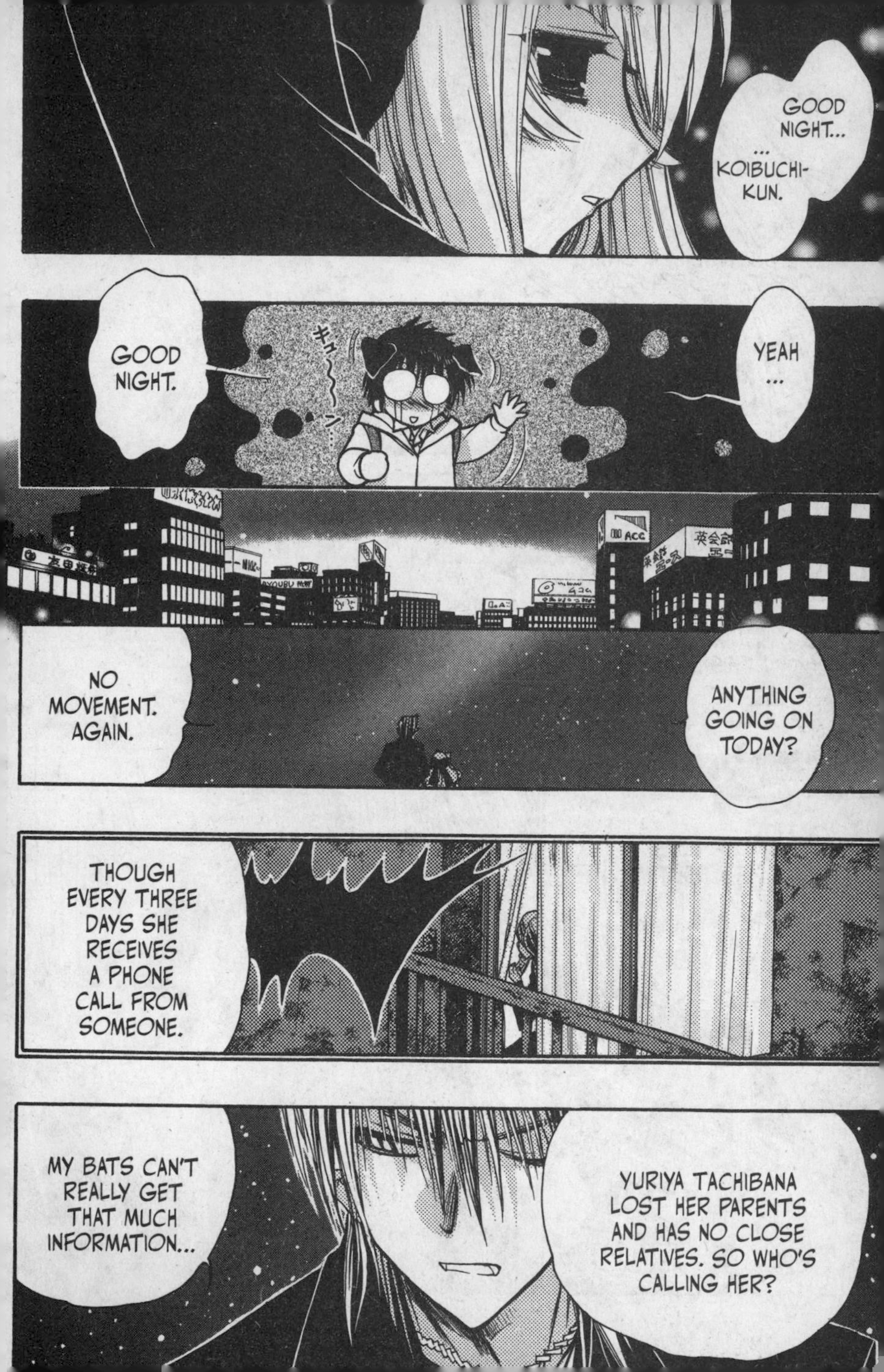
GOOD NIGHT... ...KOIBUCHI-KUN.
YEAH ...
GOOD NIGHT.
ANYTHING GOING ON TODAY?
NO MOVEMENT. AGAIN.
THOUGH EVERY THREE DAYS SHE RECEIVES A PHONE CALL FROM SOMEONE.
YURIYA TACHIBANA LOST HER PARENTS AND HAS NO CLOSE RELATIVES. SO WHO'S CALLING HER?
MY BATS CAN'T REALLY GET THAT MUCH INFORMATION...

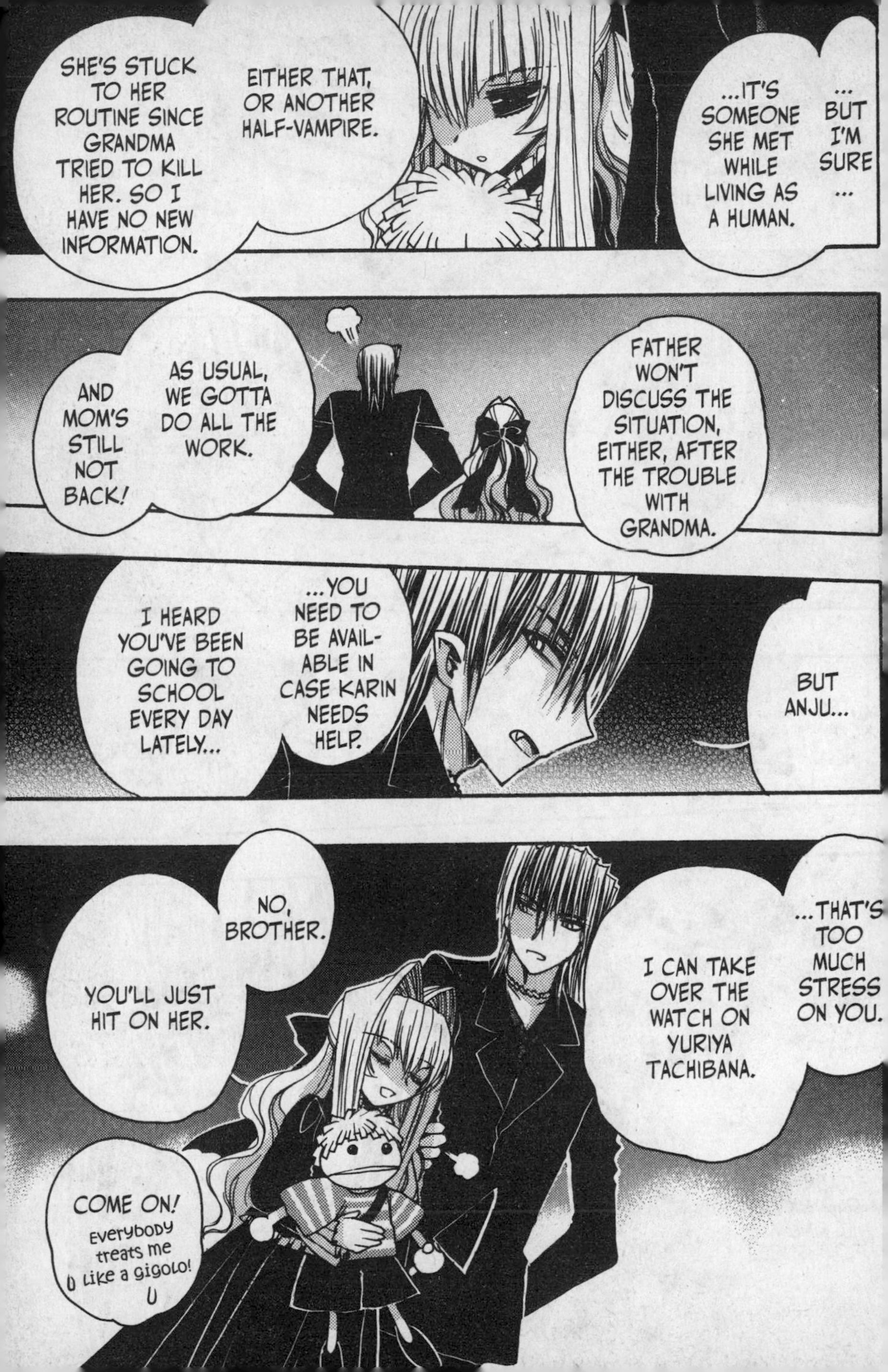
... BUT I'M SURE ...
...IT'S SOMEONE SHE MET WHILE LIVING AS A HUMAN.
EITHER THAT, OR ANOTHER HALF-VAMPIRE.
SHE'S STUCK TO HER ROUTINE SINCE GRANDMA TRIED TO KILL HER. SO I HAVE NO NEW INFORMATION.
FATHER WON'T DISCUSS THE SITUATION, EITHER, AFTER THE TROUBLE WITH GRANDMA.
AS USUAL, WE GOTTA DO ALL THE WORK.
AND MOM'S STILL NOT BACK!
BUT ANJU...
...YOU NEED TO BE AVAIL-ABLE IN CASE KARIN NEEDS HELP.
I HEARD YOU'VE BEEN GOING TO SCHOOL EVERY DAY LATELY...
...THAT'S TOO MUCH STRESS ON YOU.
I CAN TAKE OVER THE WATCH ON YURIYA TACHIBANA.
NO, BROTHER.
YOU'LL JUST HIT ON HER.
COME ON!
Everybody treats me like a gigolo!

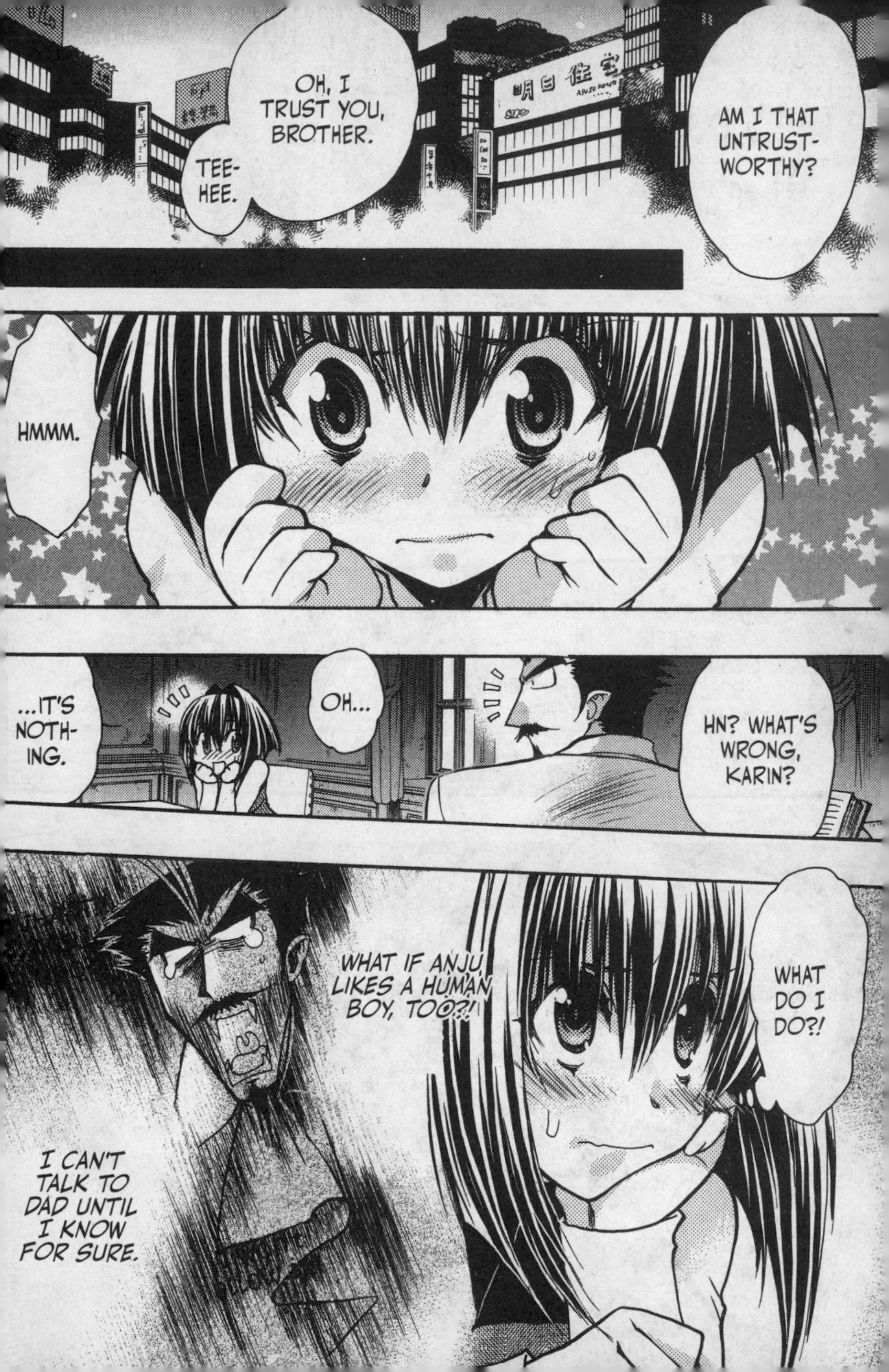
AM I THAT UNTRUST-WORTHY?
OH, I TRUST YOU, BROTHER.
TEE-HEE.
HMMM.
HN? WHAT'S WRONG, KARIN?
OH...
...IT'S NOTH-ING.
WHAT DO I DO?!
WHAT IF ANJU LIKES A HUMAN BOY, TOO?!
I CAN'T TALK TO DAD UNTIL I KNOW FOR SURE.

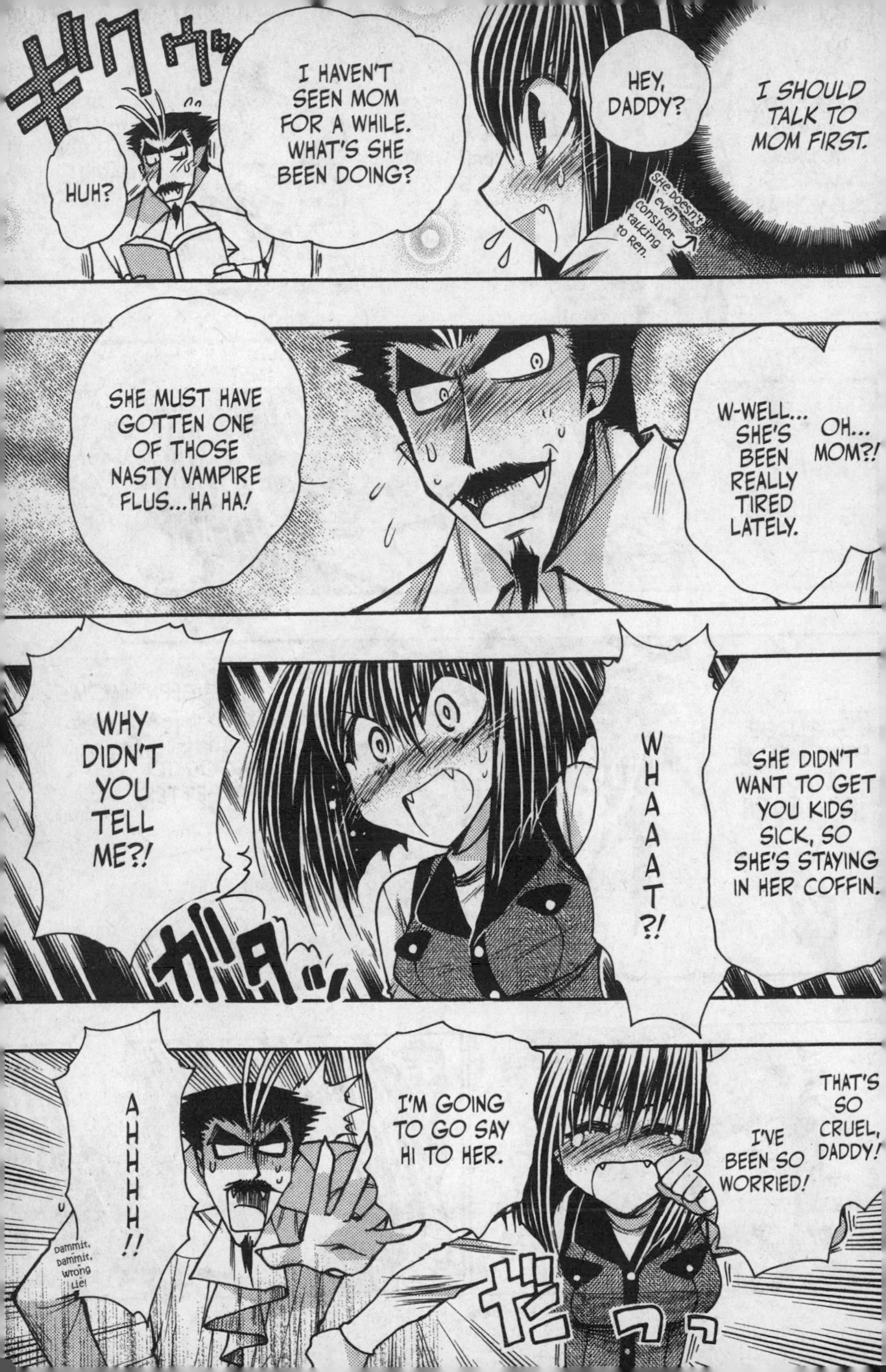
I SHOULD TALK TO MOM FIRST.
HEY, DADDY?
She doesn't even consider talking to Ren.
I HAVEN'T SEEN MOM FOR A WHILE. WHAT'S SHE BEEN DOING?
HUH?
OH... MOM?!
W-WELL... SHE'S BEEN REALLY TIRED LATELY.
SHE MUST HAVE GOTTEN ONE OF THOSE NASTY VAMPIRE FLUS...HA HA!
SHE DIDN'T WANT TO GET YOU KIDS SICK, SO SHE'S STAYING IN HER COFFIN.
WHAAAAT?!
WHY DIDN'T YOU TELL ME?!
THAT'S SO CRUEL, DADDY!
I'VE BEEN SO WORRIED!
I'M GOING TO GO SAY HI TO HER.
AHHHHH!!
Dammit, Dammit, wrong Lie!

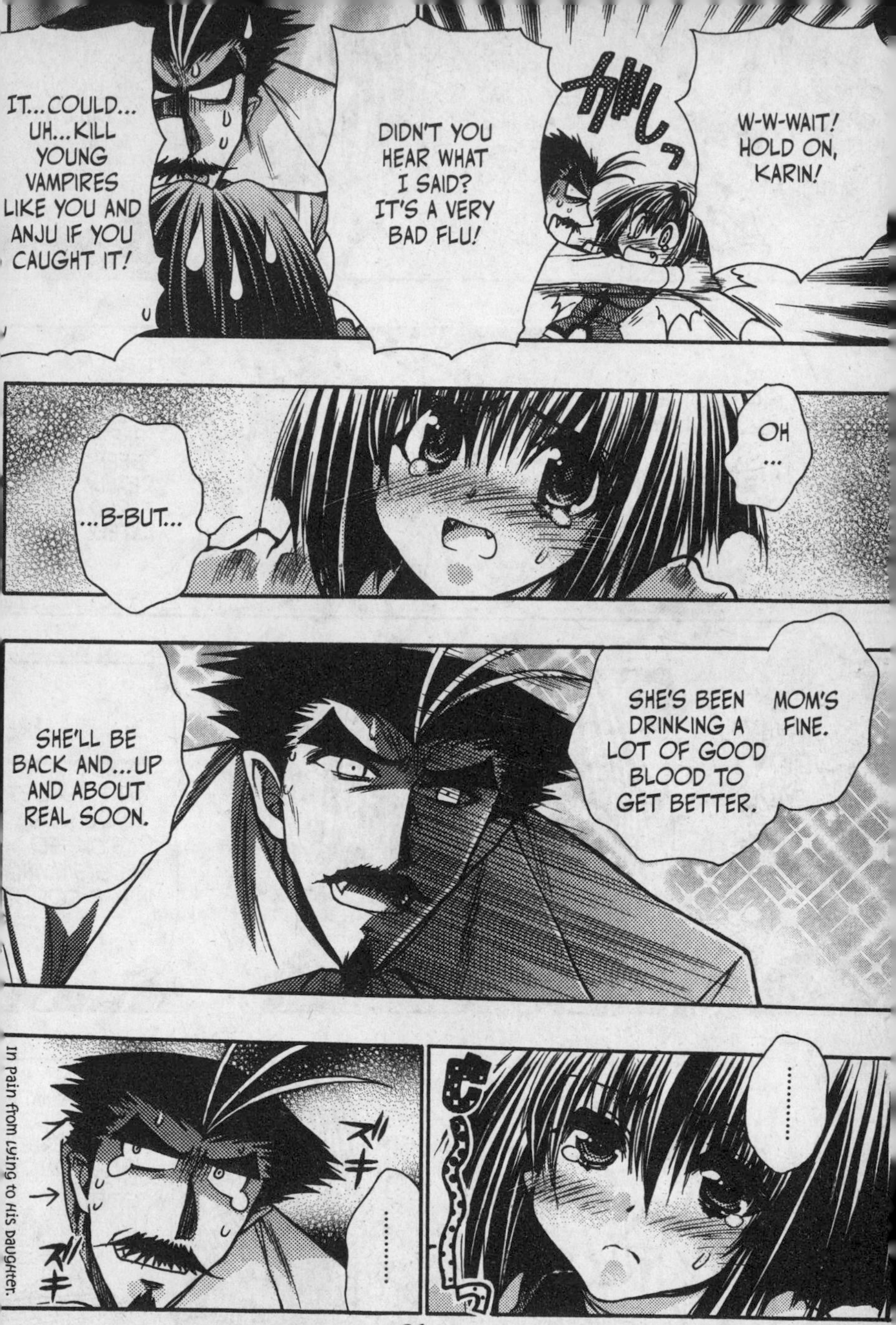
W-W-WAIT! HOLD ON, KARIN!
DIDN'T YOU HEAR WHAT I SAID? IT'S A VERY BAD FLU!
IT...COULD... UH...KILL YOUNG VAMPIRES LIKE YOU AND ANJU IF YOU CAUGHT IT!
OH ...
...B-BUT...
MOM'S FINE.
SHE'S BEEN DRINKING A LOT OF GOOD BLOOD TO GET BETTER.
SHE'LL BE BACK AND...UP AND ABOUT REAL SOON.
......
......
In Pain from Lying to His Daughter.

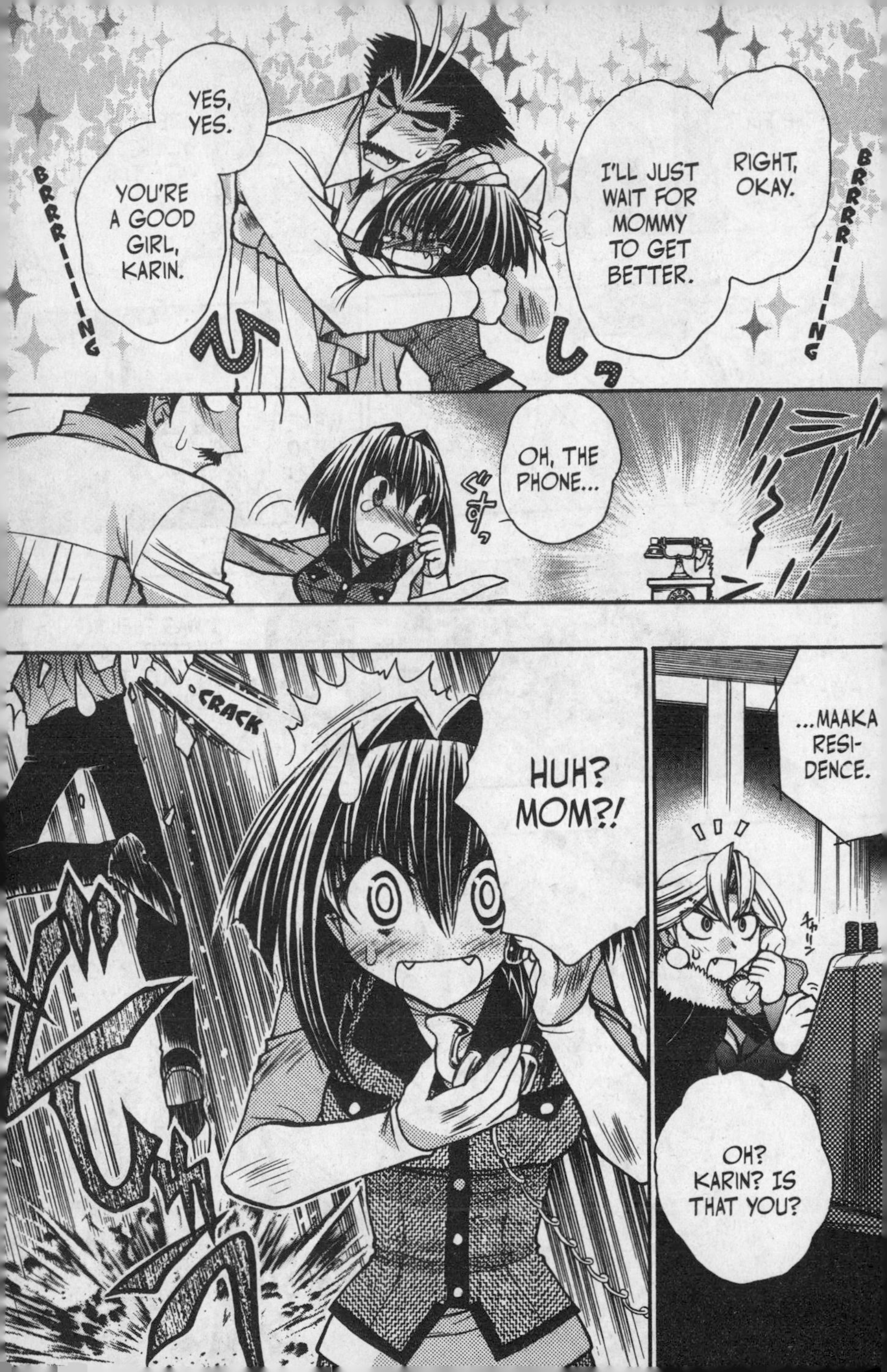
BRRRIIIING
RIGHT, OKAY.
I'LL JUST WAIT FOR MOMMY TO GET BETTER.
YES, YES.
YOU'RE A GOOD GIRL, KARIN.
BRRRIIIING
OH, THE PHONE...
ぐすっ
...MAAKA RESIDENCE.
OH? KARIN? IS THAT YOU?
HUH? MOM?!
CRACK

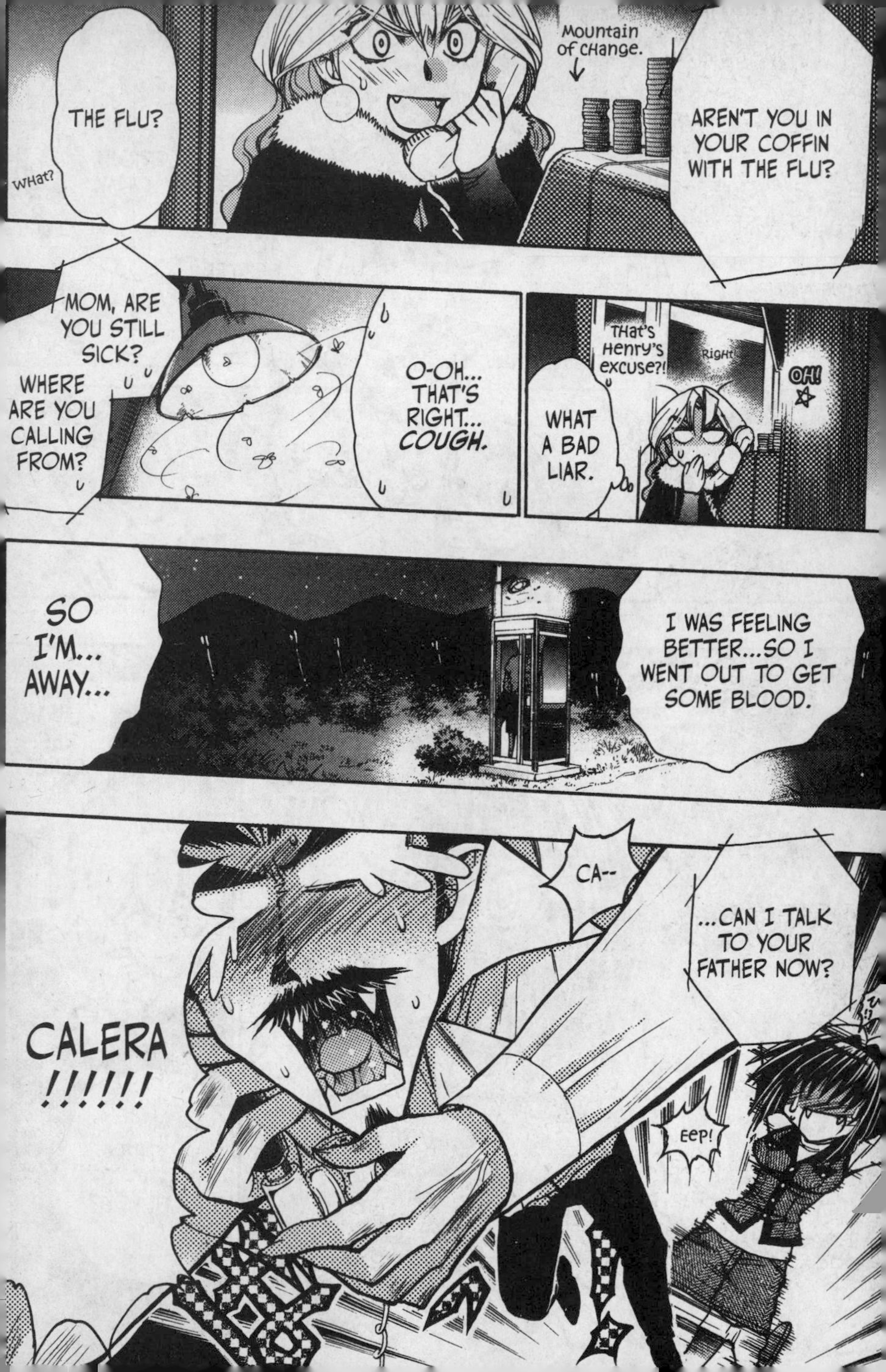

AREN'T YOU IN YOUR COFFIN WITH THE FLU?
Mountain of change.
THE FLU?
What?
Right!
OH!
That's Henry's excuse?!
WHAT A BAD LIAR.
O-OH... THAT'S RIGHT... COUGH.
MOM, ARE YOU STILL SICK?
WHERE ARE YOU CALLING FROM?
I WAS FEELING BETTER...SO I WENT OUT TO GET SOME BLOOD.
SO I'M... AWAY...
...CAN I TALK TO YOUR FATHER NOW?
CA--
CALERA !!!!!!
Eep!

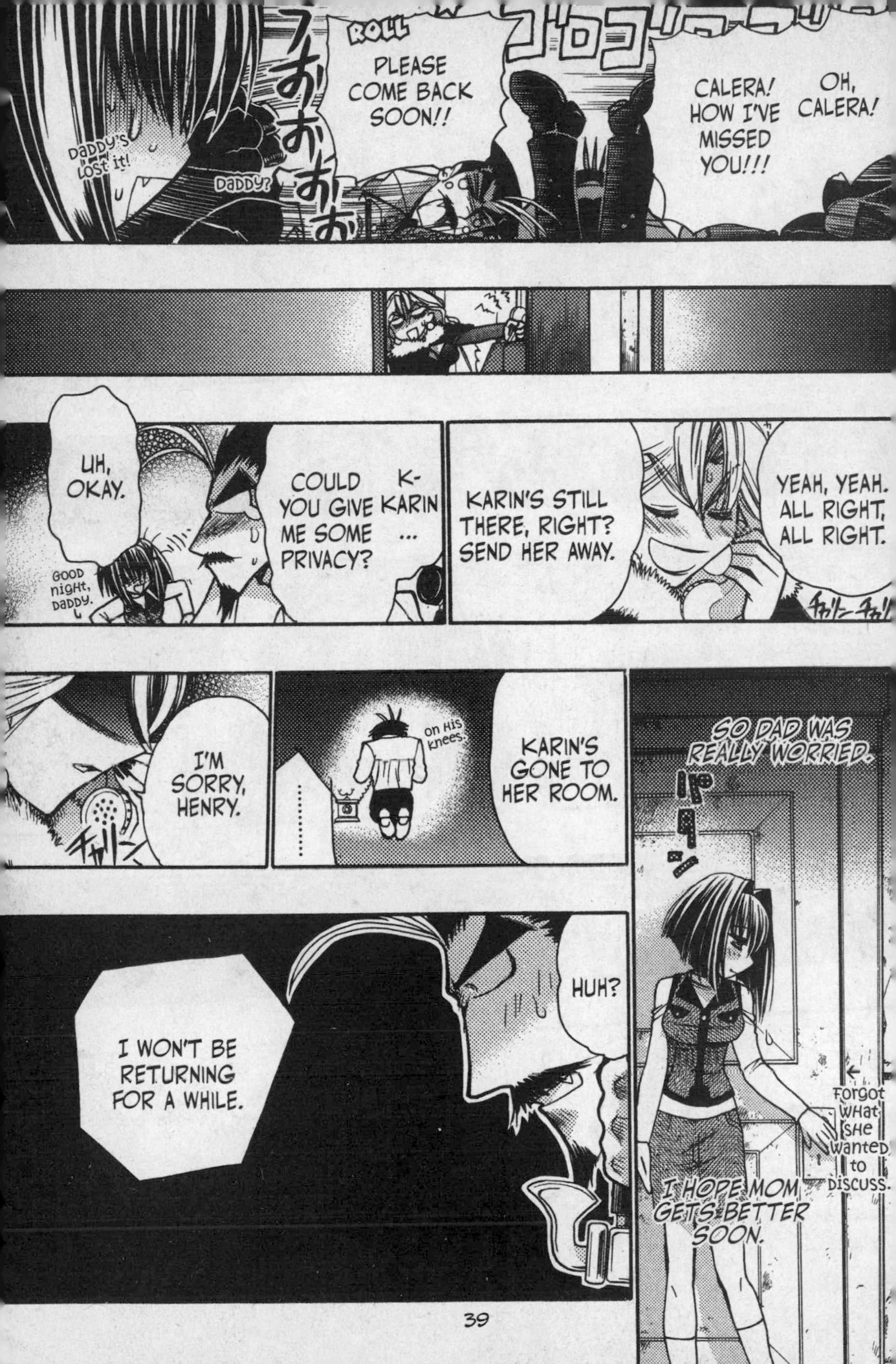
OH, CALERA!
CALERA! HOW I'VE MISSED YOU!!!
ROLL
PLEASE COME BACK SOON!!
DADDY?
Daddy's lost it!
YEAH, YEAH. ALL RIGHT, ALL RIGHT.
KARIN'S STILL THERE, RIGHT? SEND HER AWAY.
K-KARIN ...
COULD YOU GIVE ME SOME PRIVACY?
UH, OKAY.
Good night, Daddy.
SO DAD WAS REALLY WORRIED.
I HOPE MOM GETS BETTER SOON.
Forgot what she wanted to discuss.
KARIN'S GONE TO HER ROOM.
On his knees.
......
I'M SORRY, HENRY.
HUH?
I WON'T BE RETURNING FOR A WHILE.

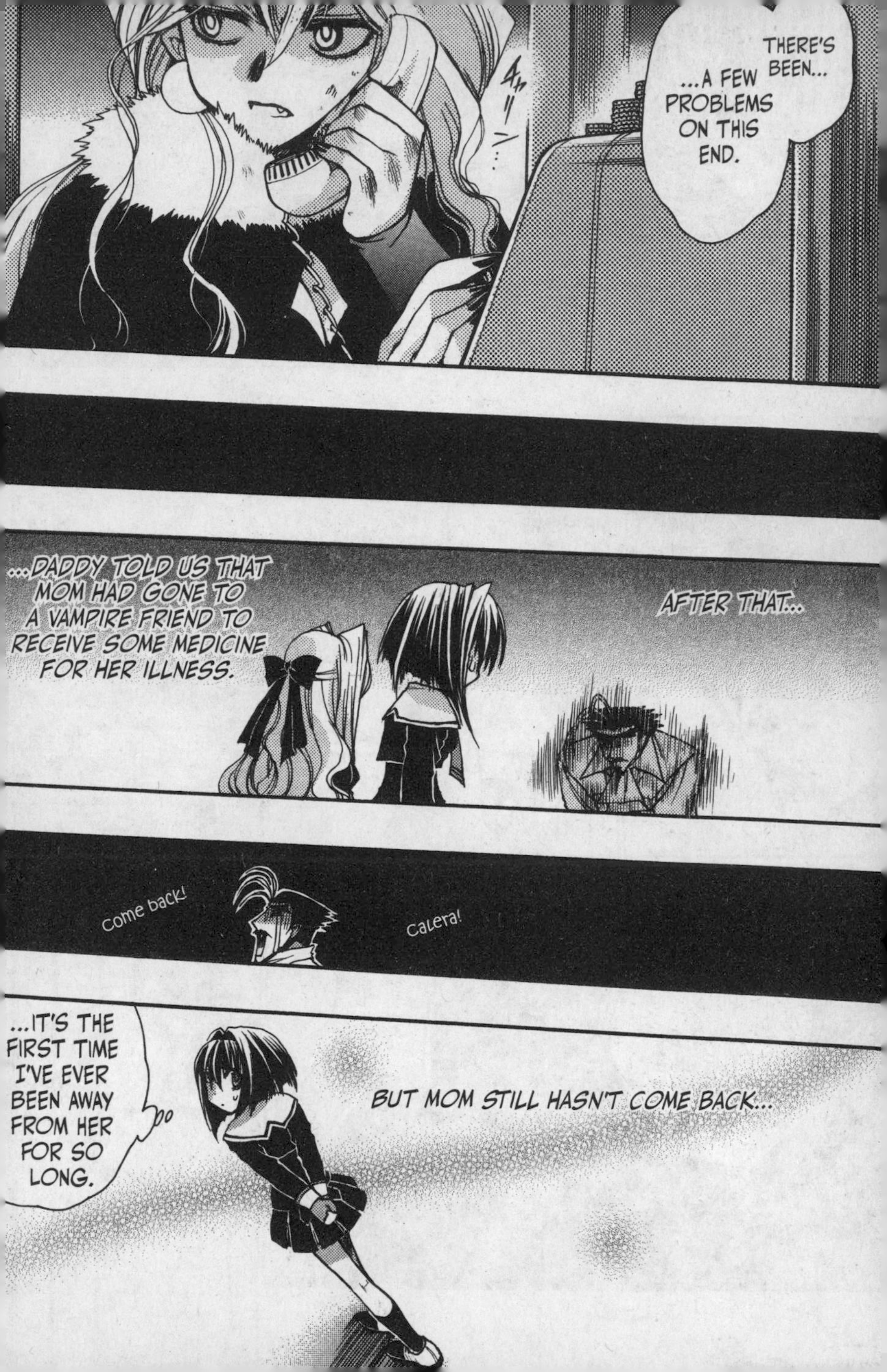
THERE'S BEEN... ...A FEW PROBLEMS ON THIS END.
AFTER THAT...
...DADDY TOLD US THAT MOM HAD GONE TO A VAMPIRE FRIEND TO RECEIVE SOME MEDICINE FOR HER ILLNESS.
Calera!
Come back!
BUT MOM STILL HASN'T COME BACK...
...IT'S THE FIRST TIME I'VE EVER BEEN AWAY FROM HER FOR SO LONG.

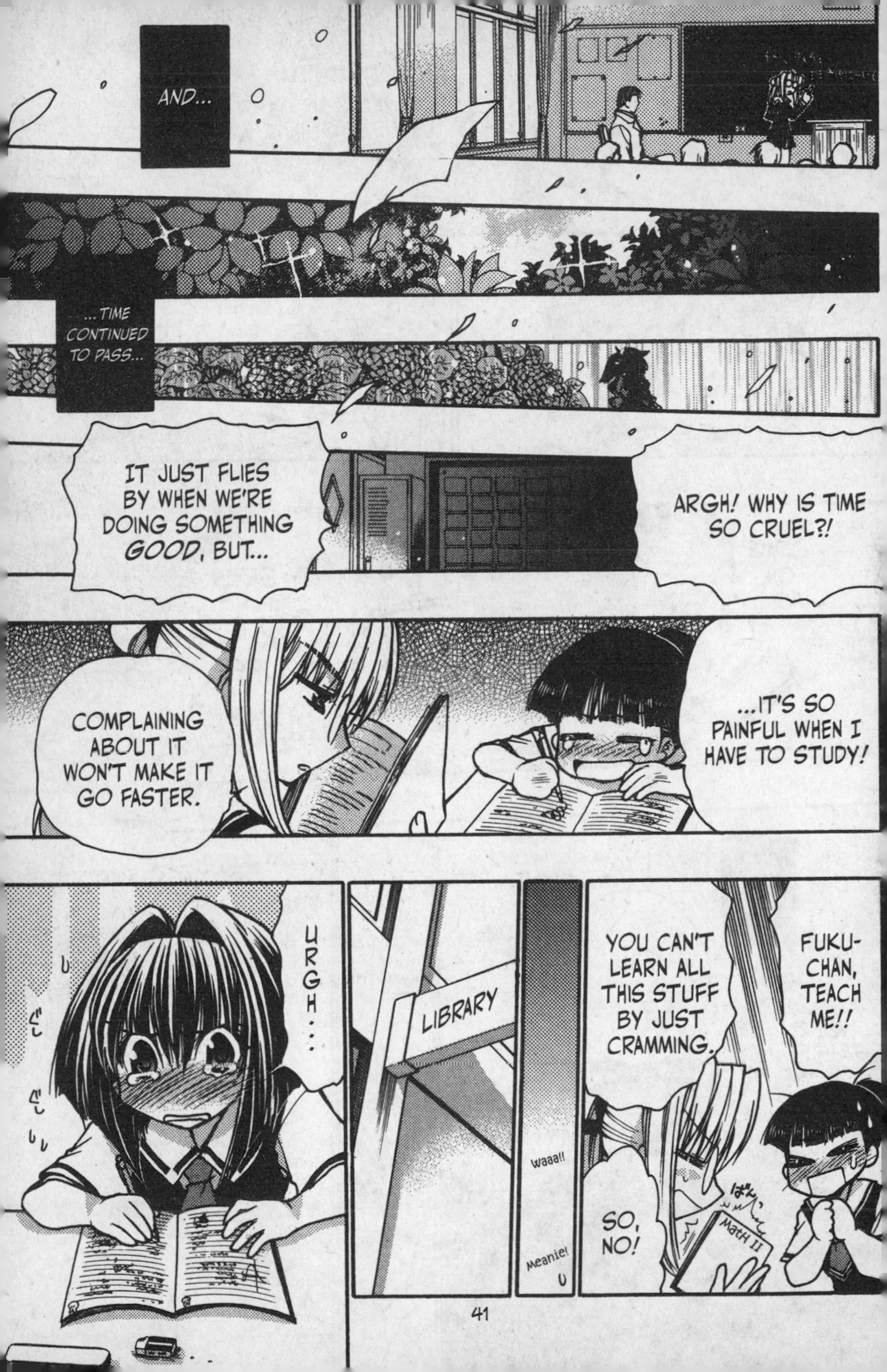
AND...
...TIME CONTINUED TO PASS...
ARGH! WHY IS TIME SO CRUEL?!
IT JUST FLIES BY WHEN WE'RE DOING SOMETHING GOOD, BUT...
...IT'S SO PAINFUL WHEN I HAVE TO STUDY!
COMPLAINING ABOUT IT WON'T MAKE IT GO FASTER.
FUKU-CHAN, TEACH ME!!
YOU CAN'T LEARN ALL THIS STUFF BY JUST CRAMMING.
SO, NO!
Math II
LIBRARY
Waaa!!
Meanie!
URGH...

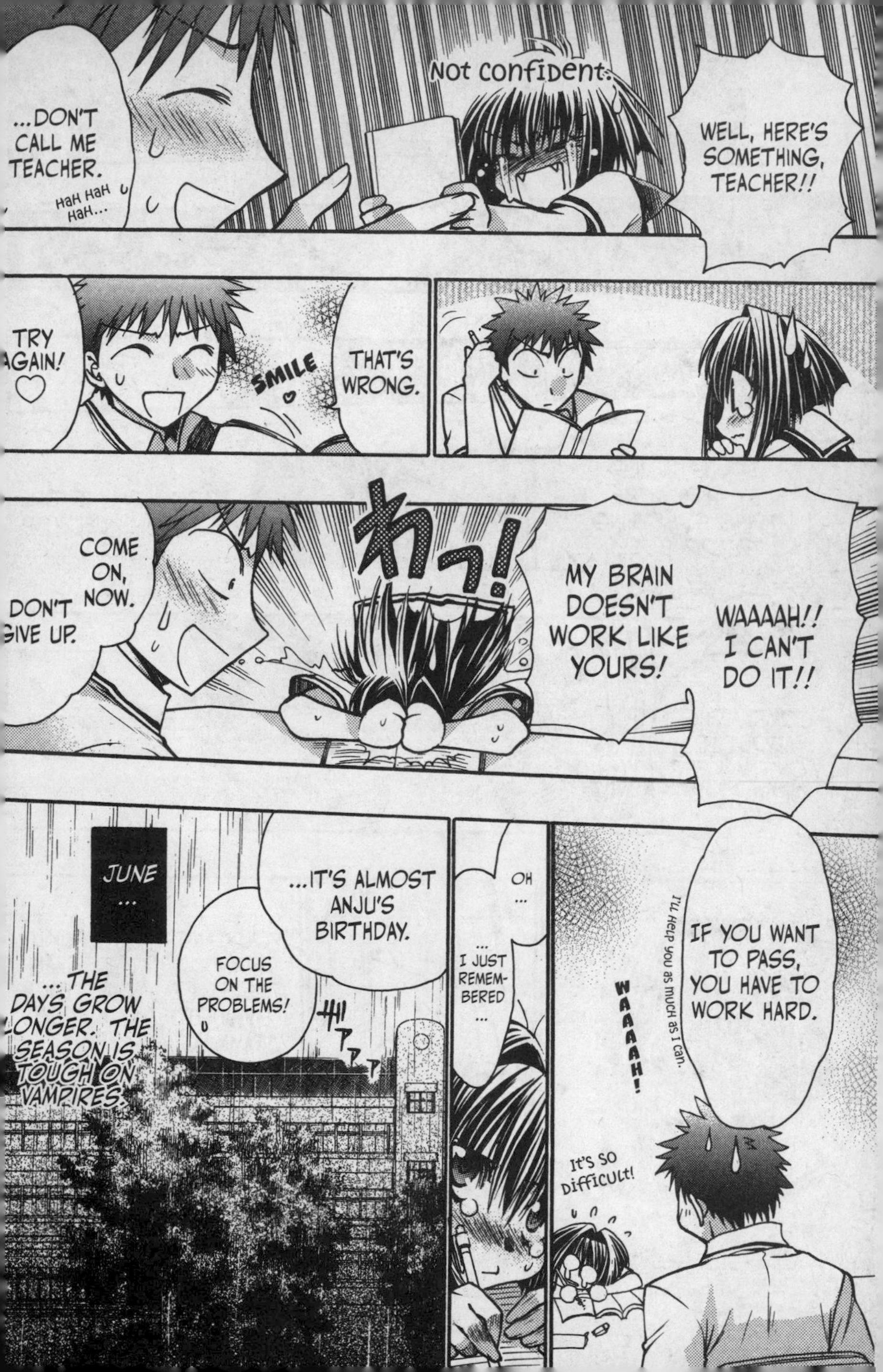
WELL, HERE'S SOMETHING, TEACHER!!
Not confident.
...DON'T CALL ME TEACHER.
HaH HaH HaH...
THAT'S WRONG.
SMILE
TRY AGAIN! ♡
WAAAAH!! I CAN'T DO IT!!
MY BRAIN DOESN'T WORK LIKE YOURS!
わっ!
COME ON, NOW.
DON'T GIVE UP.
IF YOU WANT TO PASS, YOU HAVE TO WORK HARD.
I'LL HELP YOU AS MUCH AS I CAN.
WAAAAH!
It's so difficult!
OH ...
... I JUST REMEMBERED ...
...IT'S ALMOST ANJU'S BIRTHDAY.
FOCUS ON THE PROBLEMS!
ザァァァ
JUNE ...
... THE DAYS GROW LONGER. THE SEASON IS TOUGH ON VAMPIRES.

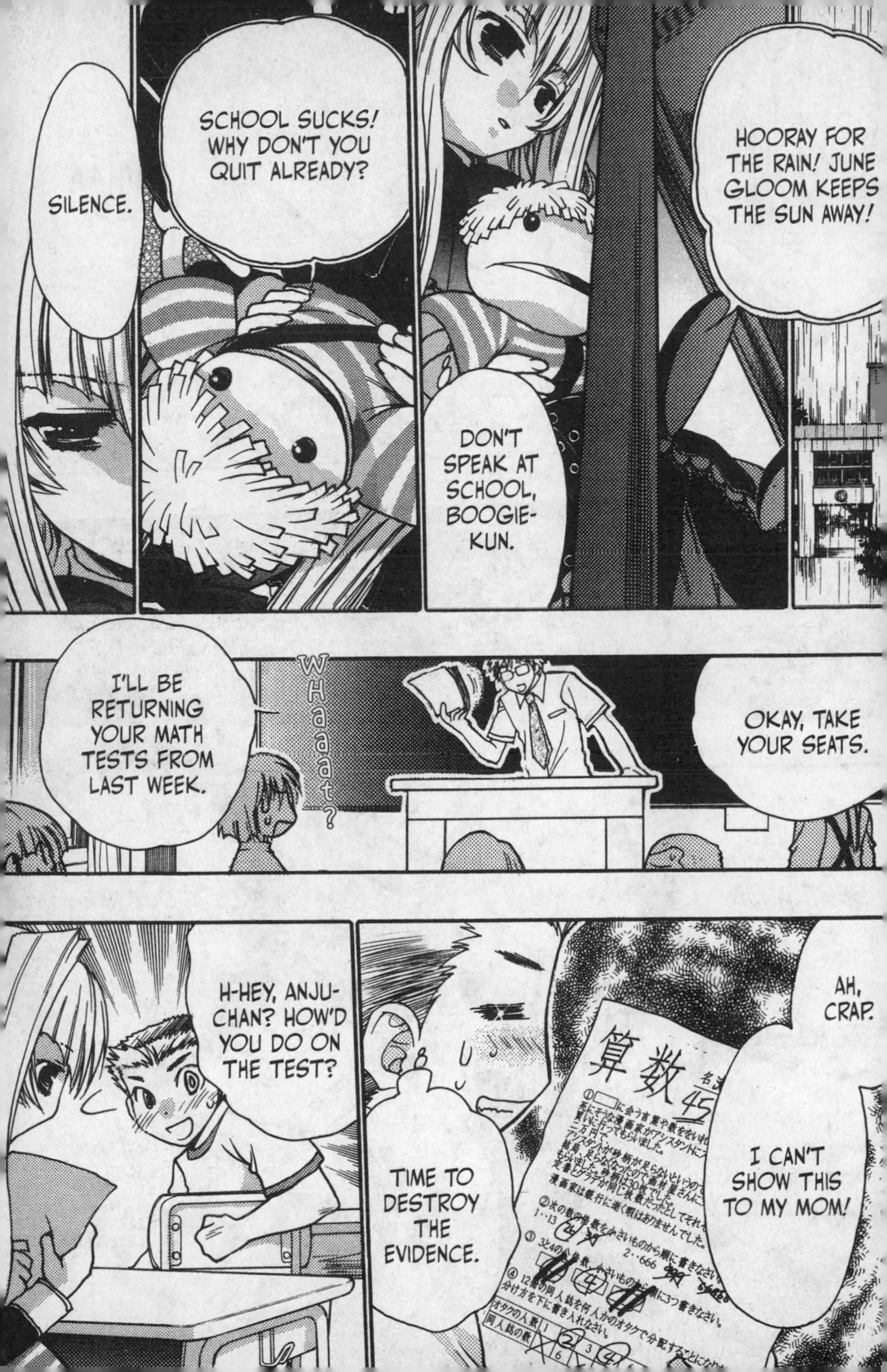
HOORAY FOR THE RAIN! JUNE GLOOM KEEPS THE SUN AWAY!
DON'T SPEAK AT SCHOOL, BOOGIE-KUN.
SCHOOL SUCKS! WHY DON'T YOU QUIT ALREADY?
SILENCE.
OKAY, TAKE YOUR SEATS.
WHaaaat?
I'LL BE RETURNING YOUR MATH TESTS FROM LAST WEEK.
AH, CRAP.
I CAN'T SHOW THIS TO MY MOM!
算数
45
TIME TO DESTROY THE EVIDENCE.
H-HEY, ANJU-CHAN? HOW'D YOU DO ON THE TEST?

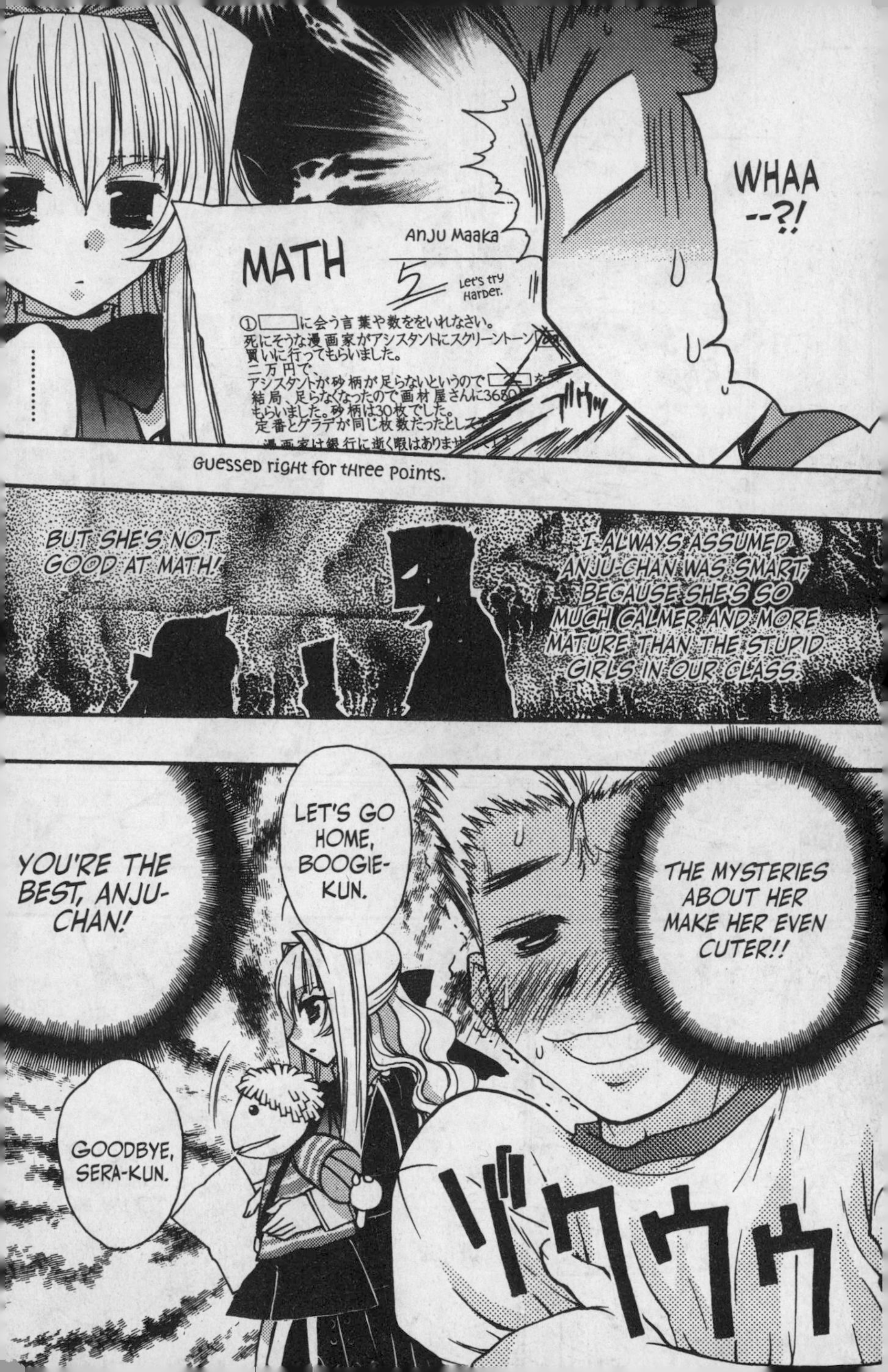
WHAA--?!
MATH
Anju Maaka
5
Let's try Harder.
①□に会う言葉や数ををいれなさい。
死にそうな漫画家がアシスタントにスクリーントーン
買いに行ってもらいました。
二万円で、
アシスタントが砂柄が足らないというので
結局、足らなくなったので画材屋さんに3680
もらいました。砂柄は30枚でした。
定番とグラデが同じ枚数だったとして
......
GUESSED RIGHT FOR THREE POINTS.
I ALWAYS ASSUMED ANJU-CHAN WAS SMART BECAUSE SHE'S SO MUCH CALMER AND MORE MATURE THAN THE STUPID GIRLS IN OUR CLASS.
BUT SHE'S NOT GOOD AT MATH!
THE MYSTERIES ABOUT HER MAKE HER EVEN CUTER!!
LET'S GO HOME, BOOGIE-KUN.
YOU'RE THE BEST, ANJU-CHAN!
GOODBYE, SERA-KUN.
ゾクウウゥ

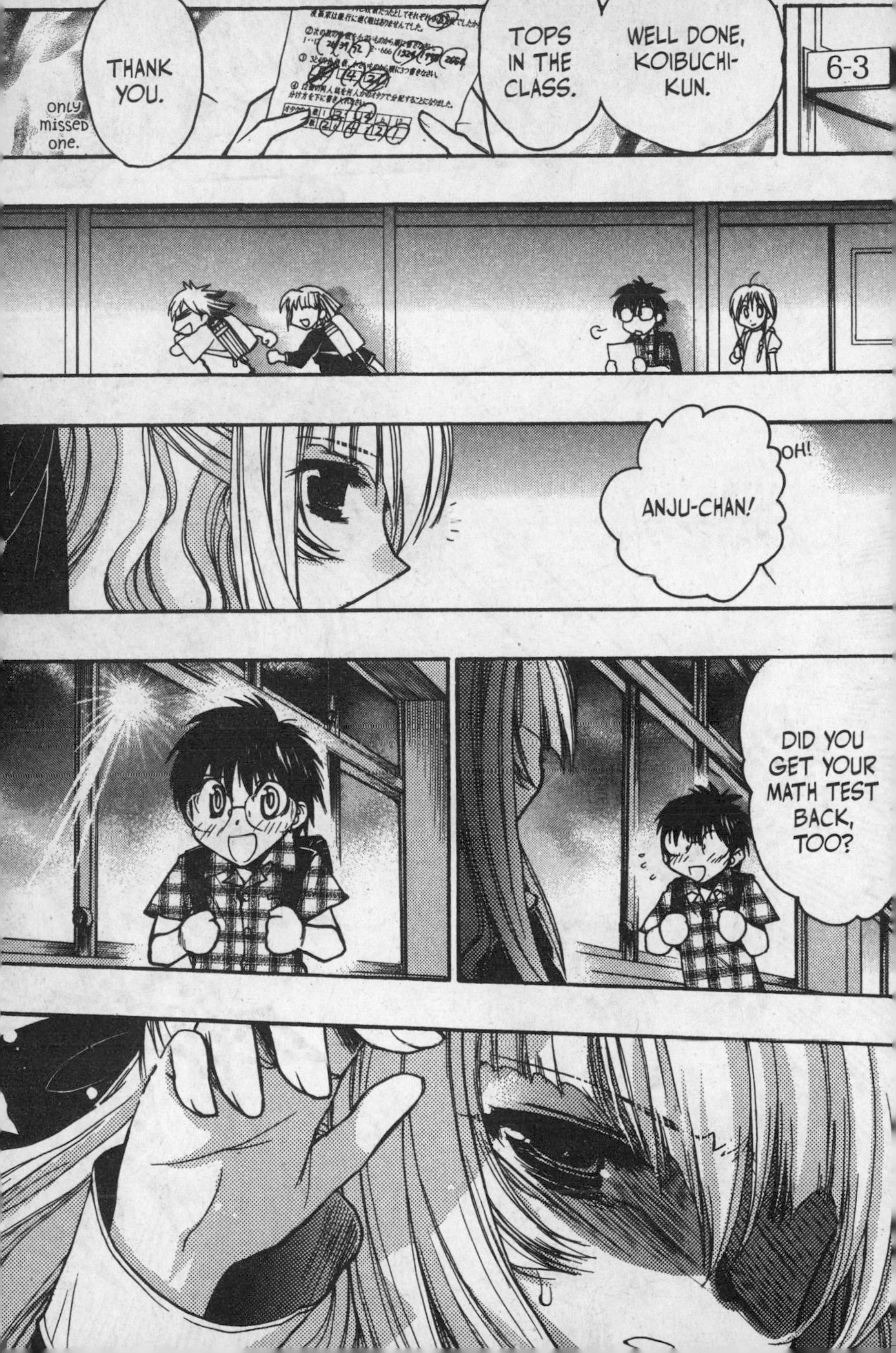
6-3
WELL DONE, KOIBUCHI-KUN.
TOPS IN THE CLASS.
THANK YOU.
only missed one.
OH!
ANJU-CHAN!
DID YOU GET YOUR MATH TEST BACK, TOO?

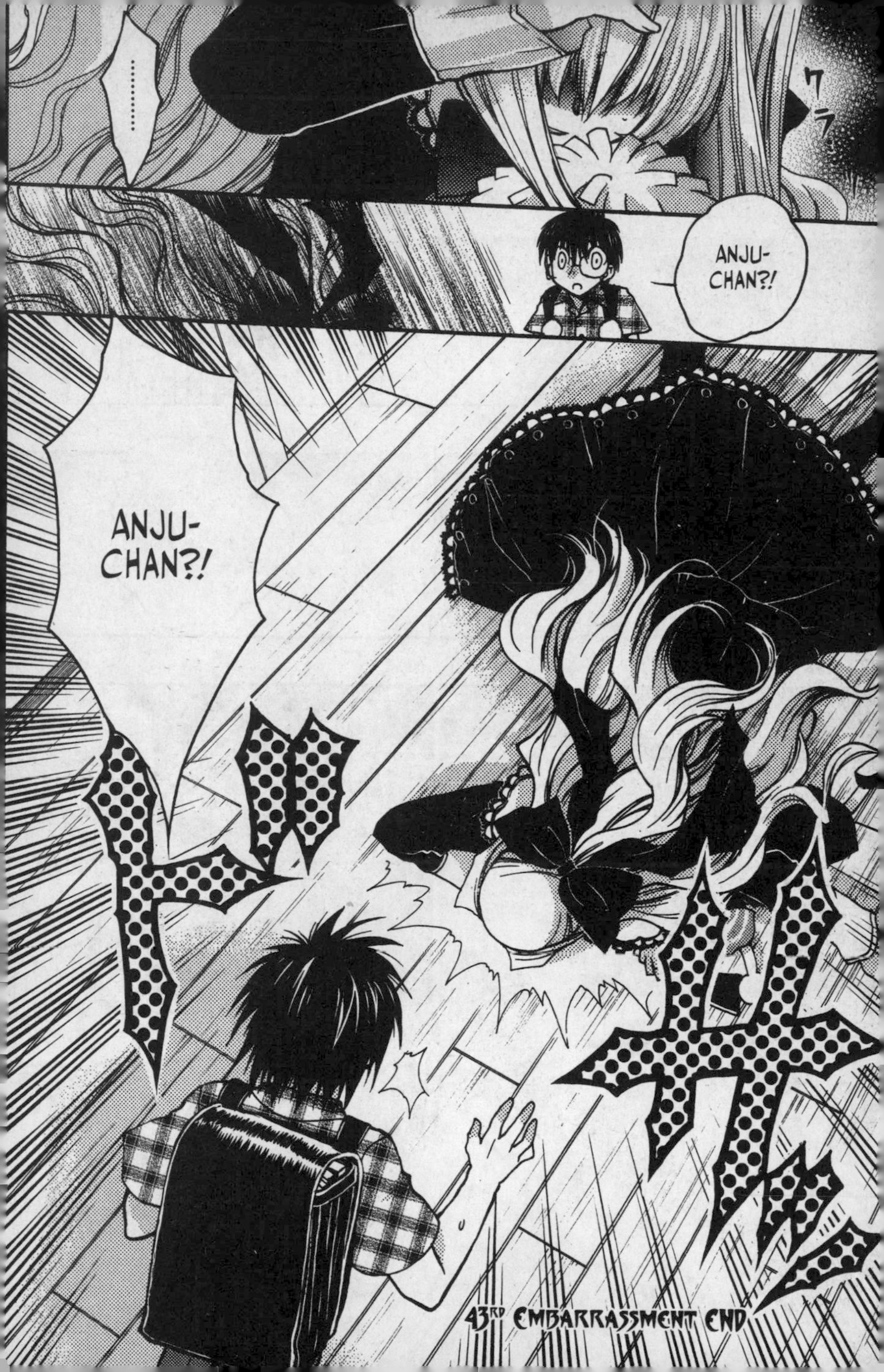
……
ANJU-CHAN?!
ANJU-CHAN?!
43RD EMBARRASSMENT END

44th Embarrassment ☽ Anju's Hesitation and Yuriya's Past

~The Past~

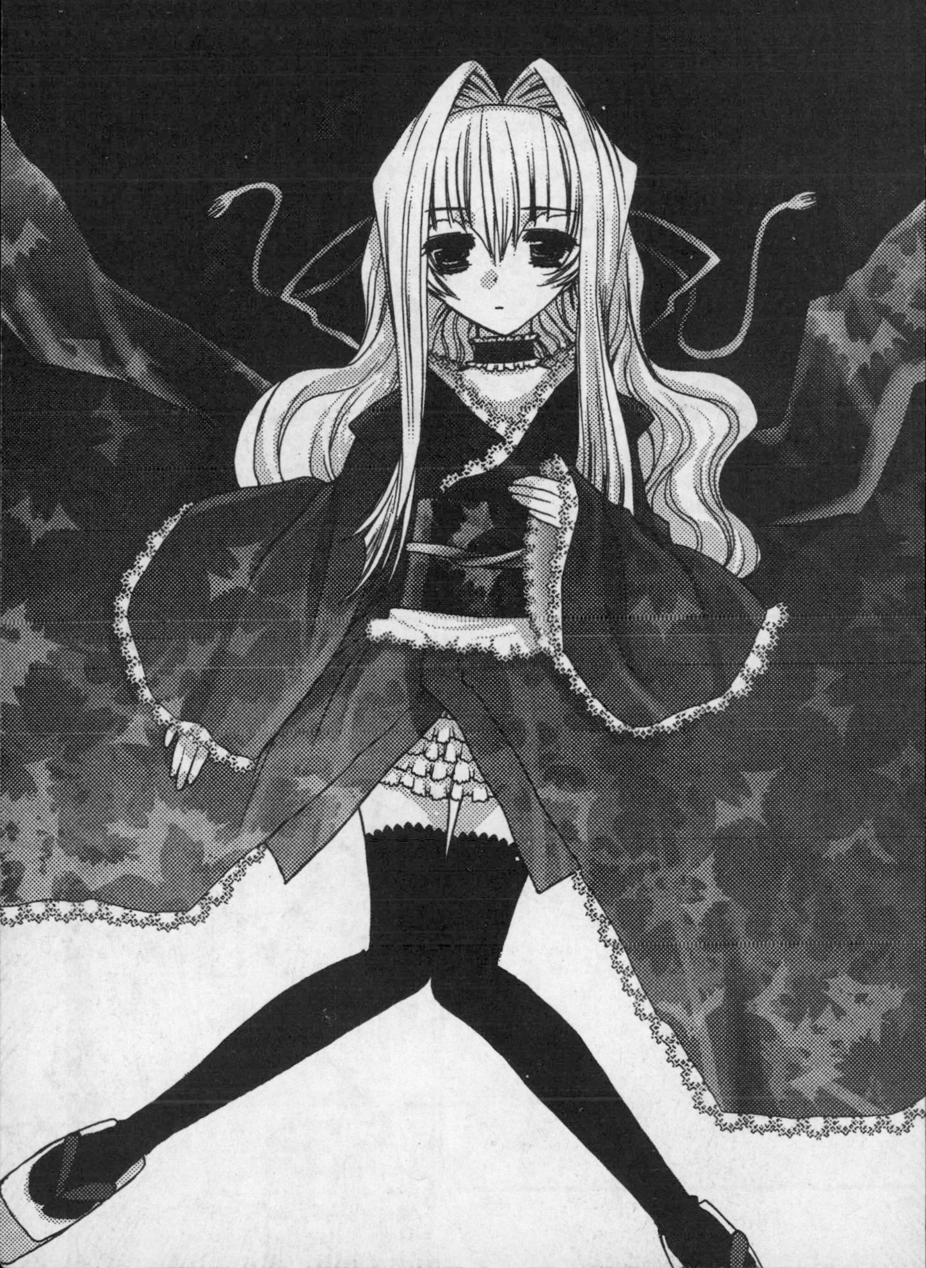

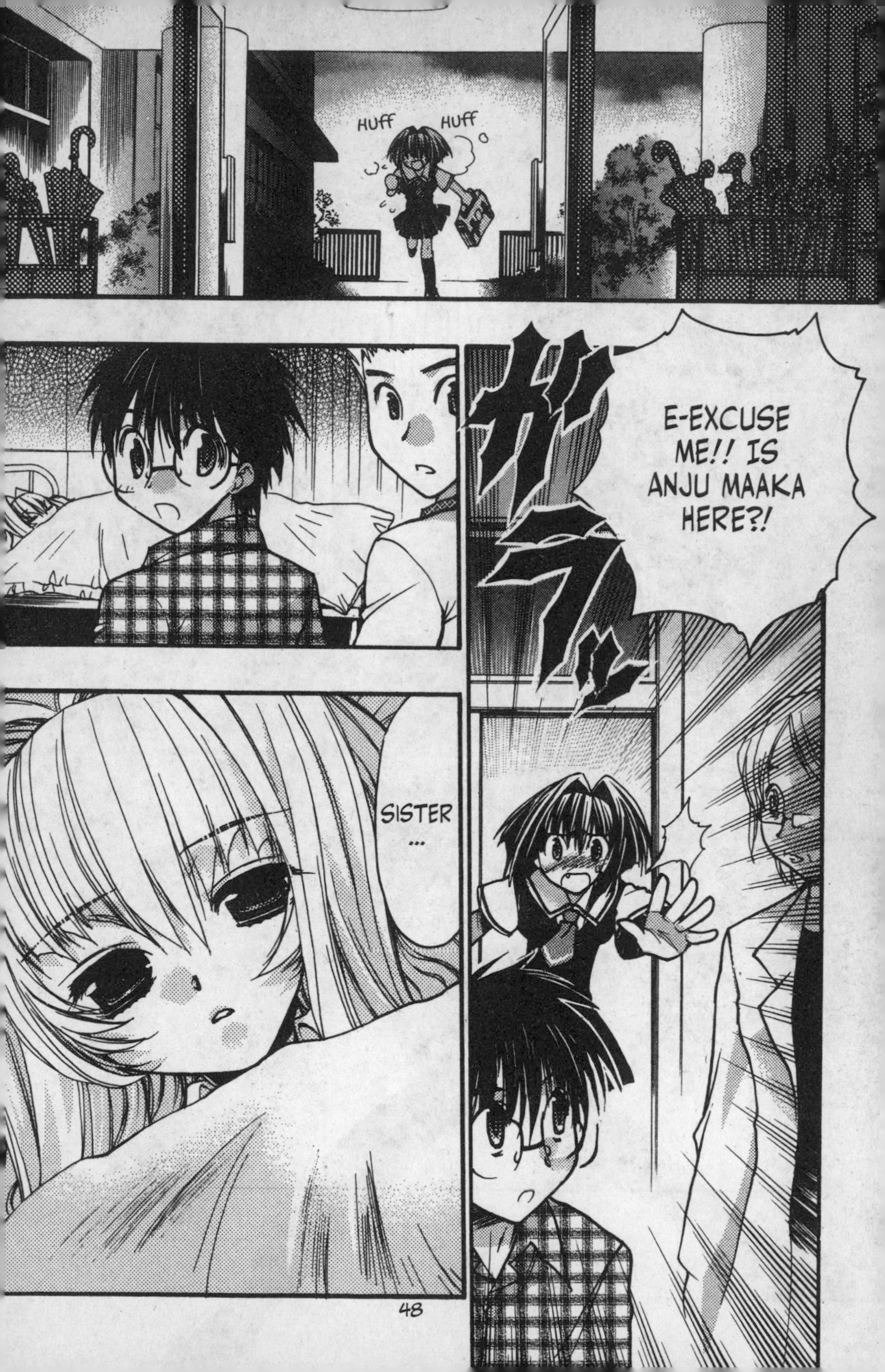
HUFF HUFF
ガラッ
E-EXCUSE ME!! IS ANJU MAAKA HERE?!
SISTER ...

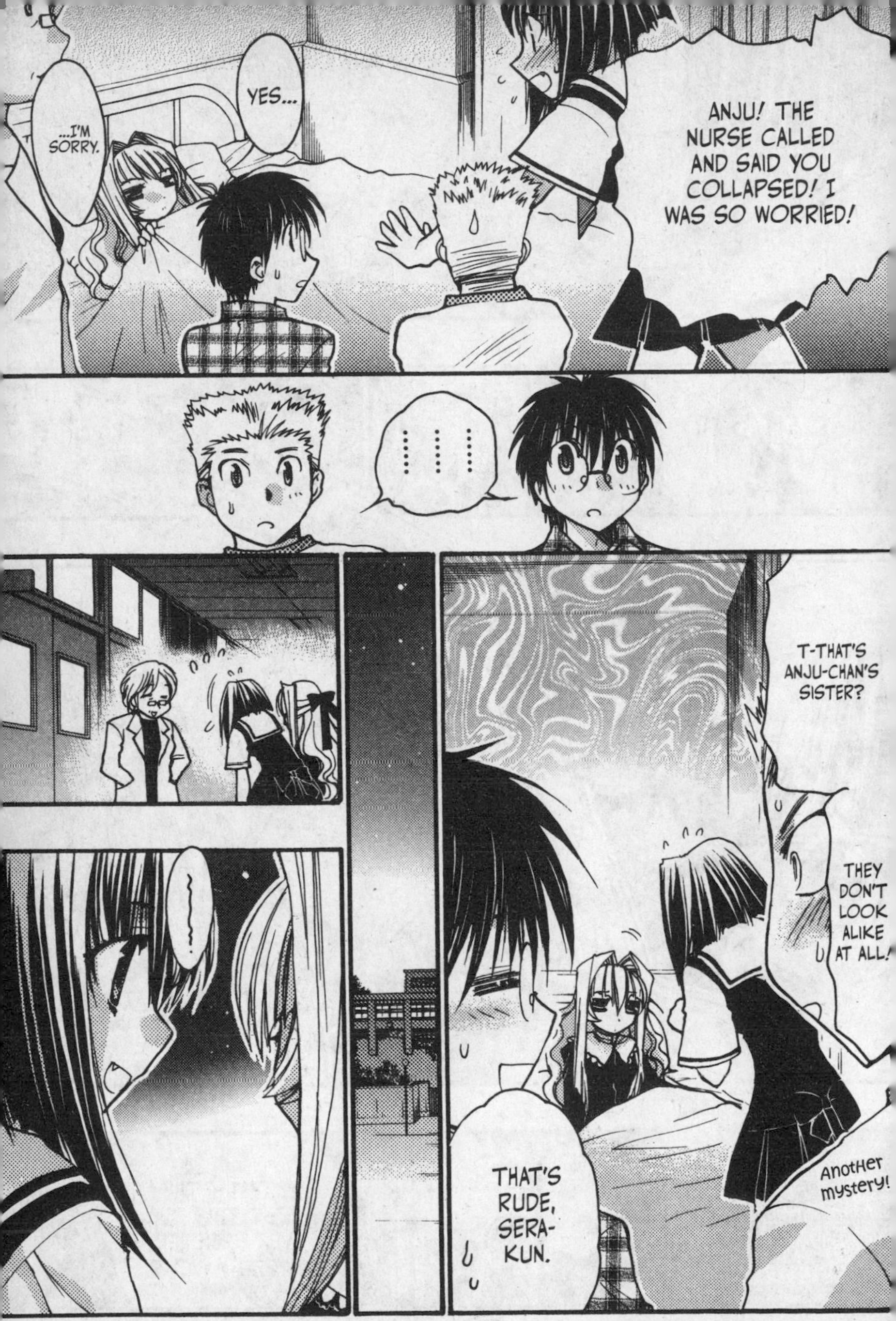
ANJU! THE NURSE CALLED AND SAID YOU COLLAPSED! I WAS SO WORRIED!
YES...
...I'M SORRY.
......
T-THAT'S ANJU-CHAN'S SISTER?
THEY DON'T LOOK ALIKE AT ALL!
THAT'S RUDE, SERA-KUN.
Another mystery!

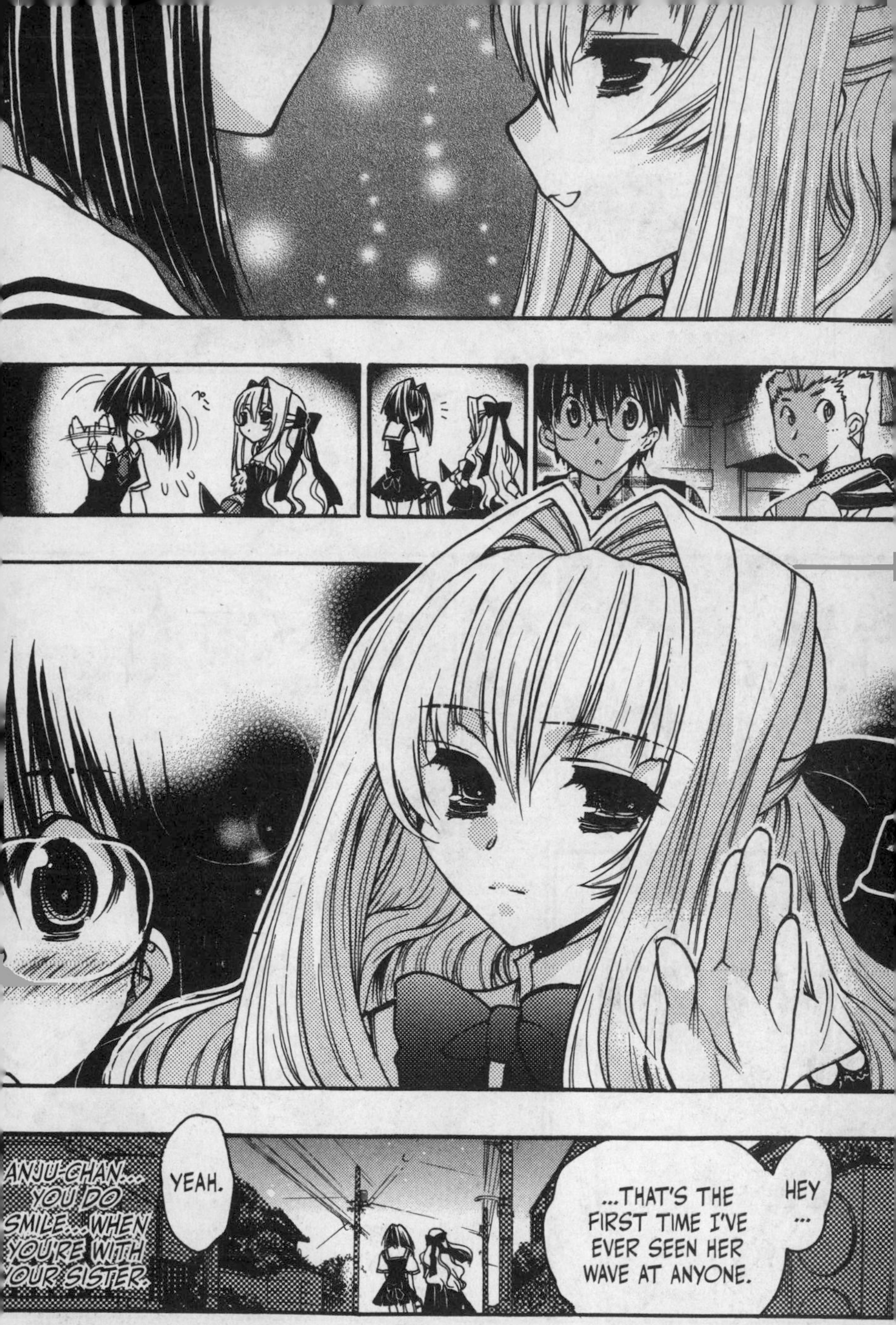
HEY ...
...THAT'S THE FIRST TIME I'VE EVER SEEN HER WAVE AT ANYONE.
YEAH.
ANJU-CHAN... YOU DO SMILE... WHEN YOU'RE WITH YOUR SISTER.

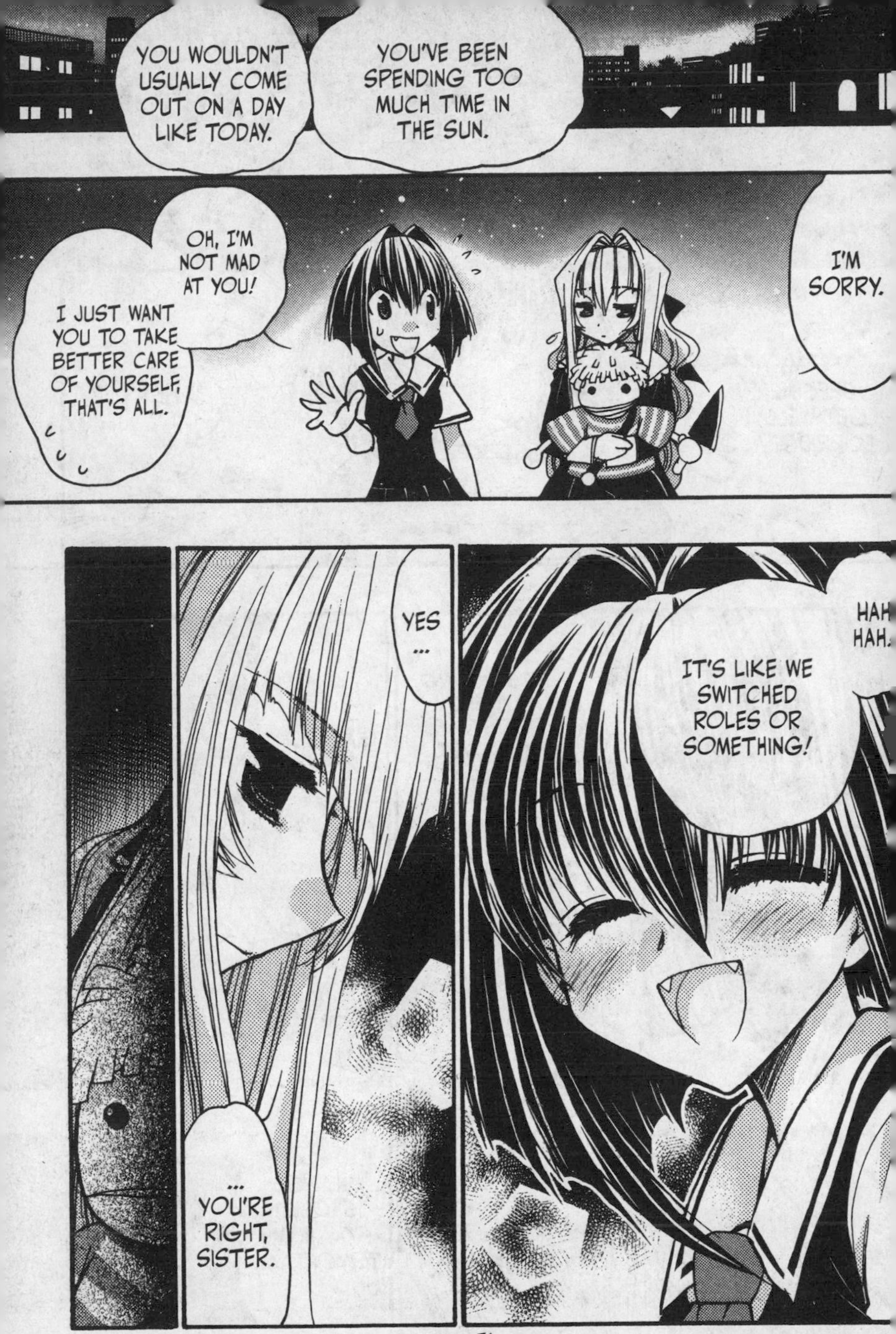
YOU'VE BEEN SPENDING TOO MUCH TIME IN THE SUN.
YOU WOULDN'T USUALLY COME OUT ON A DAY LIKE TODAY.
I'M SORRY.
OH, I'M NOT MAD AT YOU!
I JUST WANT YOU TO TAKE BETTER CARE OF YOURSELF, THAT'S ALL.
HAH HAH.
IT'S LIKE WE SWITCHED ROLES OR SOMETHING!
YES ...
... YOU'RE RIGHT, SISTER.

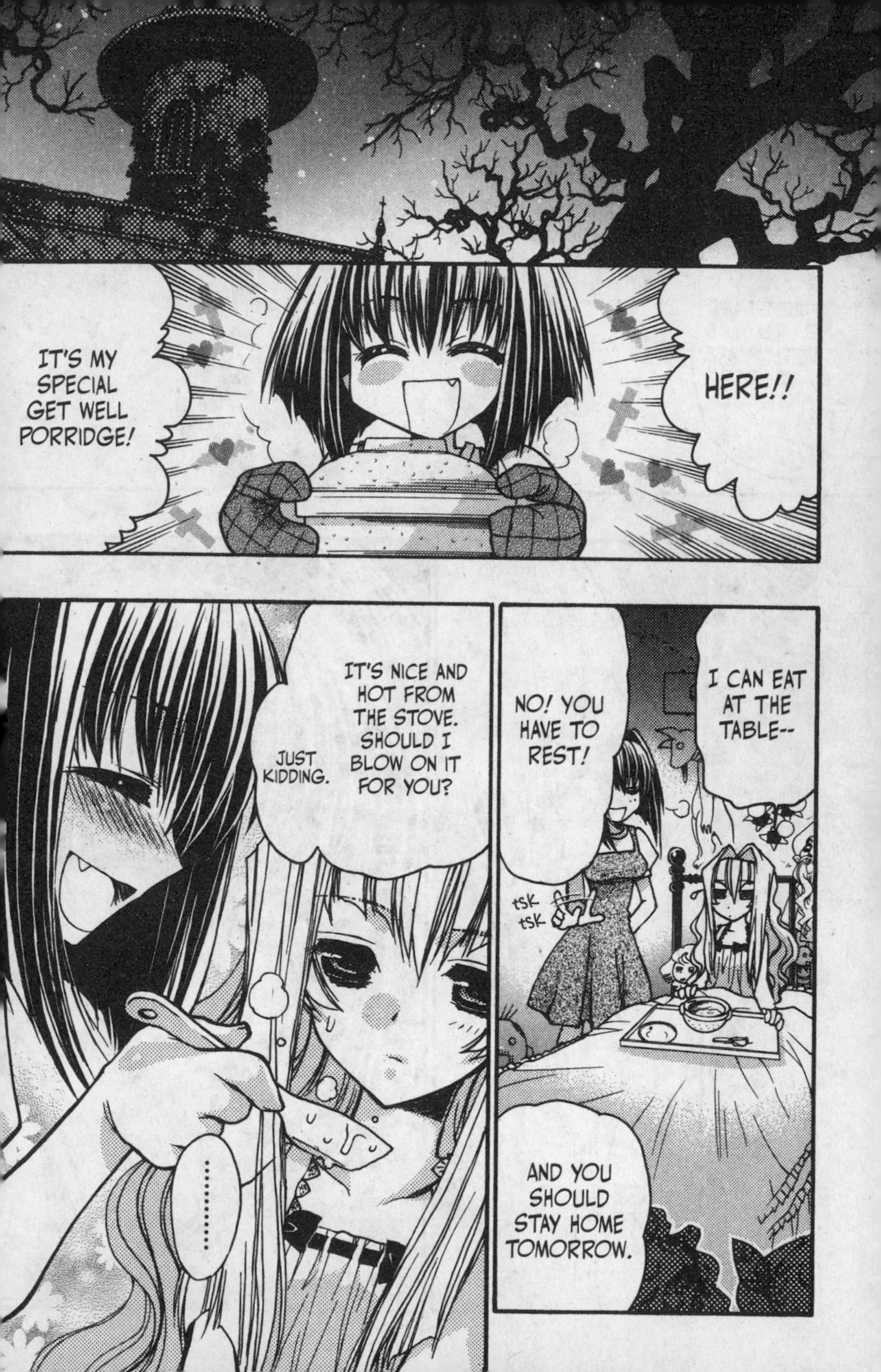
HERE!!
IT'S MY SPECIAL GET WELL PORRIDGE!
I CAN EAT AT THE TABLE--
NO! YOU HAVE TO REST!
tsk tsk
AND YOU SHOULD STAY HOME TOMORROW.
IT'S NICE AND HOT FROM THE STOVE. SHOULD I BLOW ON IT FOR YOU?
JUST KIDDING.
....

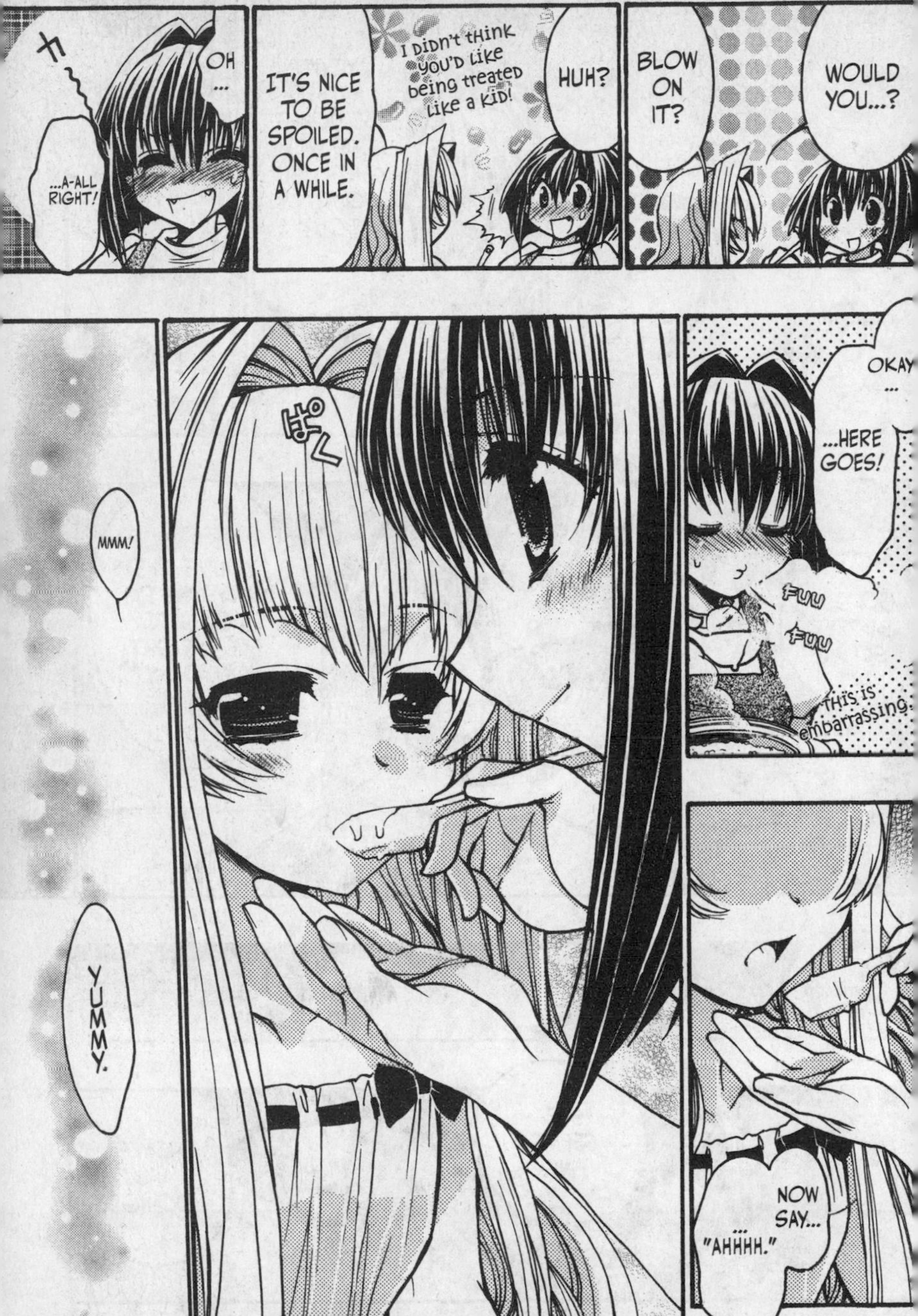
WOULD YOU...?
BLOW ON IT?
HUH?
I DIDN'T THINK YOU'D LIKE being treated like a KID!
IT'S NICE TO BE SPOILED. ONCE IN A WHILE.
OH ...
...A-ALL RIGHT!
OKAY ...
...HERE GOES!
FUU
FUU
THIS IS embarrassing.
NOW SAY... ... "AHHHH."
MMM!
YUMMY.

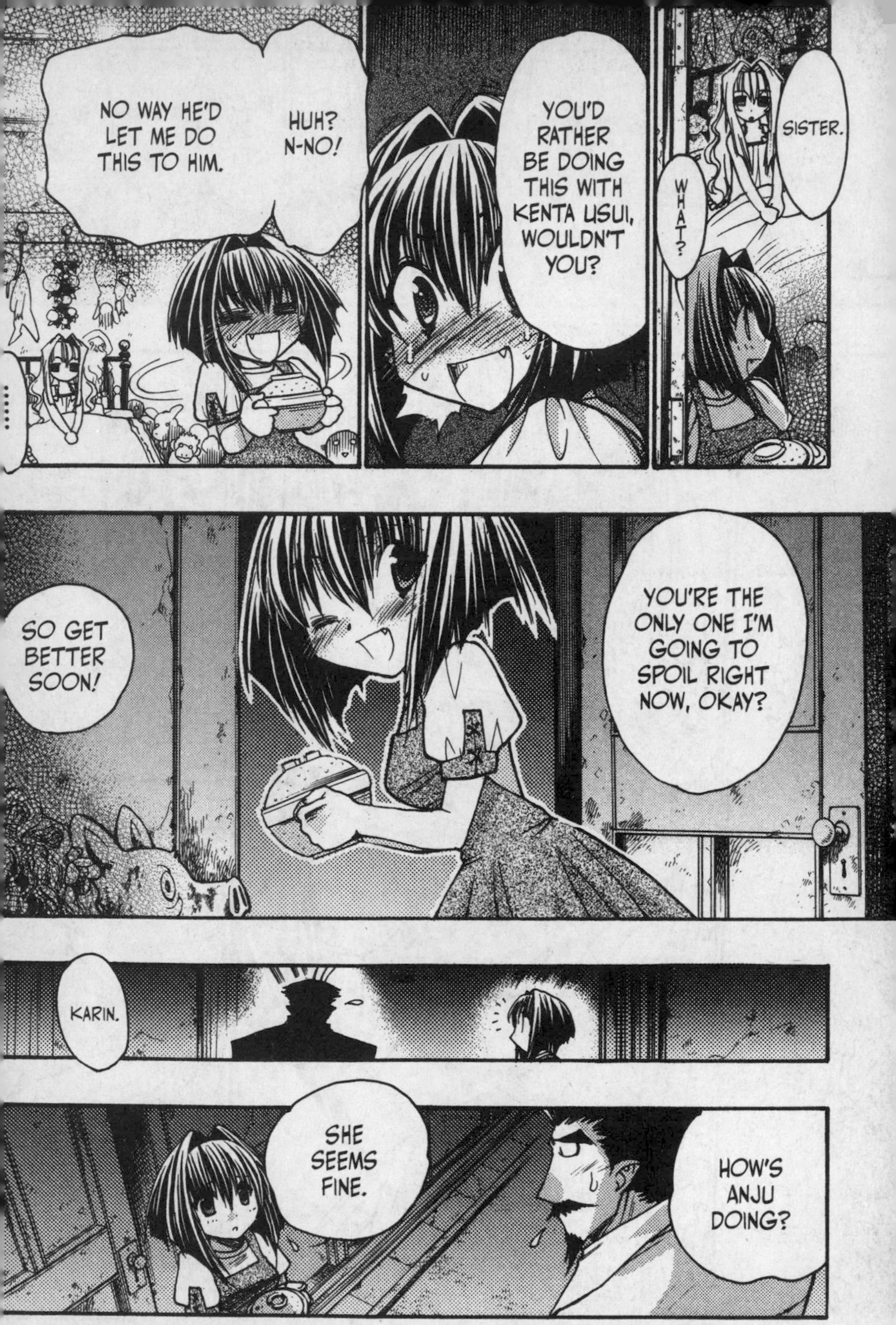
SISTER.
WHAT?
YOU'D RATHER BE DOING THIS WITH KENTA USUI, WOULDN'T YOU?
HUH? N-NO!
NO WAY HE'D LET ME DO THIS TO HIM.
......
YOU'RE THE ONLY ONE I'M GOING TO SPOIL RIGHT NOW, OKAY?
SO GET BETTER SOON!
KARIN.
HOW'S ANJU DOING?
SHE SEEMS FINE.

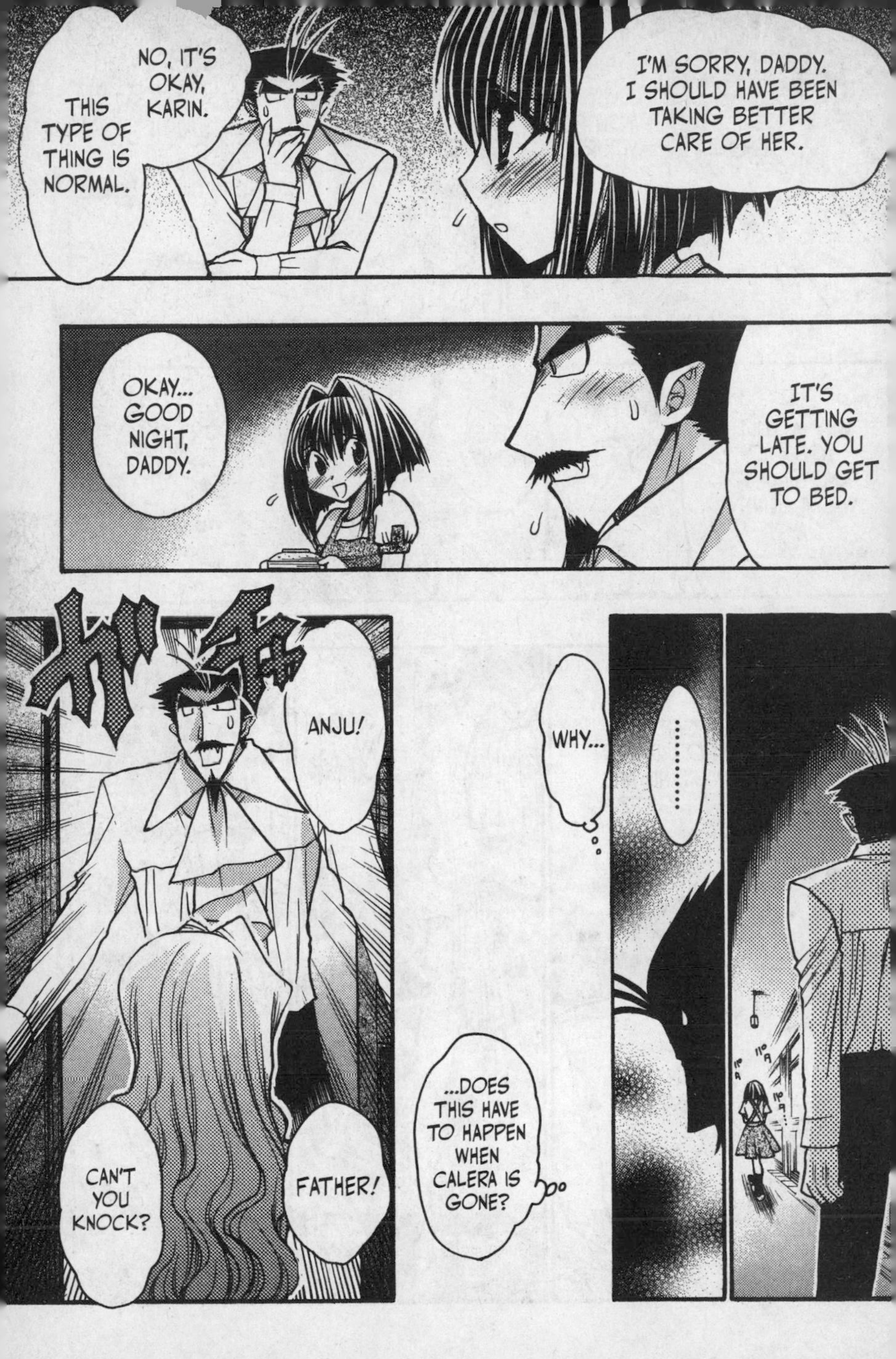
I'M SORRY, DADDY. I SHOULD HAVE BEEN TAKING BETTER CARE OF HER.
NO, IT'S OKAY, KARIN.
THIS TYPE OF THING IS NORMAL.
IT'S GETTING LATE. YOU SHOULD GET TO BED.
OKAY... GOOD NIGHT, DADDY.
......
WHY...
...DOES THIS HAVE TO HAPPEN WHEN CALERA IS GONE?
ガチャ
ANJU!
FATHER!
CAN'T YOU KNOCK?

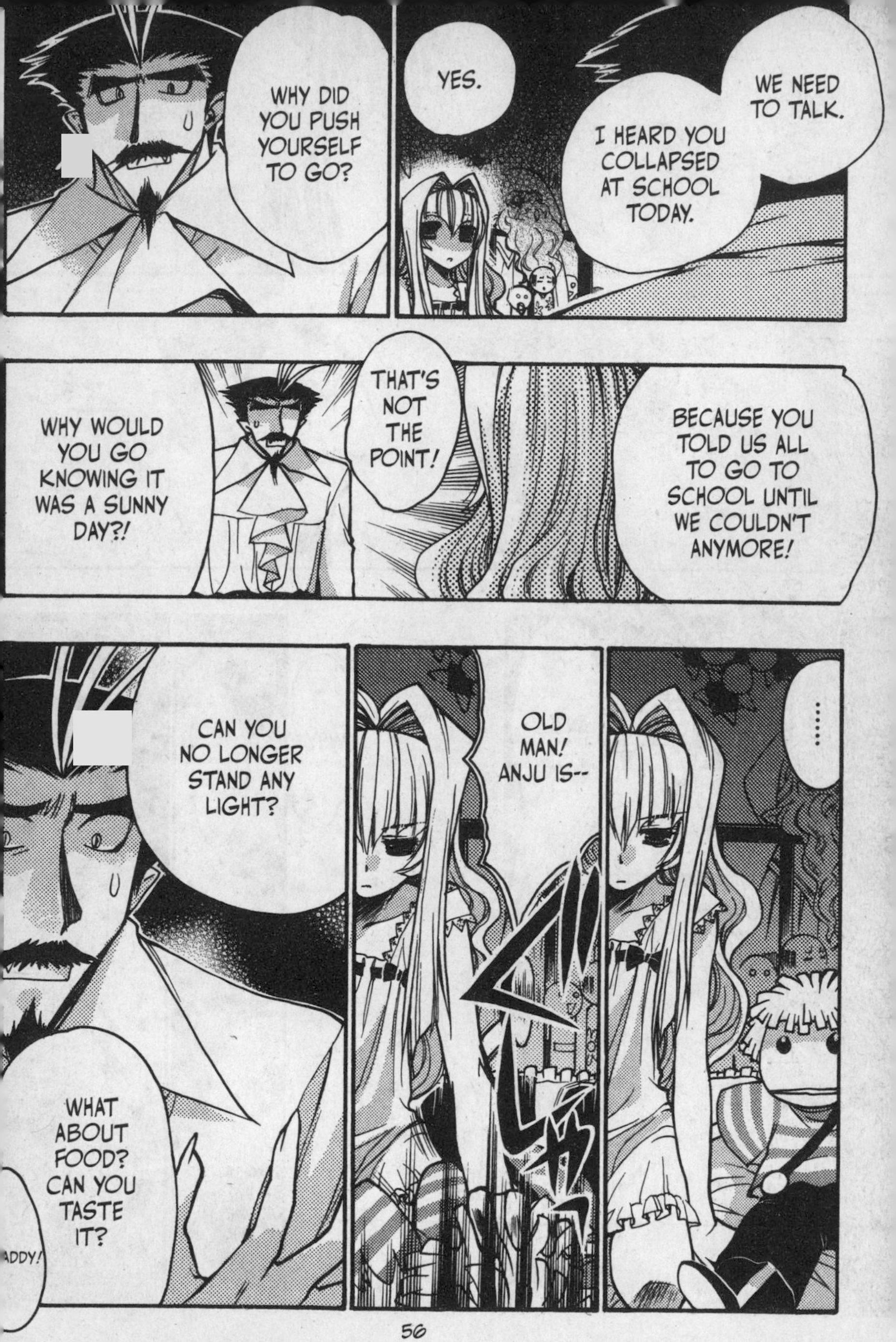
WE NEED TO TALK.
I HEARD YOU COLLAPSED AT SCHOOL TODAY.
YES.
WHY DID YOU PUSH YOURSELF TO GO?
BECAUSE YOU TOLD US ALL TO GO TO SCHOOL UNTIL WE COULDN'T ANYMORE!
THAT'S NOT THE POINT!
WHY WOULD YOU GO KNOWING IT WAS A SUNNY DAY?!
......
OLD MAN! ANJU IS--
CAN YOU NO LONGER STAND ANY LIGHT?
WHAT ABOUT FOOD? CAN YOU TASTE IT?

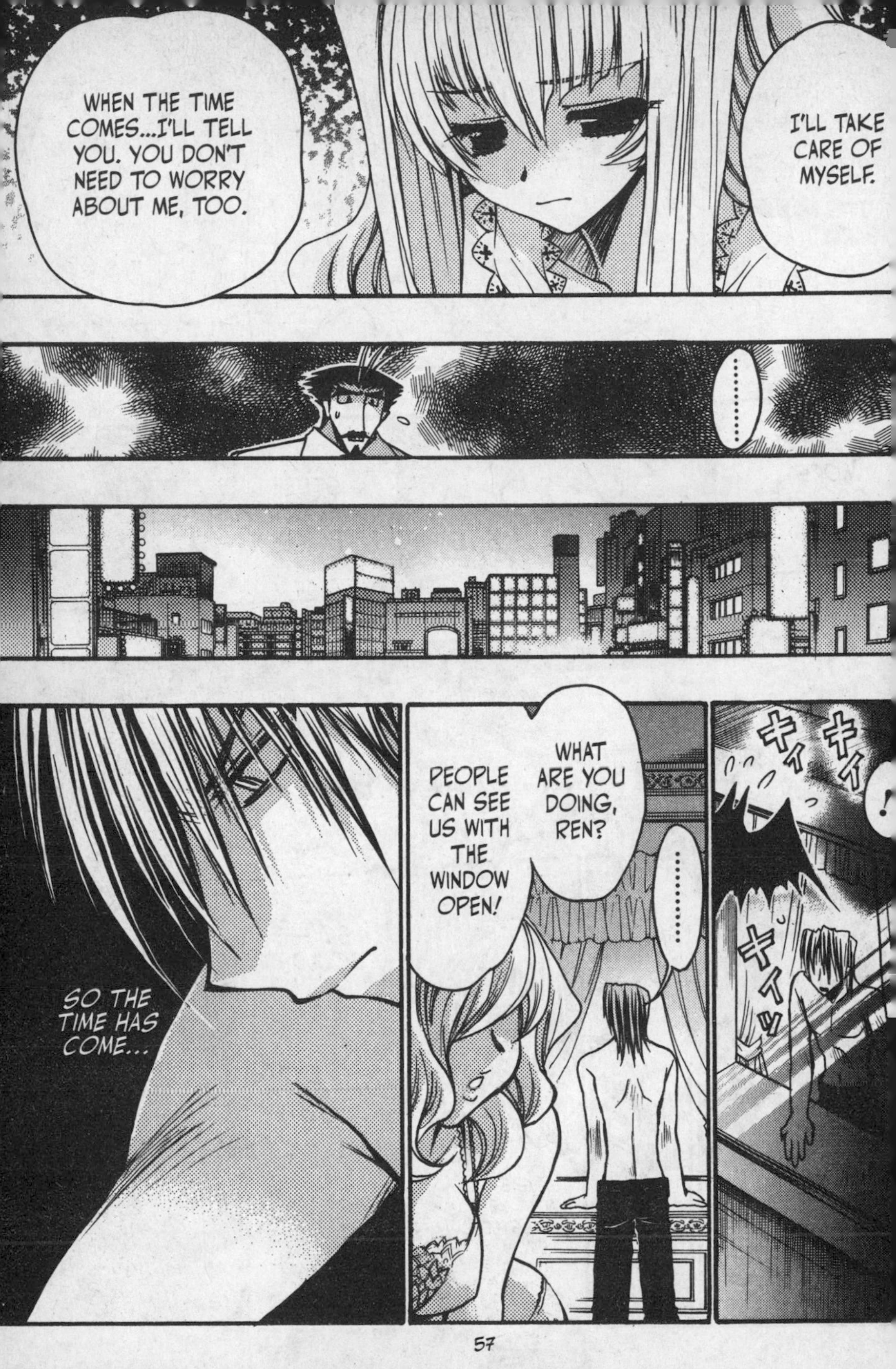
I'LL TAKE CARE OF MYSELF.
WHEN THE TIME COMES...I'LL TELL YOU. YOU DON'T NEED TO WORRY ABOUT ME, TOO.
......
!
キィ キィ
キィッ
WHAT ARE YOU DOING, REN?
PEOPLE CAN SEE US WITH THE WINDOW OPEN!
......
SO THE TIME HAS COME...

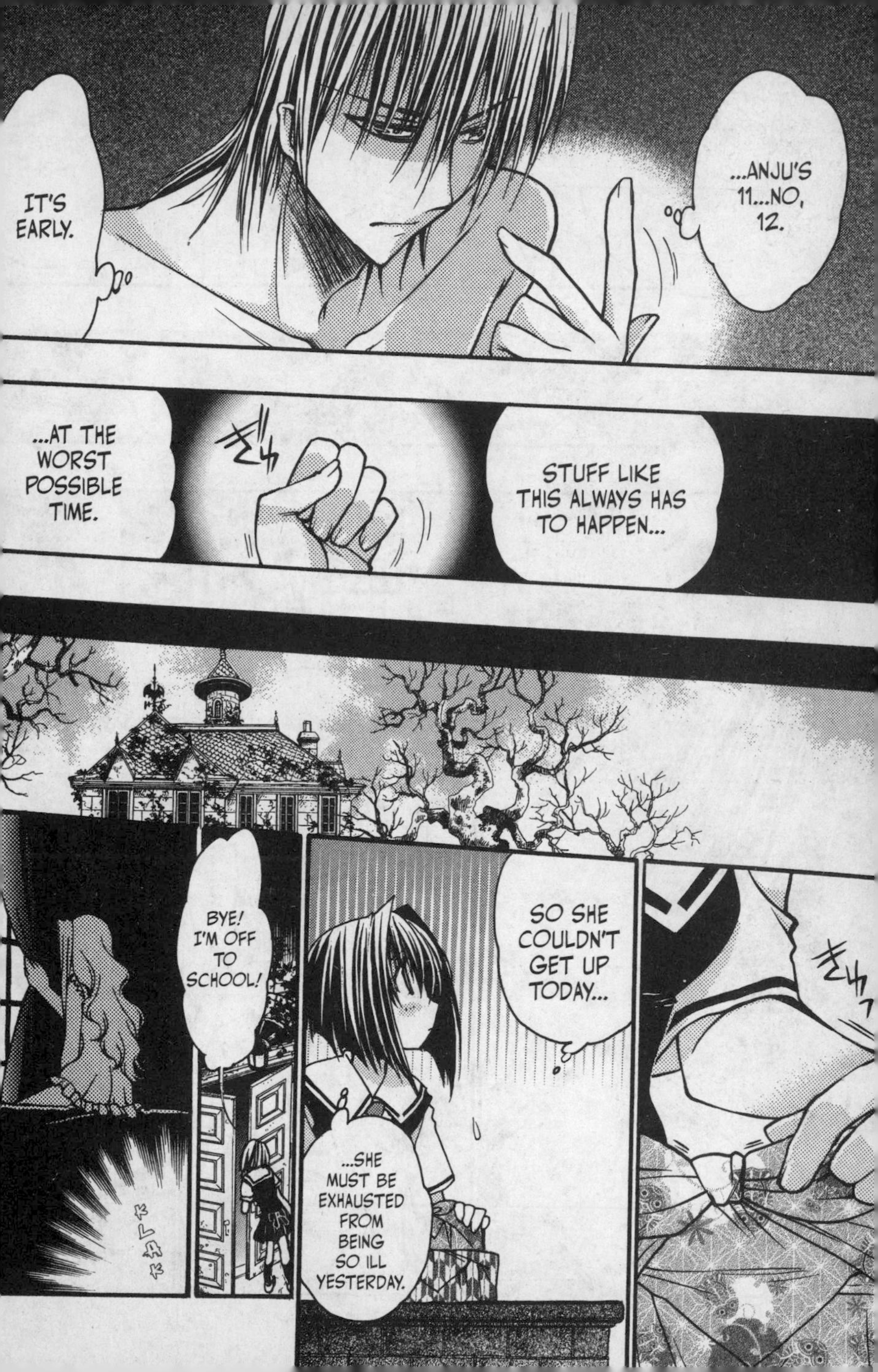
...ANJU'S 11...NO, 12.
IT'S EARLY.
STUFF LIKE THIS ALWAYS HAS TO HAPPEN...
...AT THE WORST POSSIBLE TIME.
SO SHE COULDN'T GET UP TODAY...
...SHE MUST BE EXHAUSTED FROM BEING SO ILL YESTERDAY.
BYE! I'M OFF TO SCHOOL!
KLAK

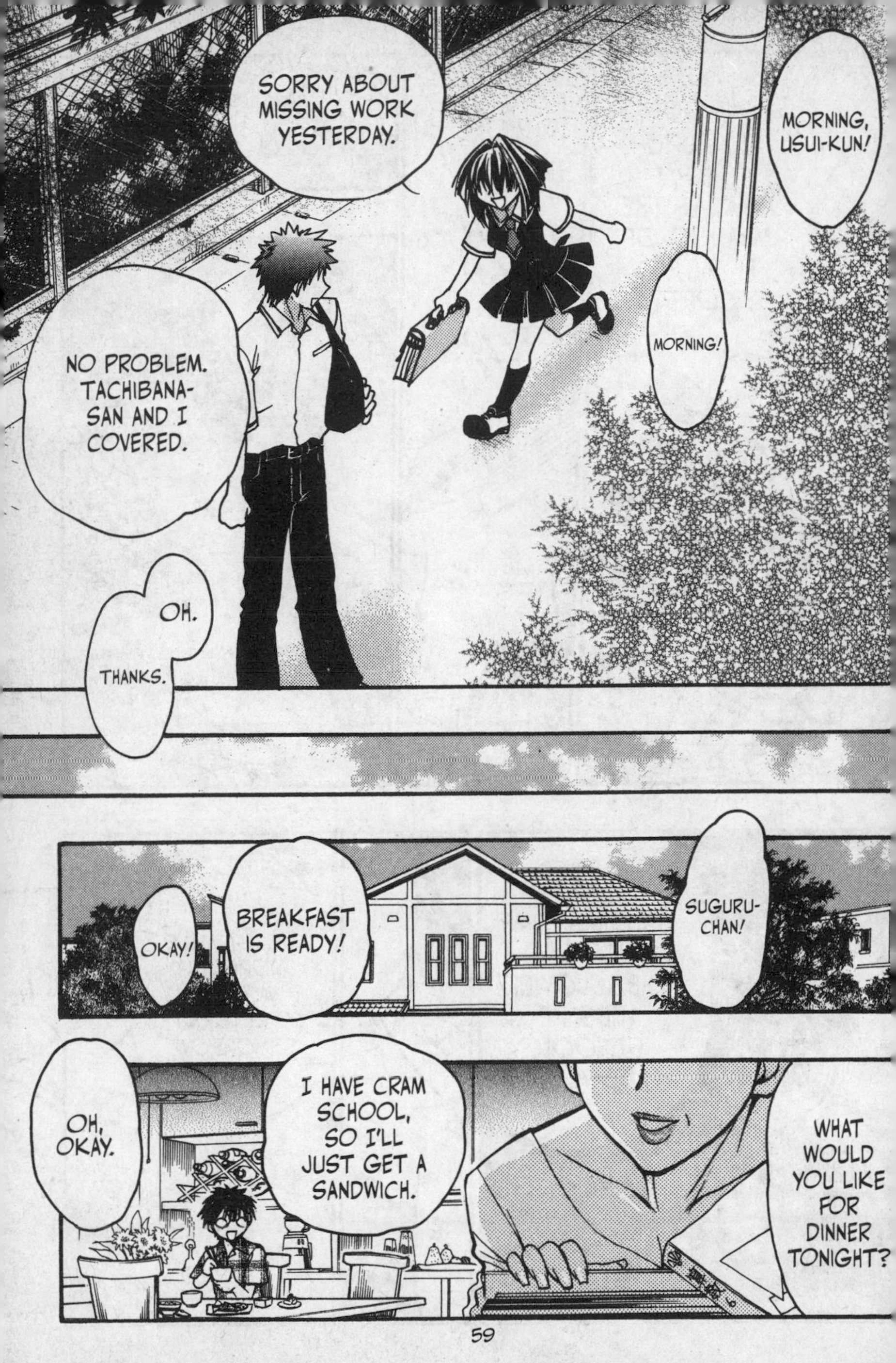
MORNING, USUI-KUN!
MORNING!
SORRY ABOUT MISSING WORK YESTERDAY.
NO PROBLEM. TACHIBANA-SAN AND I COVERED.
OH.
THANKS.
SUGURU-CHAN!
BREAKFAST IS READY!
OKAY!
WHAT WOULD YOU LIKE FOR DINNER TONIGHT?
I HAVE CRAM SCHOOL, SO I'LL JUST GET A SANDWICH.
OH, OKAY.

OH, THERE'S A PAPER IN YOUR BAG...

S-S-S-SUGURU-CHAN!! WHAT IS THE MEANING OF THIS TEST SCORE?!

OH!

AH HHHHHHHHHH!!!

WHAT'S WRONG?!

MOM?!

算数

① □に合う言葉や数な
死にそうな漫画家がアシスタ
買いに行ってもらいました。
アシスタントが砂柄が足らな
枯長…足らなくなったので画材屋
もらいました。砂柄はい皮でした
定番ビクタテが同じ枚数だった

漫画家は銀行に逆戦はありませ

② 次の数の倍数を小さいものから順に
1…13   2…666

③ 3と4の公倍数 小さいものから順に

④

話を何人かのオタクで分
き入れなさい。

YOU AREN'T WASTING TIME TUTORING THE...SLOWER KIDS AT SCHOOL, ARE YOU?

SUGURU-CHAN.

....

A CLASSMATE DROPPED IT. I WAS GOING TO RETURN IT TOMORROW.

N-NO, MOM.

I SHOWED YOU MY TEST, READ THE NAME ON TOP. remember?

O-OH, RIGHT. PHEW.

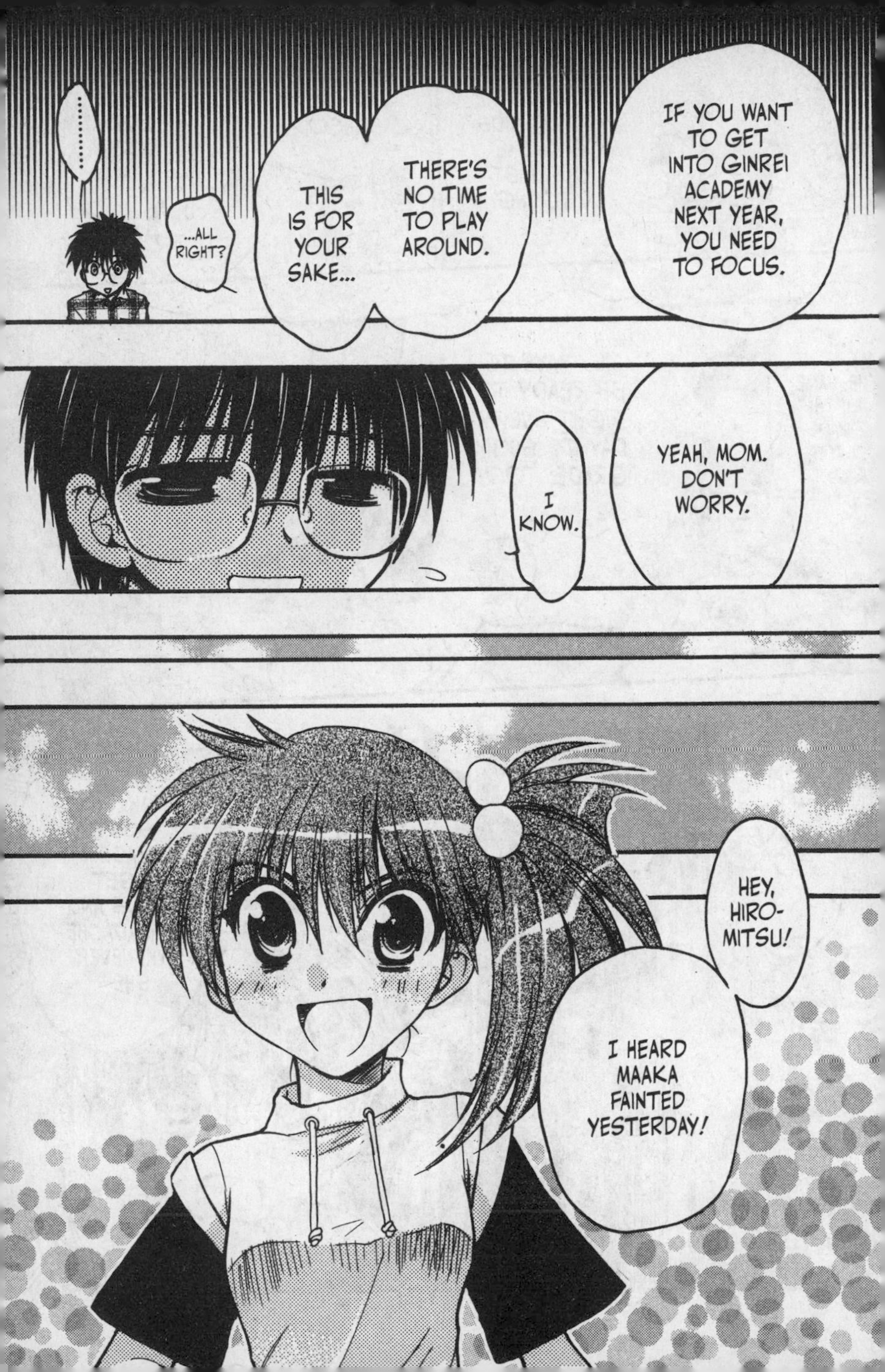
IF YOU WANT TO GET INTO GINREI ACADEMY NEXT YEAR, YOU NEED TO FOCUS.
THERE'S NO TIME TO PLAY AROUND.
THIS IS FOR YOUR SAKE...
...ALL RIGHT?
......
YEAH, MOM. DON'T WORRY.
I KNOW.
HEY, HIRO-MITSU!
I HEARD MAAKA FAINTED YESTERDAY!

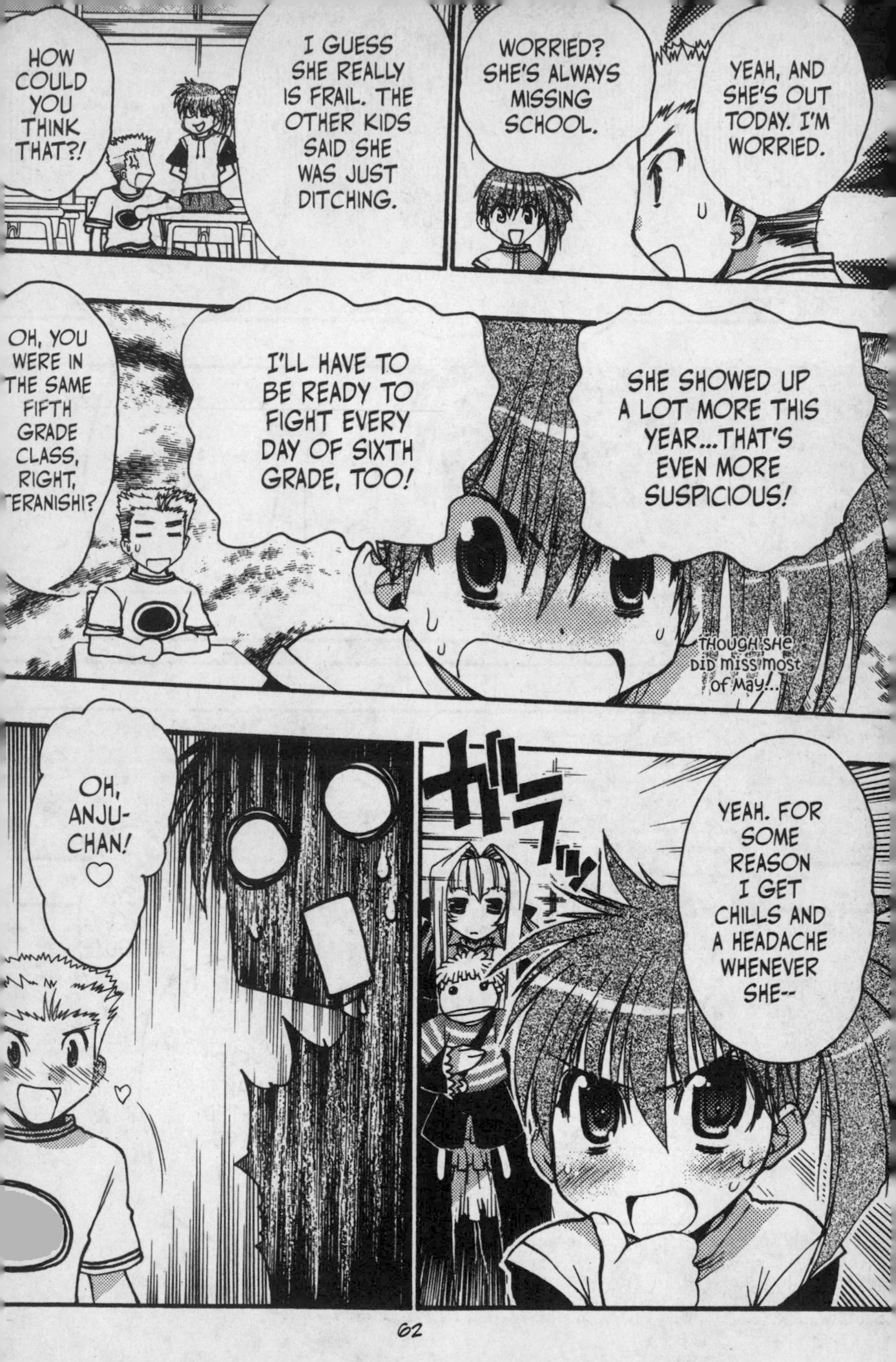
YEAH, AND SHE'S OUT TODAY. I'M WORRIED.
WORRIED? SHE'S ALWAYS MISSING SCHOOL.
I GUESS SHE REALLY IS FRAIL. THE OTHER KIDS SAID SHE WAS JUST DITCHING.
HOW COULD YOU THINK THAT?!
SHE SHOWED UP A LOT MORE THIS YEAR...THAT'S EVEN MORE SUSPICIOUS!
THOUGH SHE DID MISS MOST OF MAY...
I'LL HAVE TO BE READY TO FIGHT EVERY DAY OF SIXTH GRADE, TOO!
OH, YOU WERE IN THE SAME FIFTH GRADE CLASS, RIGHT, TERANISHI?
ガラッ
YEAH. FOR SOME REASON I GET CHILLS AND A HEADACHE WHENEVER SHE--
OH, ANJU-CHAN! ♡

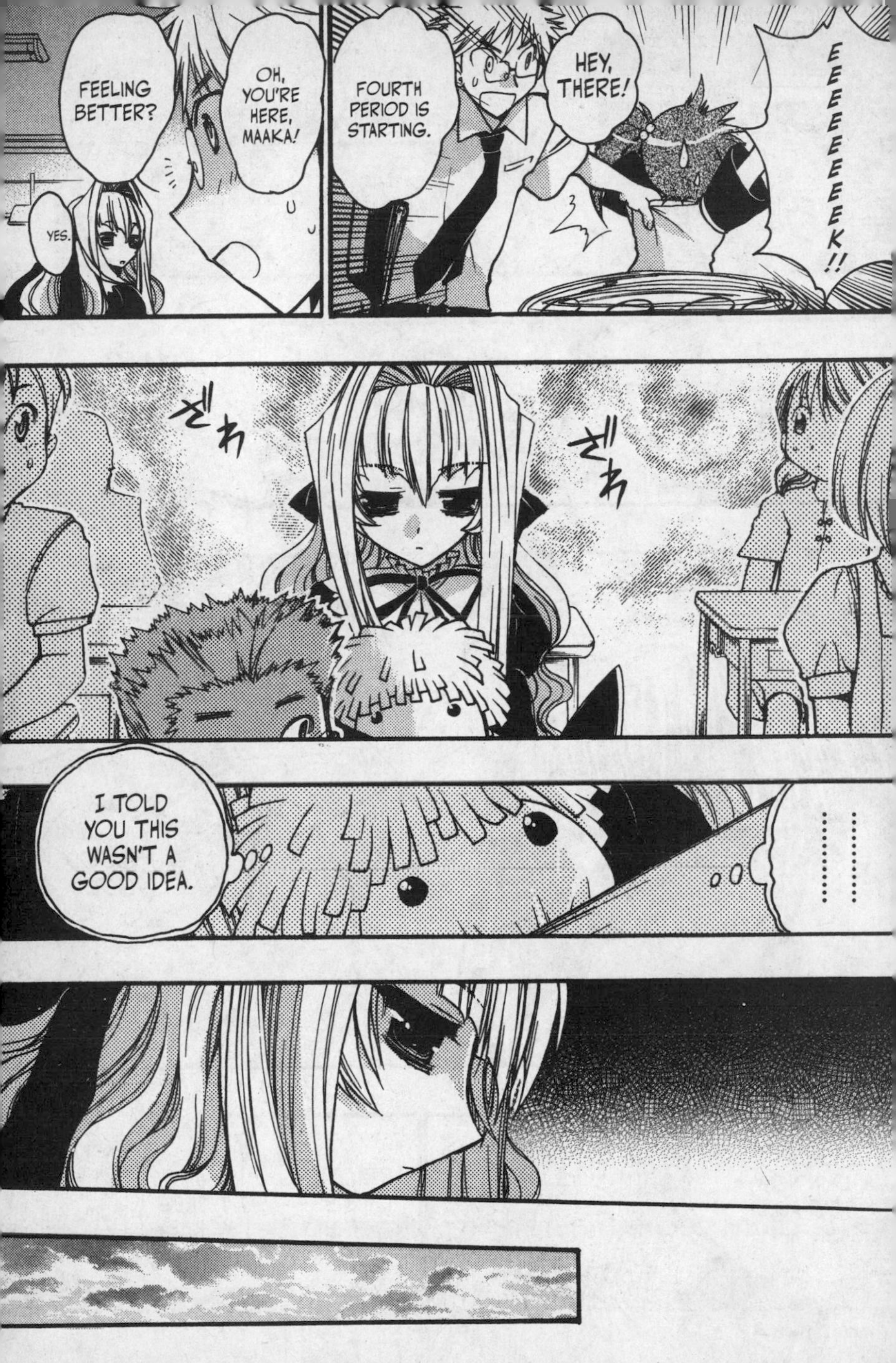
EEEEEEEEEK!!
HEY, THERE!
FOURTH PERIOD IS STARTING.
OH, YOU'RE HERE, MAAKA!
FEELING BETTER?
YES.
ざわ
ざわ
……
I TOLD YOU THIS WASN'T A GOOD IDEA.

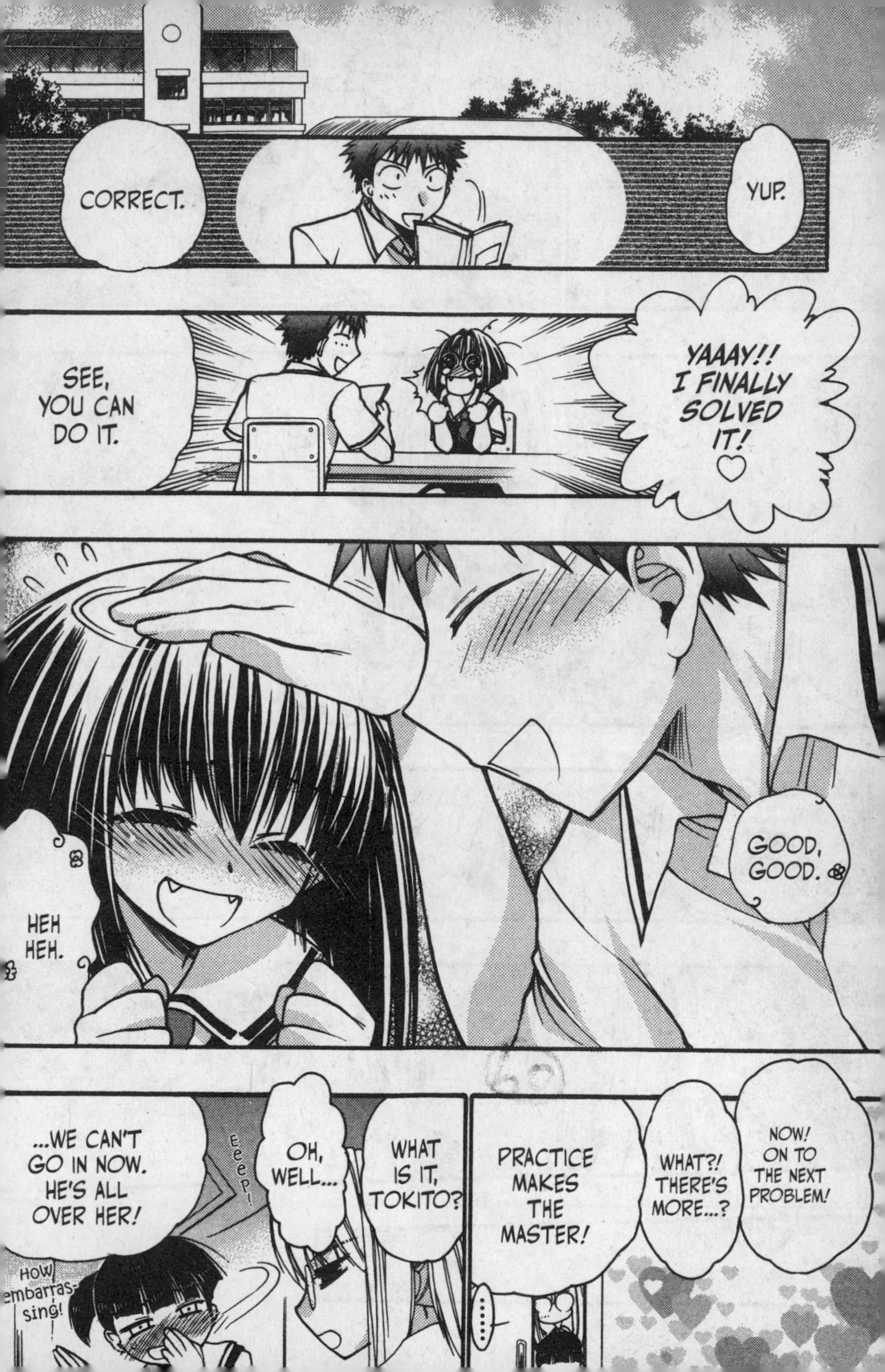
YUP.
CORRECT.
YAAAY!! I FINALLY SOLVED IT! ♡
SEE, YOU CAN DO IT.
GOOD, GOOD.
HEH HEH.
NOW! ON TO THE NEXT PROBLEM!
WHAT?! THERE'S MORE...?
PRACTICE MAKES THE MASTER!
......
WHAT IS IT, TOKITO?
OH, WELL...
EEEP!
...WE CAN'T GO IN NOW. HE'S ALL OVER HER!
HOW embarrassing!

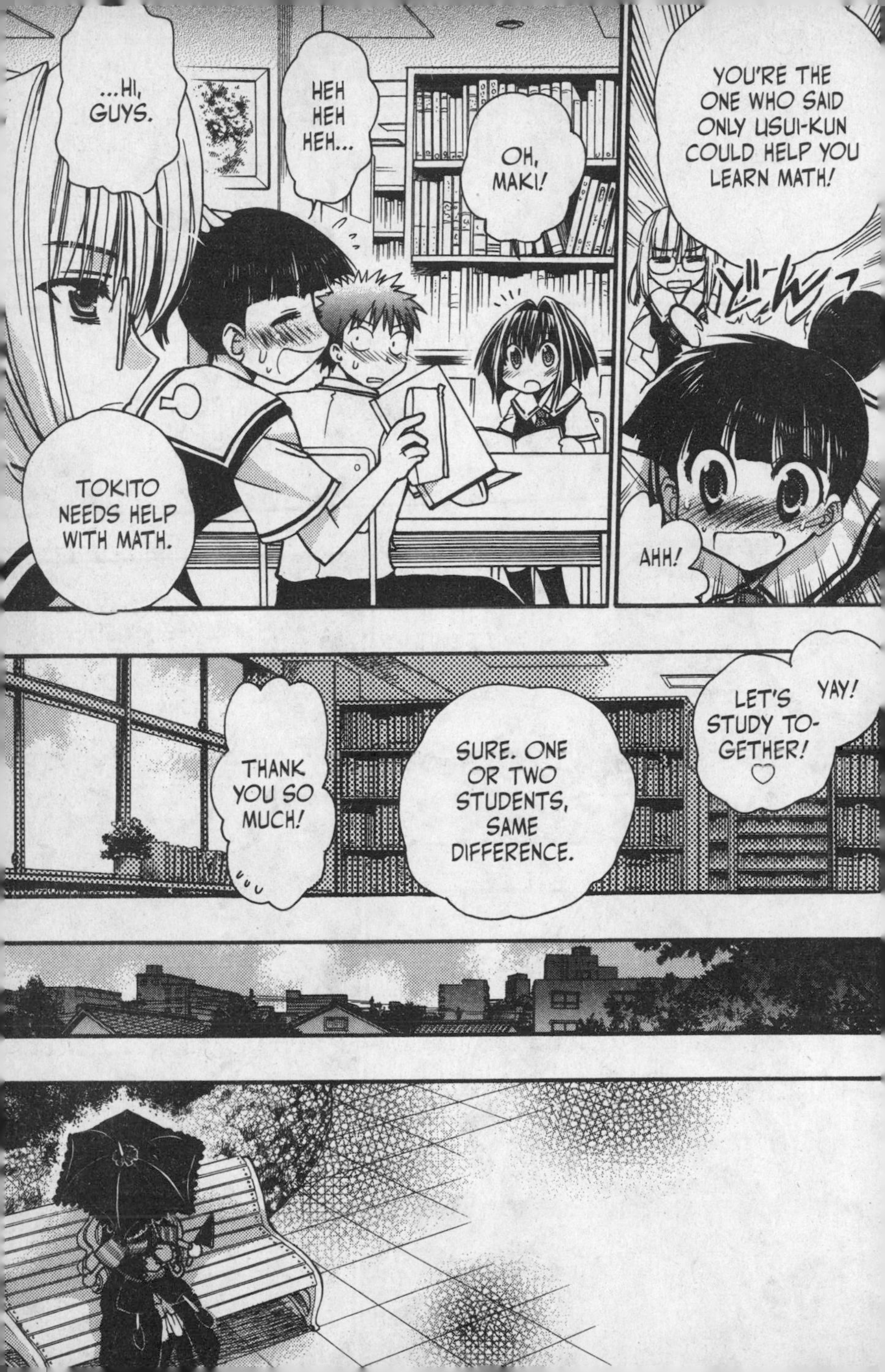
YOU'RE THE ONE WHO SAID ONLY USUI-KUN COULD HELP YOU LEARN MATH!
AHH!
OH, MAKI!
HEH HEH HEH...
...HI, GUYS.
TOKITO NEEDS HELP WITH MATH.
YAY!
LET'S STUDY TOGETHER! ♡
SURE. ONE OR TWO STUDENTS, SAME DIFFERENCE.
THANK YOU SO MUCH!

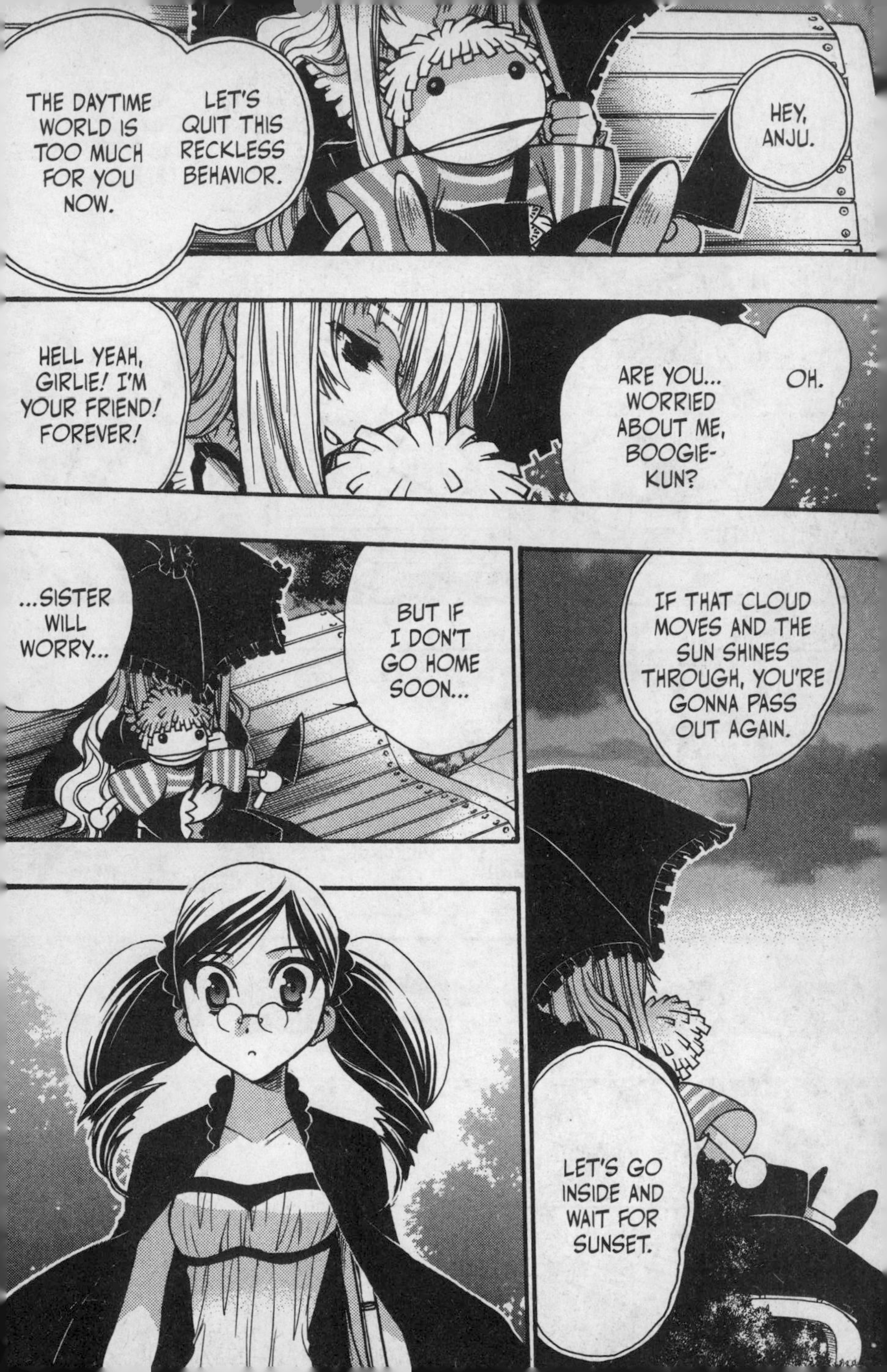
HEY, ANJU.
LET'S QUIT THIS RECKLESS BEHAVIOR.
THE DAYTIME WORLD IS TOO MUCH FOR YOU NOW.
OH.
ARE YOU... WORRIED ABOUT ME, BOOGIE-KUN?
HELL YEAH, GIRLIE! I'M YOUR FRIEND! FOREVER!
IF THAT CLOUD MOVES AND THE SUN SHINES THROUGH, YOU'RE GONNA PASS OUT AGAIN.
LET'S GO INSIDE AND WAIT FOR SUNSET.
BUT IF I DON'T GO HOME SOON...
...SISTER WILL WORRY...

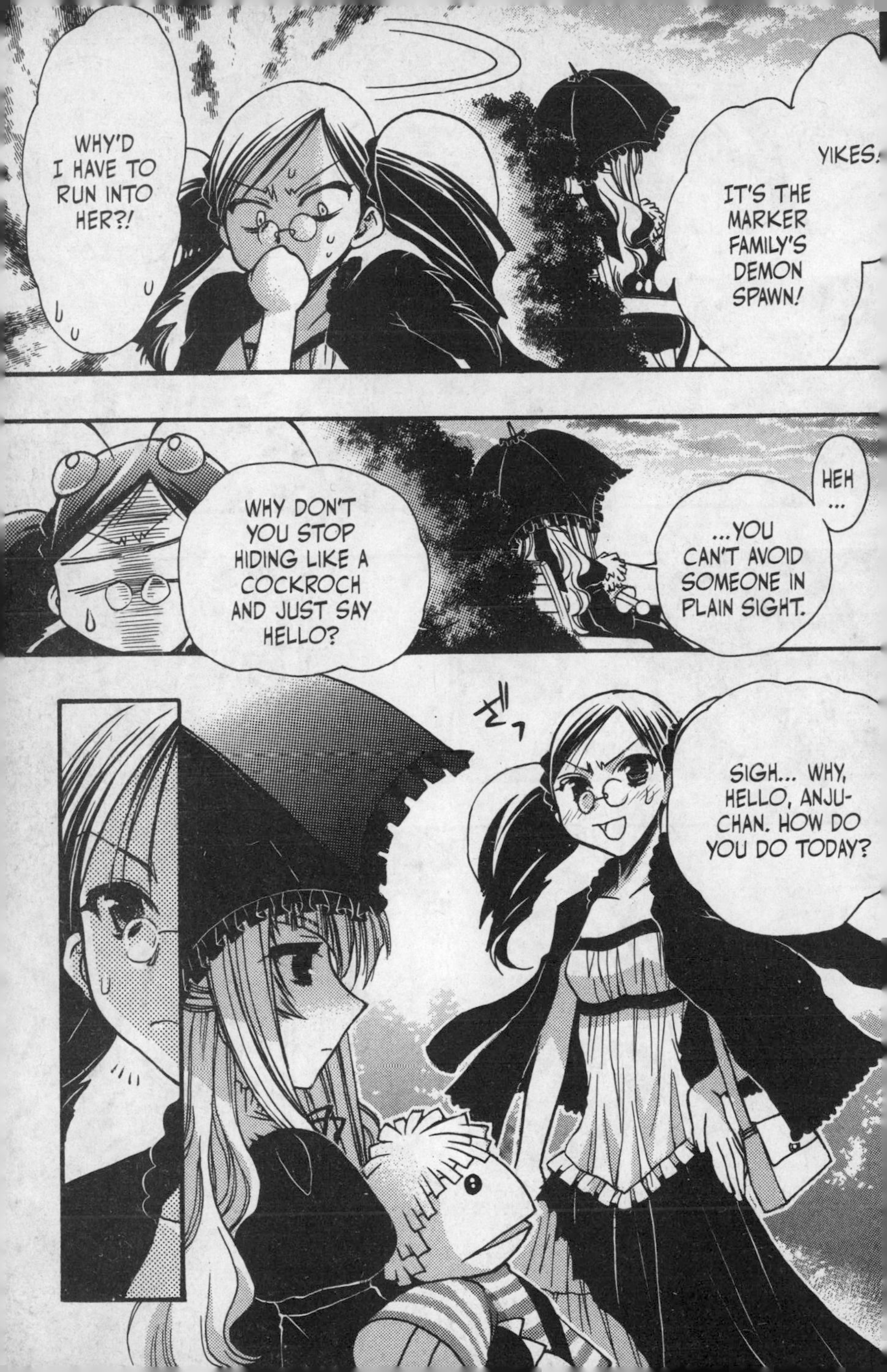
YIKES. IT'S THE MARKER FAMILY'S DEMON SPAWN!
WHY'D I HAVE TO RUN INTO HER?!
HEH...
...YOU CAN'T AVOID SOMEONE IN PLAIN SIGHT.
WHY DON'T YOU STOP HIDING LIKE A COCKROCH AND JUST SAY HELLO?
SIGH... WHY, HELLO, ANJU-CHAN. HOW DO YOU DO TODAY?

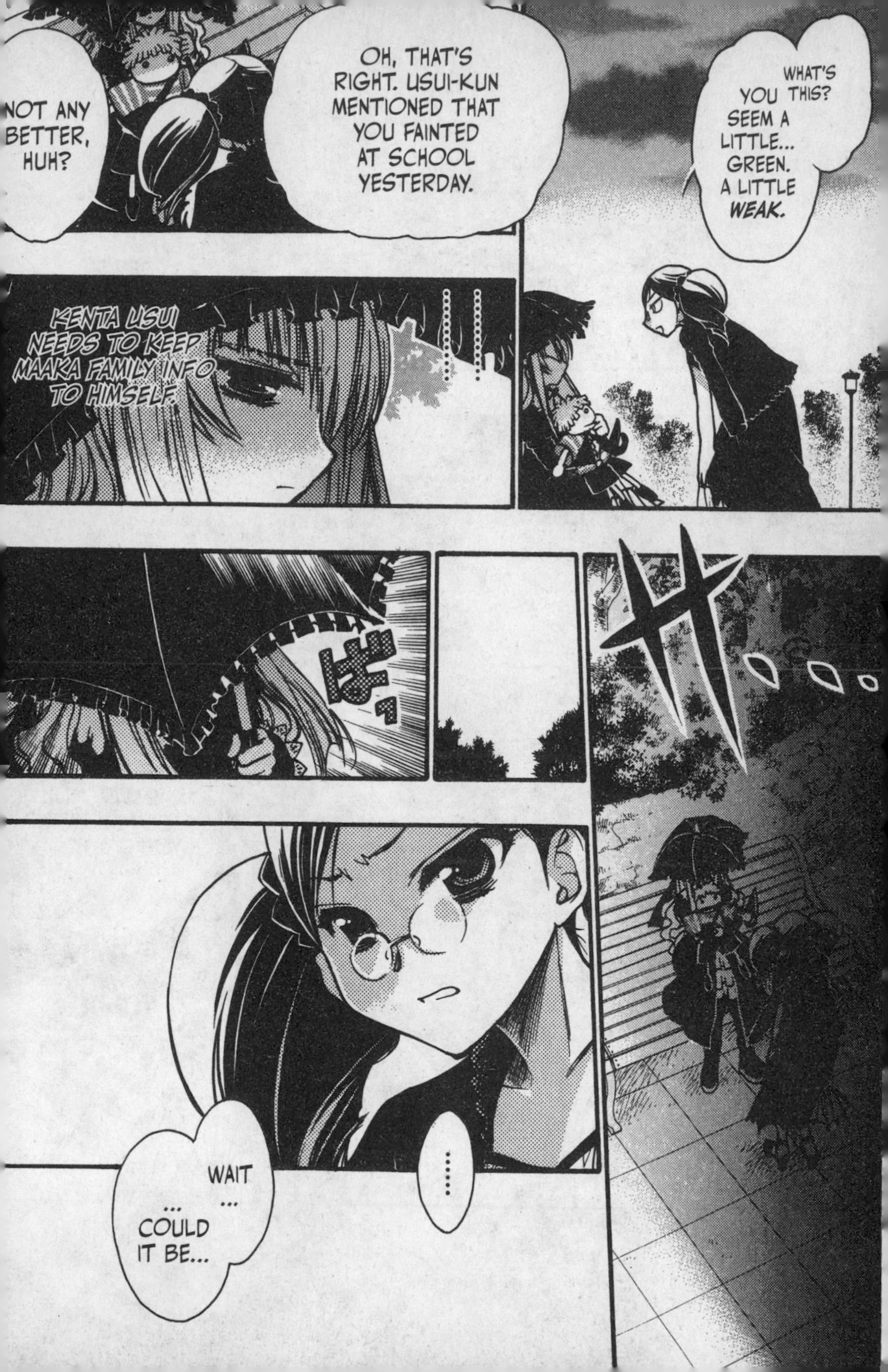
WHAT'S THIS? YOU SEEM A LITTLE... GREEN. A LITTLE WEAK.
OH, THAT'S RIGHT. USUI-KUN MENTIONED THAT YOU FAINTED AT SCHOOL YESTERDAY.
NOT ANY BETTER, HUH?
KENTA USUI NEEDS TO KEEP MAAKA FAMILY INFO TO HIMSELF.
ぱっ
......
WAIT ... ... COULD IT BE...

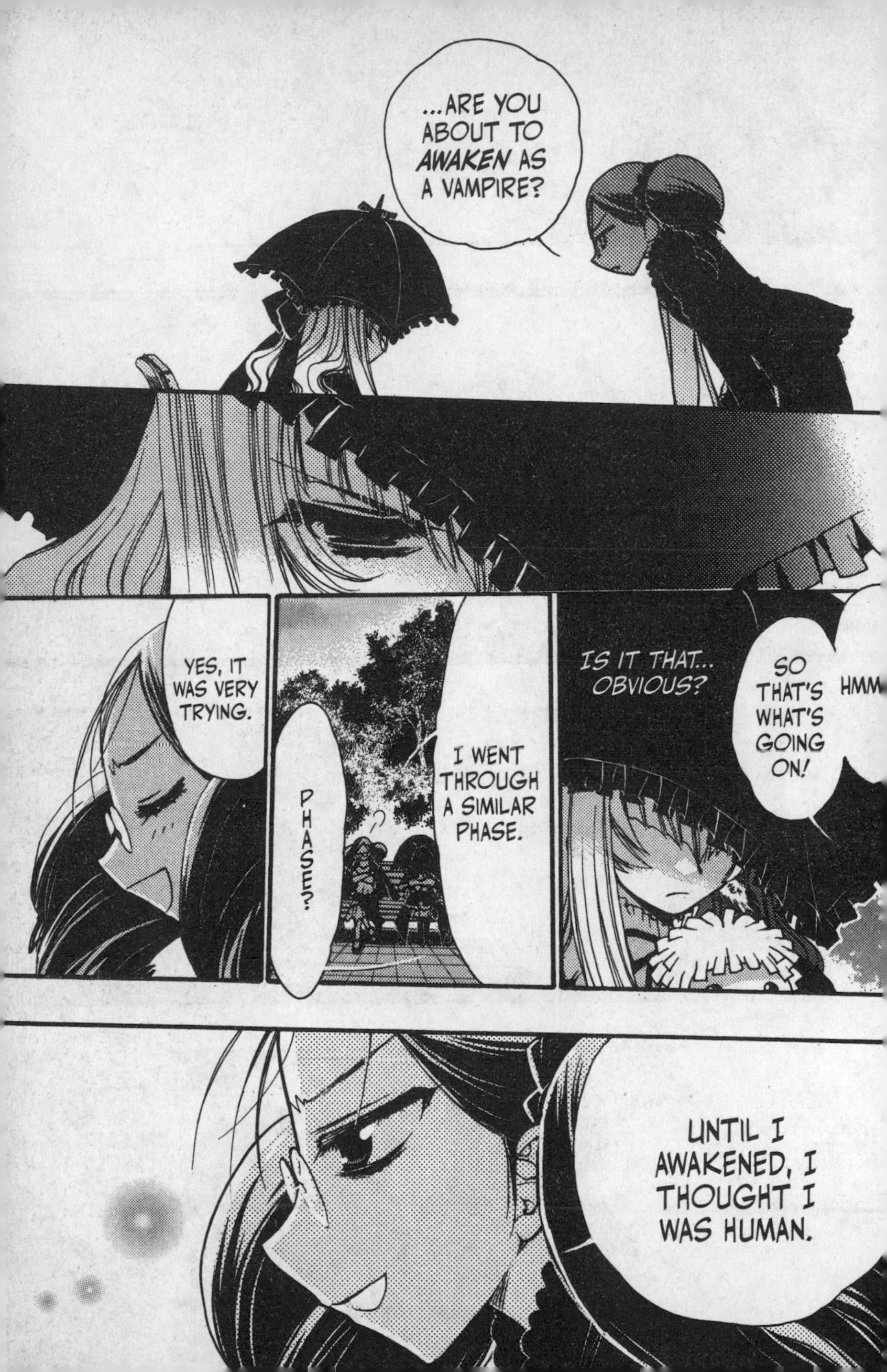
...ARE YOU ABOUT TO AWAKEN AS A VAMPIRE?
HMM
SO THAT'S WHAT'S GOING ON!
IS IT THAT... OBVIOUS?
I WENT THROUGH A SIMILAR PHASE.
PHASE?
YES, IT WAS VERY TRYING.
UNTIL I AWAKENED, I THOUGHT I WAS HUMAN.

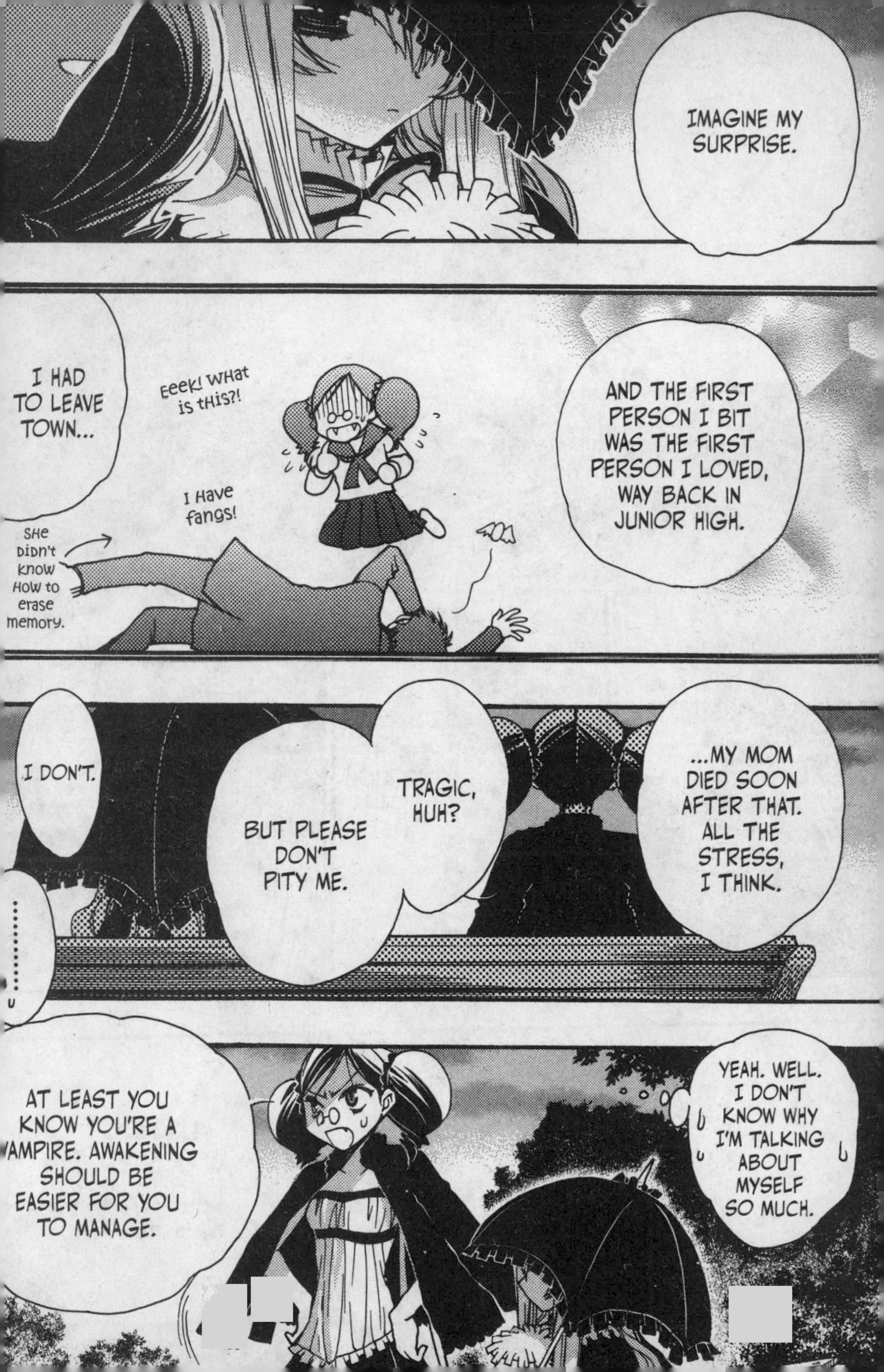
IMAGINE MY SURPRISE.
AND THE FIRST PERSON I BIT WAS THE FIRST PERSON I LOVED, WAY BACK IN JUNIOR HIGH.
Eeek! What is this?!
I have fangs!
I HAD TO LEAVE TOWN...
She didn't know how to erase memory.
...MY MOM DIED SOON AFTER THAT. ALL THE STRESS, I THINK.
TRAGIC, HUH?
BUT PLEASE DON'T PITY ME.
I DON'T.
....
YEAH. WELL. I DON'T KNOW WHY I'M TALKING ABOUT MYSELF SO MUCH.
AT LEAST YOU KNOW YOU'RE A VAMPIRE. AWAKENING SHOULD BE EASIER FOR YOU TO MANAGE.

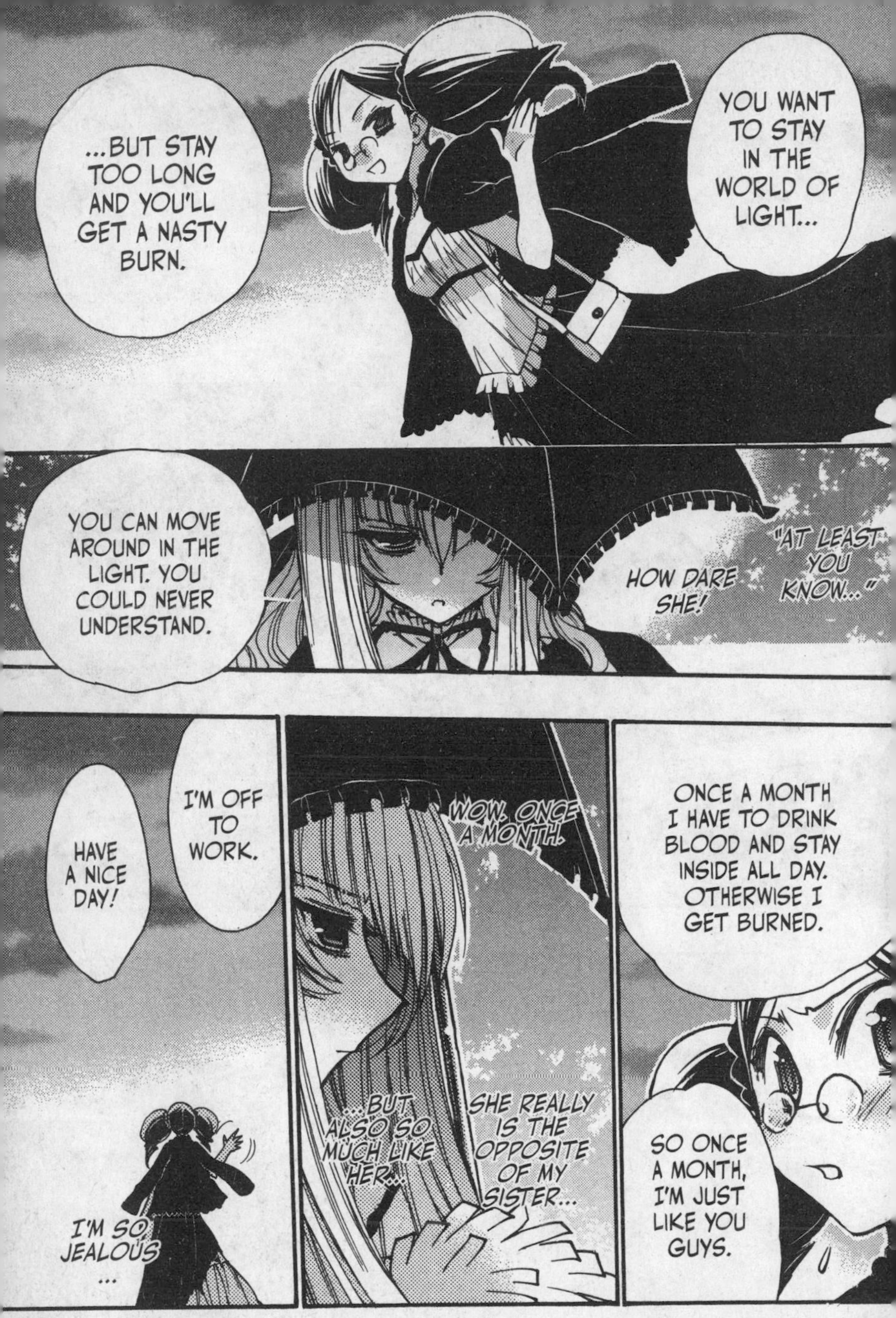
YOU WANT TO STAY IN THE WORLD OF LIGHT...
...BUT STAY TOO LONG AND YOU'LL GET A NASTY BURN.
"AT LEAST YOU KNOW..."
HOW DARE SHE!
YOU CAN MOVE AROUND IN THE LIGHT. YOU COULD NEVER UNDERSTAND.
ONCE A MONTH I HAVE TO DRINK BLOOD AND STAY INSIDE ALL DAY. OTHERWISE I GET BURNED.
SO ONCE A MONTH, I'M JUST LIKE YOU GUYS.
WOW. ONCE A MONTH.
SHE REALLY IS THE OPPOSITE OF MY SISTER...
...BUT ALSO SO MUCH LIKE HER...
I'M OFF TO WORK.
HAVE A NICE DAY!
I'M SO JEALOUS ...

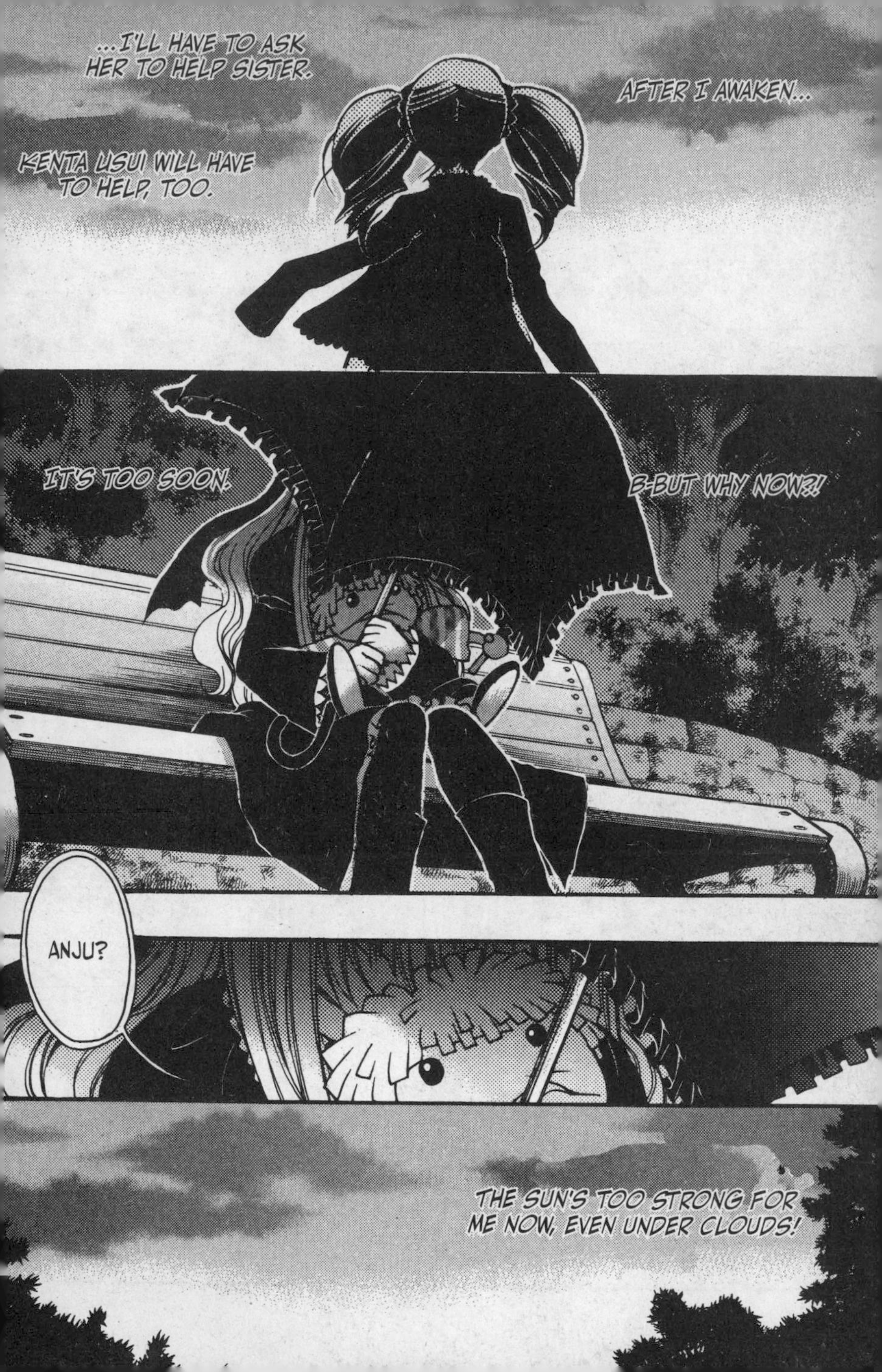
AFTER I AWAKEN...
...I'LL HAVE TO ASK HER TO HELP SISTER.
KENTA USUI WILL HAVE TO HELP, TOO.
B-BUT WHY NOW?!
IT'S TOO SOON.
ANJU?
THE SUN'S TOO STRONG FOR ME NOW, EVEN UNDER CLOUDS!

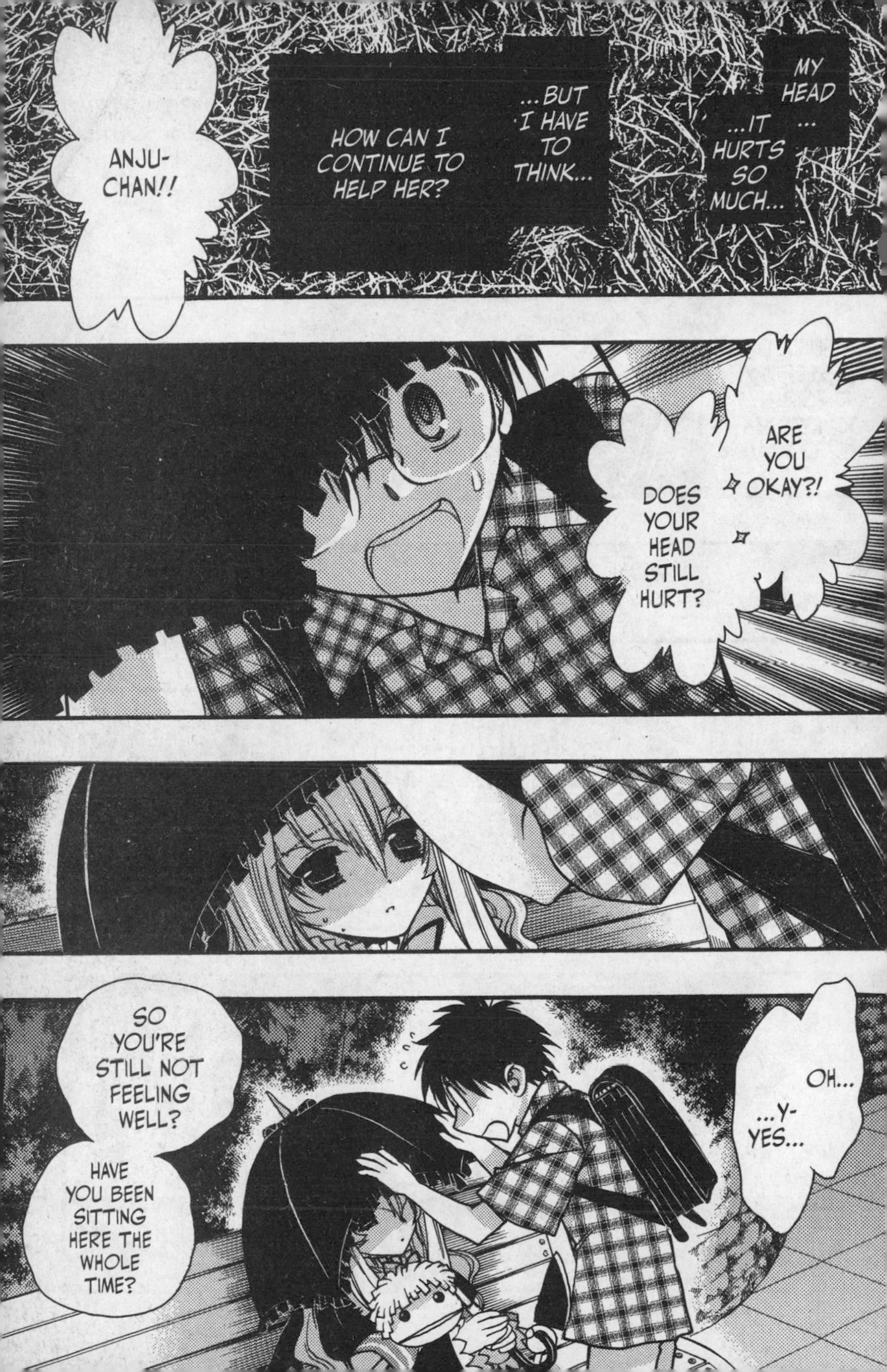
MY HEAD ...
...IT HURTS SO MUCH...
...BUT I HAVE TO THINK...
HOW CAN I CONTINUE TO HELP HER?
ANJU-CHAN!!
ARE YOU OKAY?!
DOES YOUR HEAD STILL HURT?
OH... ...Y-YES...
SO YOU'RE STILL NOT FEELING WELL?
HAVE YOU BEEN SITTING HERE THE WHOLE TIME?

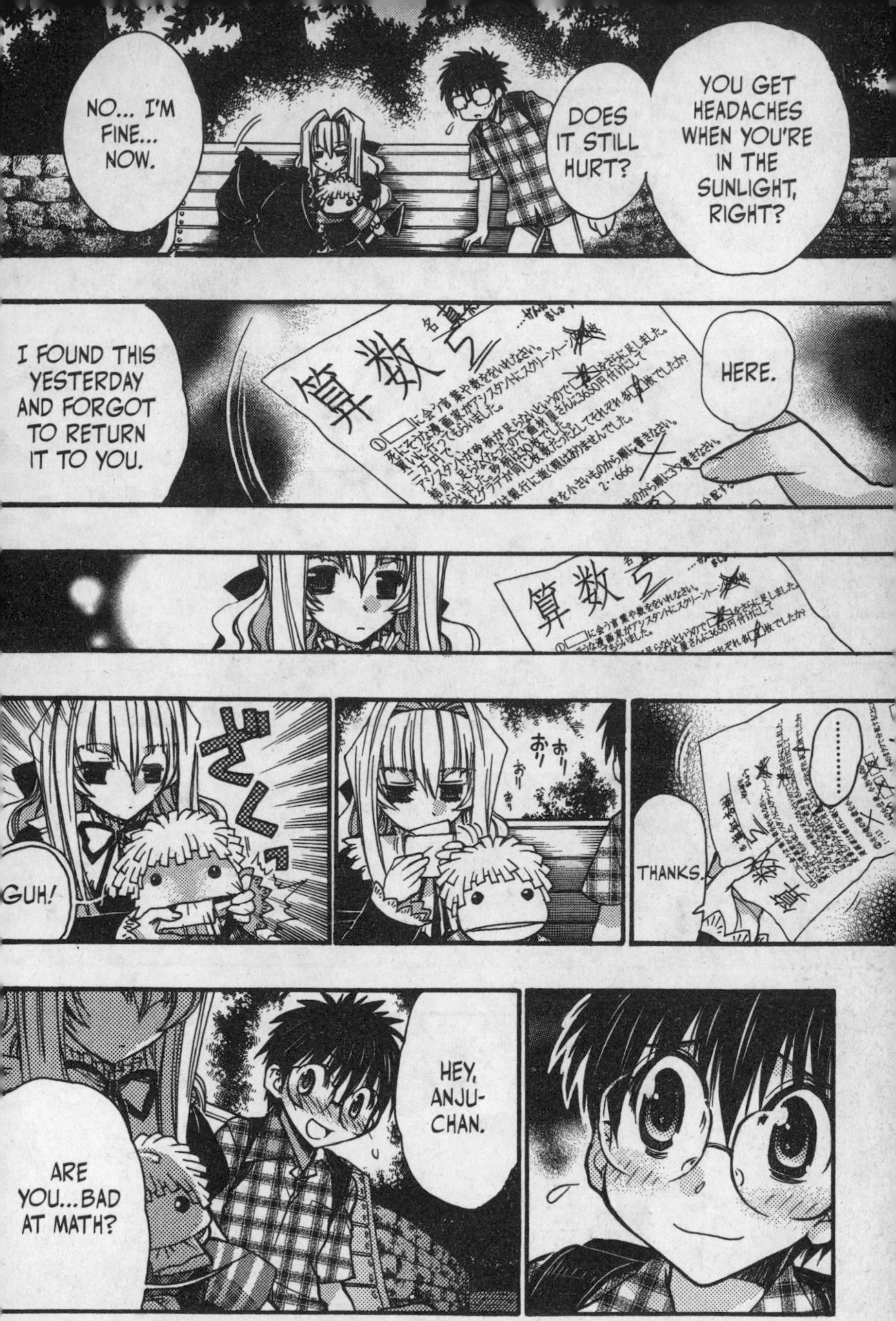
YOU GET HEADACHES WHEN YOU'RE IN THE SUNLIGHT, RIGHT?
DOES IT STILL HURT?
NO... I'M FINE... NOW.
HERE.
算数
I FOUND THIS YESTERDAY AND FORGOT TO RETURN IT TO YOU.
算数
......
THANKS.
おり おり おり おり
ざく
GUH!
HEY, ANJU-CHAN.
ARE YOU...BAD AT MATH?

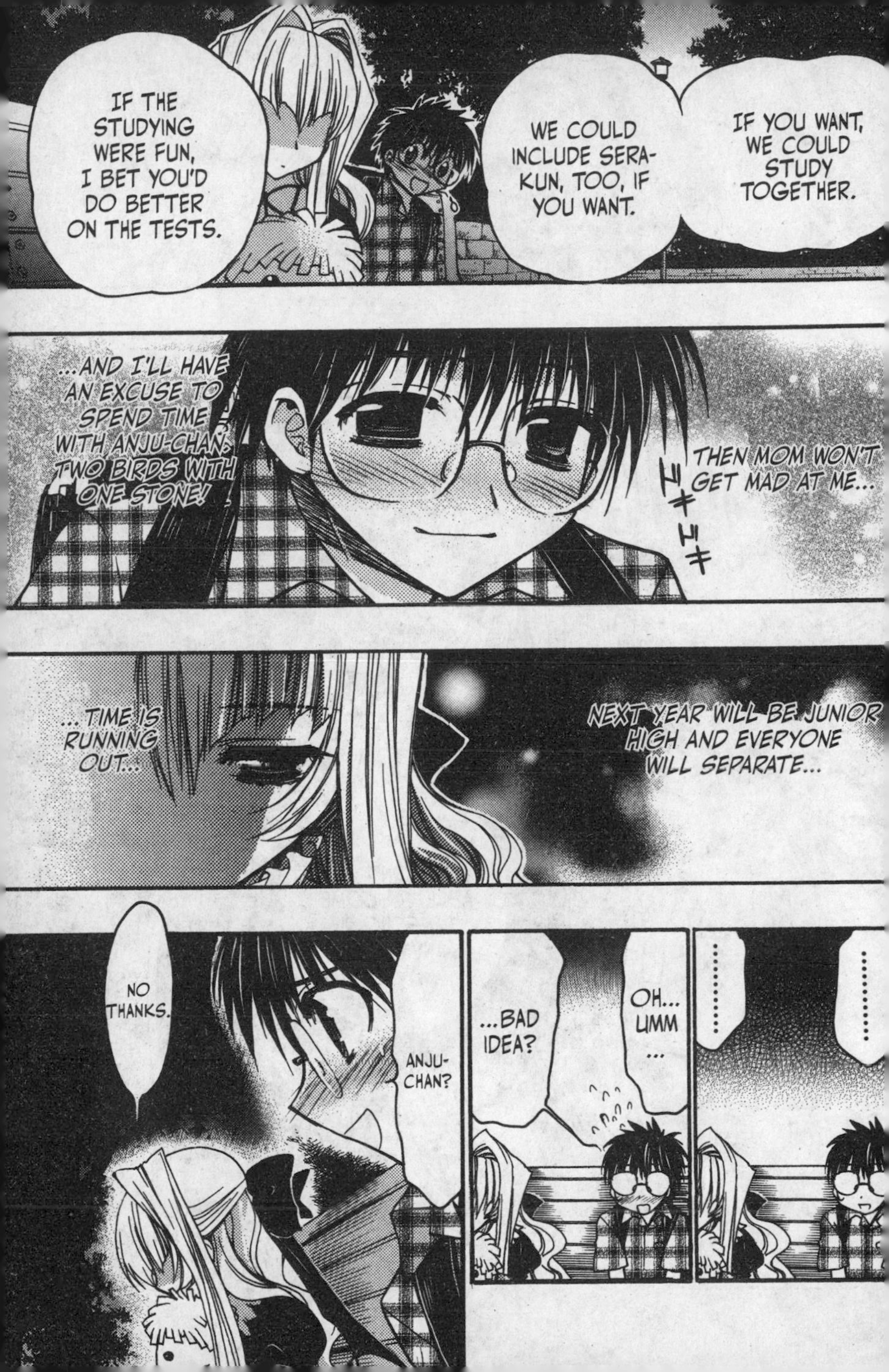
IF YOU WANT, WE COULD STUDY TOGETHER.
WE COULD INCLUDE SERA-KUN, TOO, IF YOU WANT.
IF THE STUDYING WERE FUN, I BET YOU'D DO BETTER ON THE TESTS.
THEN MOM WON'T GET MAD AT ME...
...AND I'LL HAVE AN EXCUSE TO SPEND TIME WITH ANJU-CHAN. TWO BIRDS WITH ONE STONE!
NEXT YEAR WILL BE JUNIOR HIGH AND EVERYONE WILL SEPARATE...
... TIME IS RUNNING OUT...
....
....
OH... UMM ...
...BAD IDEA?
ANJU-CHAN?
NO THANKS.

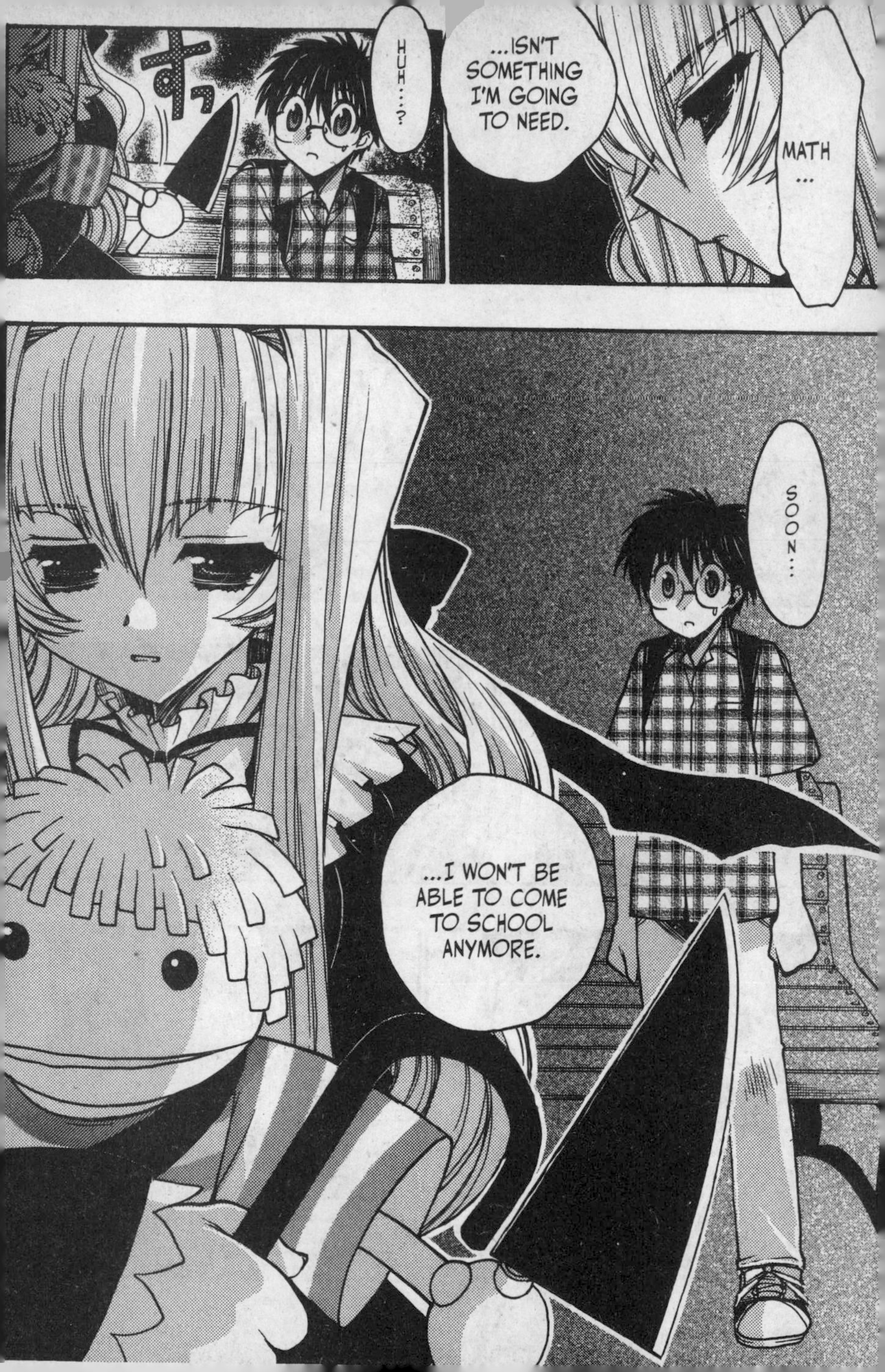
MATH ...
...ISN'T SOMETHING I'M GOING TO NEED.
HUH...?
すっ
SOON...
...I WON'T BE ABLE TO COME TO SCHOOL ANYMORE.

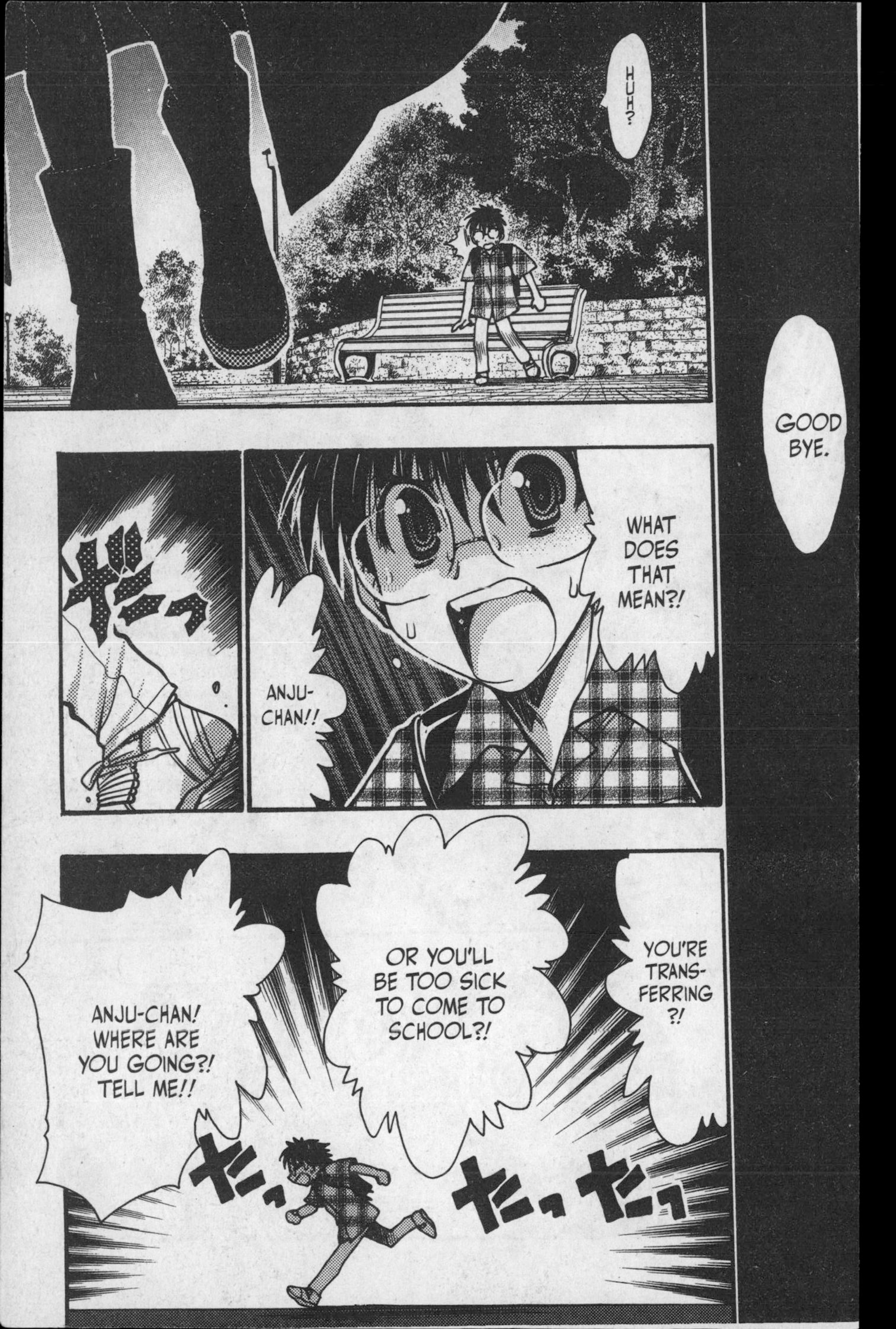
GOOD BYE.
HUH?!
WHAT DOES THAT MEAN?!
ANJU-CHAN!!
YOU'RE TRANS-FERRING?!
OR YOU'LL BE TOO SICK TO COME TO SCHOOL?!
ANJU-CHAN! WHERE ARE YOU GOING?! TELL ME!!
ダッ
ダッ
ダッ

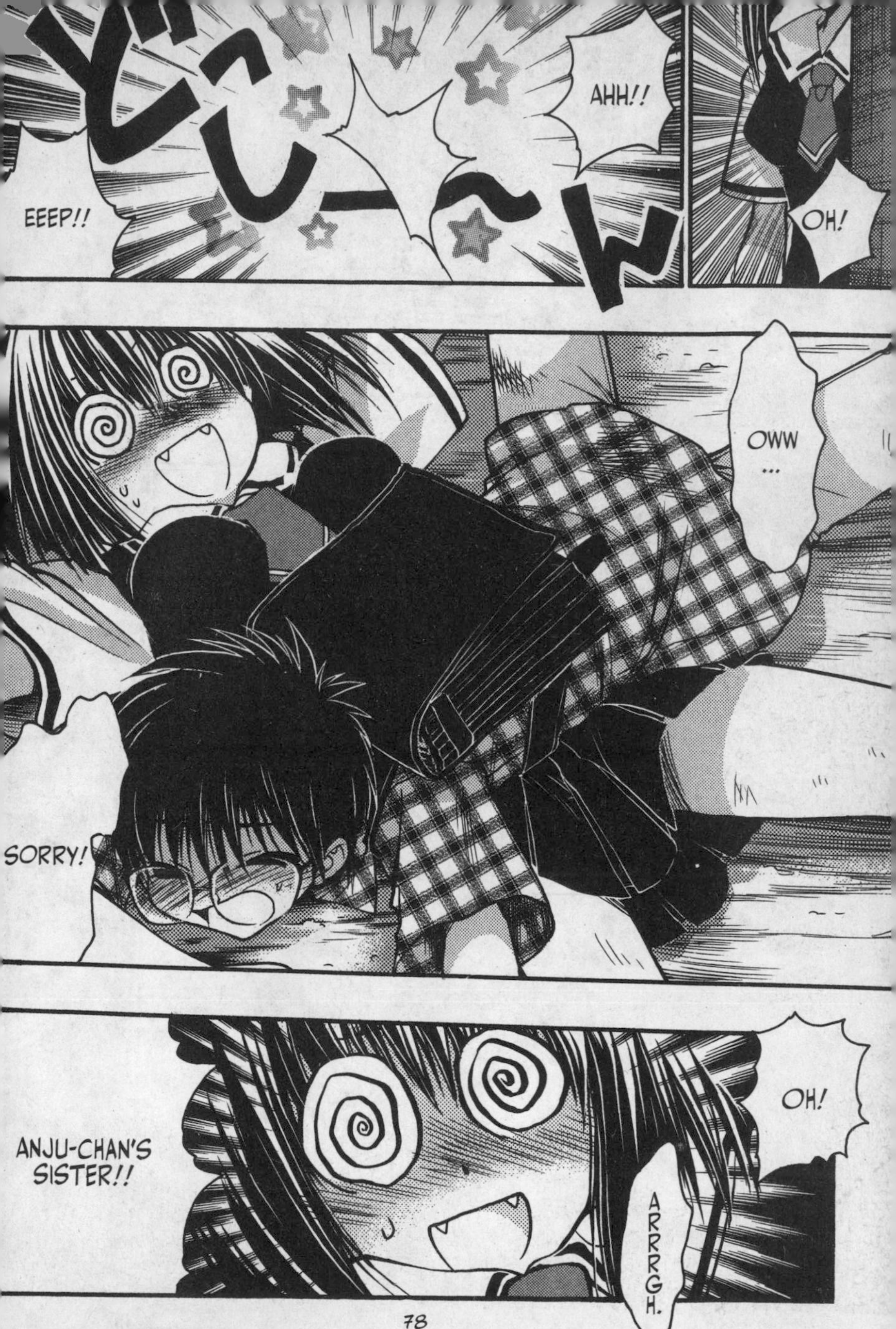
OH!
AHH!!
EEEP!!
OWW ...
SORRY!
OH!
ARRRGH.
ANJU-CHAN'S SISTER!!

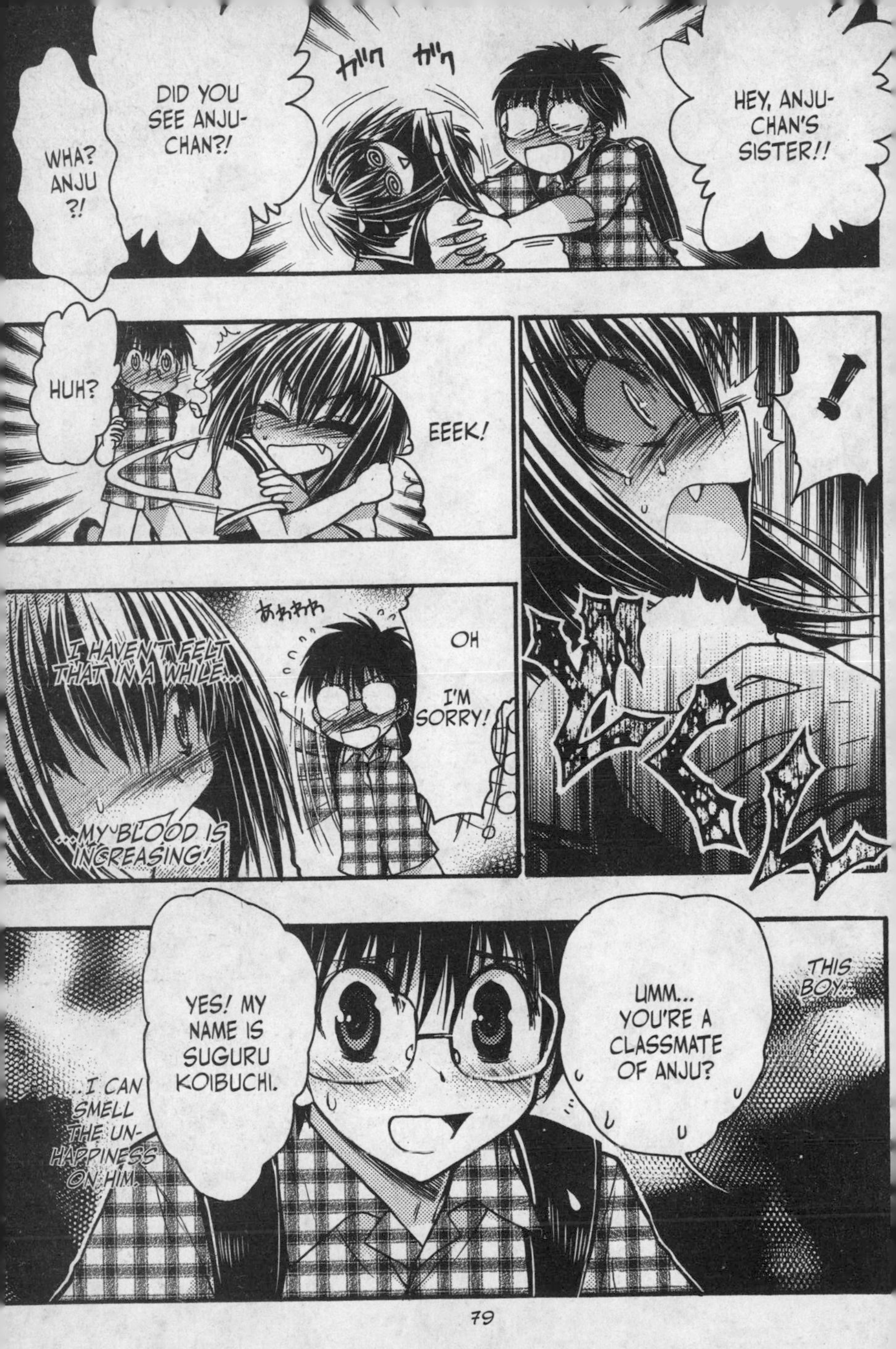
HEY, ANJU-CHAN'S SISTER!!
DID YOU SEE ANJU-CHAN?!
WHA? ANJU ?!
!
EEEK!
HUH?
OH
I'M SORRY!
I HAVEN'T FELT THAT IN A WHILE...
...MY BLOOD IS INCREASING!
THIS BOY...
UMM... YOU'RE A CLASSMATE OF ANJU?
YES! MY NAME IS SUGURU KOIBUCHI.
...I CAN SMELL THE UN-HAPPINESS ON HIM.

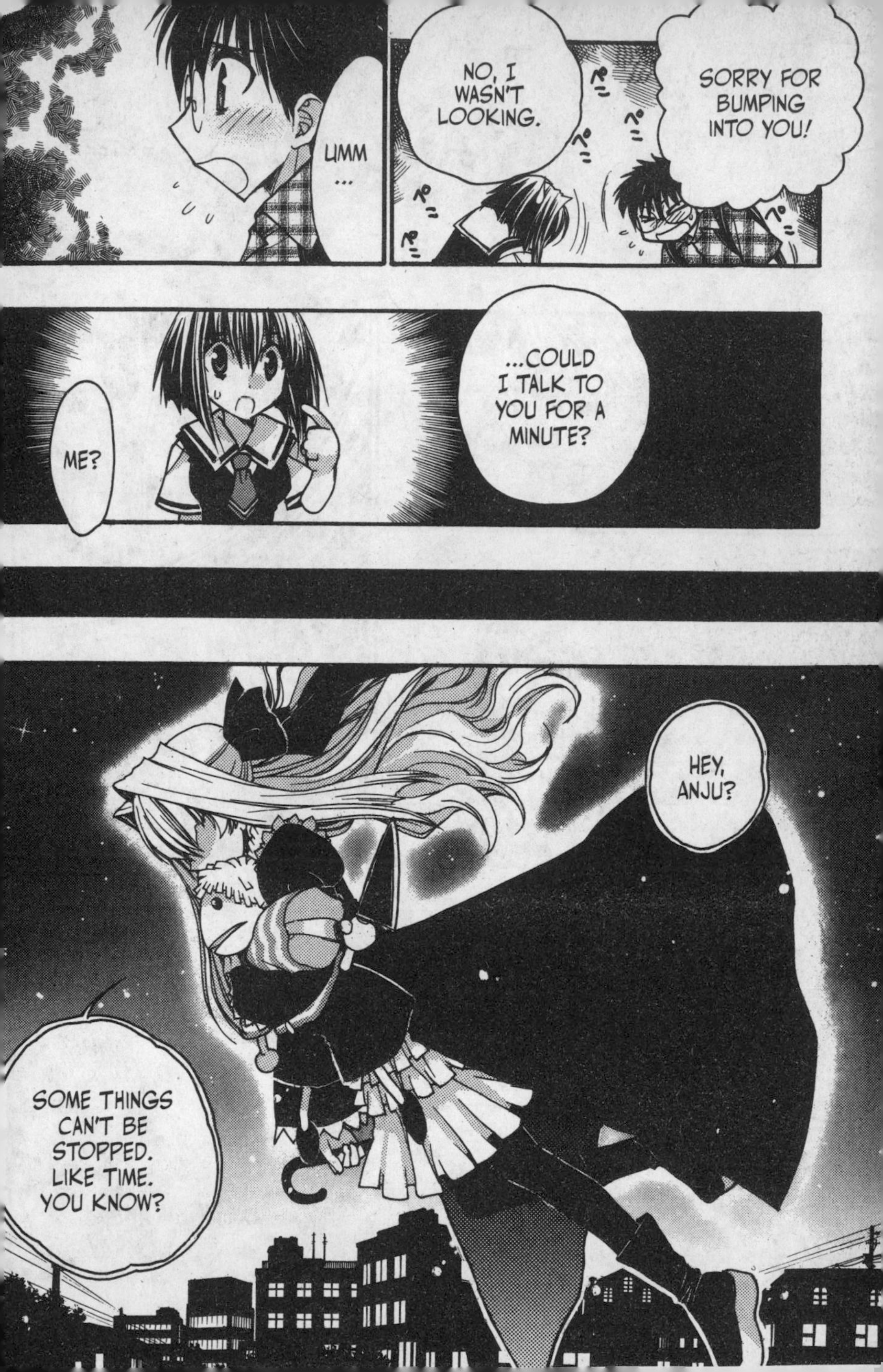
SORRY FOR BUMPING INTO YOU!
NO, I WASN'T LOOKING.
UMM ...
...COULD I TALK TO YOU FOR A MINUTE?
ME?
HEY, ANJU?
SOME THINGS CAN'T BE STOPPED. LIKE TIME. YOU KNOW?

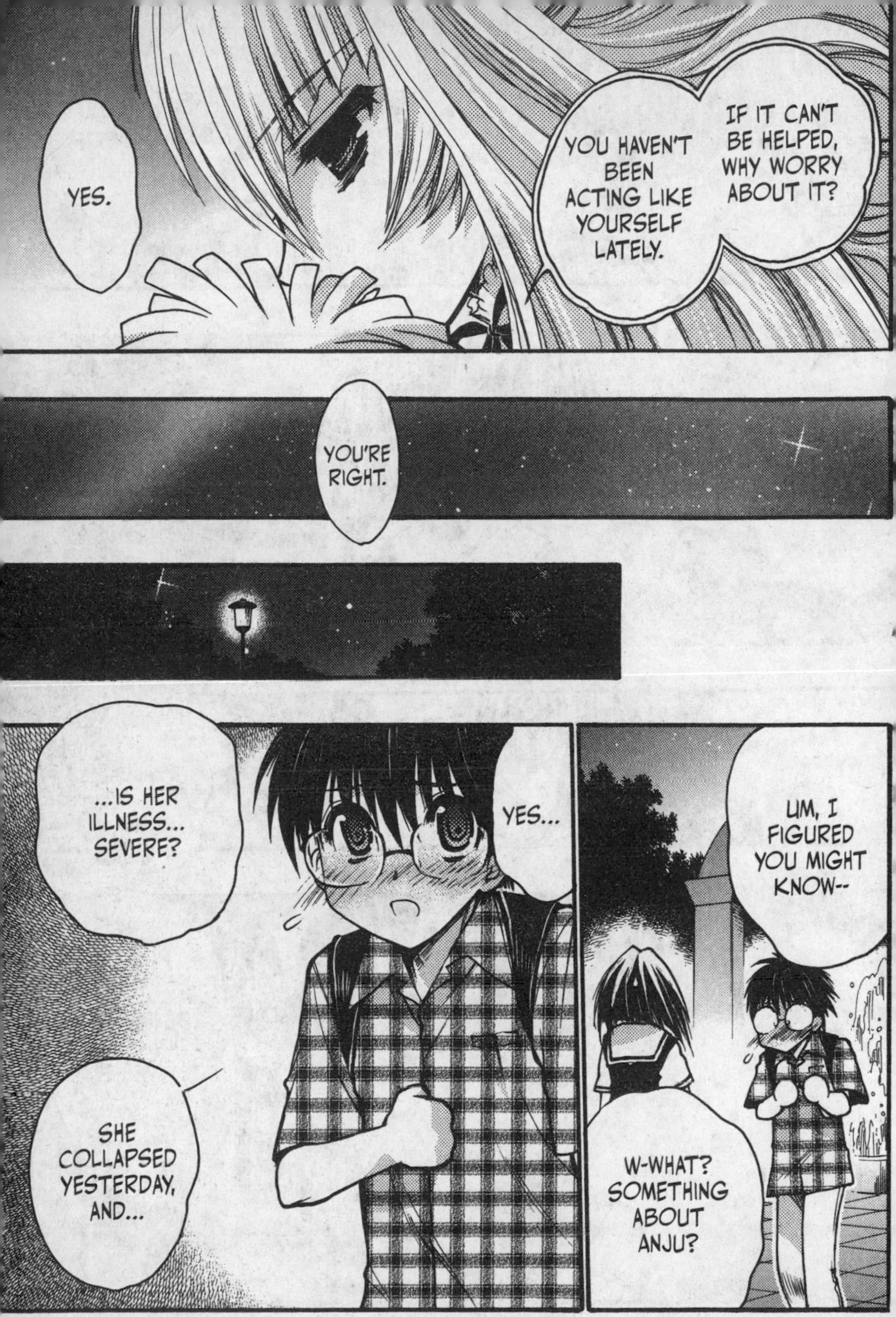
IF IT CAN'T BE HELPED, WHY WORRY ABOUT IT?
YOU HAVEN'T BEEN ACTING LIKE YOURSELF LATELY.
YES.
YOU'RE RIGHT.
UM, I FIGURED YOU MIGHT KNOW--
W-WHAT? SOMETHING ABOUT ANJU?
YES...
...IS HER ILLNESS... SEVERE?
SHE COLLAPSED YESTERDAY, AND...

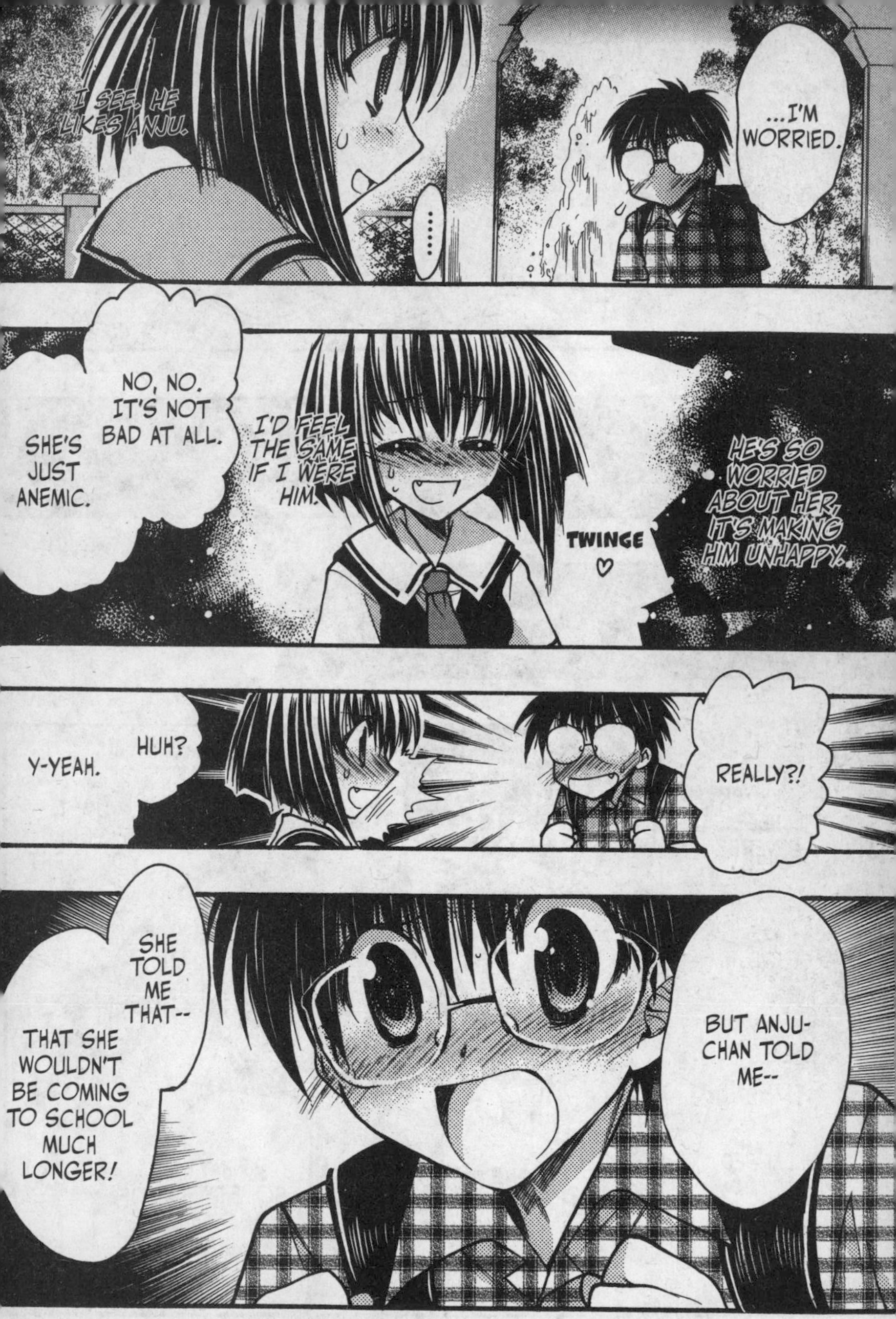
...I'M WORRIED.
I SEE, HE LIKES ANJU.
......
HE'S SO WORRIED ABOUT HER, IT'S MAKING HIM UNHAPPY.
TWINGE ♡
I'D FEEL THE SAME IF I WERE HIM.
NO, NO. IT'S NOT BAD AT ALL.
SHE'S JUST ANEMIC.
REALLY?!
HUH?
Y-YEAH.
BUT ANJU-CHAN TOLD ME--
SHE TOLD ME THAT--
THAT SHE WOULDN'T BE COMING TO SCHOOL MUCH LONGER!

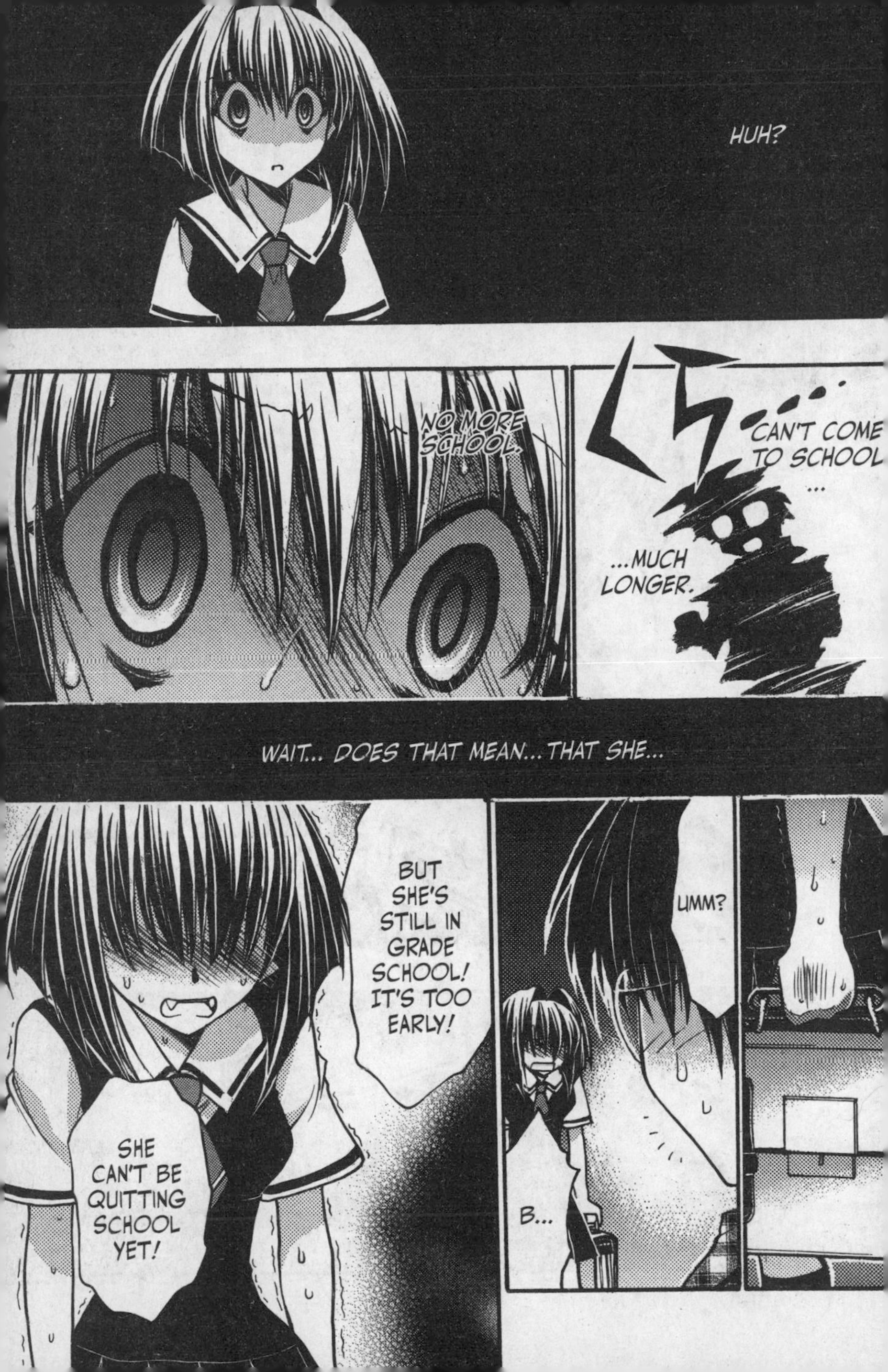
HUH?
...CAN'T COME TO SCHOOL...
...MUCH LONGER.
NO MORE SCHOOL.
WAIT... DOES THAT MEAN... THAT SHE...
UMM?
B...
BUT SHE'S STILL IN GRADE SCHOOL! IT'S TOO EARLY!
SHE CAN'T BE QUITTING SCHOOL YET!

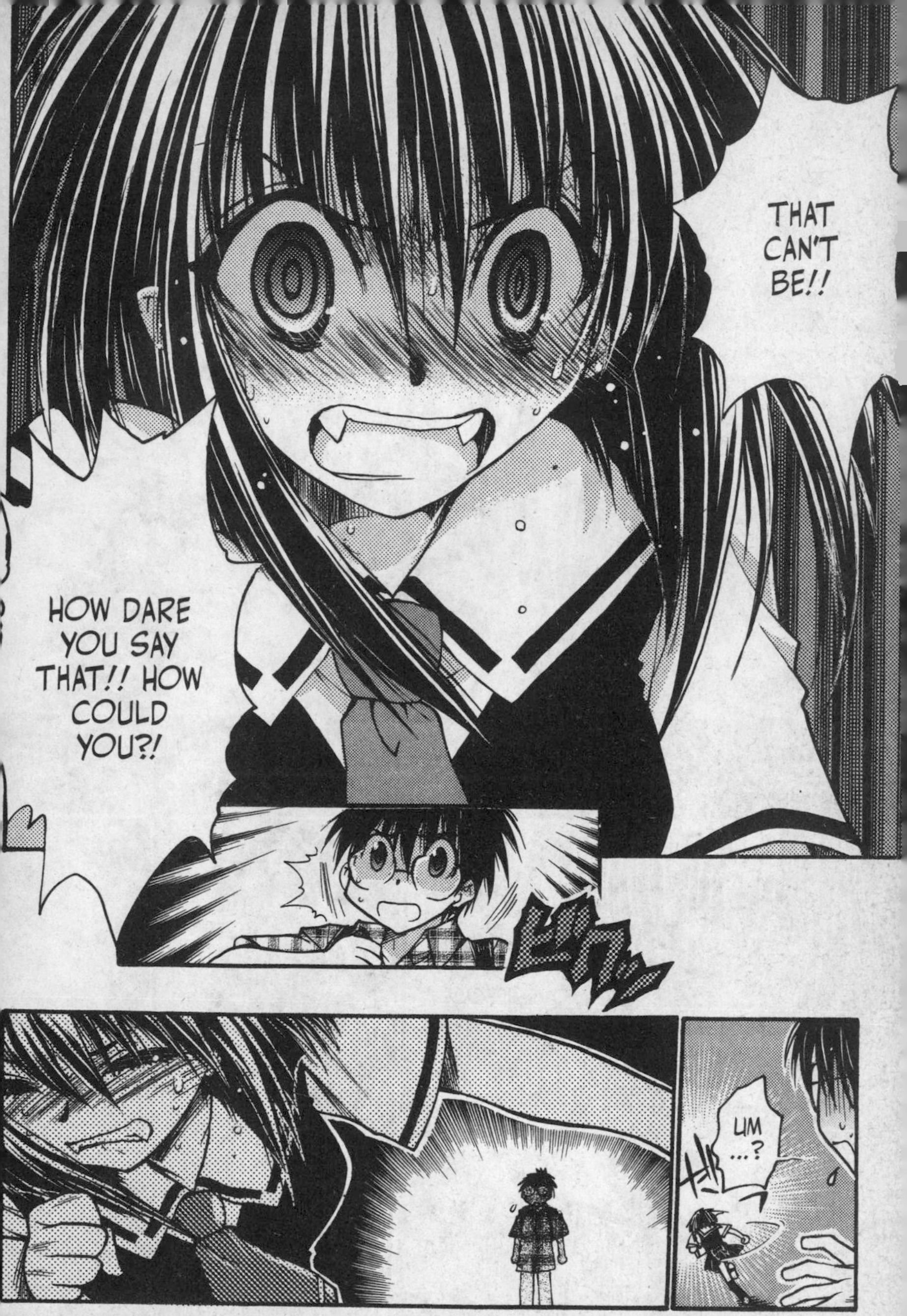
THAT CAN'T BE!!
HOW DARE YOU SAY THAT!! HOW COULD YOU?!
UM ...?

44TH EMBARRASSMENT END

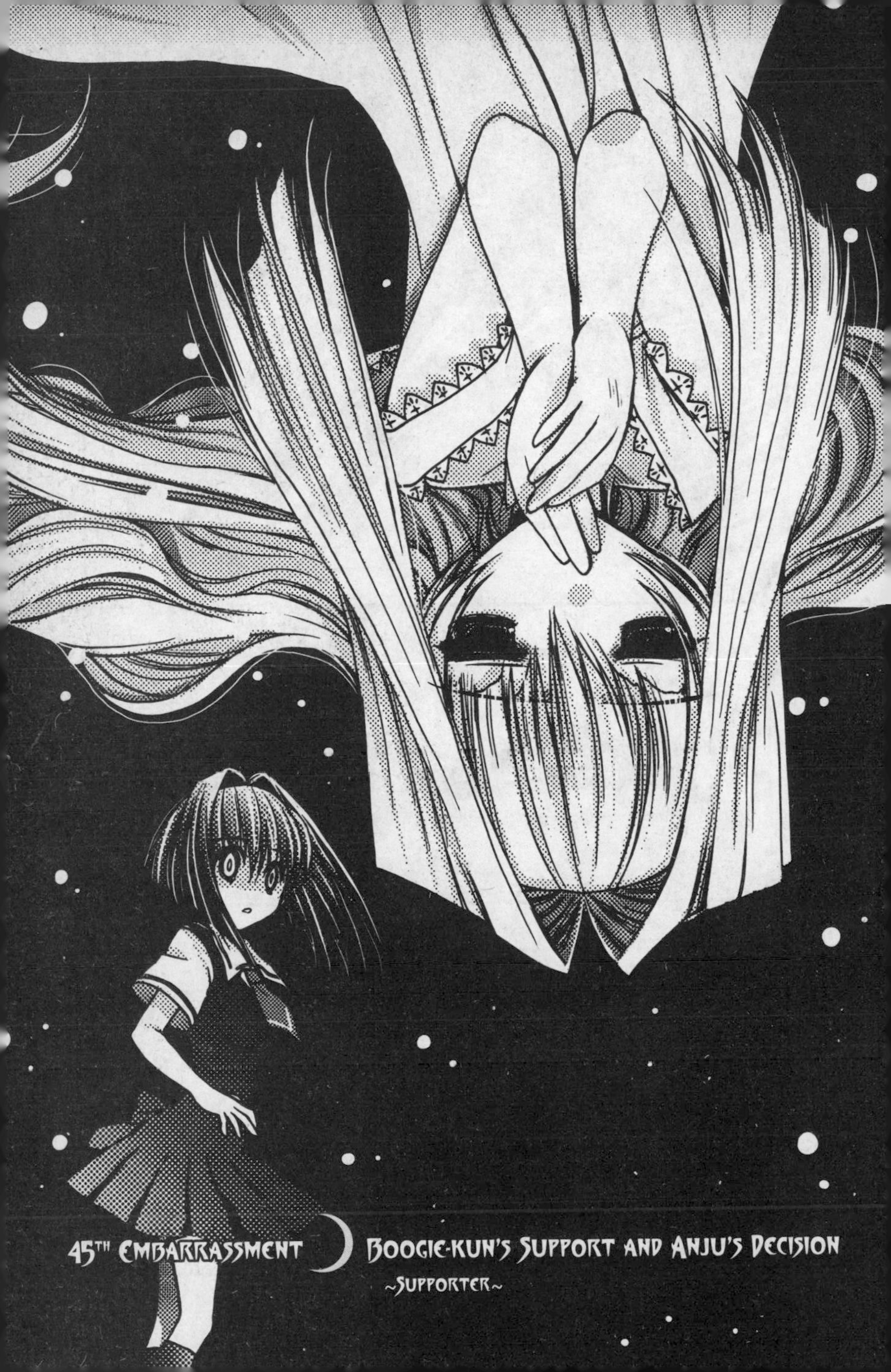
45TH EMBARRASSMENT
BOOGIE-KUN'S SUPPORT AND ANJU'S DECISION
~SUPPORTER~

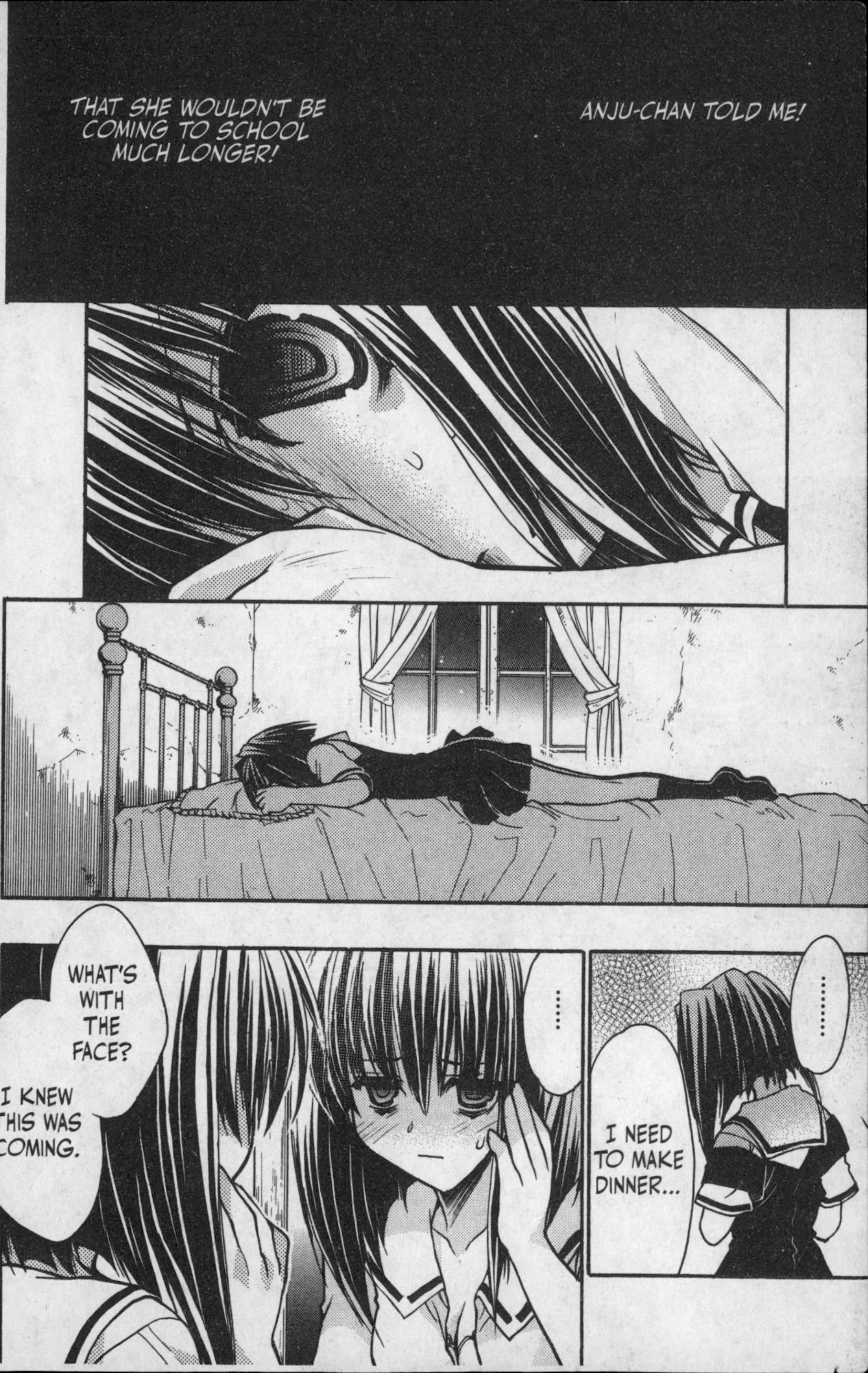
ANJU-CHAN TOLD ME!
THAT SHE WOULDN'T BE COMING TO SCHOOL MUCH LONGER!
...
......
I NEED TO MAKE DINNER...
......
WHAT'S WITH THE FACE?
I KNEW THIS WAS COMING.

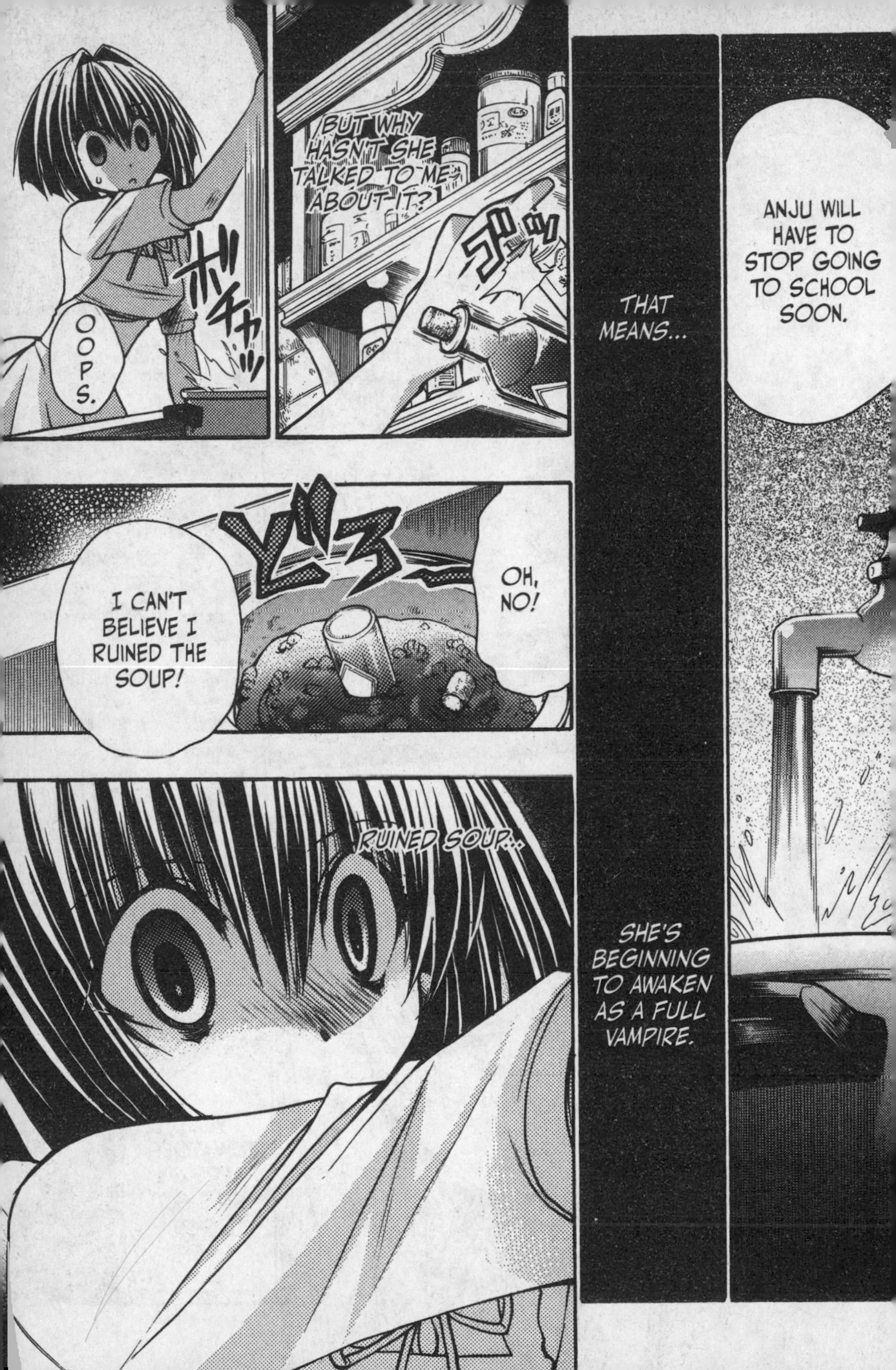
ANJU WILL HAVE TO STOP GOING TO SCHOOL SOON.
THAT MEANS...
SHE'S BEGINNING TO AWAKEN AS A FULL VAMPIRE.
BUT WHY HASN'T SHE TALKED TO ME ABOUT IT?
OOPS.
OH, NO!
I CAN'T BELIEVE I RUINED THE SOUP!
RUINED SOUP...

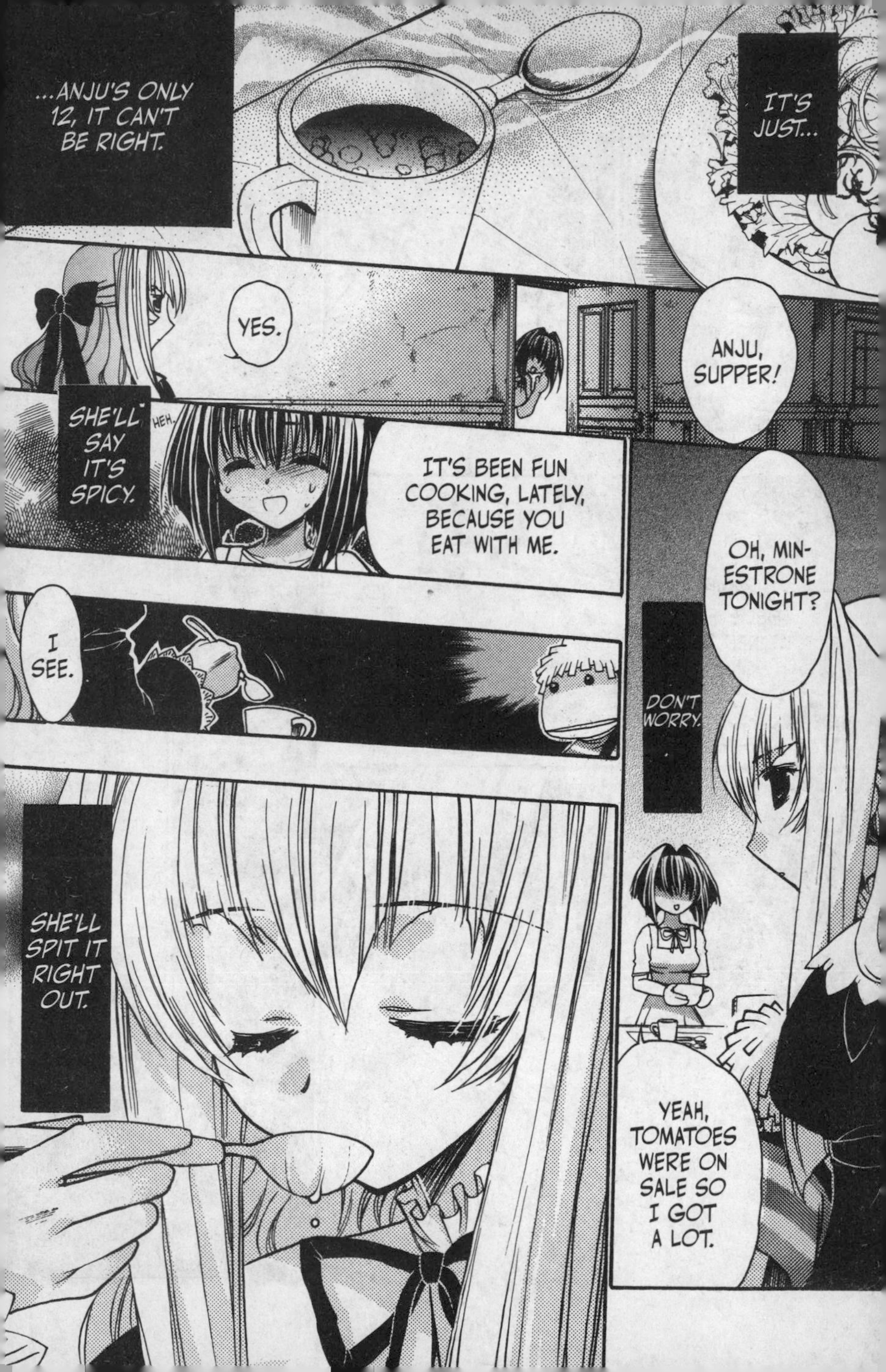
IT'S JUST...
...ANJU'S ONLY 12, IT CAN'T BE RIGHT.
ANJU, SUPPER!
YES.
OH, MIN-ESTRONE TONIGHT?
YEAH, TOMATOES WERE ON SALE SO I GOT A LOT.
DON'T WORRY.
IT'S BEEN FUN COOKING, LATELY, BECAUSE YOU EAT WITH ME.
HEH.
SHE'LL SAY IT'S SPICY.
I SEE.
SHE'LL SPIT IT RIGHT OUT.

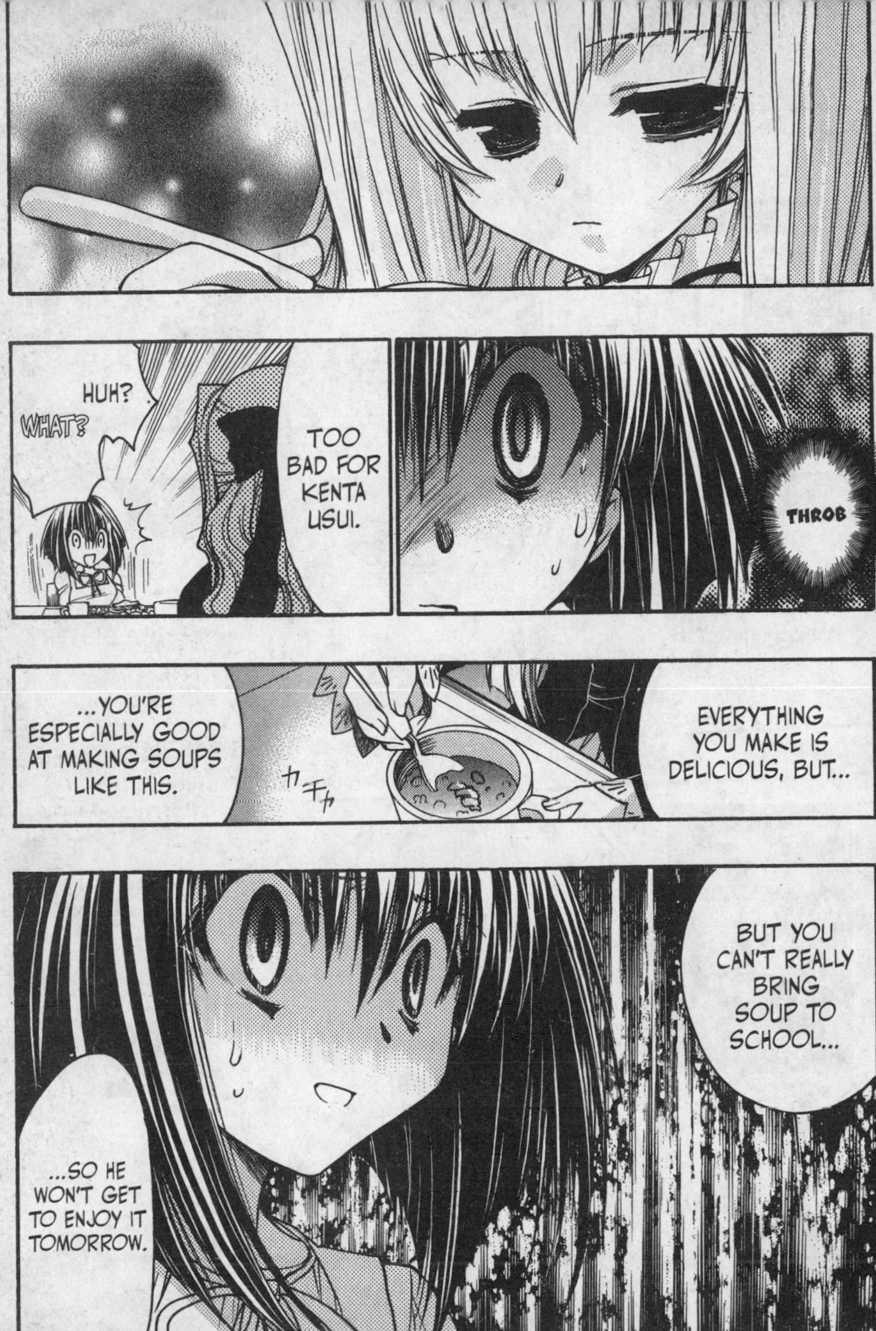
THROB
TOO BAD FOR KENTA USUI.
HUH?
WHAT?
EVERYTHING YOU MAKE IS DELICIOUS, BUT...
カチャ
...YOU'RE ESPECIALLY GOOD AT MAKING SOUPS LIKE THIS.
BUT YOU CAN'T REALLY BRING SOUP TO SCHOOL...
...SO HE WON'T GET TO ENJOY IT TOMORROW.

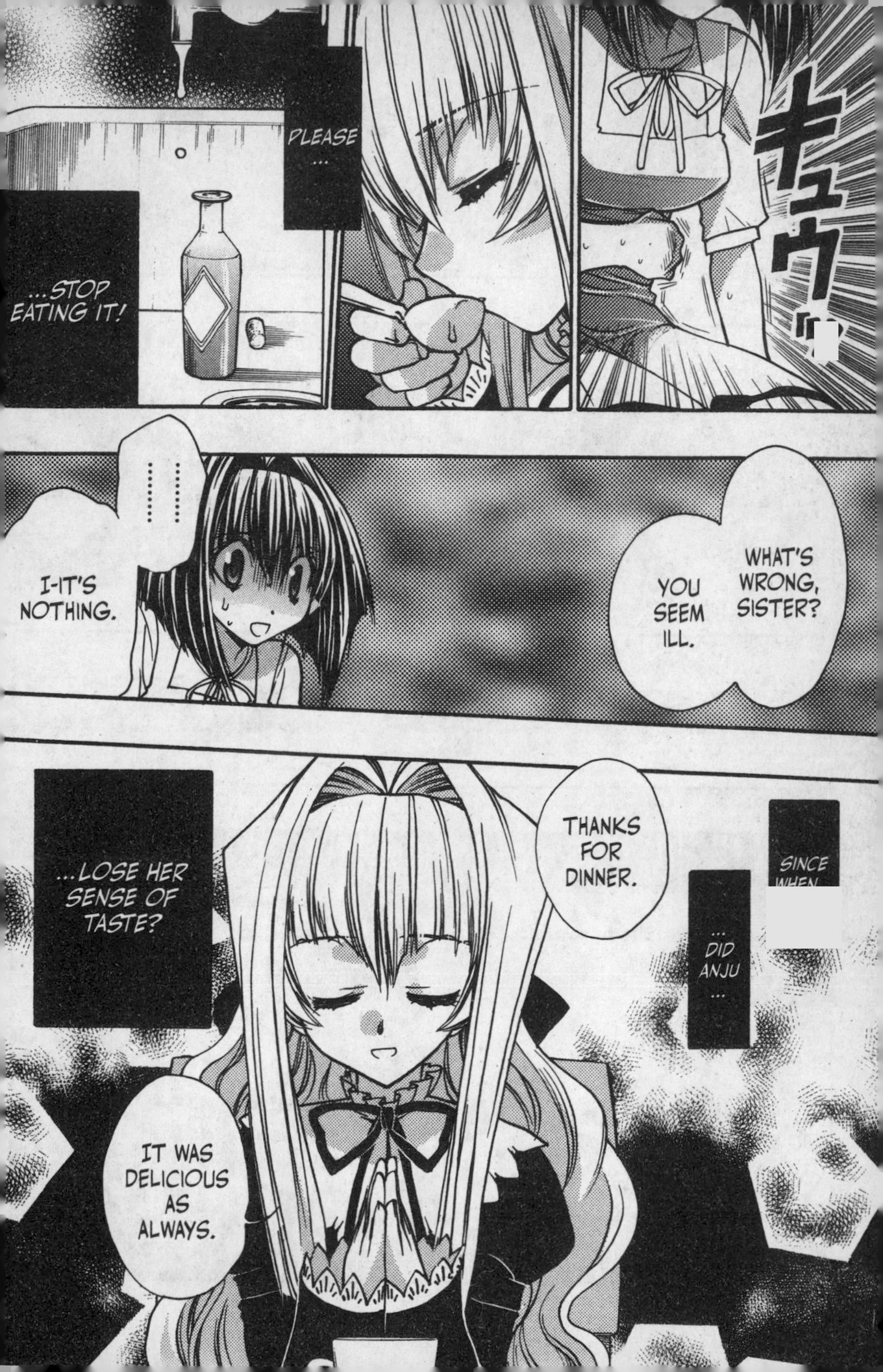
キュウ
PLEASE ...
...STOP EATING IT!
WHAT'S WRONG, SISTER?
YOU SEEM ILL.
......
I-IT'S NOTHING.
SINCE WHEN
... DID ANJU ...
THANKS FOR DINNER.
...LOSE HER SENSE OF TASTE?
IT WAS DELICIOUS AS ALWAYS.

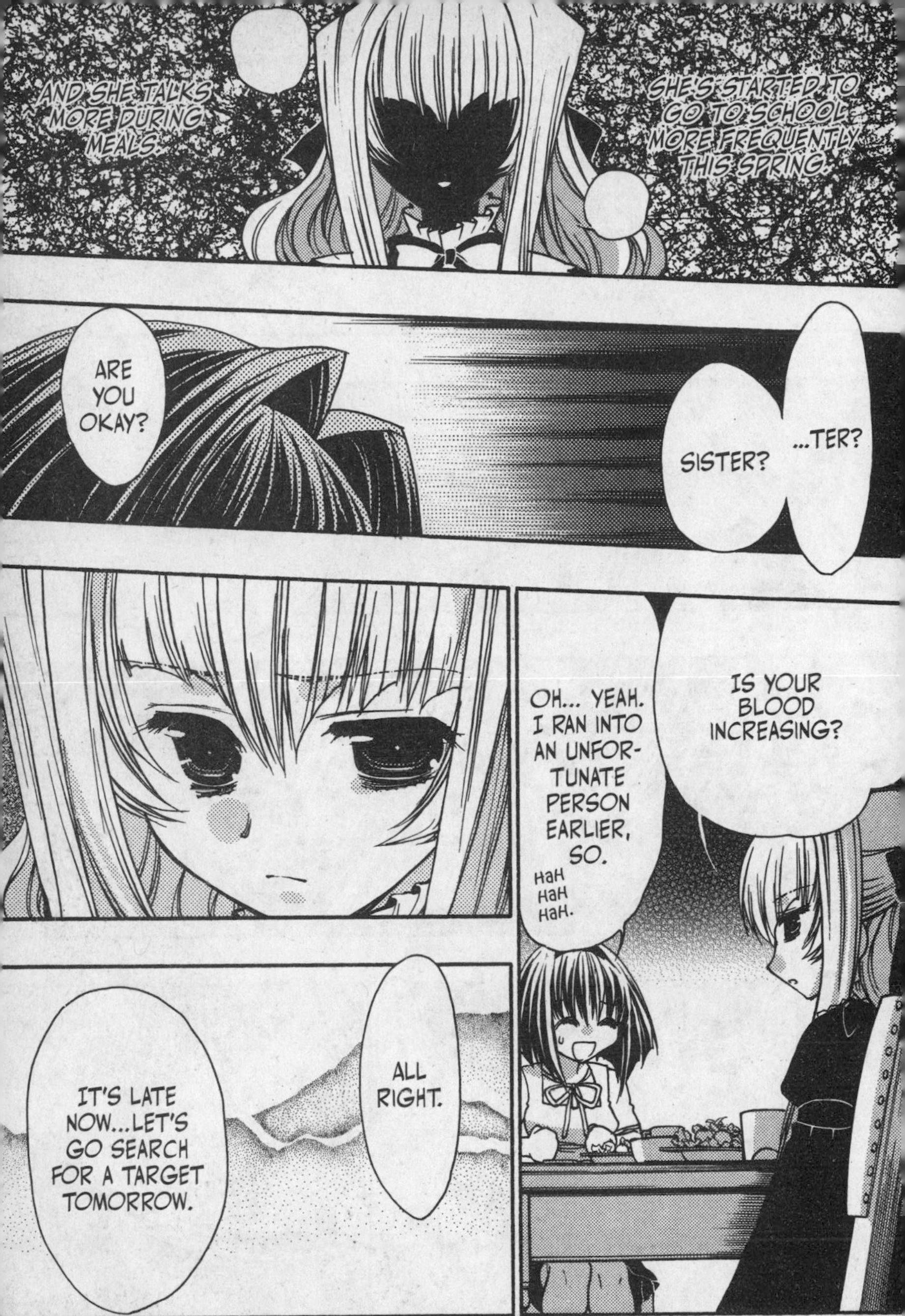
SHE'S STARTED TO GO TO SCHOOL MORE FREQUENTLY THIS SPRING.
AND SHE TALKS MORE DURING MEALS.
...TER?
SISTER?
ARE YOU OKAY?
IS YOUR BLOOD INCREASING?
OH... YEAH. I RAN INTO AN UNFORTUNATE PERSON EARLIER, SO.
HAH HAH HAH.
ALL RIGHT.
IT'S LATE NOW...LET'S GO SEARCH FOR A TARGET TOMORROW.

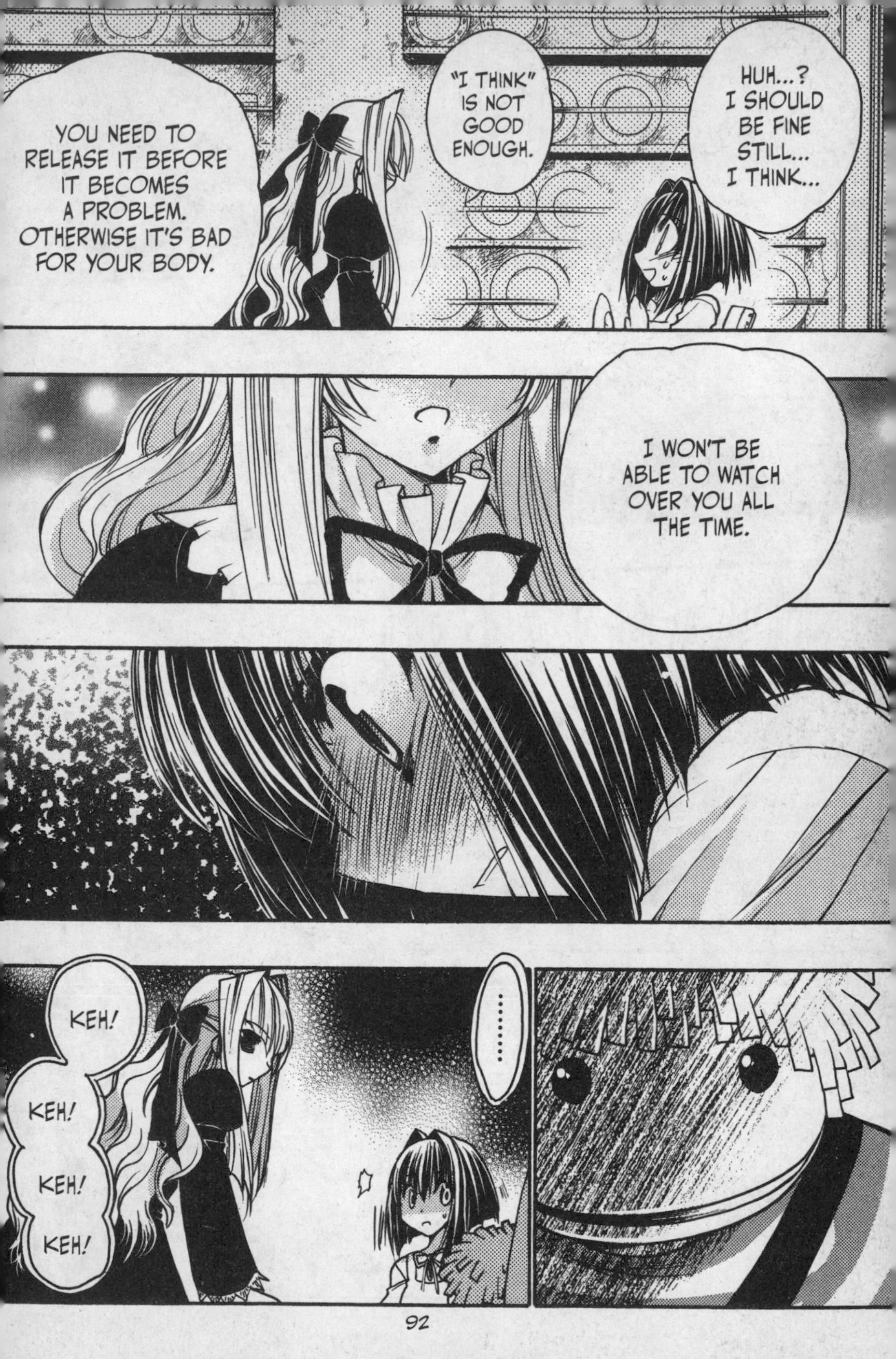
HUH...? I SHOULD BE FINE STILL... I THINK...
"I THINK" IS NOT GOOD ENOUGH.
YOU NEED TO RELEASE IT BEFORE IT BECOMES A PROBLEM. OTHERWISE IT'S BAD FOR YOUR BODY.
I WON'T BE ABLE TO WATCH OVER YOU ALL THE TIME.
......
KEH!
KEH!
KEH!
KEH!

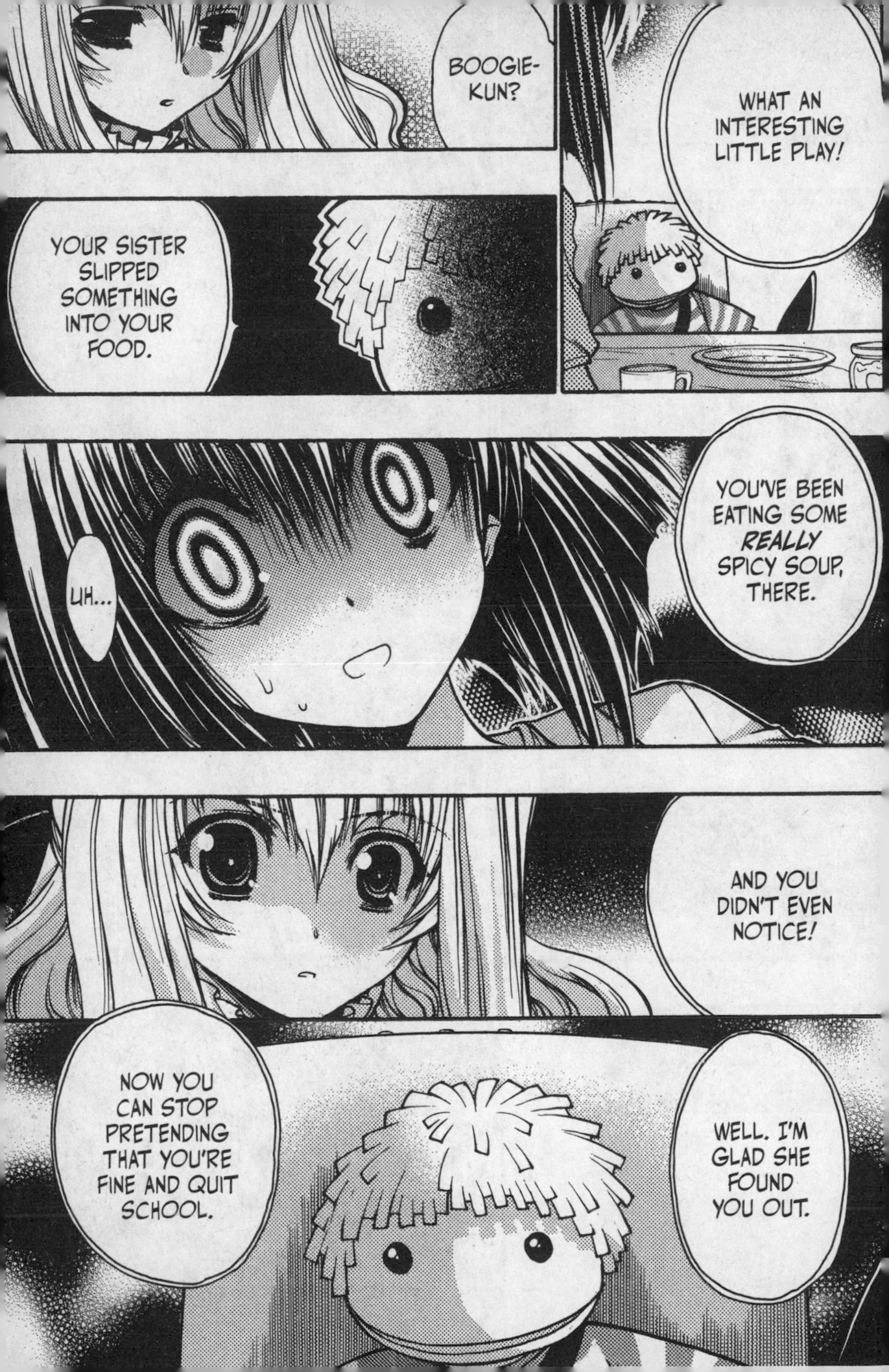
WHAT AN INTERESTING LITTLE PLAY!
BOOGIE-KUN?
YOUR SISTER SLIPPED SOMETHING INTO YOUR FOOD.
YOU'VE BEEN EATING SOME *REALLY* SPICY SOUP, THERE.
UH...
AND YOU DIDN'T EVEN NOTICE!
WELL. I'M GLAD SHE FOUND YOU OUT.
NOW YOU CAN STOP PRETENDING THAT YOU'RE FINE AND QUIT SCHOOL.

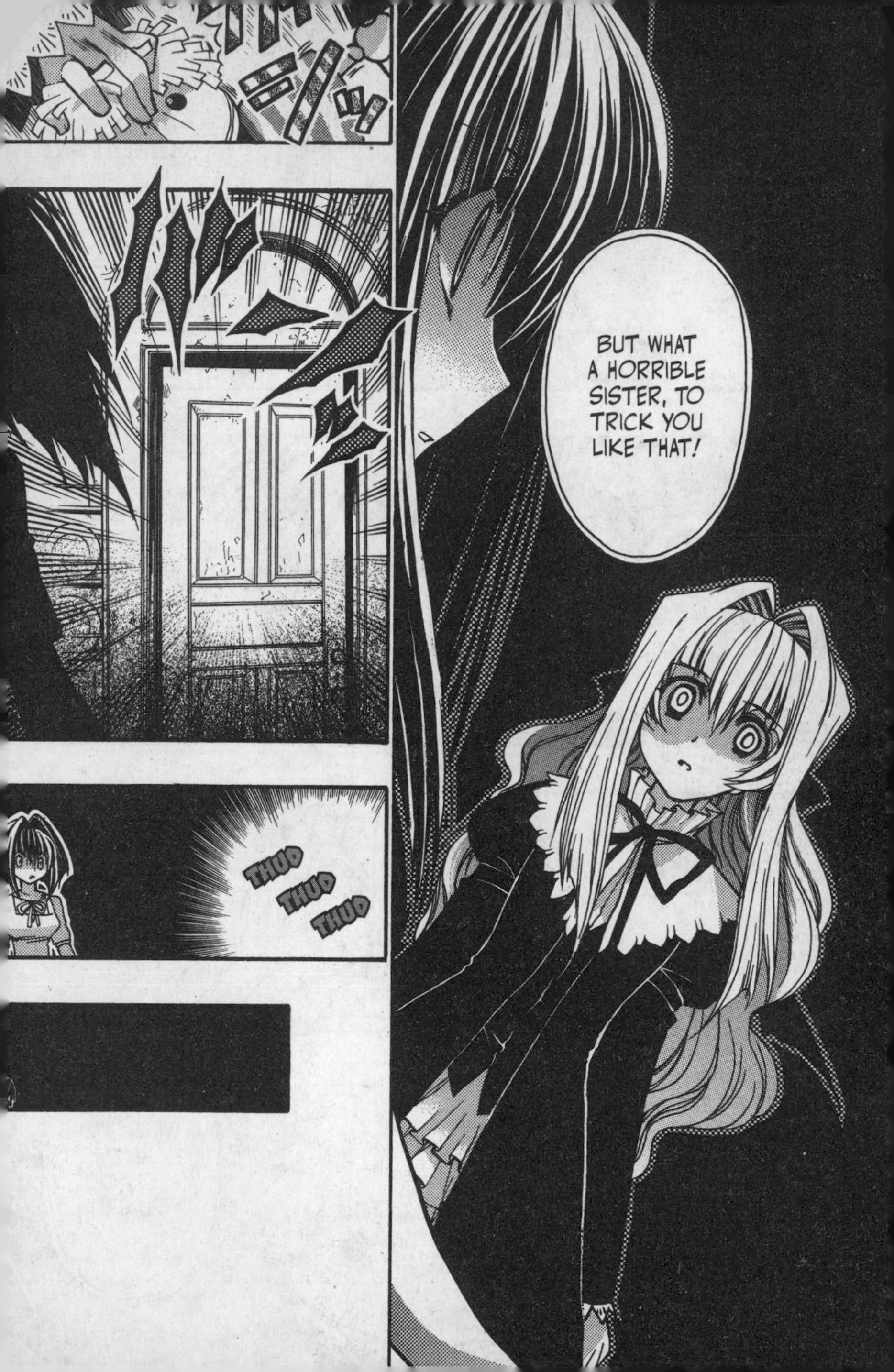
BUT WHAT A HORRIBLE SISTER, TO TRICK YOU LIKE THAT!
THUD THUD THUD

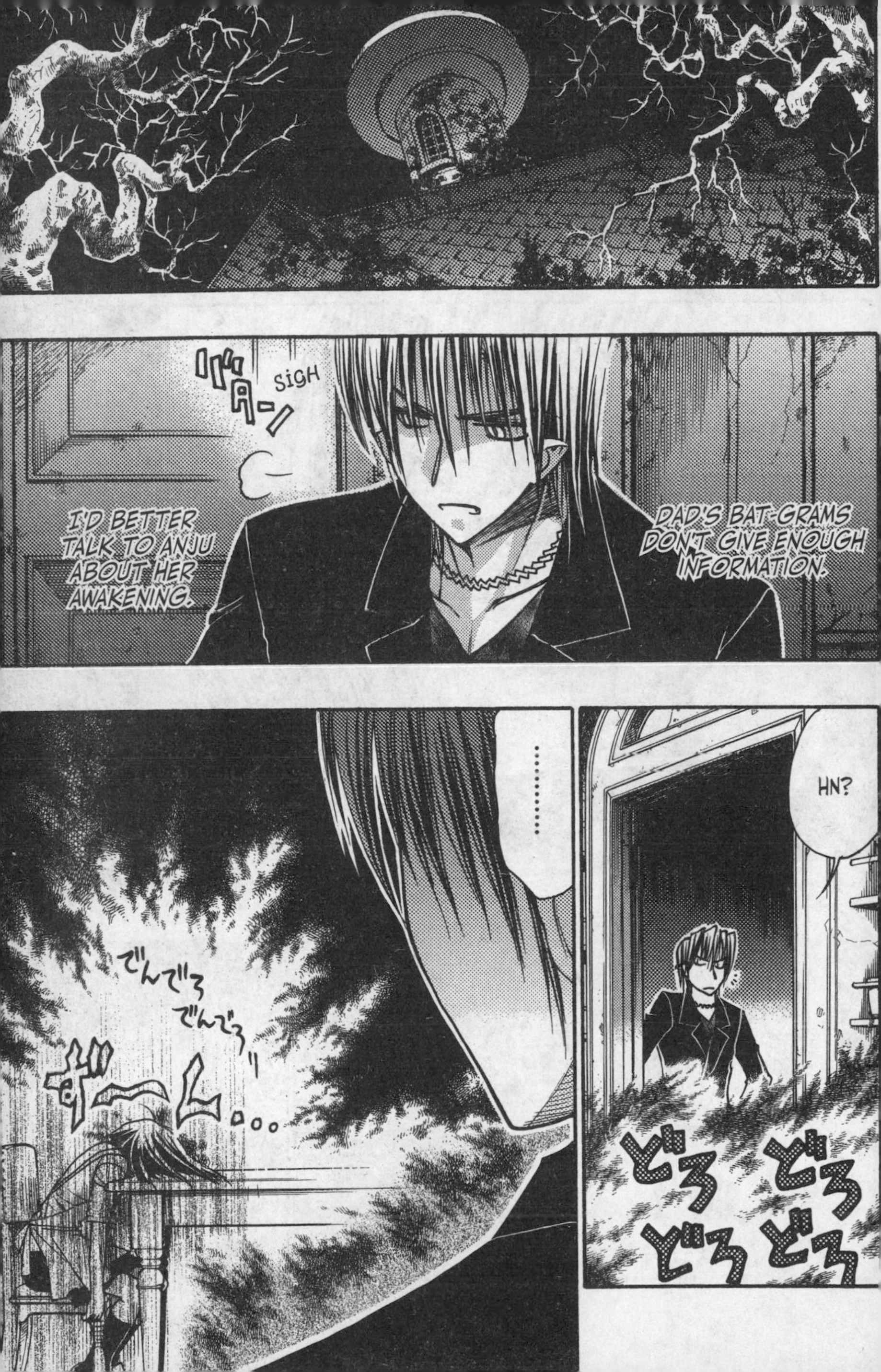
DAD'S BAT-GRAMS DON'T GIVE ENOUGH INFORMATION.
SIGH
I'D BETTER TALK TO ANJU ABOUT HER AWAKENING.
HN?
どろ どろ どろ どろ
……
でんでろ でんでろ
ずーん…

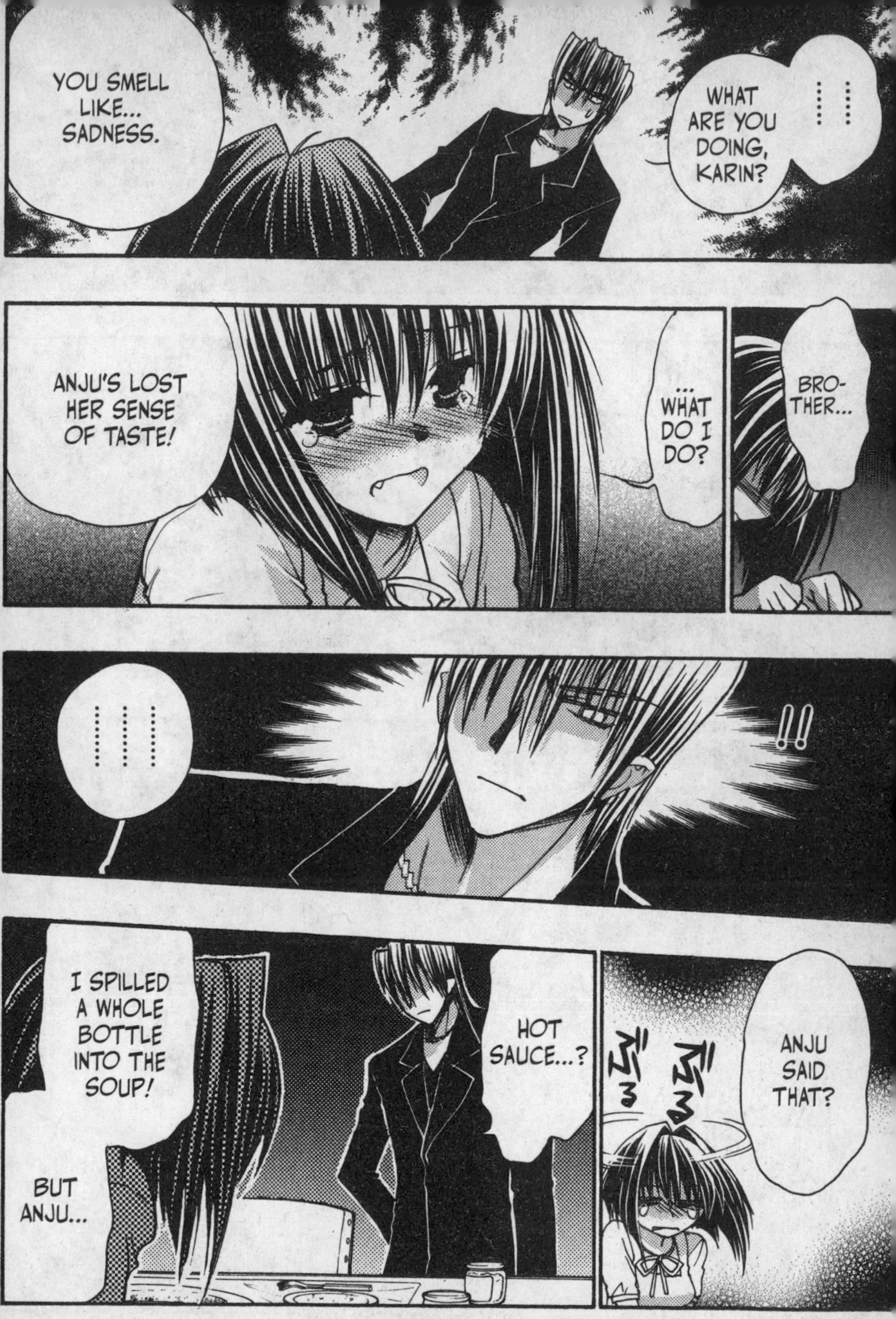
......
WHAT ARE YOU DOING, KARIN?
YOU SMELL LIKE... SADNESS.
BRO-THER...
...WHAT DO I DO?
ANJU'S LOST HER SENSE OF TASTE!
!!
......
ANJU SAID THAT?
HOT SAUCE...?
I SPILLED A WHOLE BOTTLE INTO THE SOUP!
BUT ANJU...

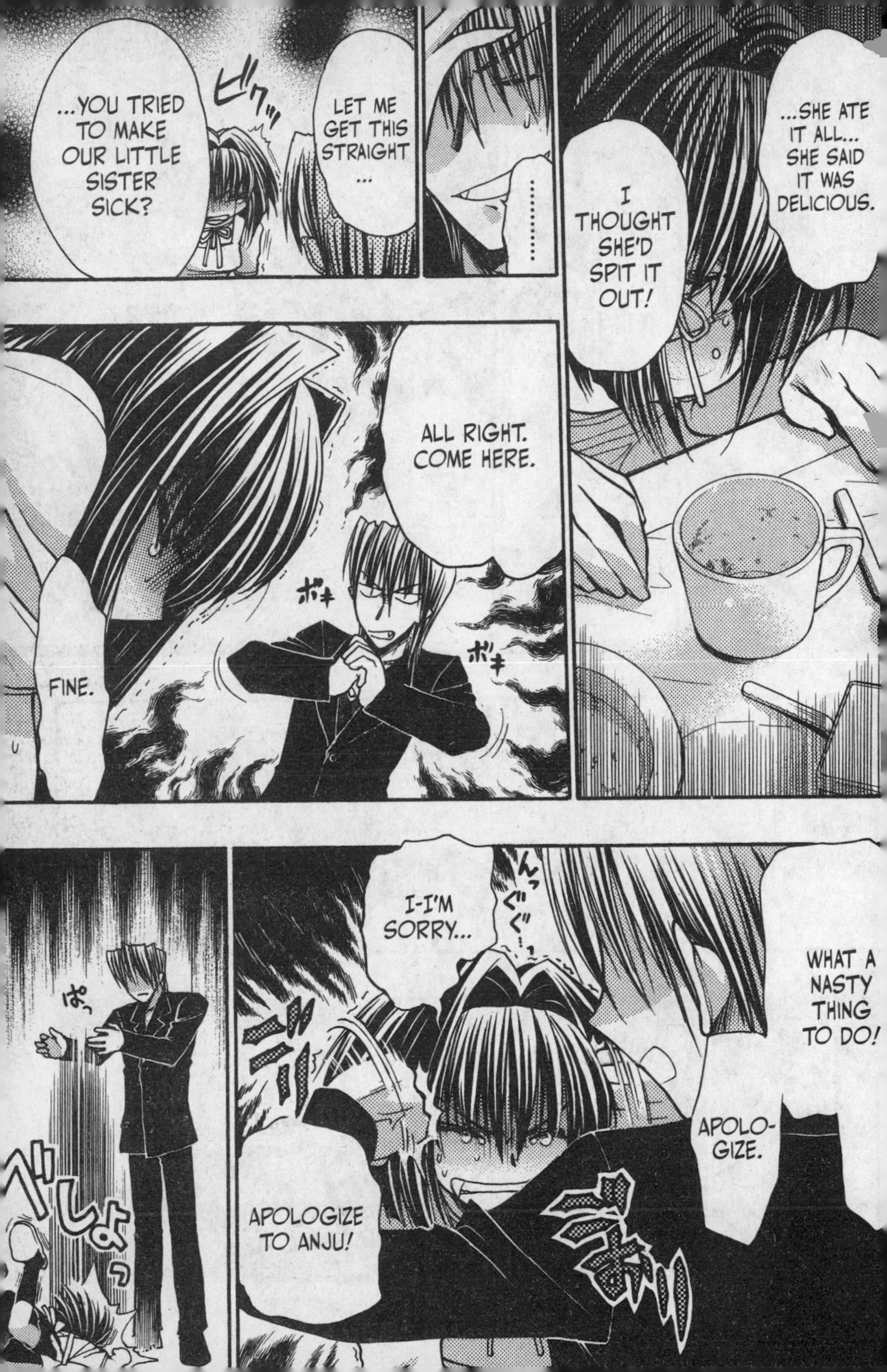
...SHE ATE IT ALL... SHE SAID IT WAS DELICIOUS.
I THOUGHT SHE'D SPIT IT OUT!
......
LET ME GET THIS STRAIGHT ...
ビクッ
...YOU TRIED TO MAKE OUR LITTLE SISTER SICK?
ALL RIGHT. COME HERE.
ボキ
ボキ
FINE.
WHAT A NASTY THING TO DO!
APOLOGIZE.
APOLOGIZE TO ANJU!
I-I'M SORRY...
ぱっ
べしょっ

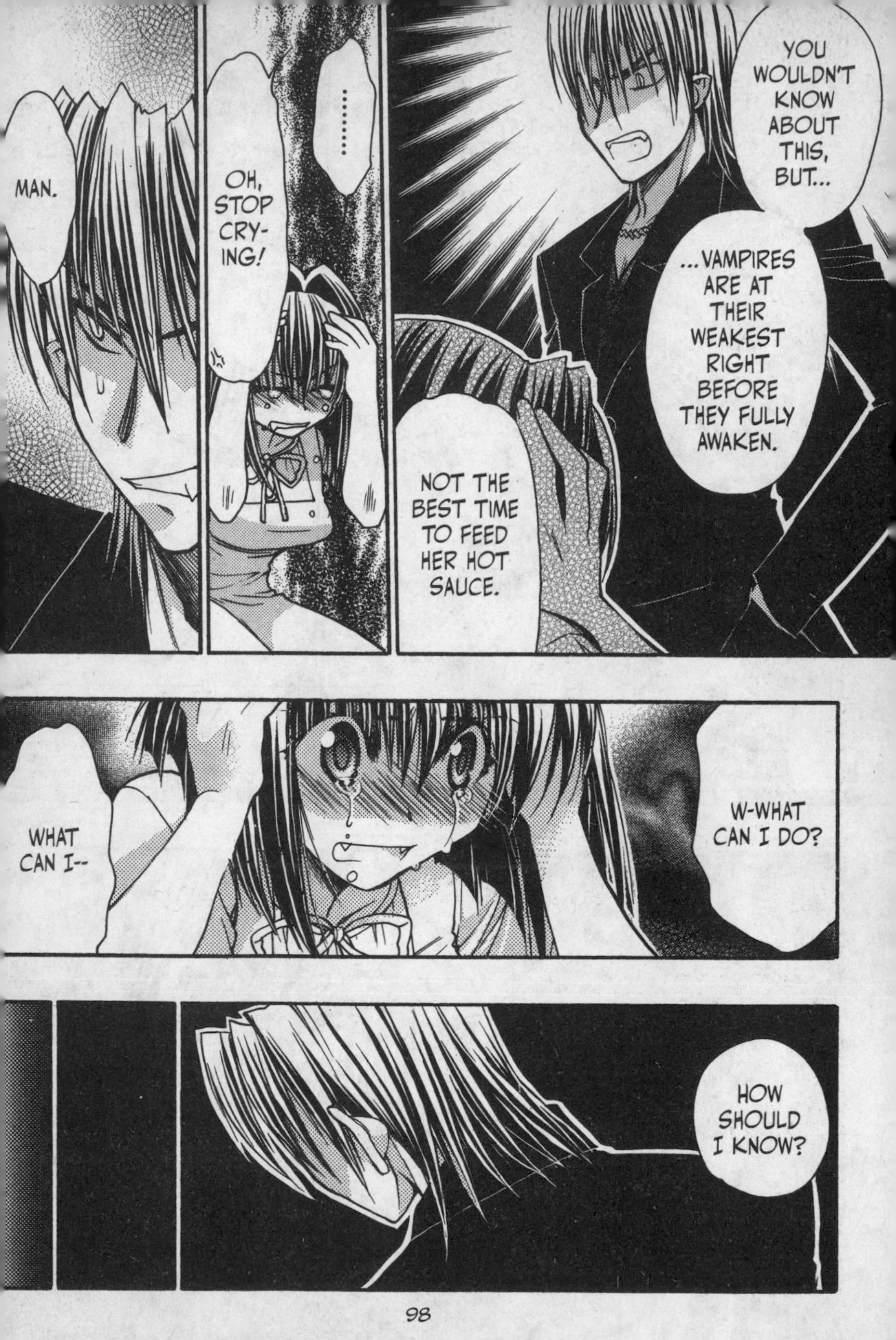
YOU WOULDN'T KNOW ABOUT THIS, BUT...
...VAMPIRES ARE AT THEIR WEAKEST RIGHT BEFORE THEY FULLY AWAKEN.
NOT THE BEST TIME TO FEED HER HOT SAUCE.
......
OH, STOP CRY-ING!
MAN.
W-WHAT CAN I DO?
WHAT CAN I--
HOW SHOULD I KNOW?

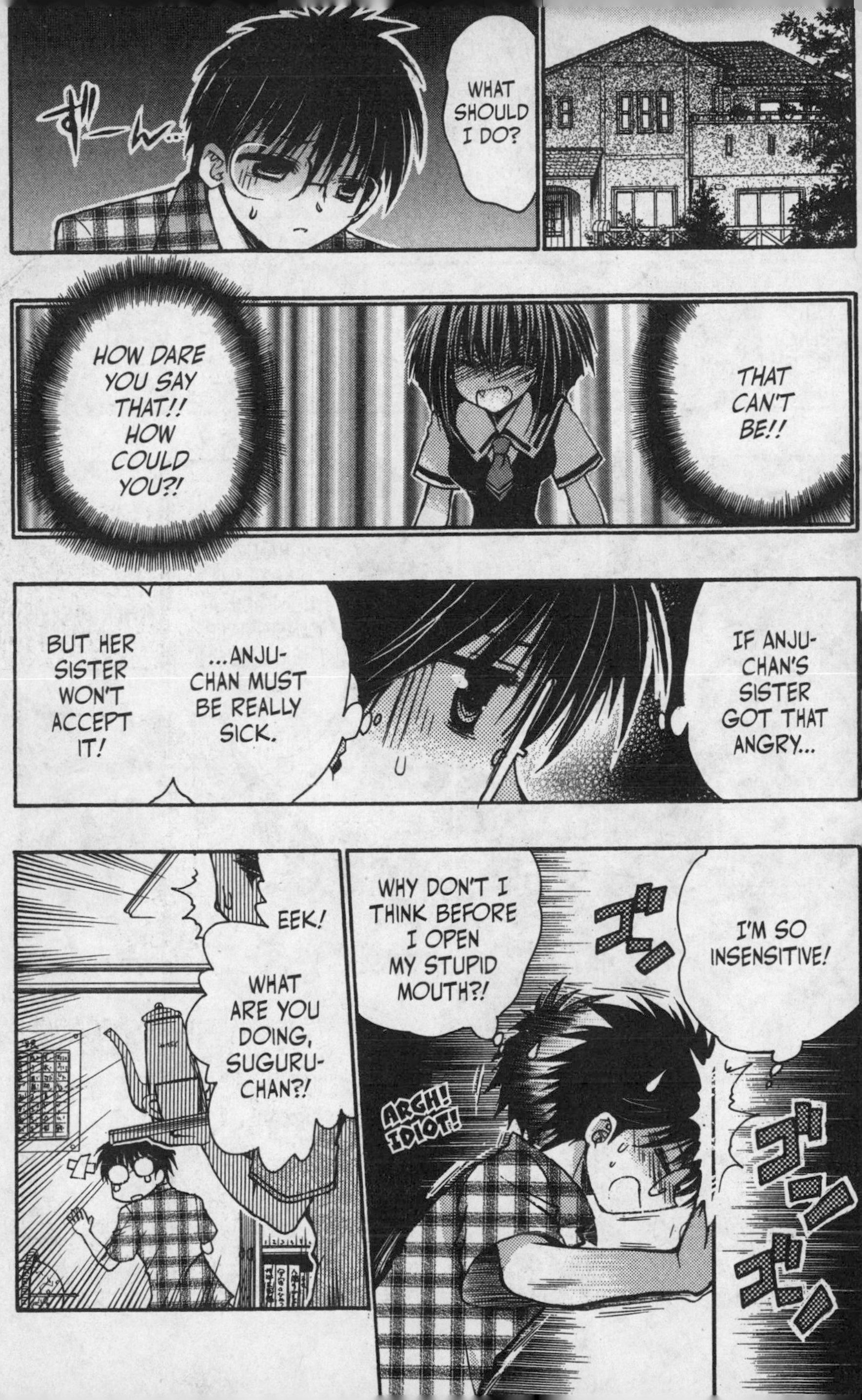
WHAT SHOULD I DO?
THAT CAN'T BE!!
HOW DARE YOU SAY THAT!! HOW COULD YOU?!
IF ANJU-CHAN'S SISTER GOT THAT ANGRY...
...ANJU-CHAN MUST BE REALLY SICK.
BUT HER SISTER WON'T ACCEPT IT!
I'M SO INSENSITIVE!
WHY DON'T I THINK BEFORE I OPEN MY STUPID MOUTH?!
ARGH! IDIOT!
EEK!
WHAT ARE YOU DOING, SUGURU-CHAN?!

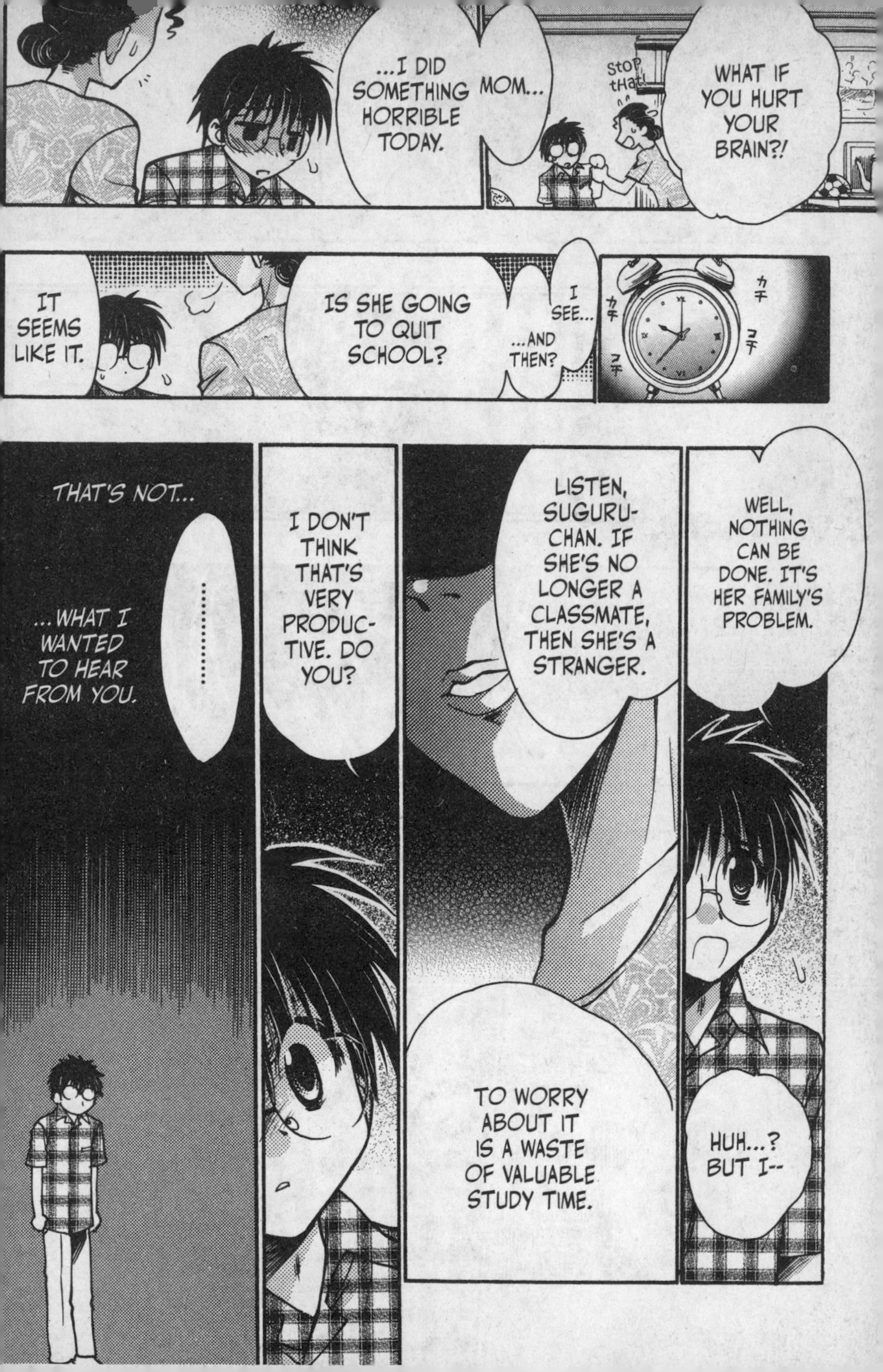
Stop that!
WHAT IF YOU HURT YOUR BRAIN?!
MOM...
...I DID SOMETHING HORRIBLE TODAY.
カチ コチ カチ コチ
I SEE...
...AND THEN?
IS SHE GOING TO QUIT SCHOOL?
IT SEEMS LIKE IT.
WELL, NOTHING CAN BE DONE. IT'S HER FAMILY'S PROBLEM.
HUH...? BUT I--
LISTEN, SUGURU-CHAN. IF SHE'S NO LONGER A CLASSMATE, THEN SHE'S A STRANGER.
TO WORRY ABOUT IT IS A WASTE OF VALUABLE STUDY TIME.
I DON'T THINK THAT'S VERY PRODUCTIVE. DO YOU?
......
THAT'S NOT...
...WHAT I WANTED TO HEAR FROM YOU.

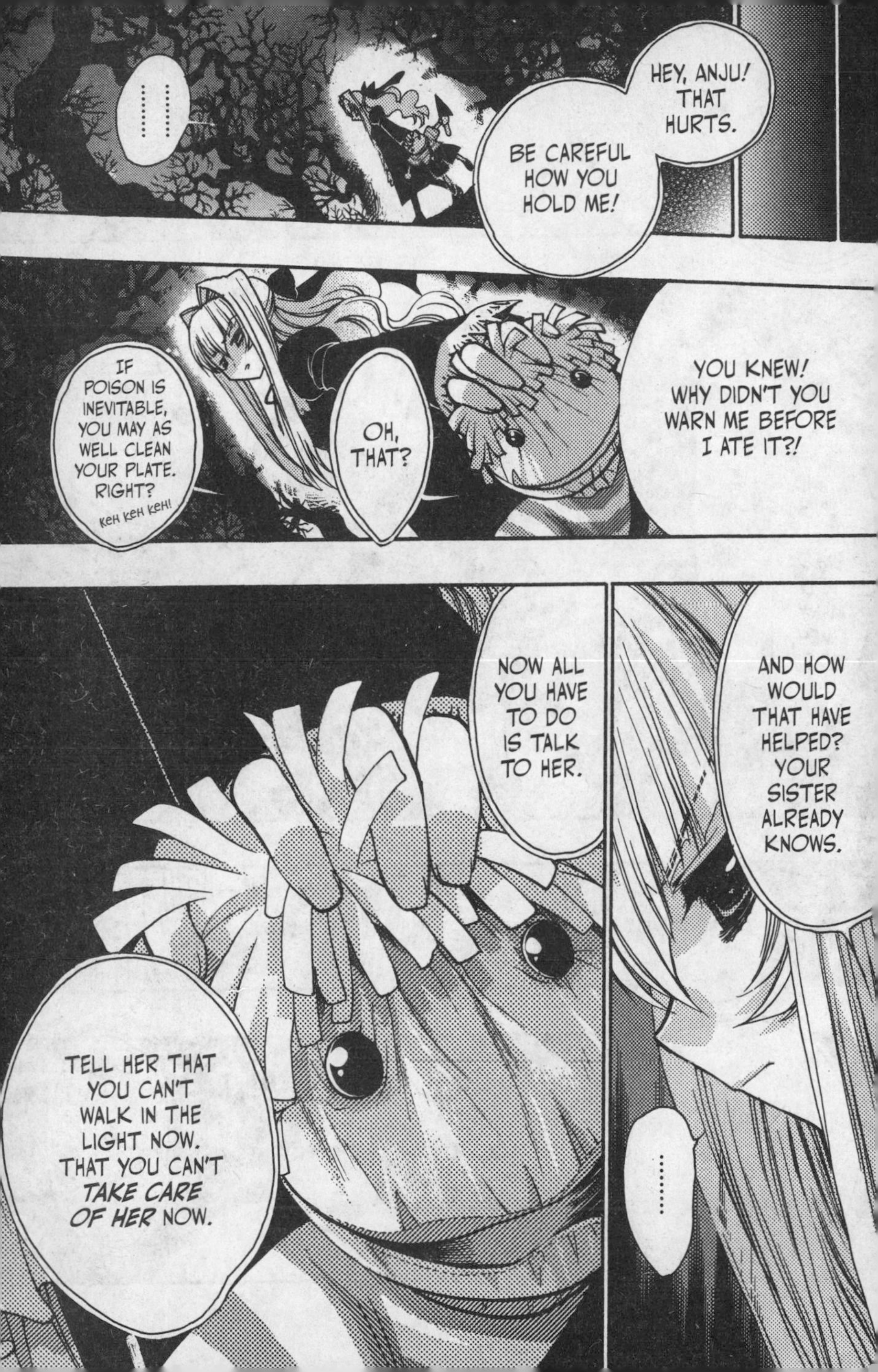
HEY, ANJU! THAT HURTS.
BE CAREFUL HOW YOU HOLD ME!
......
YOU KNEW! WHY DIDN'T YOU WARN ME BEFORE I ATE IT?!
OH, THAT?
IF POISON IS INEVITABLE, YOU MAY AS WELL CLEAN YOUR PLATE. RIGHT?
KEH KEH KEH!
AND HOW WOULD THAT HAVE HELPED? YOUR SISTER ALREADY KNOWS.
......
NOW ALL YOU HAVE TO DO IS TALK TO HER.
TELL HER THAT YOU CAN'T WALK IN THE LIGHT NOW. THAT YOU CAN'T *TAKE CARE OF HER* NOW.

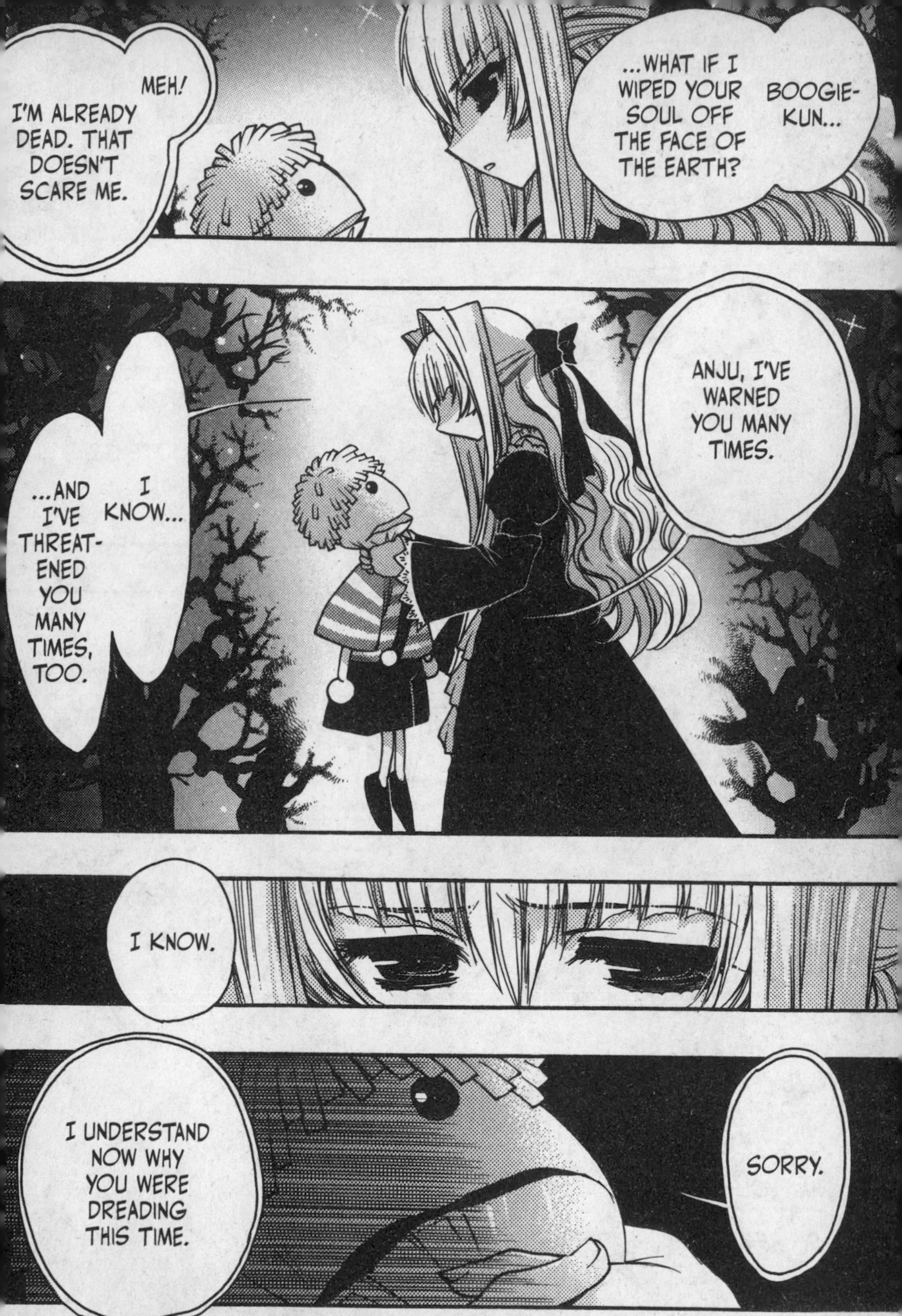
BOOGIE-KUN...
...WHAT IF I WIPED YOUR SOUL OFF THE FACE OF THE EARTH?
MEH!
I'M ALREADY DEAD. THAT DOESN'T SCARE ME.
ANJU, I'VE WARNED YOU MANY TIMES.
I KNOW...
...AND I'VE THREATENED YOU MANY TIMES, TOO.
I KNOW.
SORRY.
I UNDERSTAND NOW WHY YOU WERE DREADING THIS TIME.

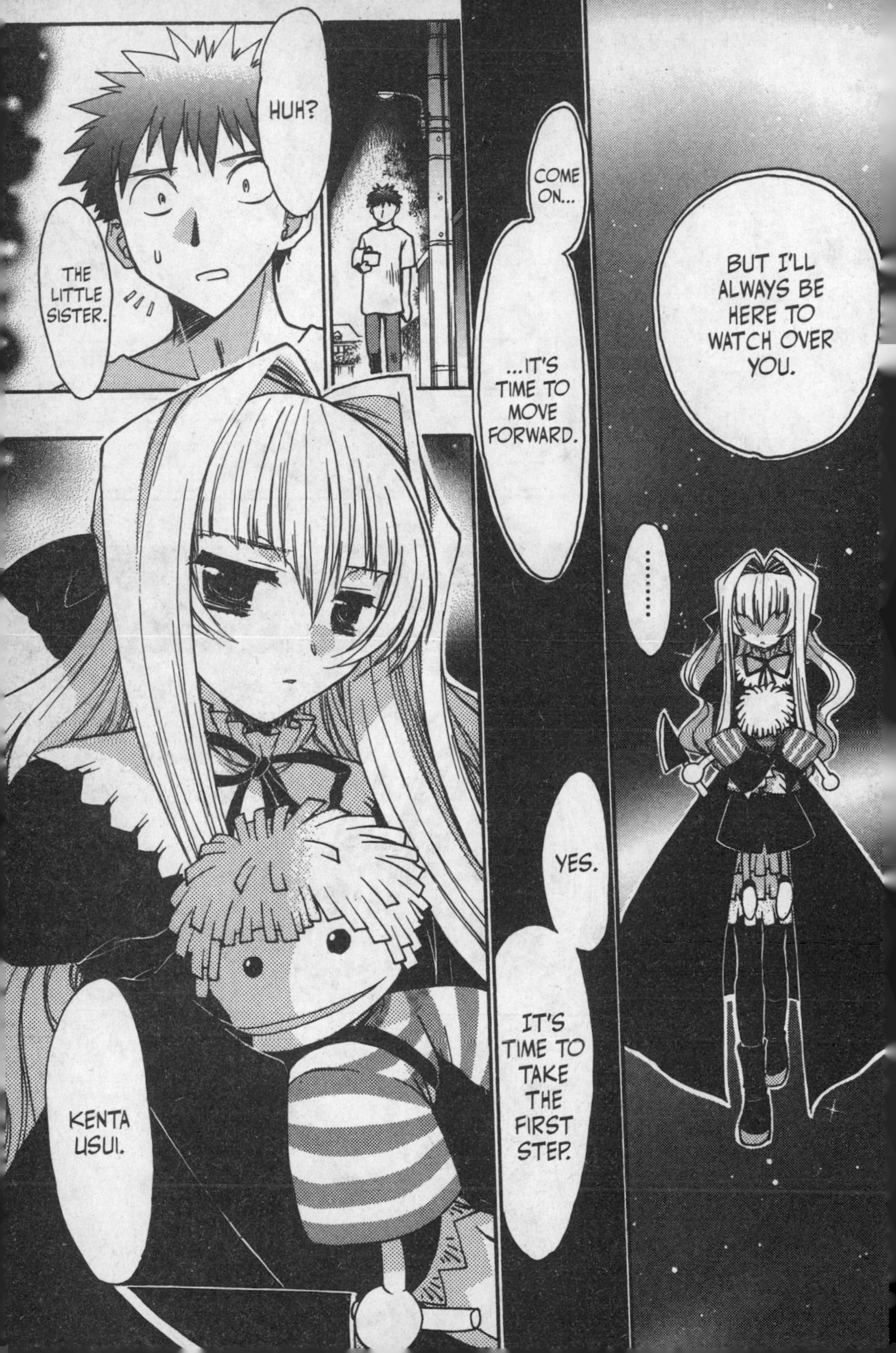
BUT I'LL ALWAYS BE HERE TO WATCH OVER YOU.
......
COME ON...
...IT'S TIME TO MOVE FORWARD.
YES.
IT'S TIME TO TAKE THE FIRST STEP.
HUH?
THE LITTLE SISTER.
KENTA USUI.

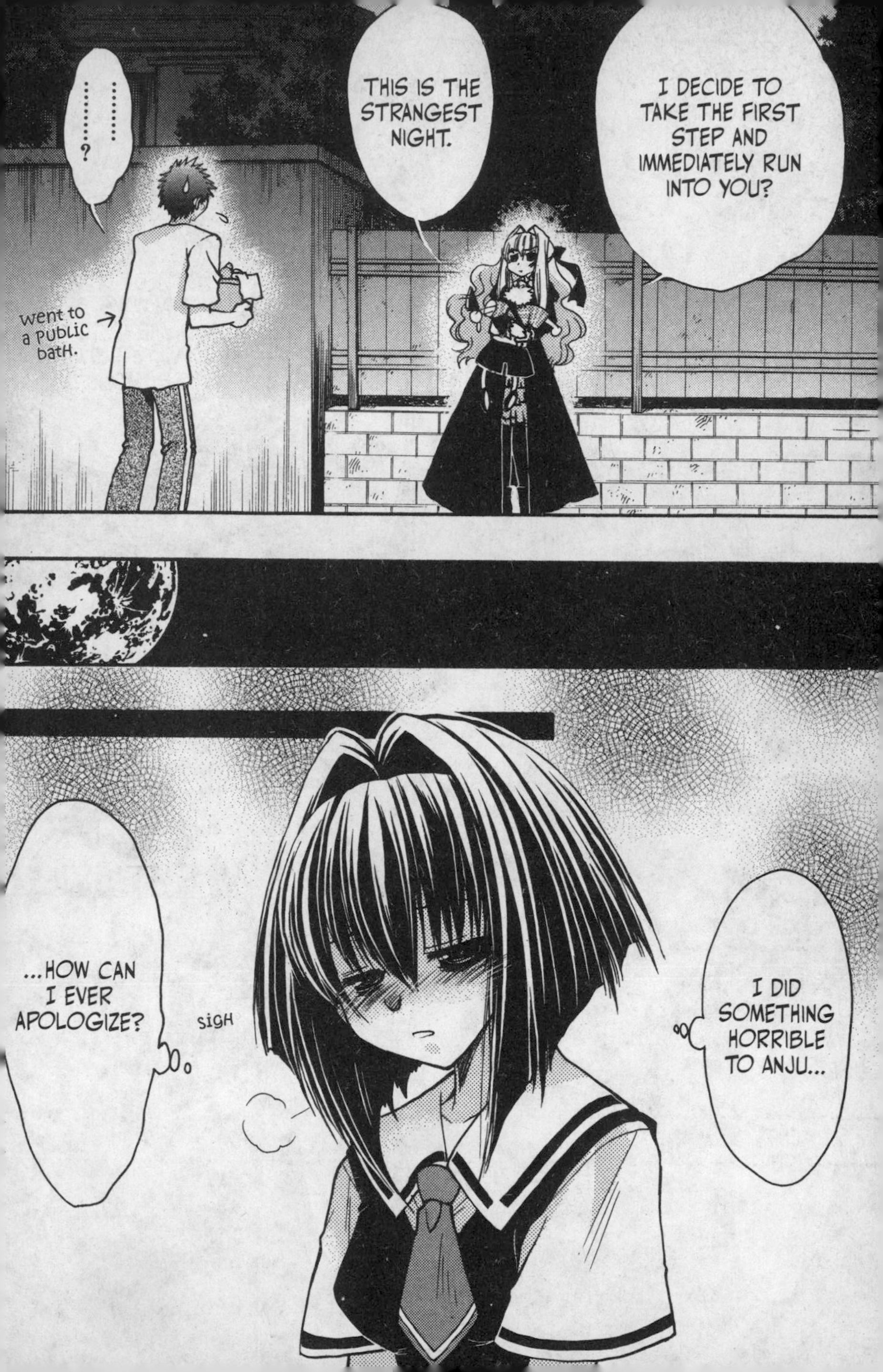

I DECIDE TO TAKE THE FIRST STEP AND IMMEDIATELY RUN INTO YOU?
THIS IS THE STRANGEST NIGHT.
......?
went to a public bath.
I DID SOMETHING HORRIBLE TO ANJU...
SIGH
...HOW CAN I EVER APOLOGIZE?

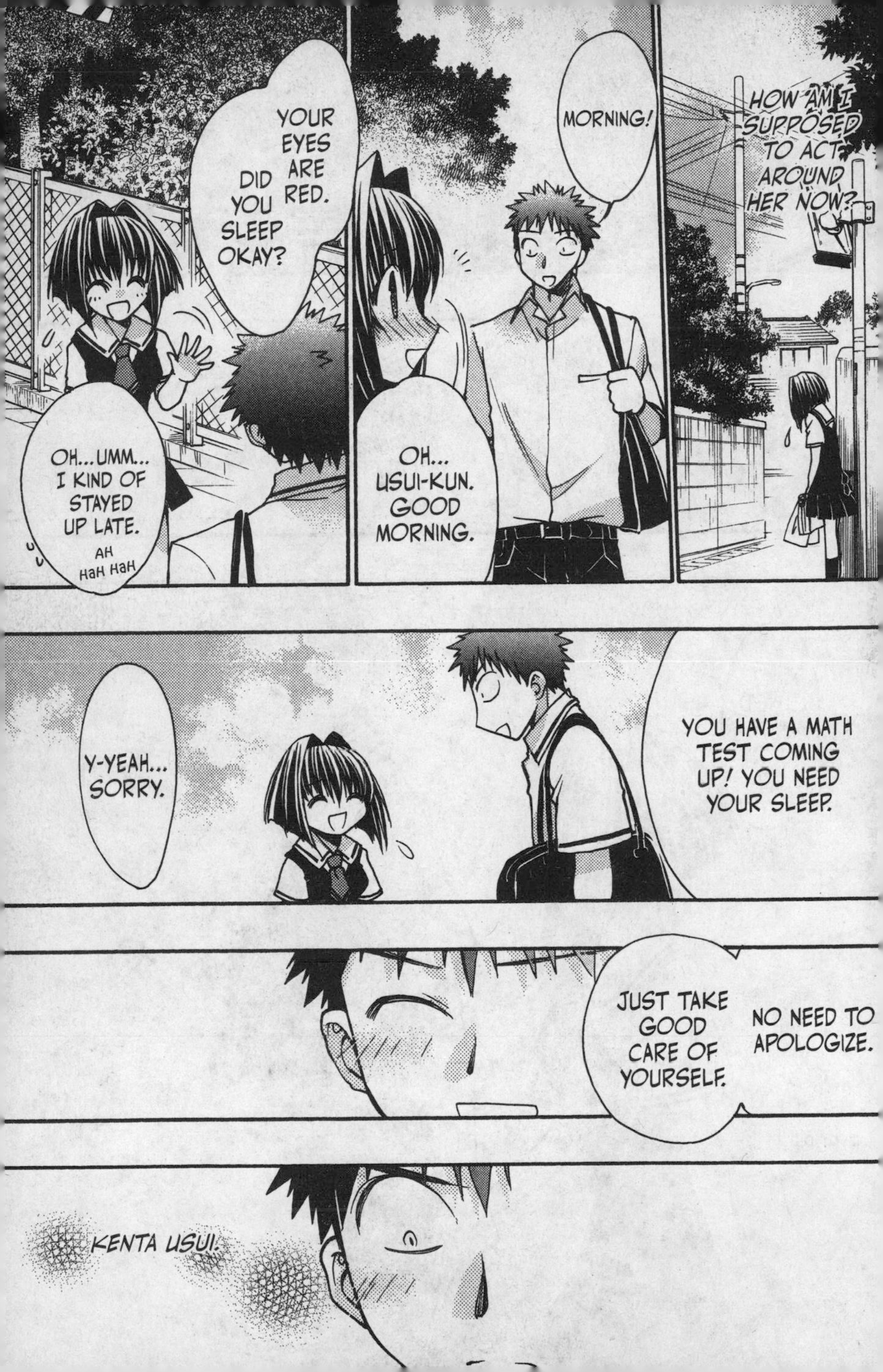
HOW AM I SUPPOSED TO ACT AROUND HER NOW?
MORNING!
OH... USUI-KUN. GOOD MORNING.
YOUR EYES ARE RED.
DID YOU SLEEP OKAY?
OH...UMM... I KIND OF STAYED UP LATE.
AH HAH HAH
YOU HAVE A MATH TEST COMING UP! YOU NEED YOUR SLEEP.
Y-YEAH... SORRY.
NO NEED TO APOLOGIZE.
JUST TAKE GOOD CARE OF YOURSELF.
KENTA USUI.

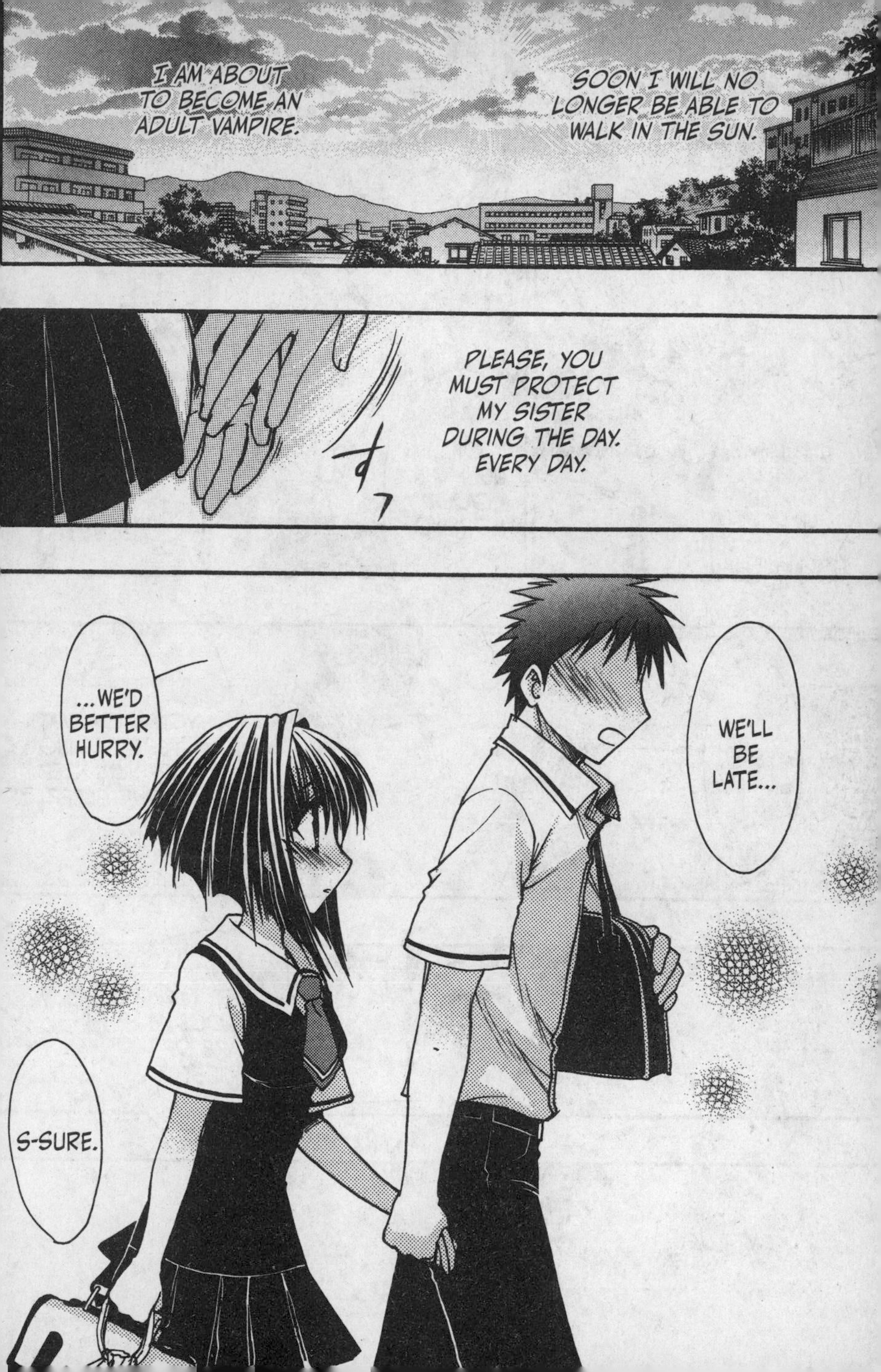
SOON I WILL NO LONGER BE ABLE TO WALK IN THE SUN.
I AM ABOUT TO BECOME AN ADULT VAMPIRE.
PLEASE, YOU MUST PROTECT MY SISTER DURING THE DAY. EVERY DAY.
すっ
WE'LL BE LATE...
...WE'D BETTER HURRY.
S-SURE.

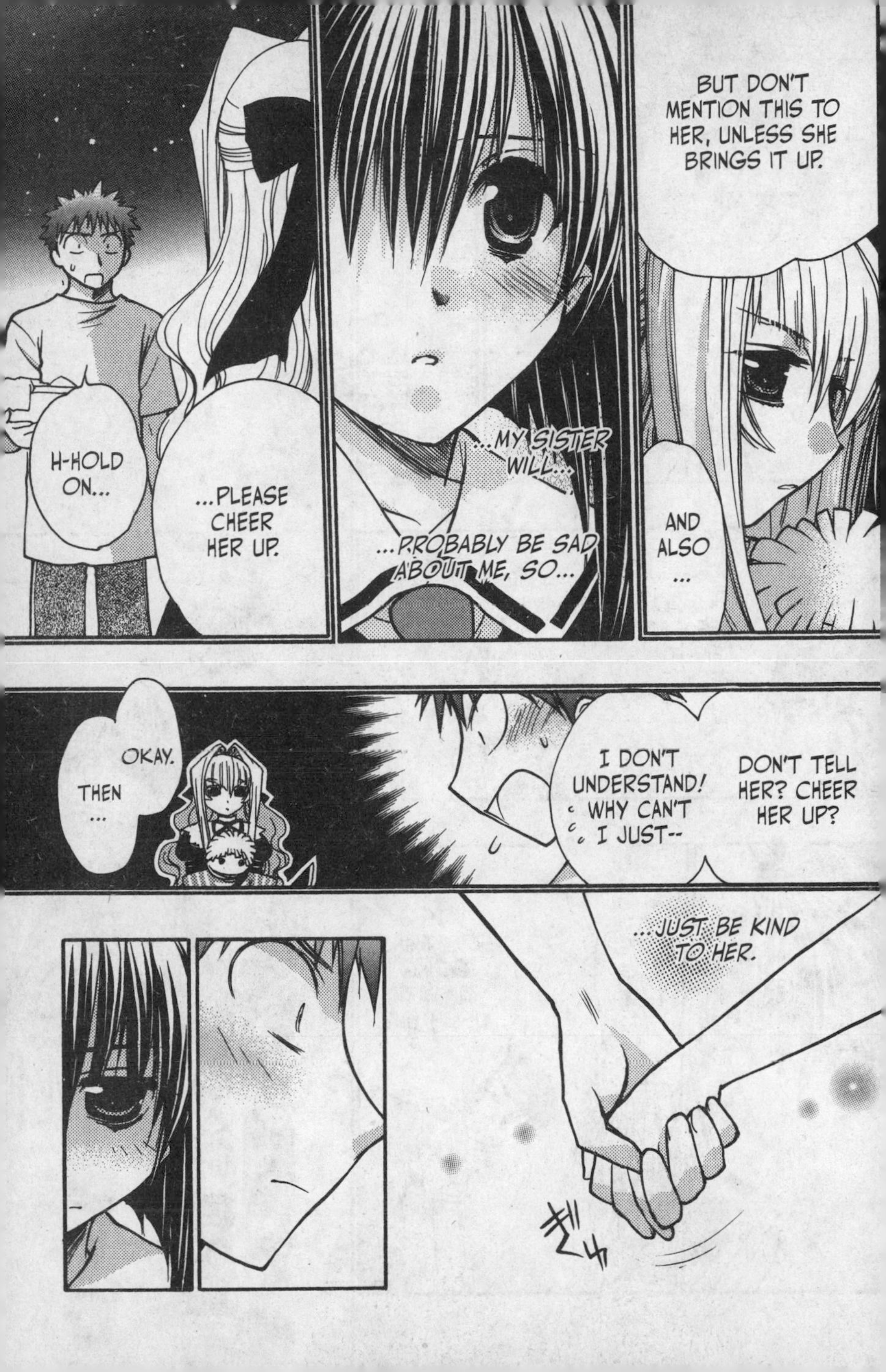
BUT DON'T MENTION THIS TO HER, UNLESS SHE BRINGS IT UP.
AND ALSO ...
...MY SISTER WILL...
...PROBABLY BE SAD ABOUT ME, SO...
...PLEASE CHEER HER UP.
H-HOLD ON...
DON'T TELL HER? CHEER HER UP?
I DON'T UNDERSTAND! WHY CAN'T I JUST--
OKAY.
THEN ...
...JUST BE KIND TO HER.

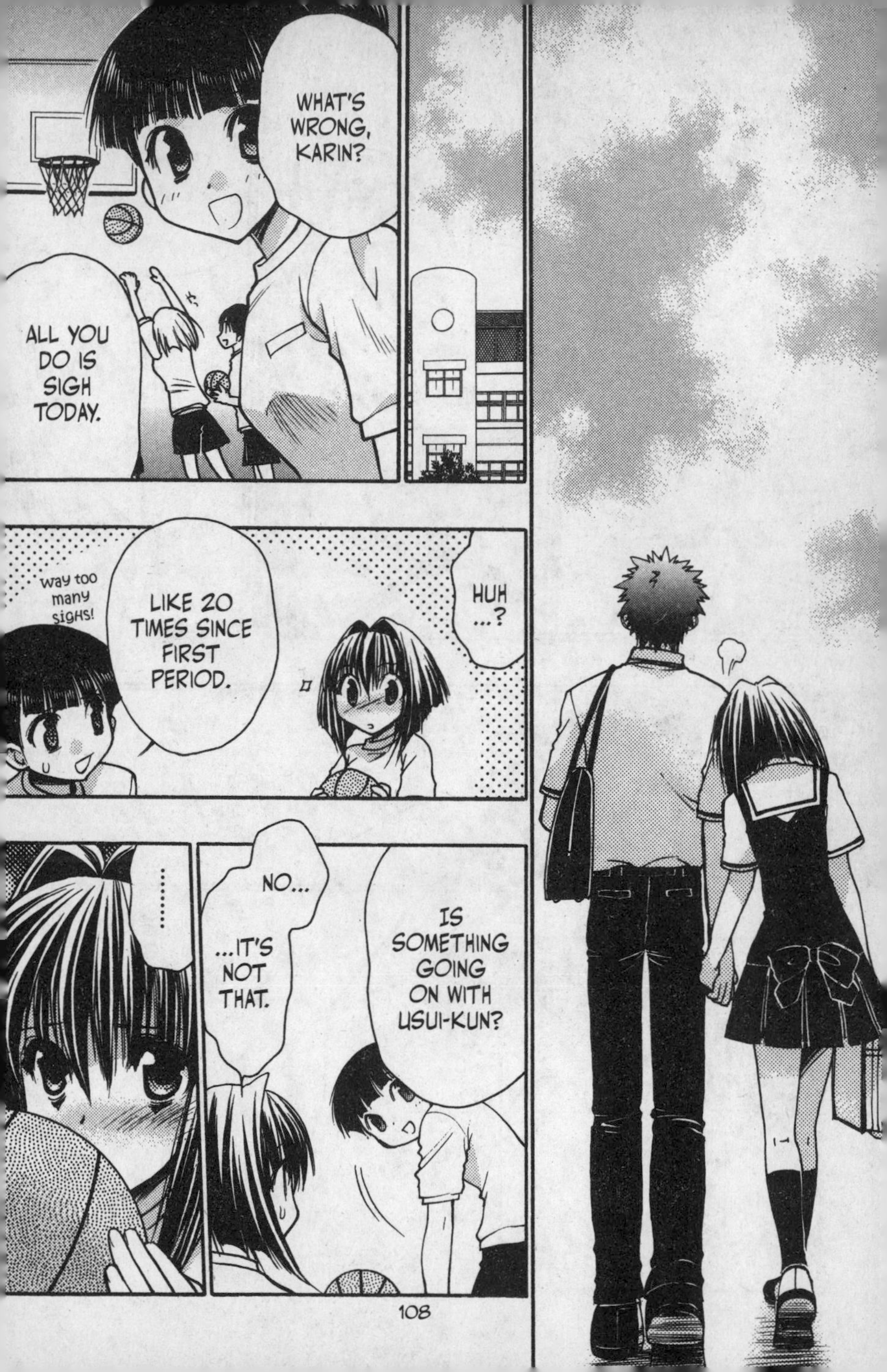
WHAT'S WRONG, KARIN?
ALL YOU DO IS SIGH TODAY.
HUH ...?
LIKE 20 TIMES SINCE FIRST PERIOD.
way too many sighs!
IS SOMETHING GOING ON WITH USUI-KUN?
NO...
...IT'S NOT THAT.
......

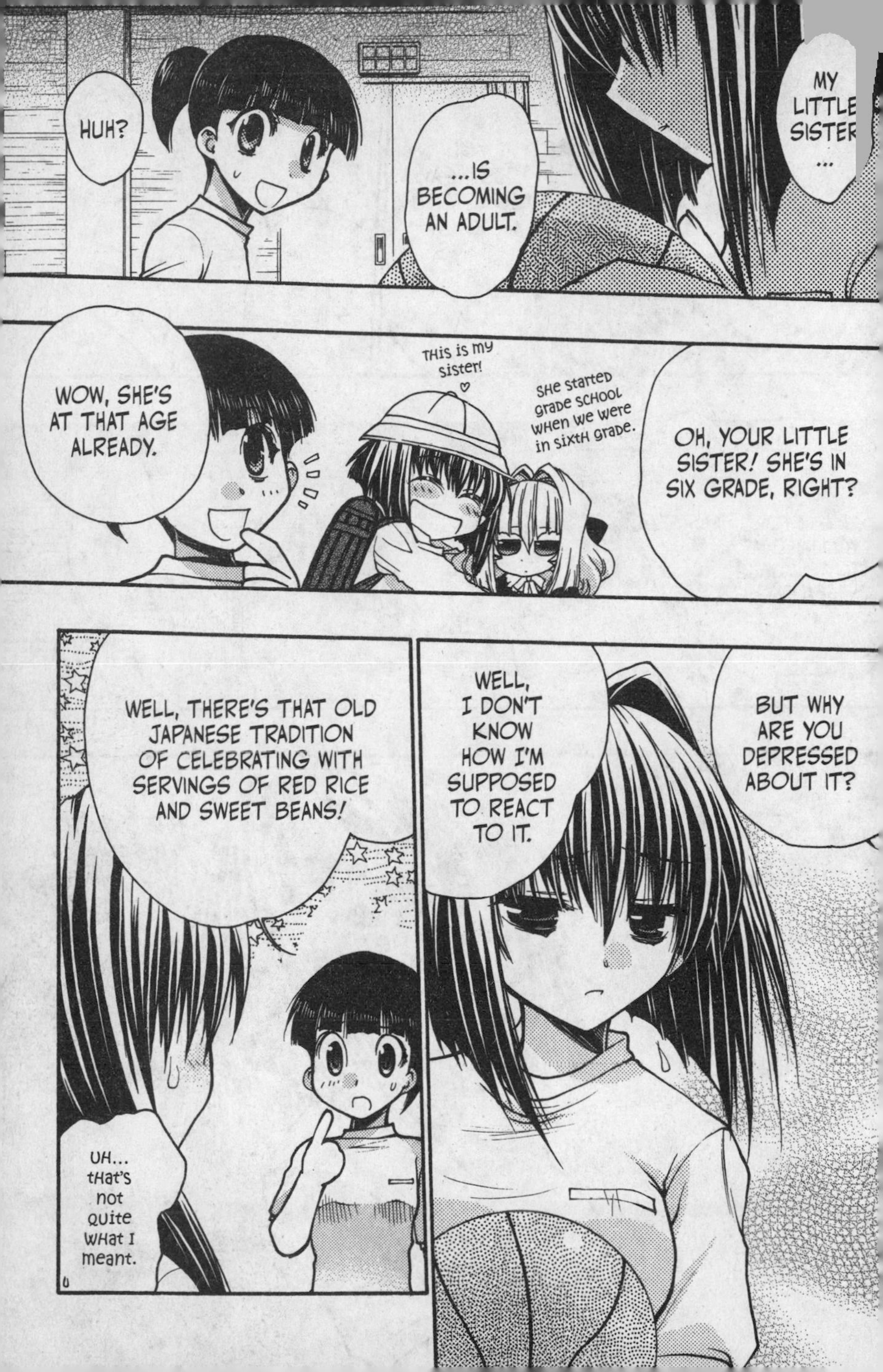
MY LITTLE SISTER...
...IS BECOMING AN ADULT.
HUH?
OH, YOUR LITTLE SISTER! SHE'S IN SIX GRADE, RIGHT?
SHE started grade SCHOOL WHEN WE were in sixth grade.
THIS is my sister! ♡
WOW, SHE'S AT THAT AGE ALREADY.
BUT WHY ARE YOU DEPRESSED ABOUT IT?
WELL, I DON'T KNOW HOW I'M SUPPOSED TO REACT TO IT.
WELL, THERE'S THAT OLD JAPANESE TRADITION OF CELEBRATING WITH SERVINGS OF RED RICE AND SWEET BEANS!
UH... that's not quite what I meant.

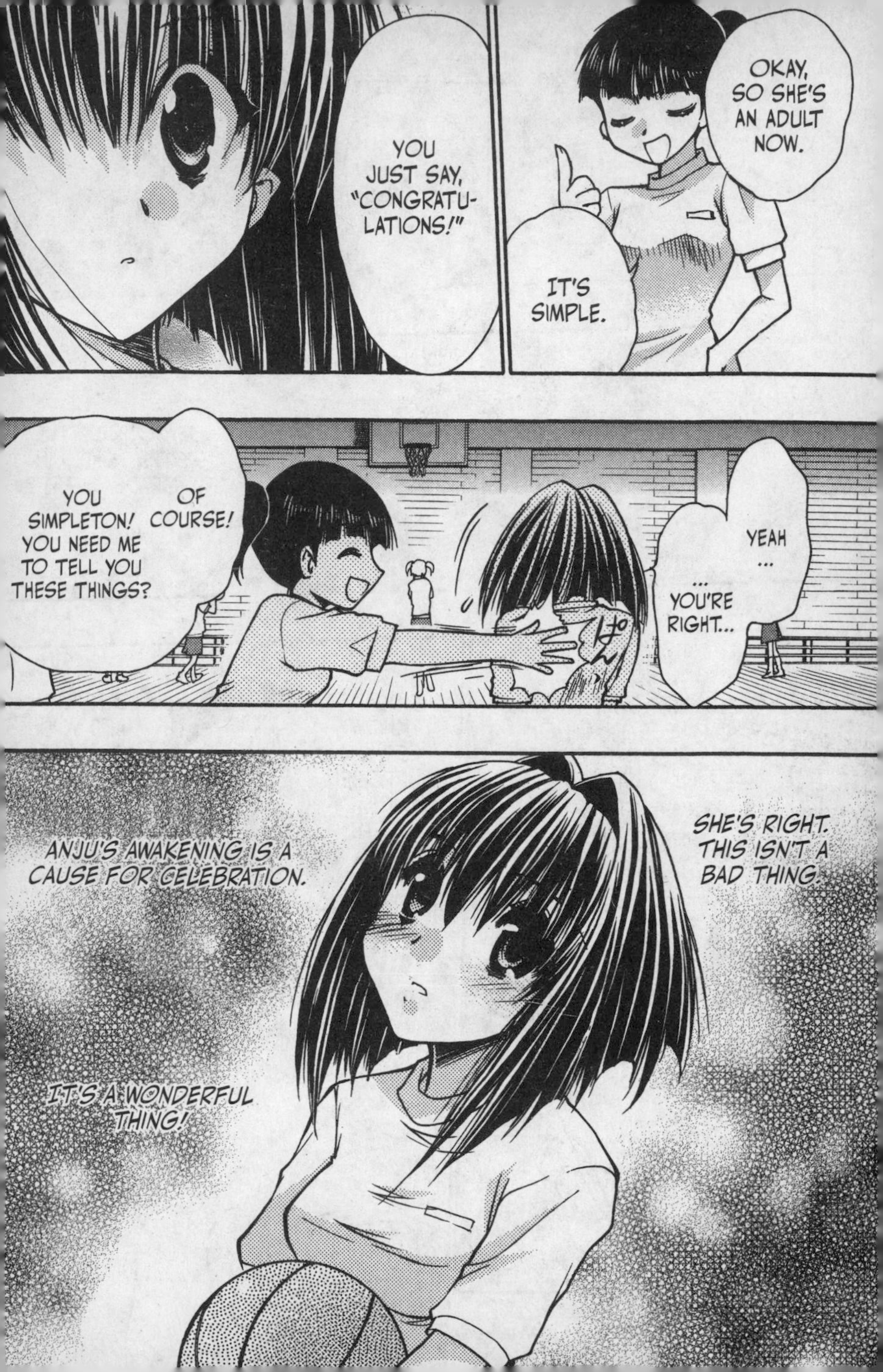
OKAY, SO SHE'S AN ADULT NOW.
IT'S SIMPLE.
YOU JUST SAY, "CONGRATULATIONS!"
YEAH ... ... YOU'RE RIGHT...
OF COURSE!
YOU SIMPLETON! YOU NEED ME TO TELL YOU THESE THINGS?
SHE'S RIGHT. THIS ISN'T A BAD THING.
ANJU'S AWAKENING IS A CAUSE FOR CELEBRATION.
IT'S A WONDERFUL THING!

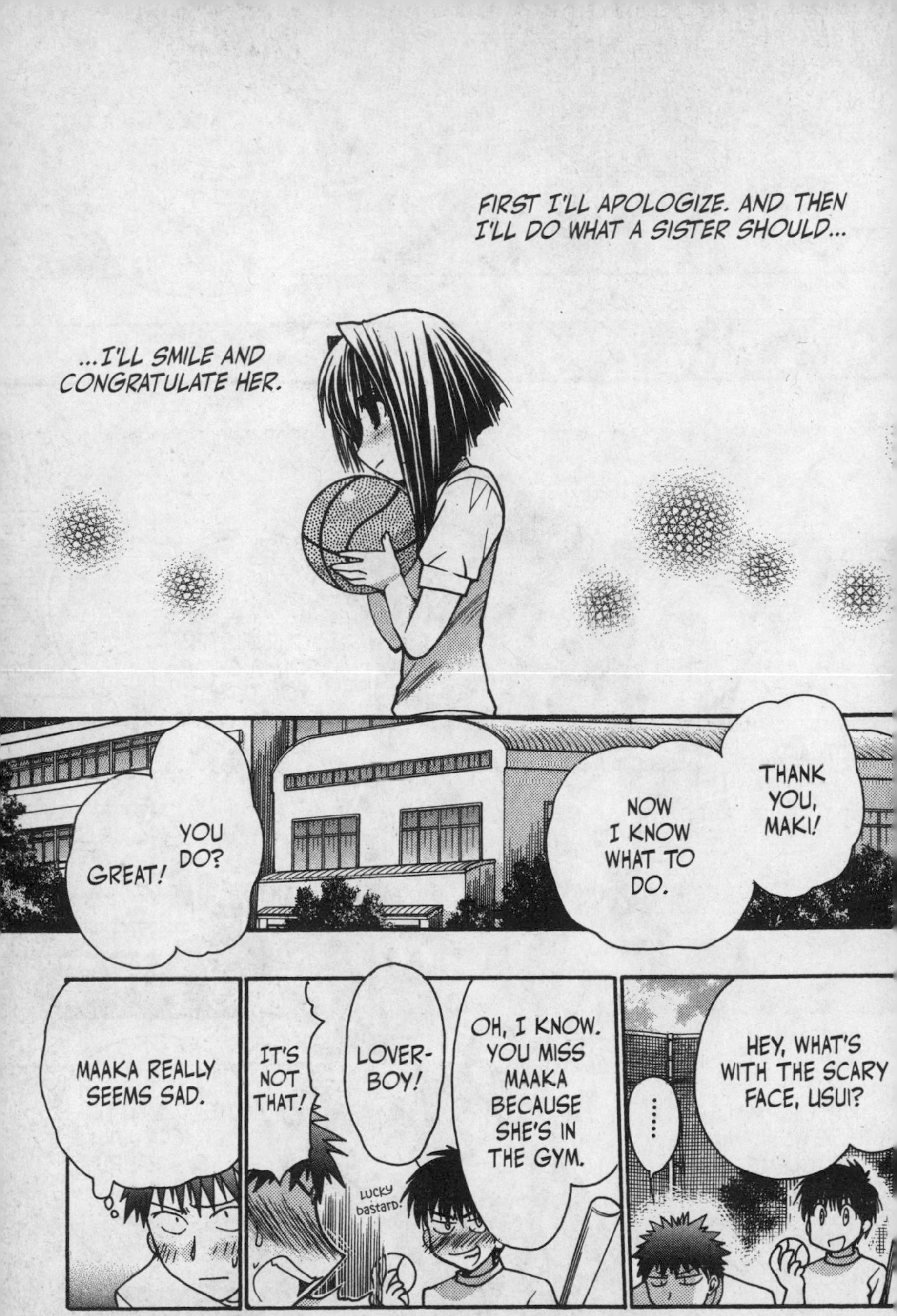
FIRST I'LL APOLOGIZE. AND THEN I'LL DO WHAT A SISTER SHOULD...
...I'LL SMILE AND CONGRATULATE HER.
THANK YOU, MAKI!
NOW I KNOW WHAT TO DO.
YOU DO?
GREAT!
HEY, WHAT'S WITH THE SCARY FACE, USUI?
......
OH, I KNOW. YOU MISS MAAKA BECAUSE SHE'S IN THE GYM.
LOVER-BOY!
IT'S NOT THAT!
LUCKY bastard.
MAAKA REALLY SEEMS SAD.

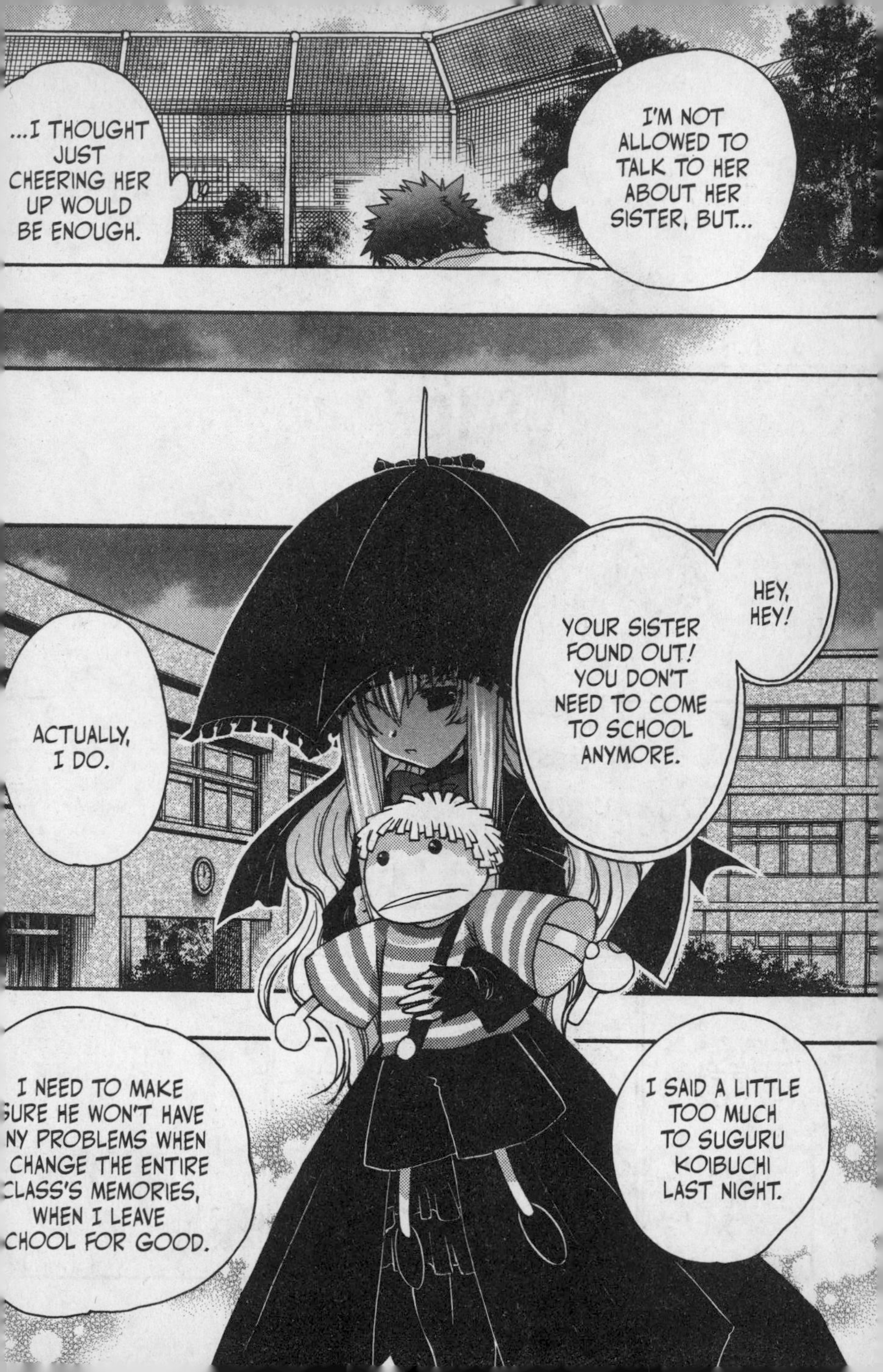
I'M NOT ALLOWED TO TALK TO HER ABOUT HER SISTER, BUT...
...I THOUGHT JUST CHEERING HER UP WOULD BE ENOUGH.
HEY, HEY!
YOUR SISTER FOUND OUT! YOU DON'T NEED TO COME TO SCHOOL ANYMORE.
ACTUALLY, I DO.
I SAID A LITTLE TOO MUCH TO SUGURU KOIBUCHI LAST NIGHT.
I NEED TO MAKE SURE HE WON'T HAVE NY PROBLEMS WHEN CHANGE THE ENTIRE CLASS'S MEMORIES, WHEN I LEAVE CHOOL FOR GOOD.

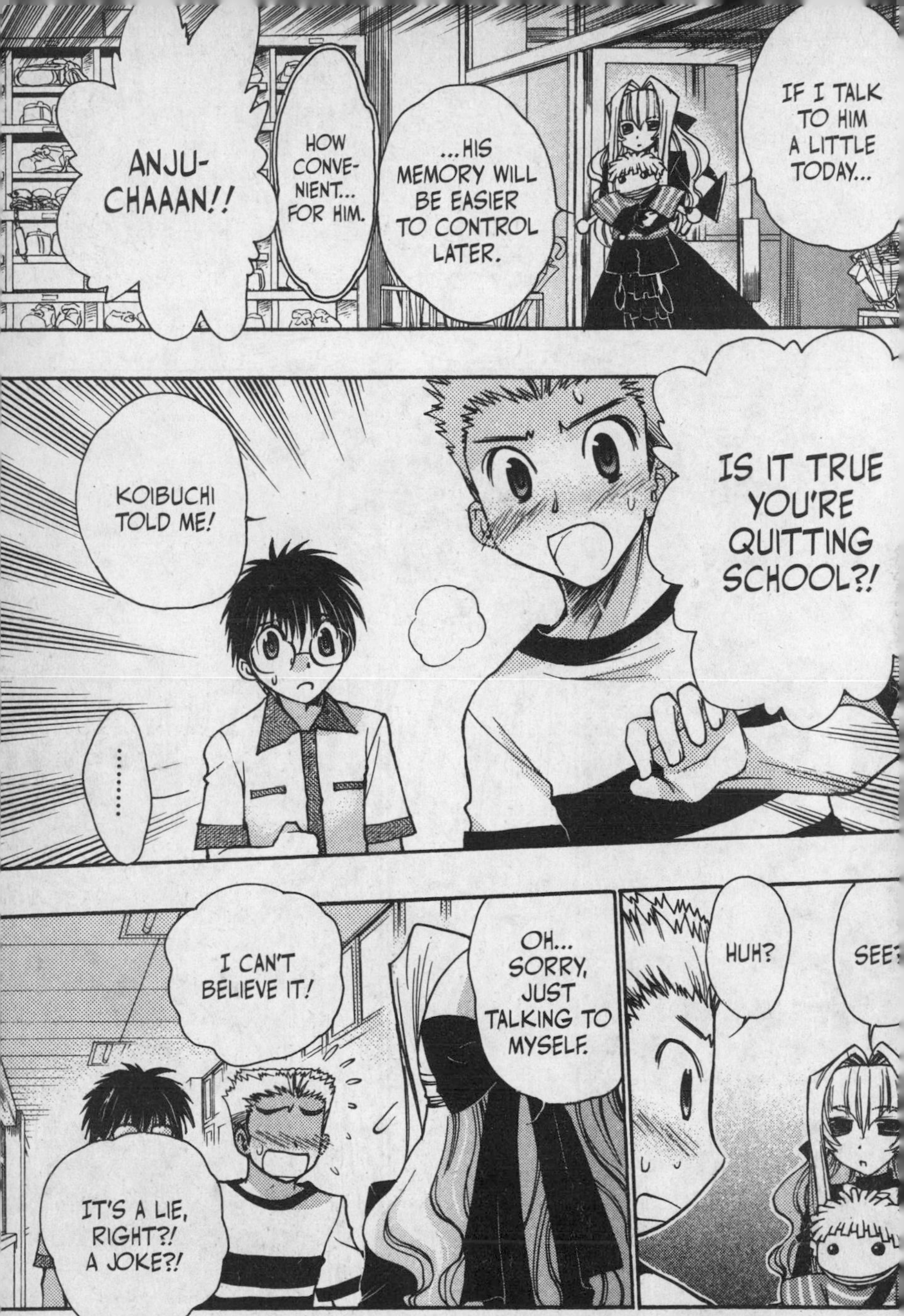
IF I TALK TO HIM A LITTLE TODAY...
...HIS MEMORY WILL BE EASIER TO CONTROL LATER.
HOW CONVENIENT... FOR HIM.
ANJU-CHAAAN!!
IS IT TRUE YOU'RE QUITTING SCHOOL?!
KOIBUCHI TOLD ME!
......
SEE
HUH?
OH... SORRY, JUST TALKING TO MYSELF.
I CAN'T BELIEVE IT!
IT'S A LIE, RIGHT?! A JOKE?!

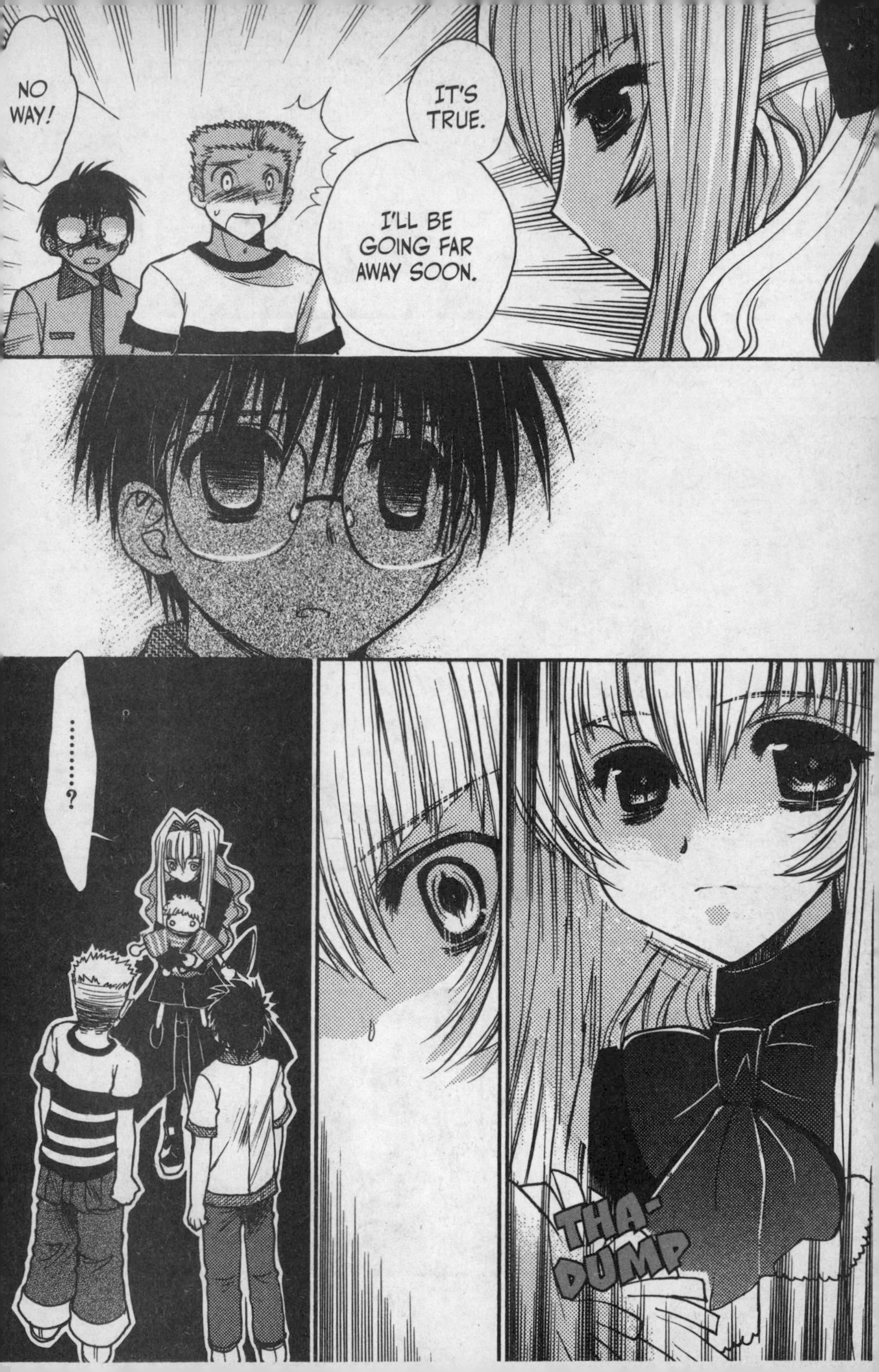
IT'S TRUE.
I'LL BE GOING FAR AWAY SOON.
NO WAY!
THA-DUMP
......?

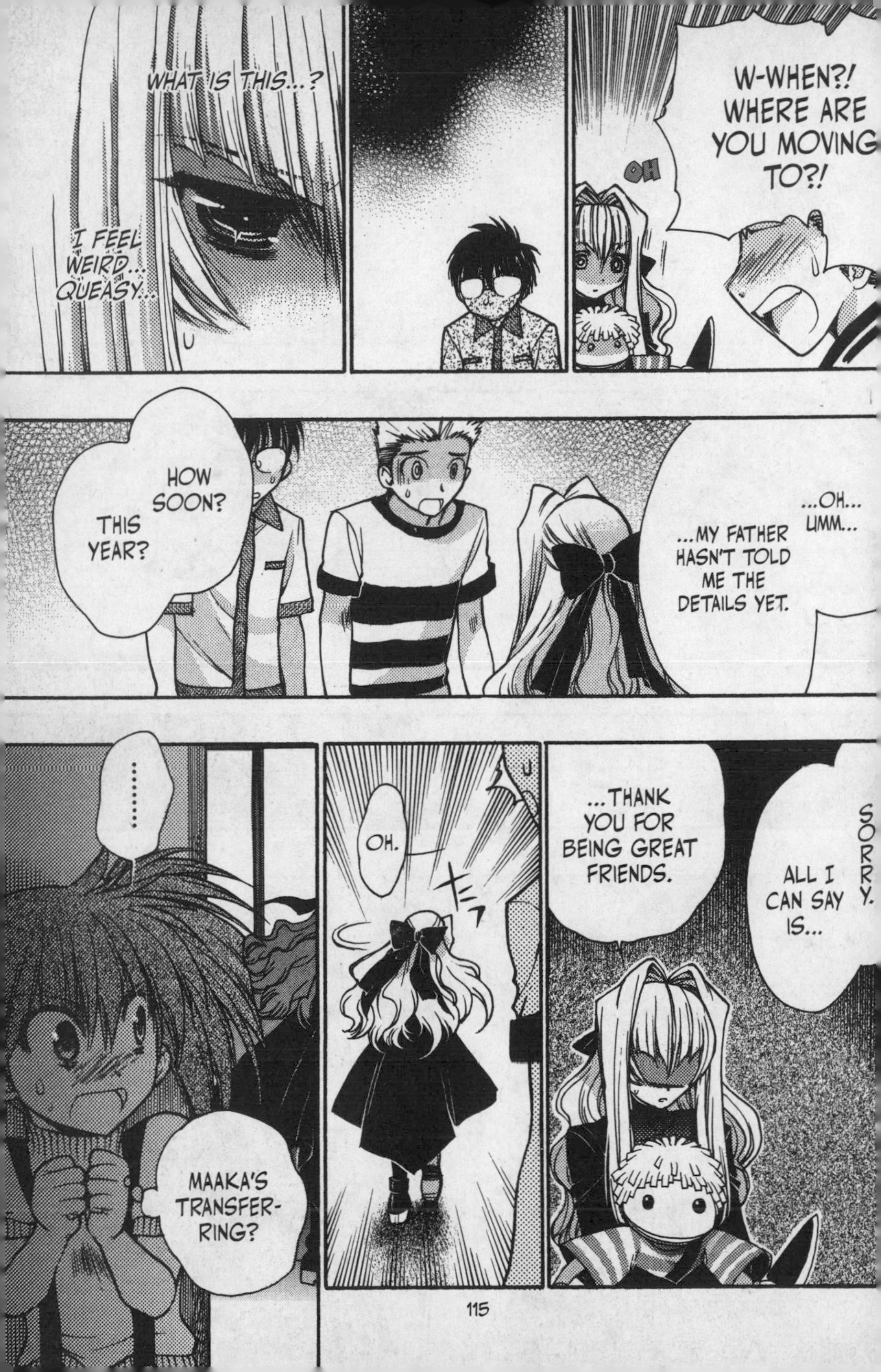
W-WHEN?! WHERE ARE YOU MOVING TO?!
OH
WHAT IS THIS...?
I FEEL WEIRD... QUEASY...
...OH... UMM...
...MY FATHER HASN'T TOLD ME THE DETAILS YET.
HOW SOON? THIS YEAR?
ALL I CAN SAY IS... SORRY.
...THANK YOU FOR BEING GREAT FRIENDS.
OH.
......
MAAKA'S TRANSFER-RING?

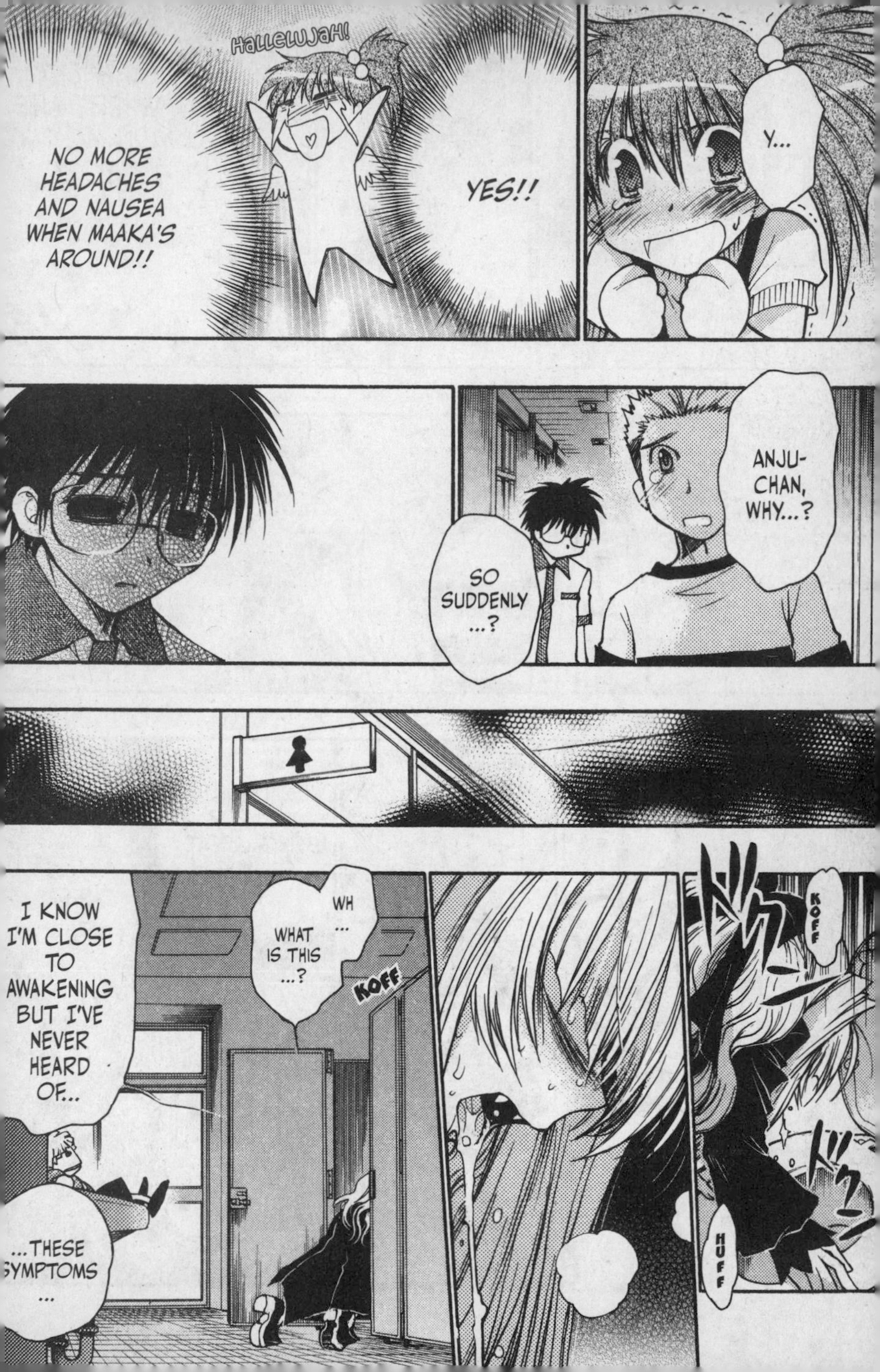
Y...
HALLELUJAH!
YES!!
NO MORE HEADACHES AND NAUSEA WHEN MAAKA'S AROUND!!
ANJU-CHAN, WHY...?
SO SUDDENLY ...?
KOFF
HUFF
WH ...
WHAT IS THIS ...?
KOFF
I KNOW I'M CLOSE TO AWAKENING BUT I'VE NEVER HEARD OF...
...THESE SYMPTOMS ...

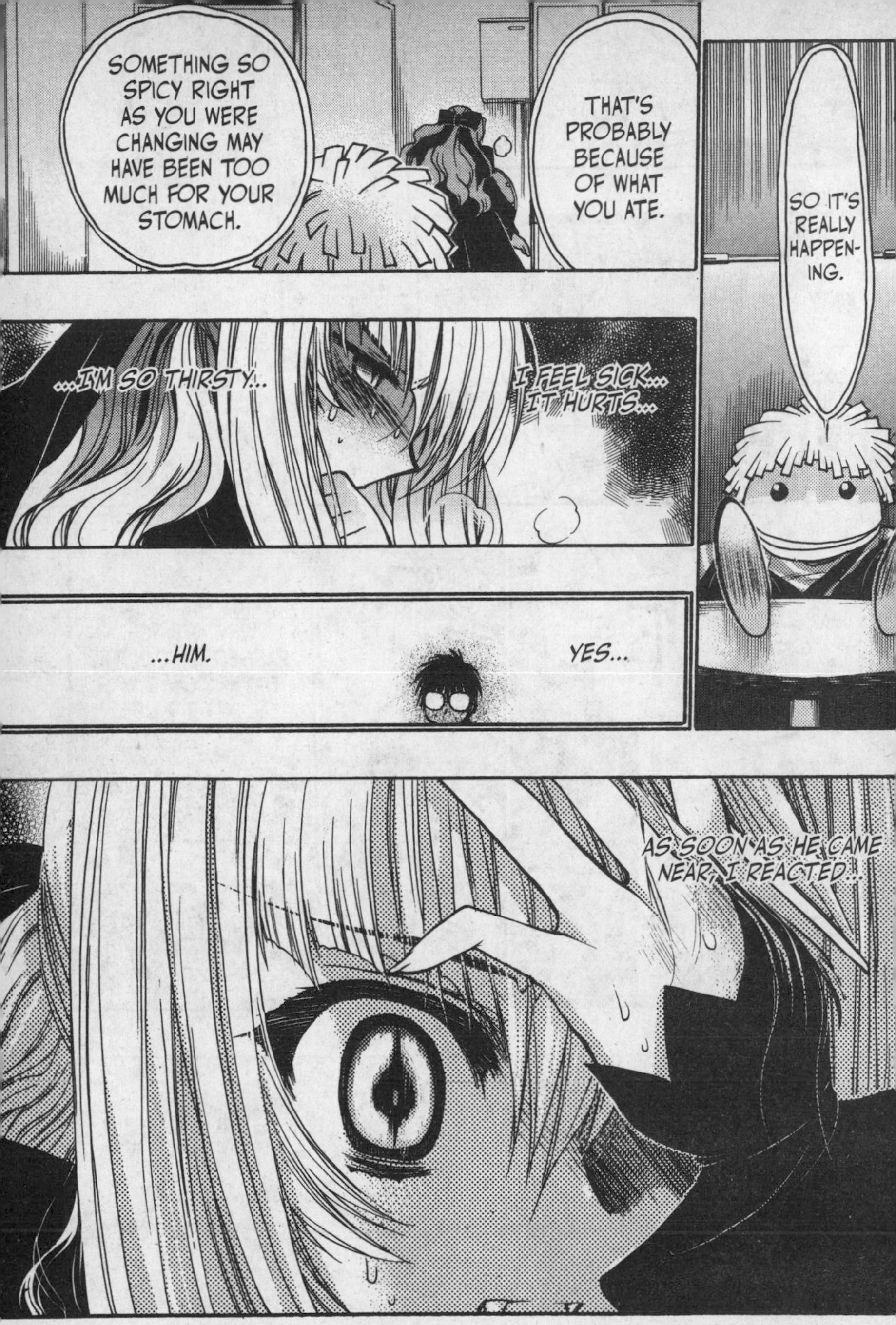
SO IT'S REALLY HAPPEN-ING.
THAT'S PROBABLY BECAUSE OF WHAT YOU ATE.
SOMETHING SO SPICY RIGHT AS YOU WERE CHANGING MAY HAVE BEEN TOO MUCH FOR YOUR STOMACH.
I FEEL SICK... IT HURTS...
...I'M SO THIRSTY...
YES...
...HIM.
AS SOON AS HE CAME NEAR, I REACTED...

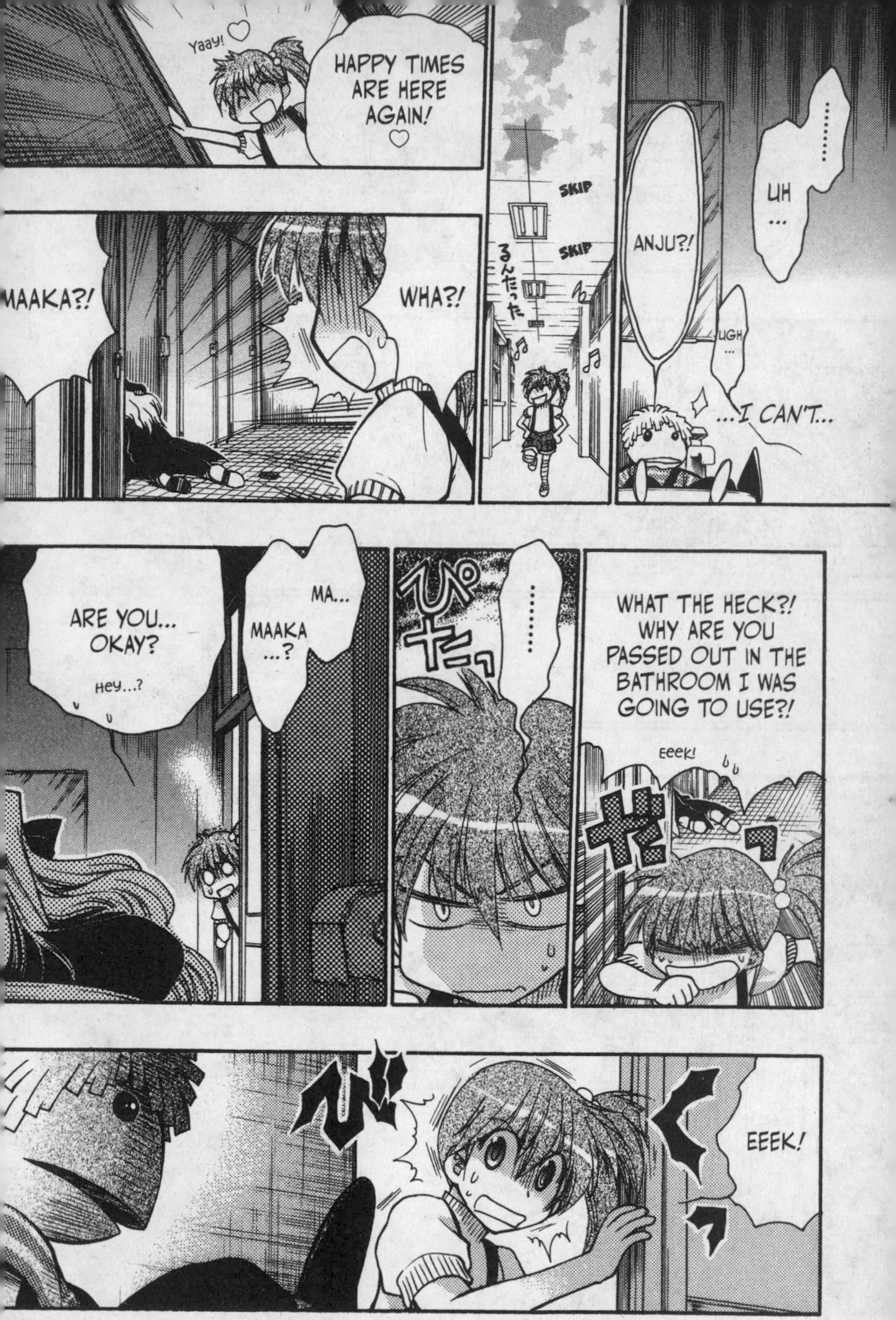
......
UH ...
ANJU?!
UGH ...
...I CAN'T...
SKIP
SKIP
るんたった
Yaay!
HAPPY TIMES ARE HERE AGAIN!
WHA?!
MAAKA?!
WHAT THE HECK?! WHY ARE YOU PASSED OUT IN THE BATHROOM I WAS GOING TO USE?!
Eeek!
......
MA... MAAKA ...?
ARE YOU... OKAY?
Hey...?
EEEK!

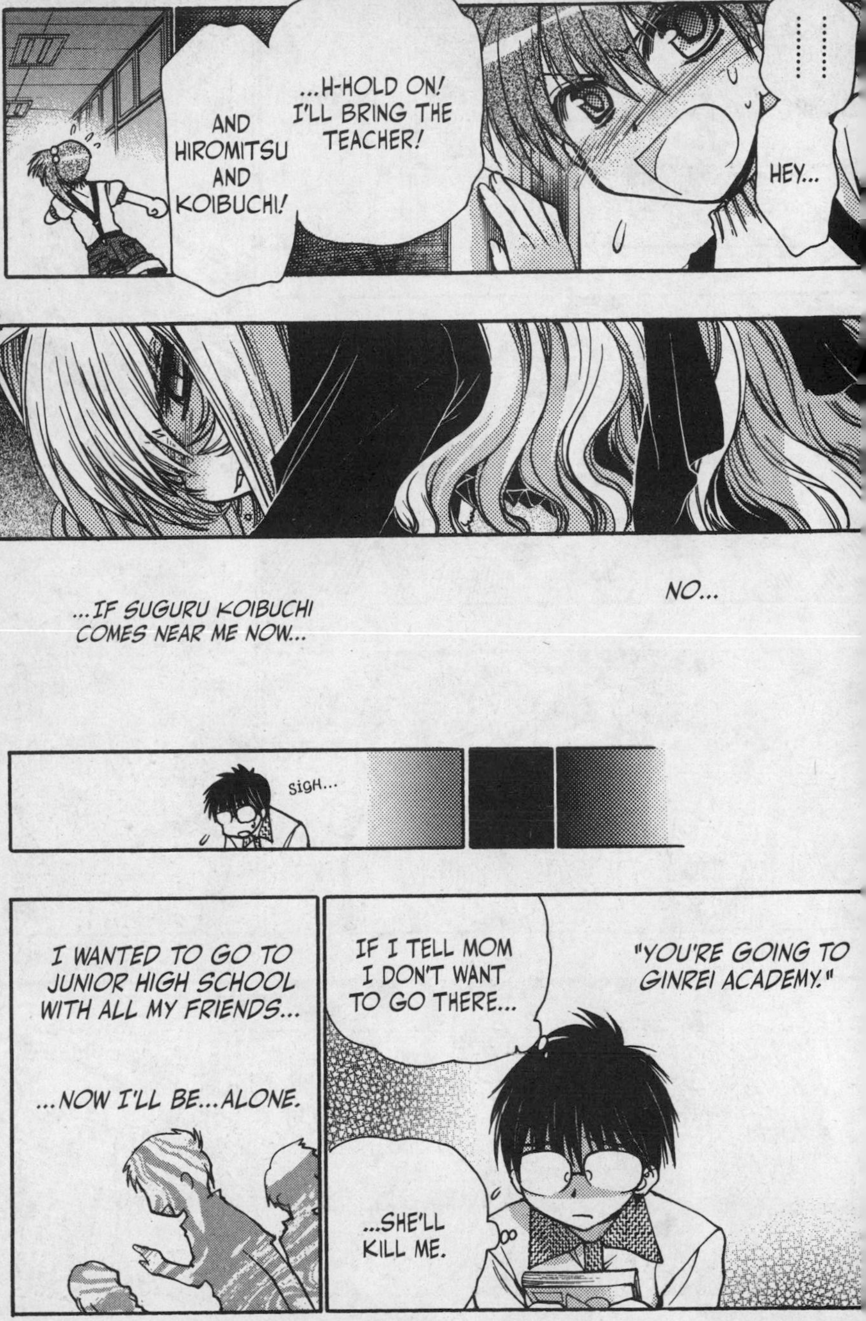
......
HEY...
...H-HOLD ON! I'LL BRING THE TEACHER!
AND HIROMITSU AND KOIBUCHI!
NO...
...IF SUGURU KOIBUCHI COMES NEAR ME NOW...
SIGH...
"YOU'RE GOING TO GINREI ACADEMY."
IF I TELL MOM I DON'T WANT TO GO THERE...
...SHE'LL KILL ME.
I WANTED TO GO TO JUNIOR HIGH SCHOOL WITH ALL MY FRIENDS...
...NOW I'LL BE...ALONE.

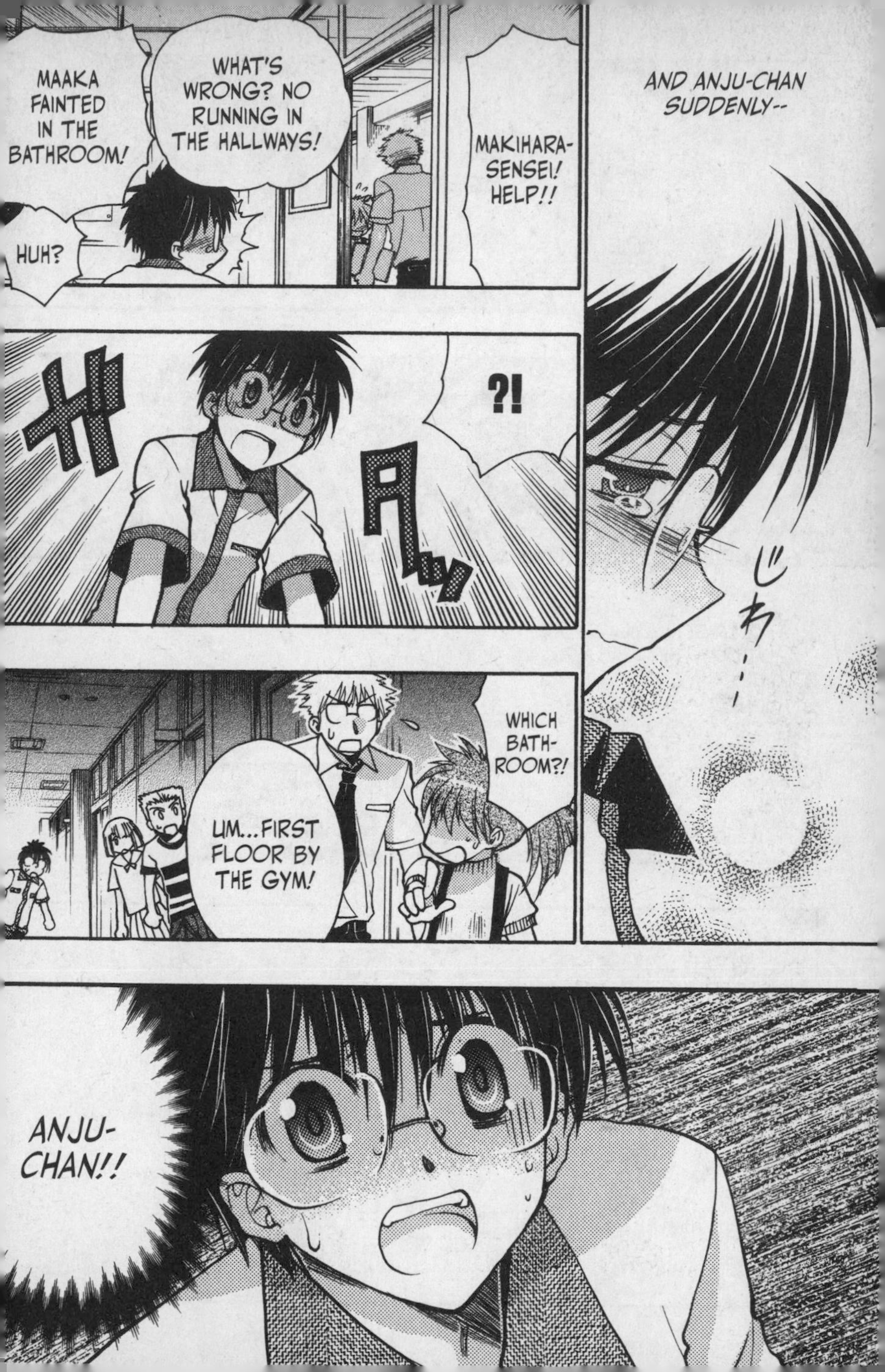
AND ANJU-CHAN SUDDENLY--
じわ…
MAKIHARA-SENSEI! HELP!!
WHAT'S WRONG? NO RUNNING IN THE HALLWAYS!
MAAKA FAINTED IN THE BATHROOM!
HUH?
?!
WHICH BATHROOM?!
UM...FIRST FLOOR BY THE GYM!
ANJU-CHAN!!

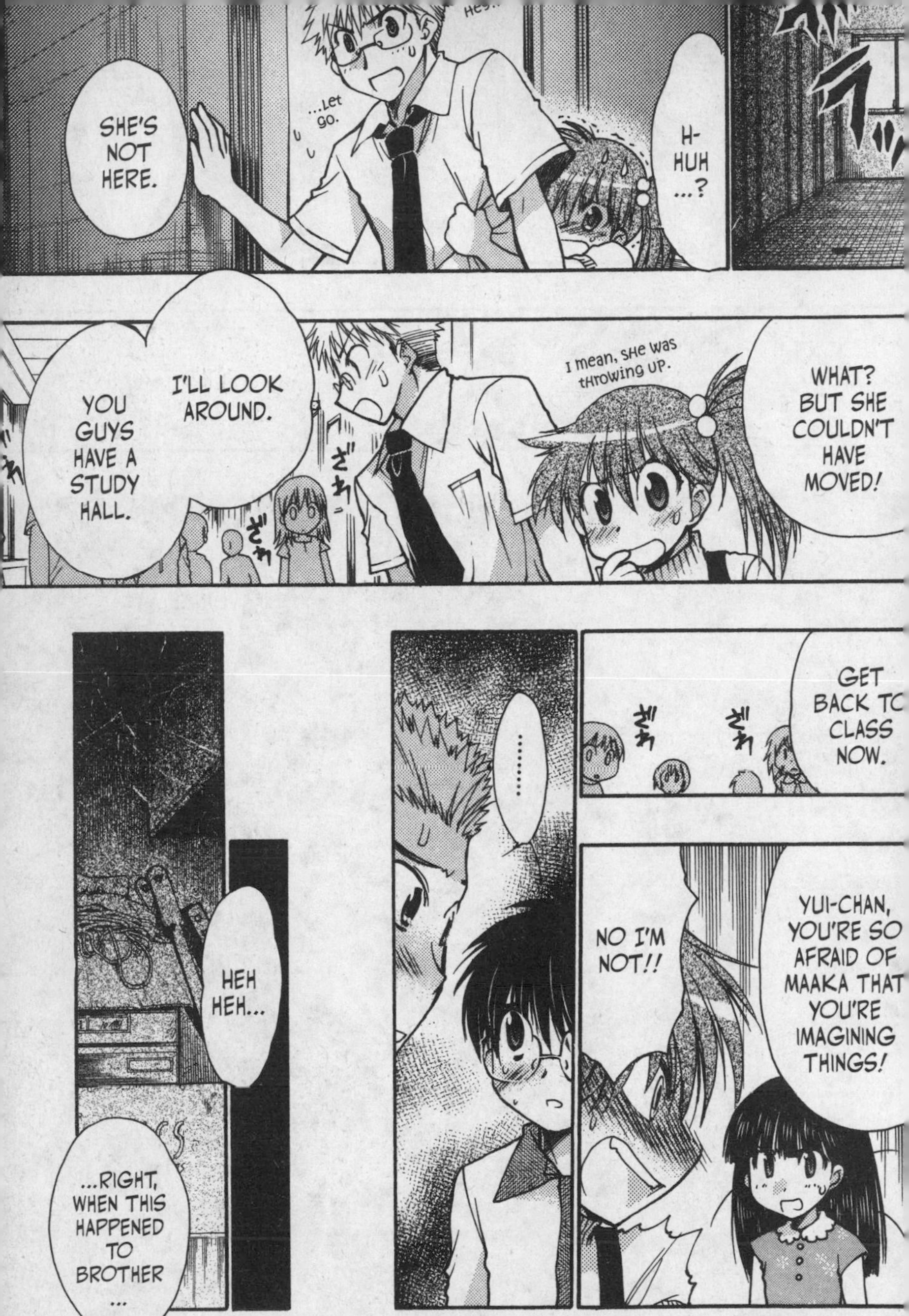
H-HUH...?
...Let go.
SHE'S NOT HERE.
WHAT? BUT SHE COULDN'T HAVE MOVED!
I mean, she was throwing up.
I'LL LOOK AROUND.
YOU GUYS HAVE A STUDY HALL.
ざわ
ざわ
GET BACK TO CLASS NOW.
ざわ
ざわ
YUI-CHAN, YOU'RE SO AFRAID OF MAAKA THAT YOU'RE IMAGINING THINGS!
NO I'M NOT!!
......
HEH HEH...
...RIGHT, WHEN THIS HAPPENED TO BROTHER ...

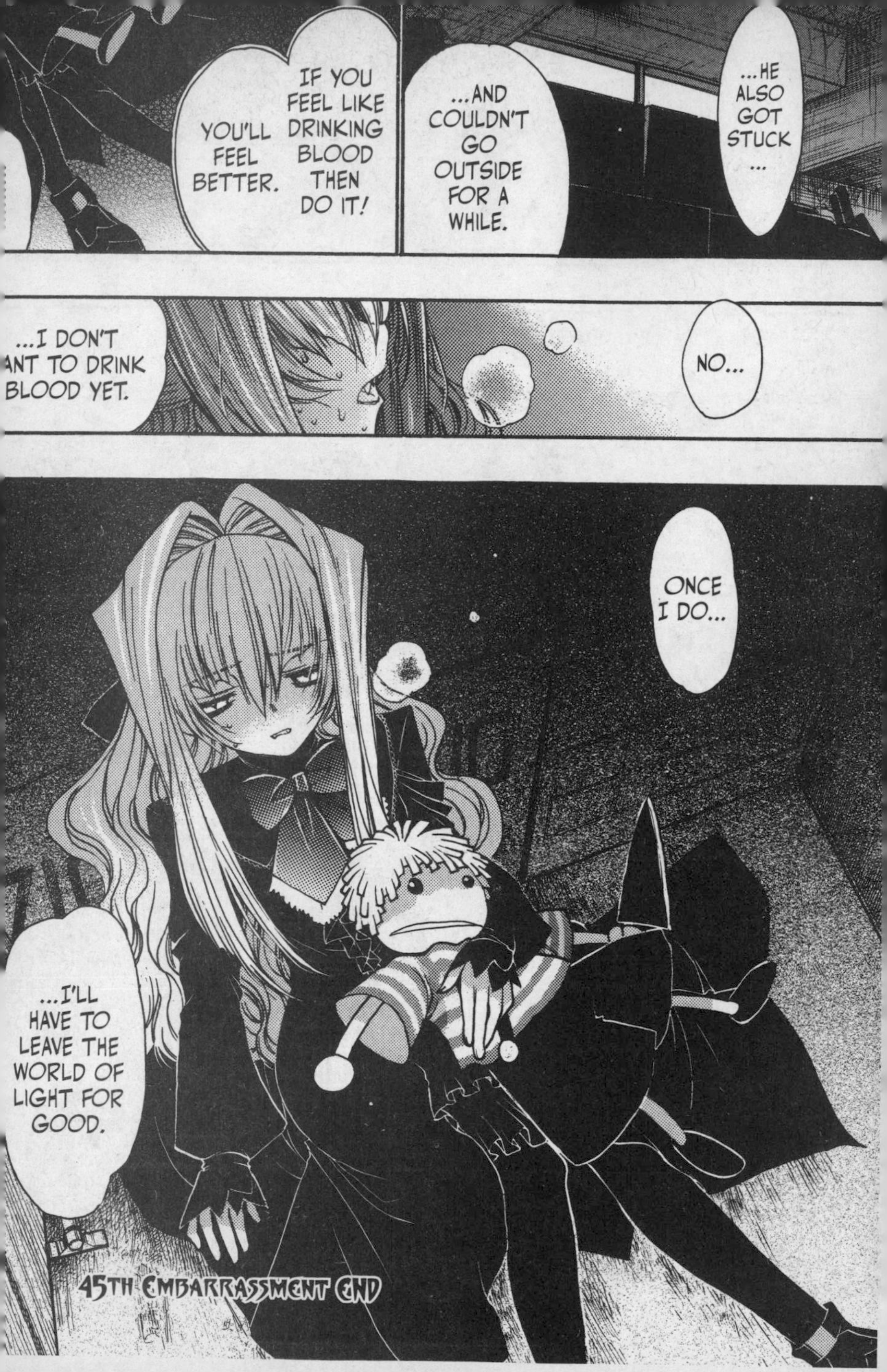
...HE ALSO GOT STUCK ...
...AND COULDN'T GO OUTSIDE FOR A WHILE.
IF YOU FEEL LIKE DRINKING BLOOD THEN DO IT!
YOU'LL FEEL BETTER.
NO...
...I DON'T ANT TO DRINK BLOOD YET.
ONCE I DO...
...I'LL HAVE TO LEAVE THE WORLD OF LIGHT FOR GOOD.
45TH EMBARRASSMENT END

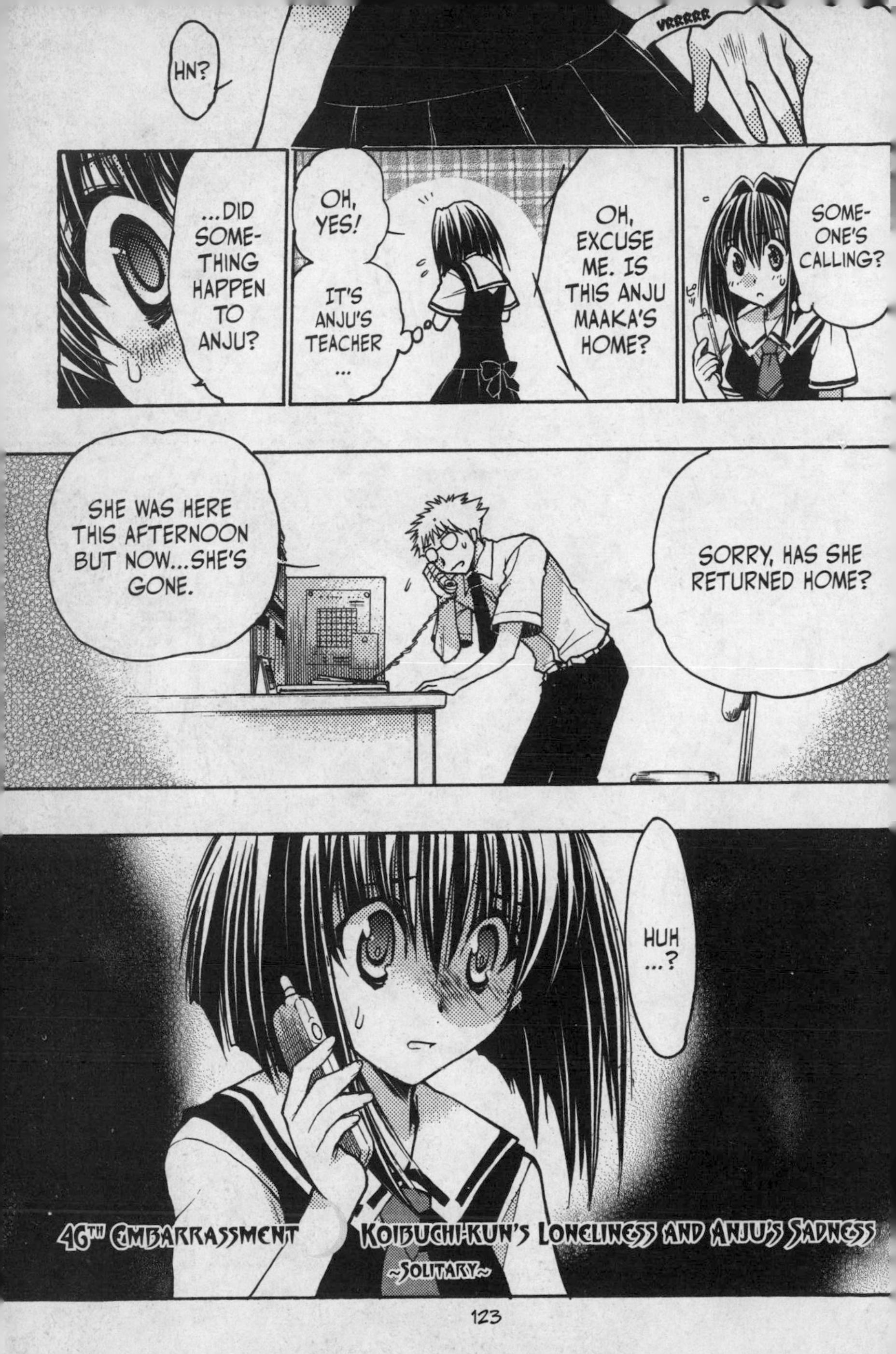
VRRRRR
HN?
SOME-ONE'S CALLING?
OH, EXCUSE ME. IS THIS ANJU MAAKA'S HOME?
OH, YES!
IT'S ANJU'S TEACHER ...
...DID SOMETHING HAPPEN TO ANJU?
SORRY, HAS SHE RETURNED HOME?
SHE WAS HERE THIS AFTERNOON BUT NOW...SHE'S GONE.
HUH ...?
46TH EMBARRASSMENT
KOIBUCHI-KUN'S LONELINESS AND ANJU'S SADNESS
~SOLITARY~

16ᵀᴴ EMBARRASSMENT ☾ KOIBUCHI-KUN'S LONELINESS AND ANJU'S SADNESS
~SOLITARY~

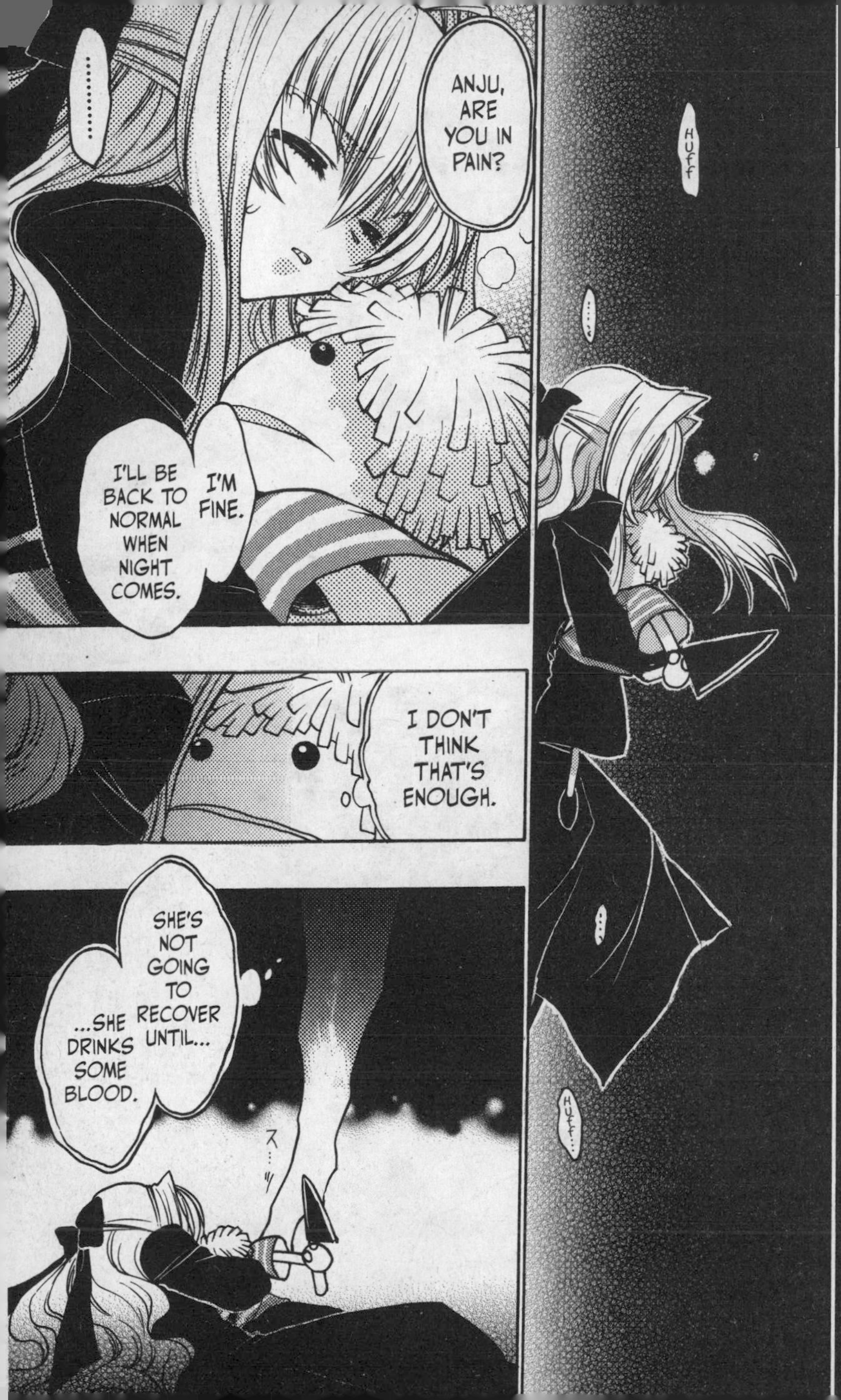
HUFF
...
...
HUFF...
ANJU, ARE YOU IN PAIN?
......
I'M FINE.
I'LL BE BACK TO NORMAL WHEN NIGHT COMES.
I DON'T THINK THAT'S ENOUGH.
SHE'S NOT GOING TO RECOVER UNTIL...
...SHE DRINKS SOME BLOOD.
ス…ッ

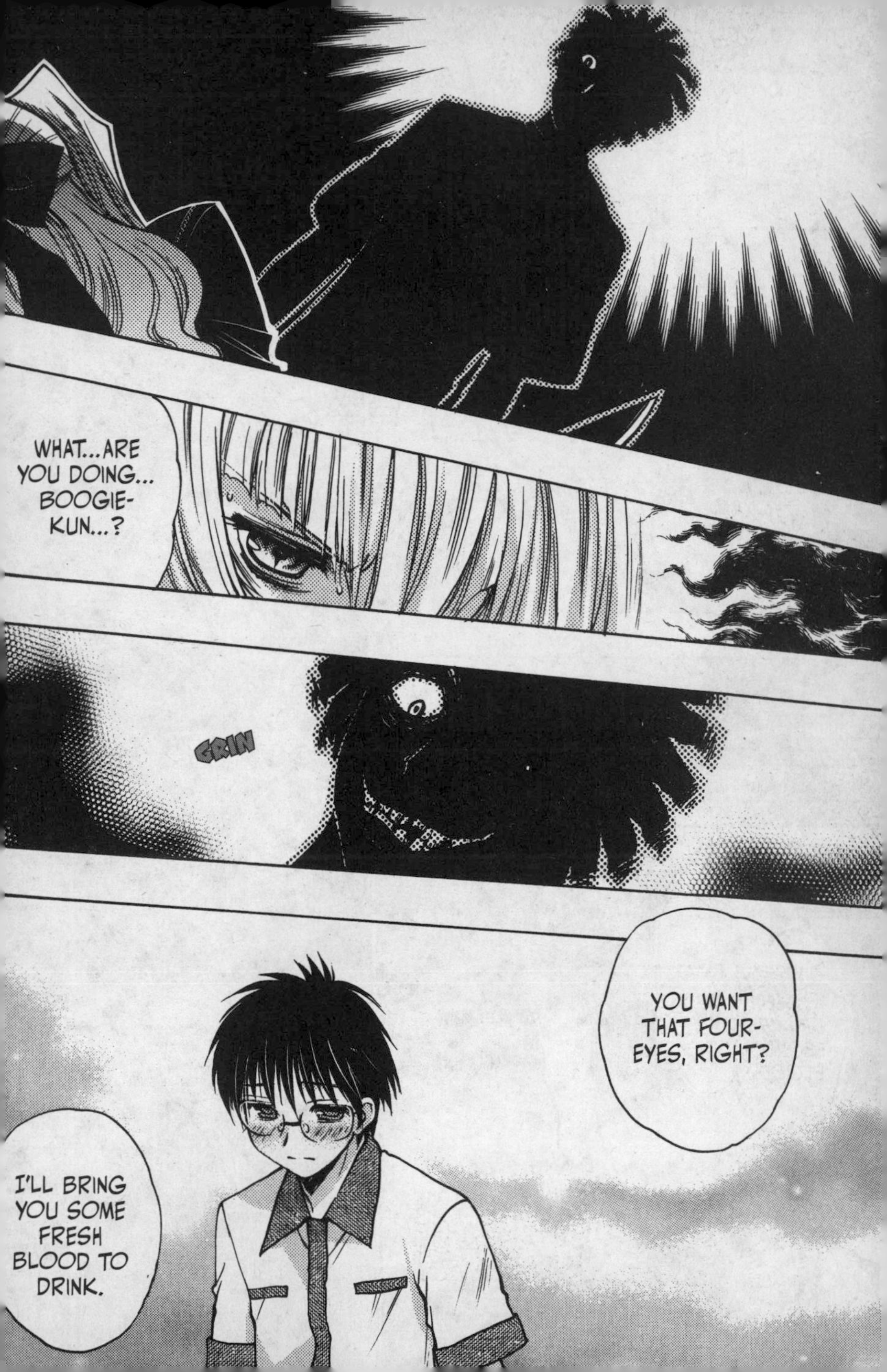
WHAT...ARE YOU DOING... BOOGIE-KUN...?
GRIN
YOU WANT THAT FOUR-EYES, RIGHT?
I'LL BRING YOU SOME FRESH BLOOD TO DRINK.

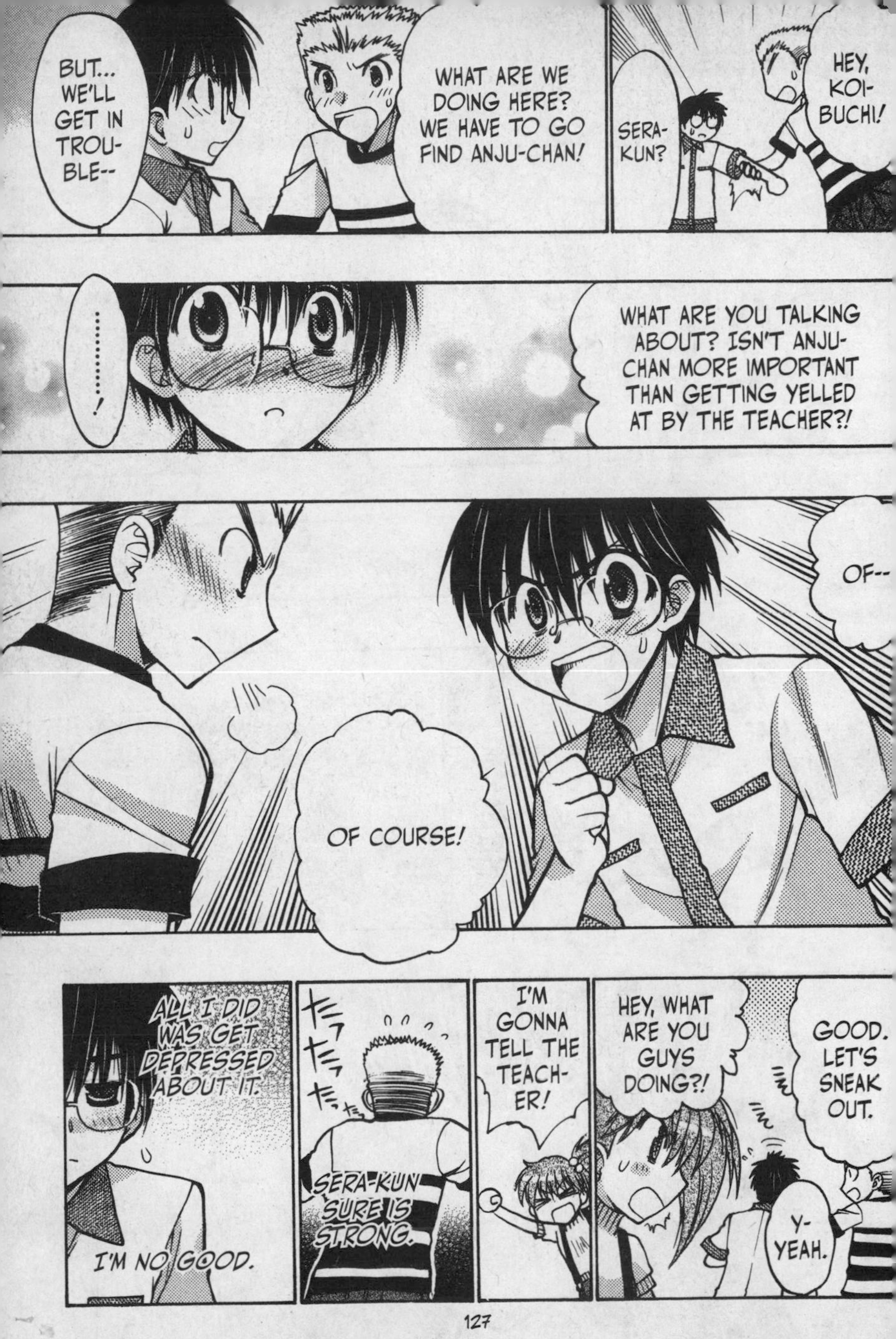
HEY, KOI-BUCHI!
SERA-KUN?
WHAT ARE WE DOING HERE? WE HAVE TO GO FIND ANJU-CHAN!
BUT... WE'LL GET IN TROU-BLE--
WHAT ARE YOU TALKING ABOUT? ISN'T ANJU-CHAN MORE IMPORTANT THAN GETTING YELLED AT BY THE TEACHER?!
.........!
OF--
OF COURSE!
GOOD. LET'S SNEAK OUT.
Y-YEAH.
HEY, WHAT ARE YOU GUYS DOING?!
I'M GONNA TELL THE TEACH-ER!
SERA-KUN SURE IS STRONG.
ALL I DID WAS GET DEPRESSED ABOUT IT.
I'M NO GOOD.

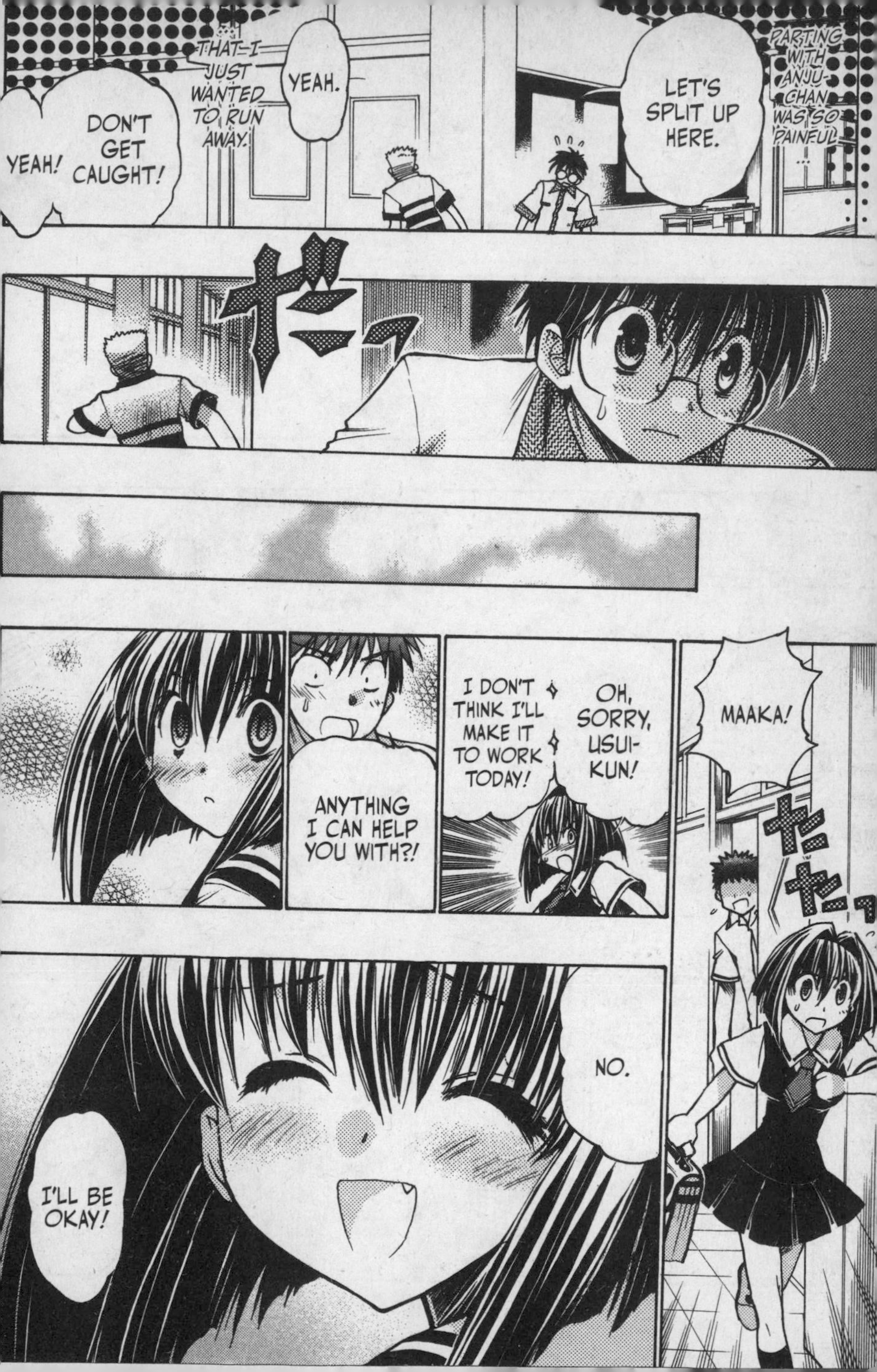
PARTING WITH ANJU-CHAN WAS SO PAINFUL...
LET'S SPLIT UP HERE.
YEAH.
THAT I JUST WANTED TO RUN AWAY.
DON'T GET CAUGHT!
YEAH!
MAAKA!
OH, SORRY, USUI-KUN!
I DON'T THINK I'LL MAKE IT TO WORK TODAY!
ANYTHING I CAN HELP YOU WITH?!
NO.
I'LL BE OKAY!

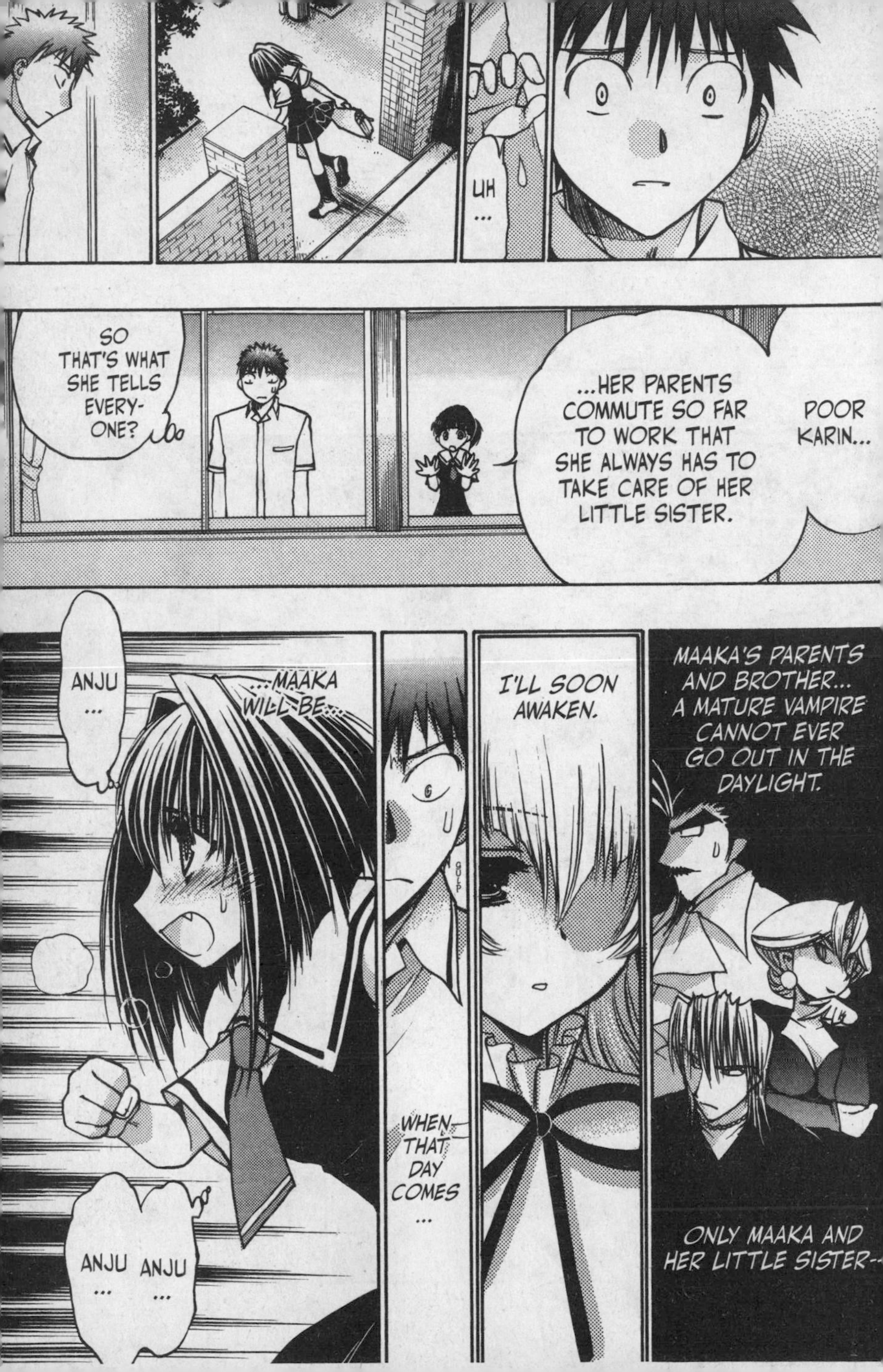
UH ...
POOR KARIN...
...HER PARENTS COMMUTE SO FAR TO WORK THAT SHE ALWAYS HAS TO TAKE CARE OF HER LITTLE SISTER.
SO THAT'S WHAT SHE TELLS EVERY-ONE?
MAAKA'S PARENTS AND BROTHER... A MATURE VAMPIRE CANNOT EVER GO OUT IN THE DAYLIGHT.
ONLY MAAKA AND HER LITTLE SISTER--
I'LL SOON AWAKEN.
GULP
WHEN THAT DAY COMES ...
...MAAKA WILL BE...
ANJU ...
ANJU ...
ANJU ...

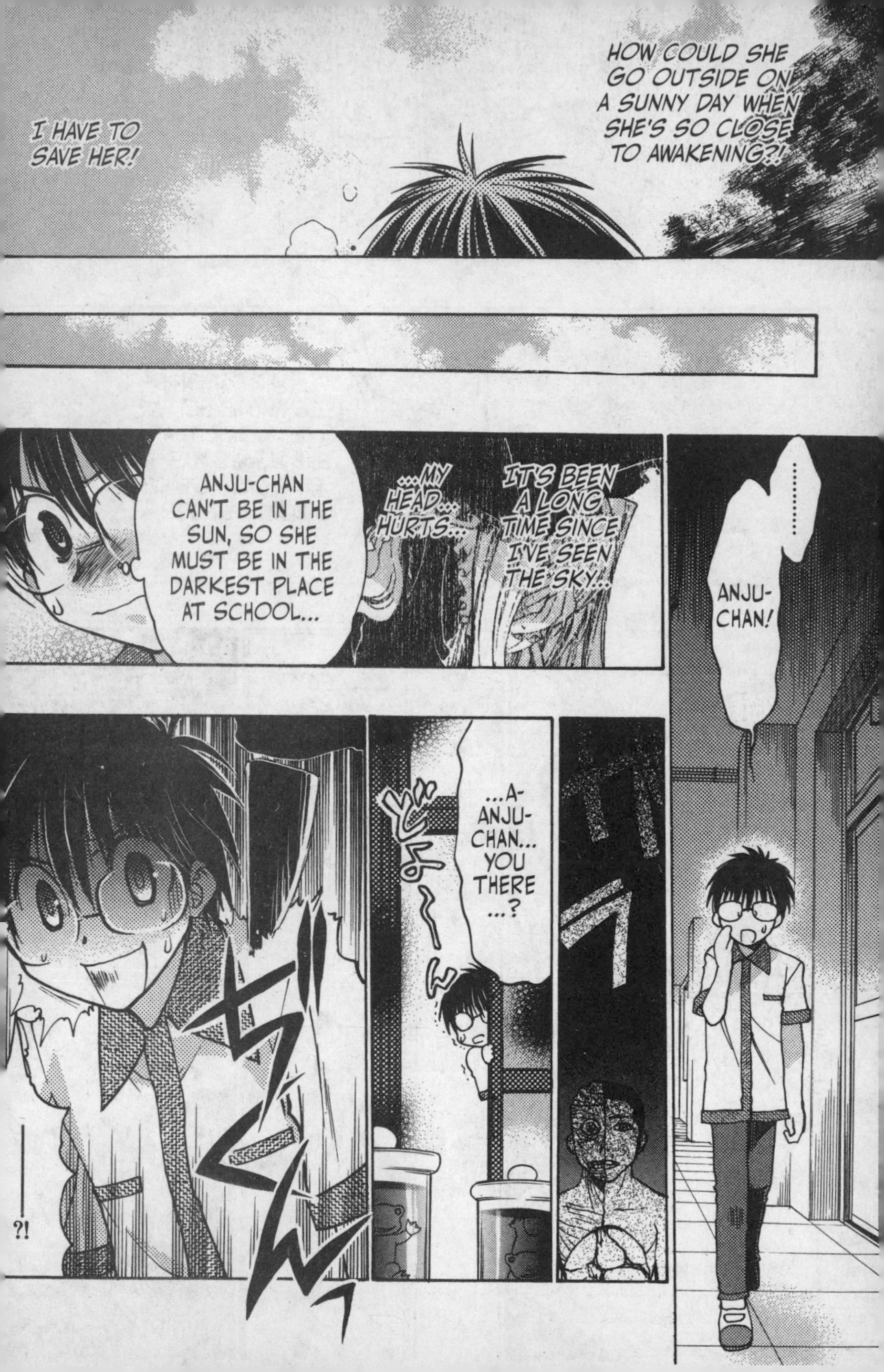
HOW COULD SHE GO OUTSIDE ON A SUNNY DAY WHEN SHE'S SO CLOSE TO AWAKENING?!
I HAVE TO SAVE HER!
......
ANJU-CHAN!
IT'S BEEN A LONG TIME SINCE I'VE SEEN THE SKY...
...MY HEAD... HURTS...
ANJU-CHAN CAN'T BE IN THE SUN, SO SHE MUST BE IN THE DARKEST PLACE AT SCHOOL...
...A-ANJU-CHAN... YOU THERE...?
?!

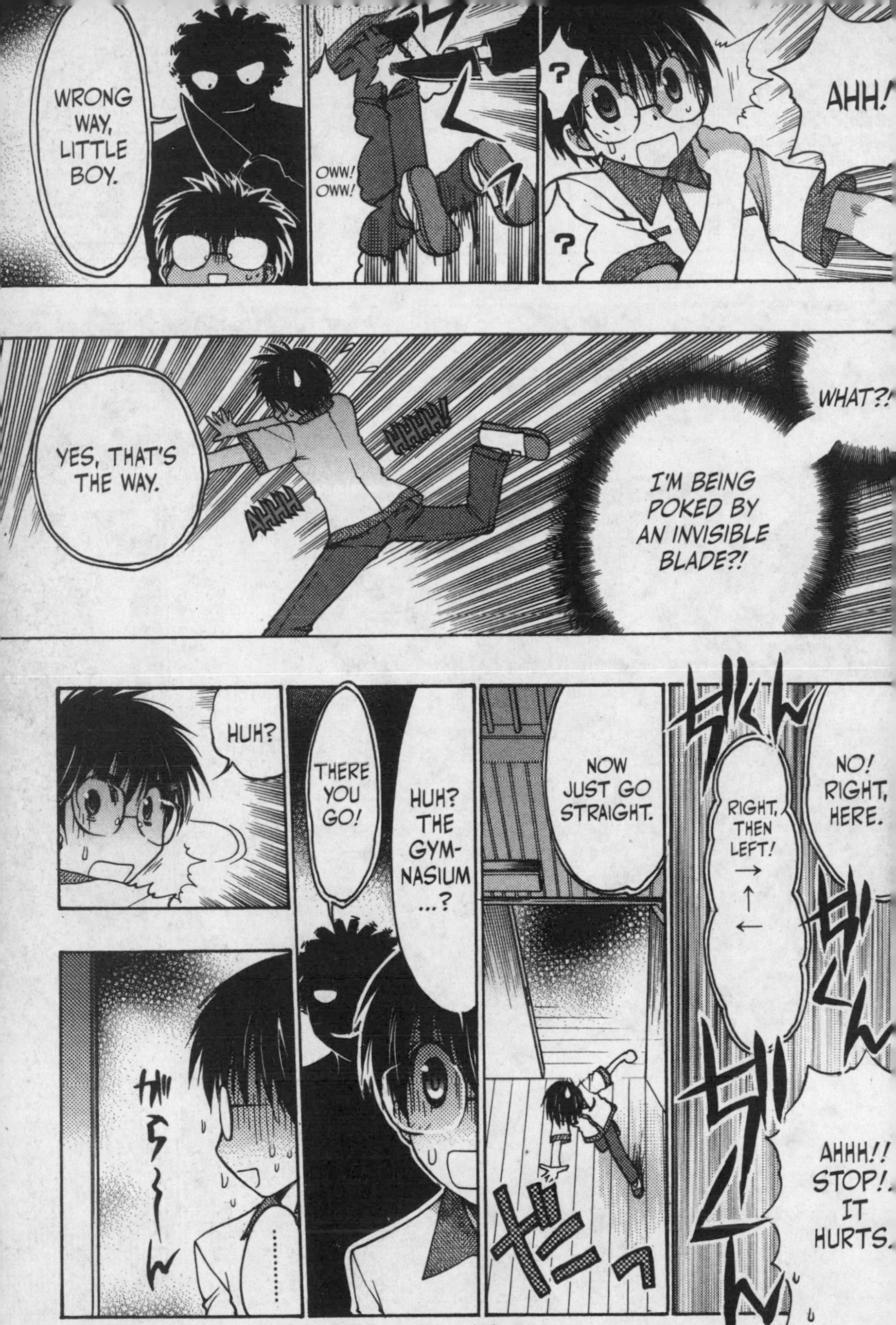
AHH!
?
?
OWW! OWW!
WRONG WAY, LITTLE BOY.
WHAT?!
I'M BEING POKED BY AN INVISIBLE BLADE?!
YES, THAT'S THE WAY.
NO! RIGHT, HERE.
RIGHT, THEN LEFT! → ↑ ←
AHHH!! STOP!. IT HURTS.
NOW JUST GO STRAIGHT.
THERE YOU GO!
HUH? THE GYM-NASIUM ...?
HUH?
......

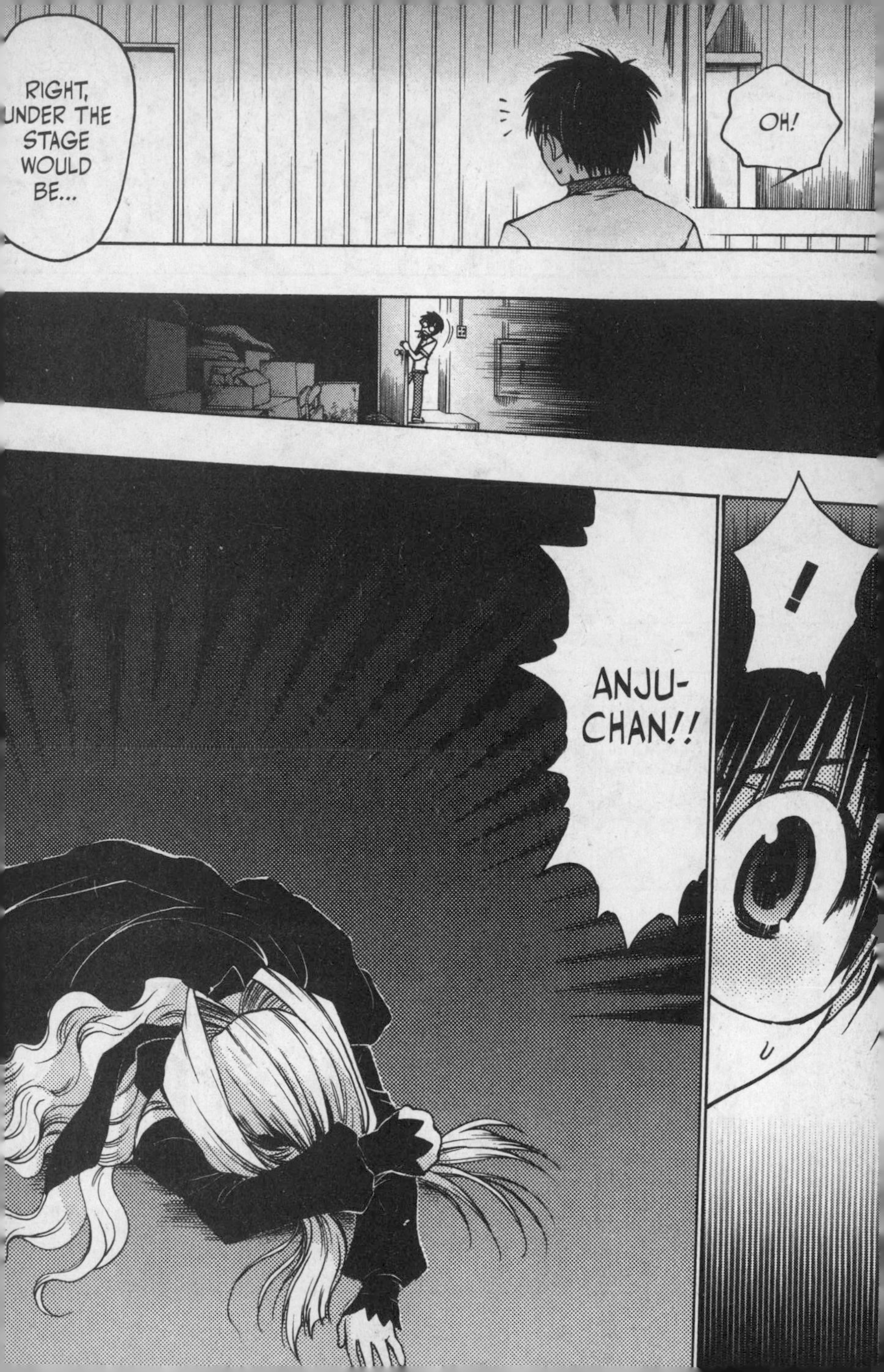
OH!
RIGHT, UNDER THE STAGE WOULD BE...
!
ANJU-CHAN!!

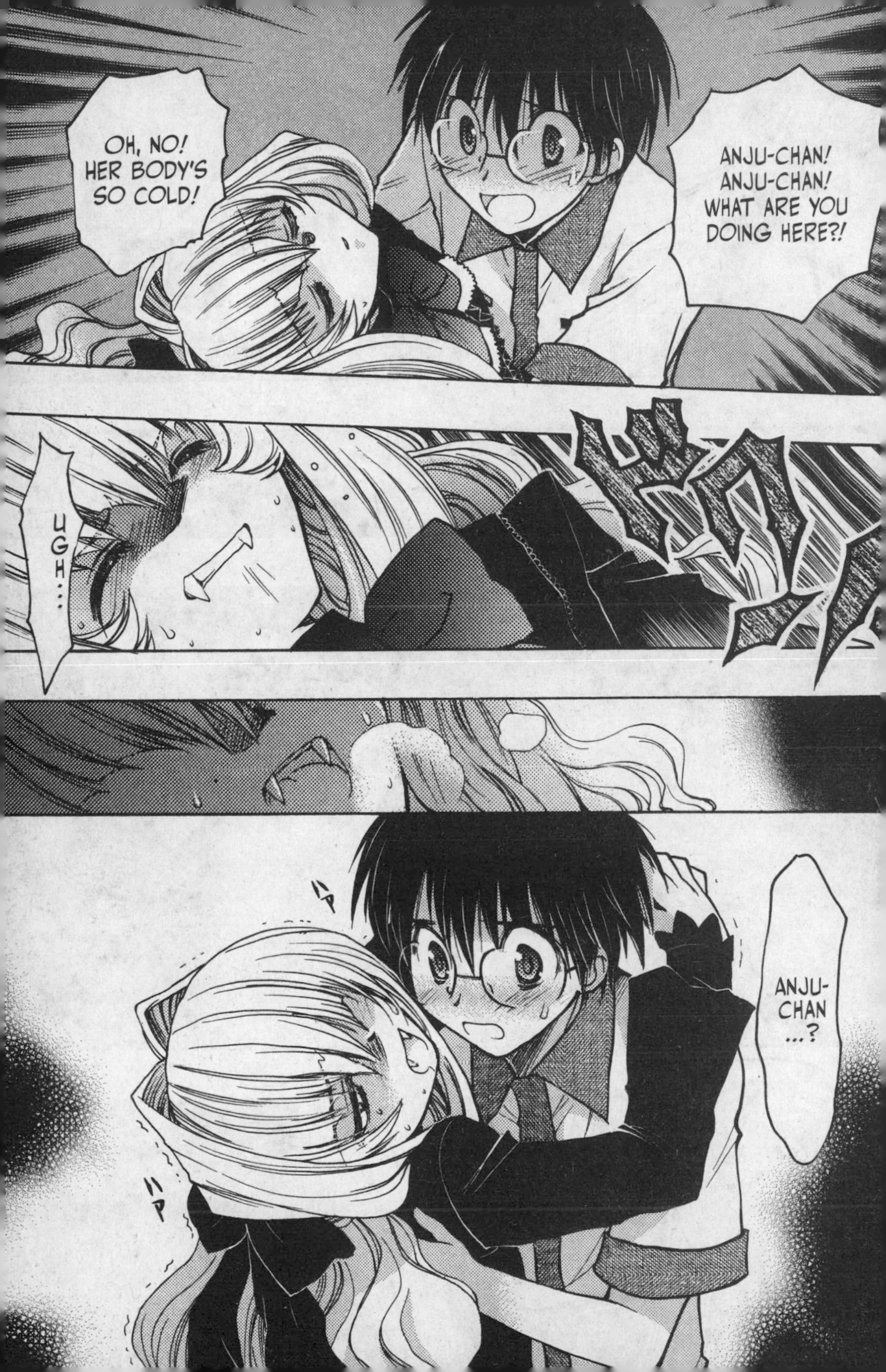
ANJU-CHAN! ANJU-CHAN! WHAT ARE YOU DOING HERE?!
OH, NO! HER BODY'S SO COLD!
UGH...
ANJU-CHAN ...?

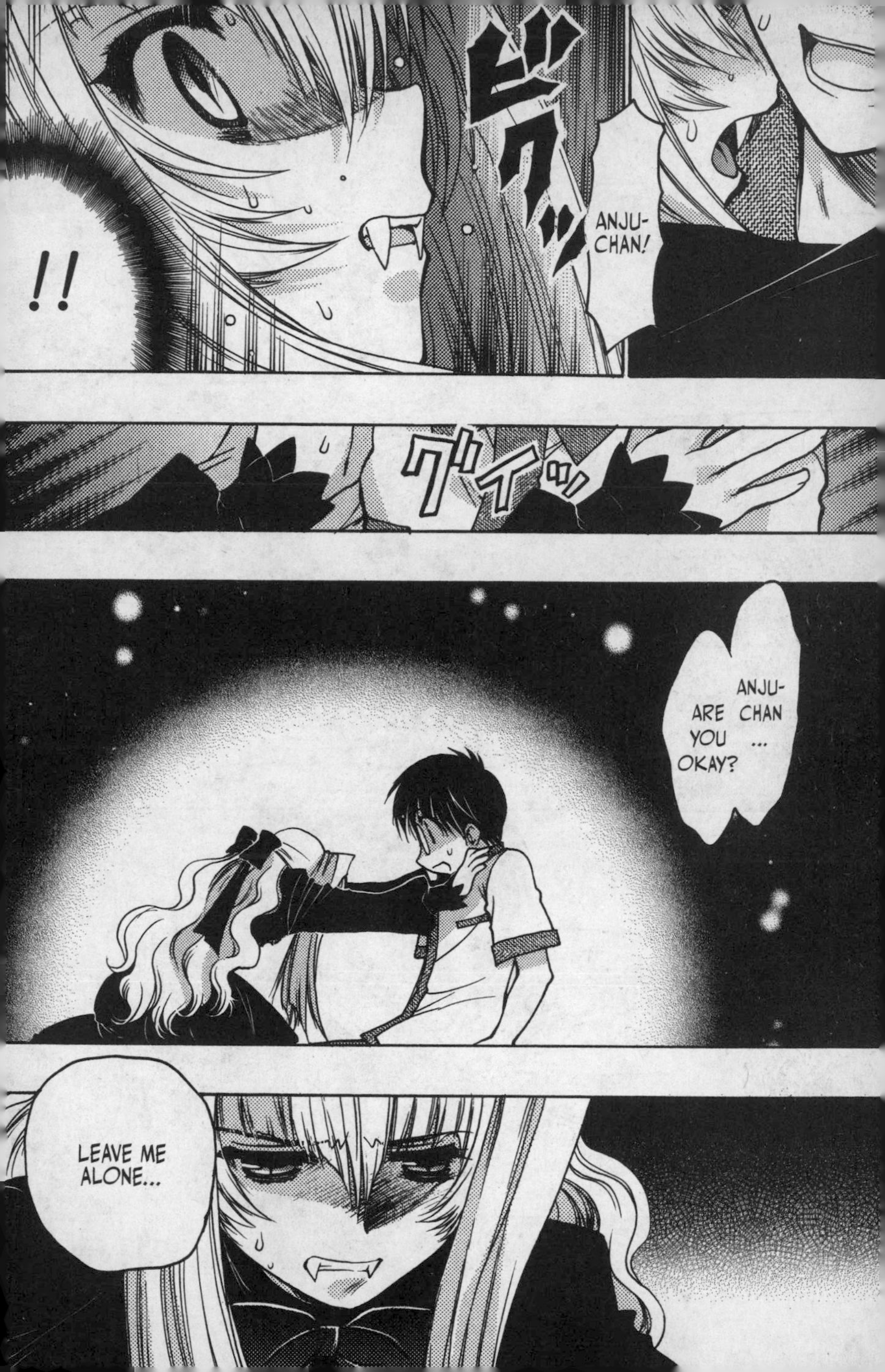
ビクッ
ANJU-CHAN!
!!
グイッ
ANJU-CHAN... ARE YOU OKAY?
LEAVE ME ALONE...

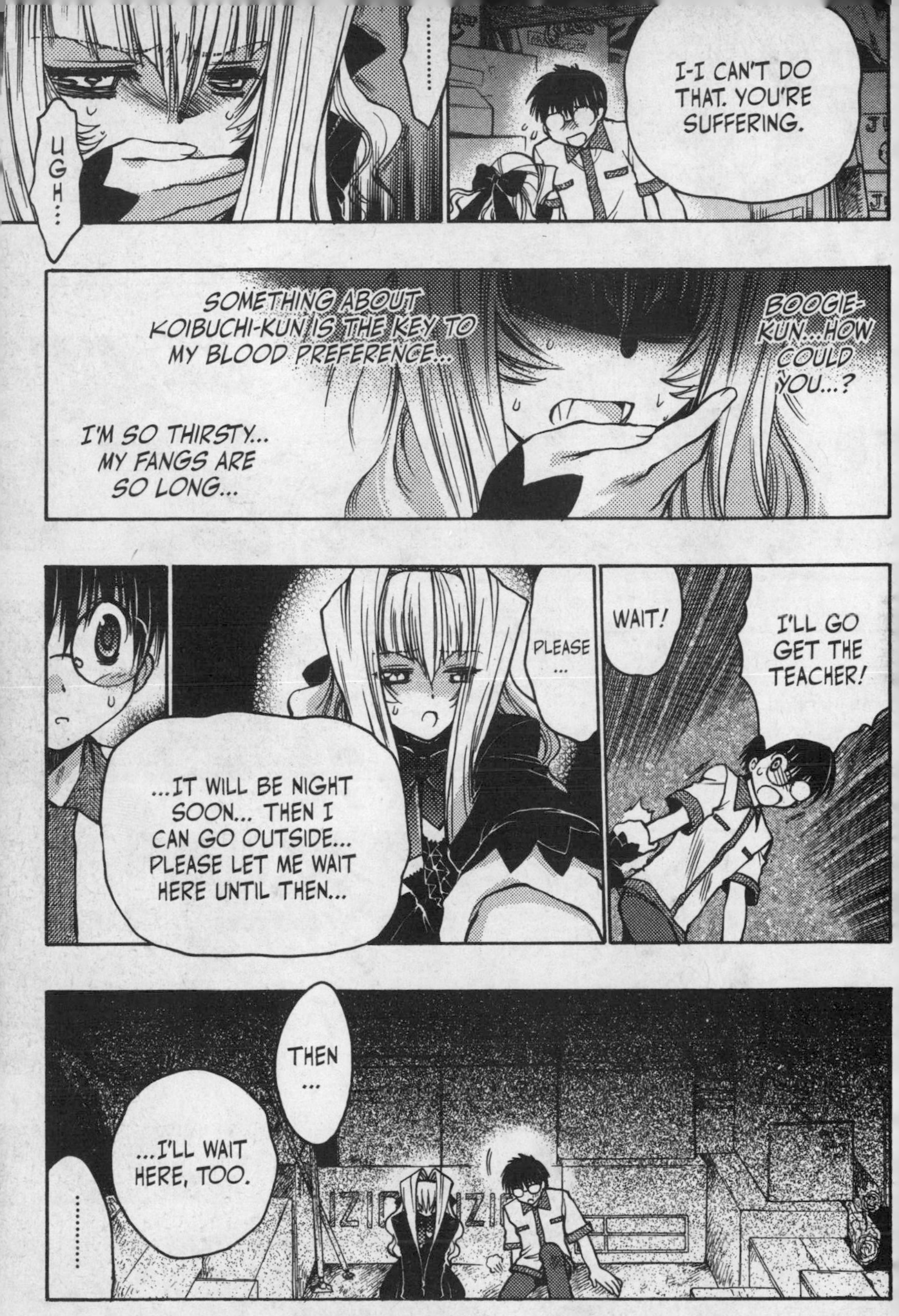
I-I CAN'T DO THAT. YOU'RE SUFFERING.
......
UGH...
BOOGIE-KUN...HOW COULD YOU...?
SOMETHING ABOUT KOIBUCHI-KUN IS THE KEY TO MY BLOOD PREFERENCE...
I'M SO THIRSTY... MY FANGS ARE SO LONG...
I'LL GO GET THE TEACHER!
WAIT!
PLEASE ...
...IT WILL BE NIGHT SOON... THEN I CAN GO OUTSIDE... PLEASE LET ME WAIT HERE UNTIL THEN...
THEN ...
...I'LL WAIT HERE, TOO.
......

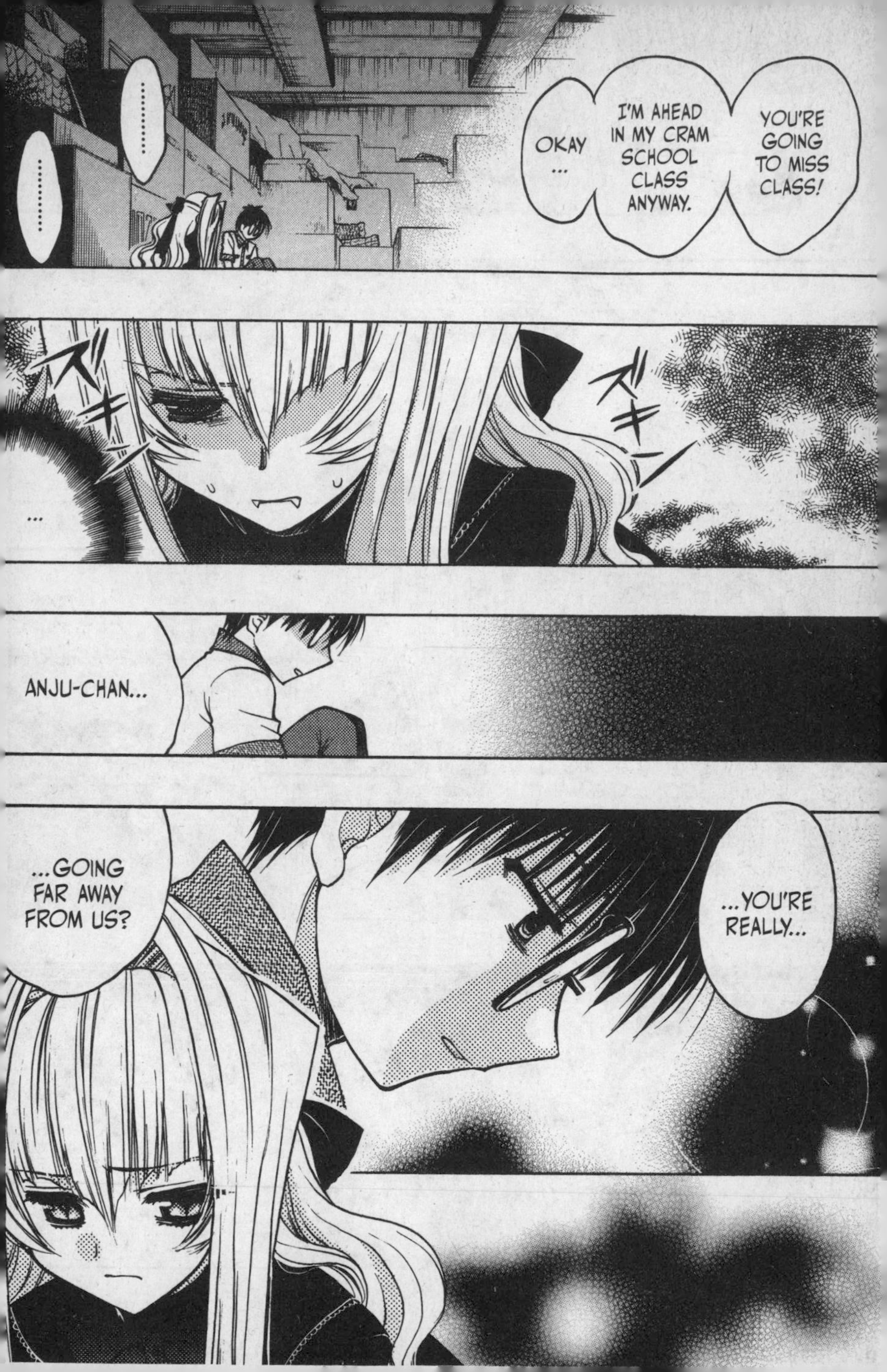
YOU'RE GOING TO MISS CLASS!
I'M AHEAD IN MY CRAM SCHOOL CLASS ANYWAY.
OKAY ...
......
......
ズキー
ズキー
...
ANJU-CHAN...
...YOU'RE REALLY...
...GOING FAR AWAY FROM US?

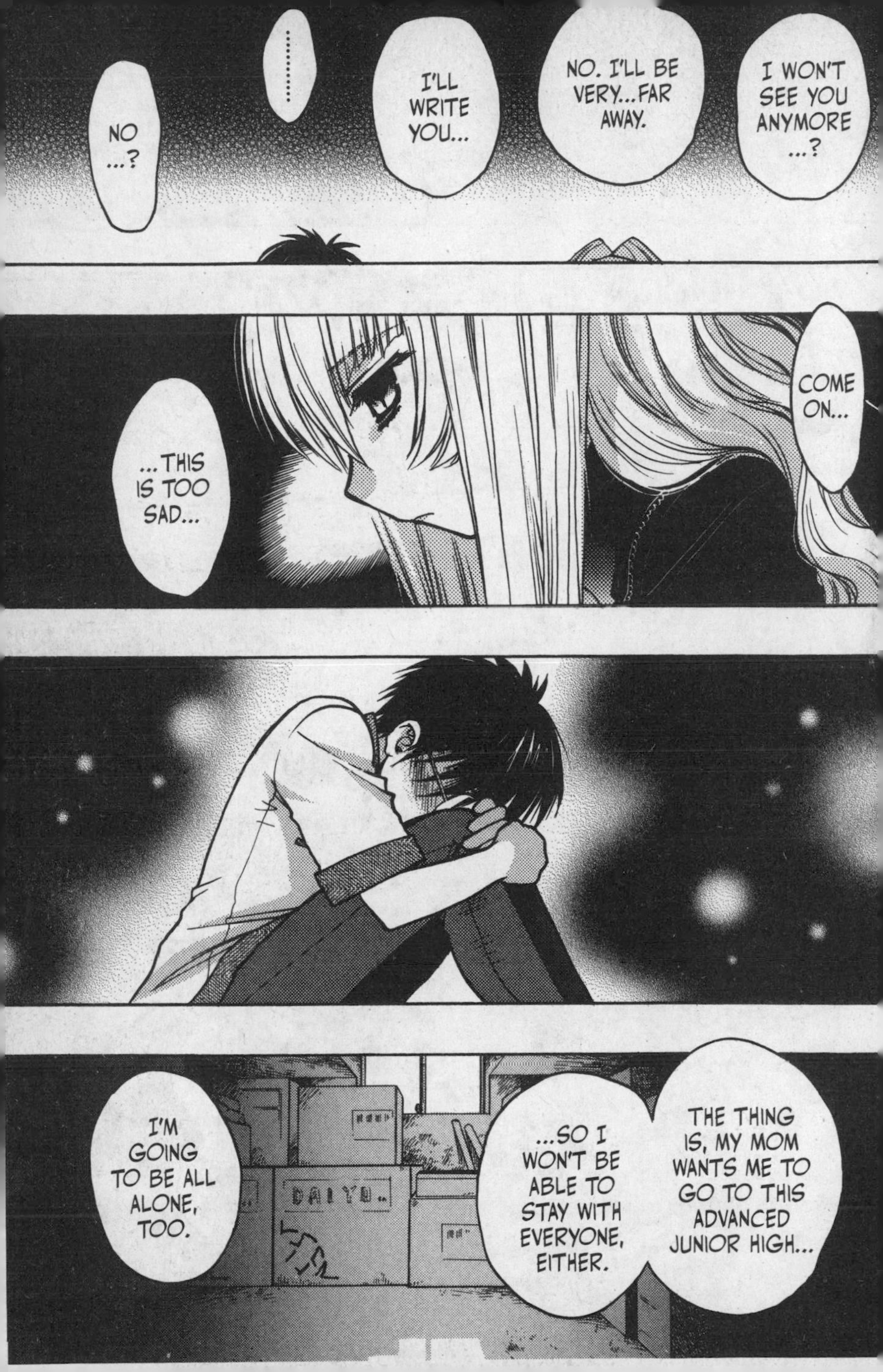
I WON'T SEE YOU ANYMORE ...?
NO. I'LL BE VERY...FAR AWAY.
I'LL WRITE YOU...
......
NO ...?
COME ON...
...THIS IS TOO SAD...
THE THING IS, MY MOM WANTS ME TO GO TO THIS ADVANCED JUNIOR HIGH...
...SO I WON'T BE ABLE TO STAY WITH EVERYONE, EITHER.
I'M GOING TO BE ALL ALONE, TOO.

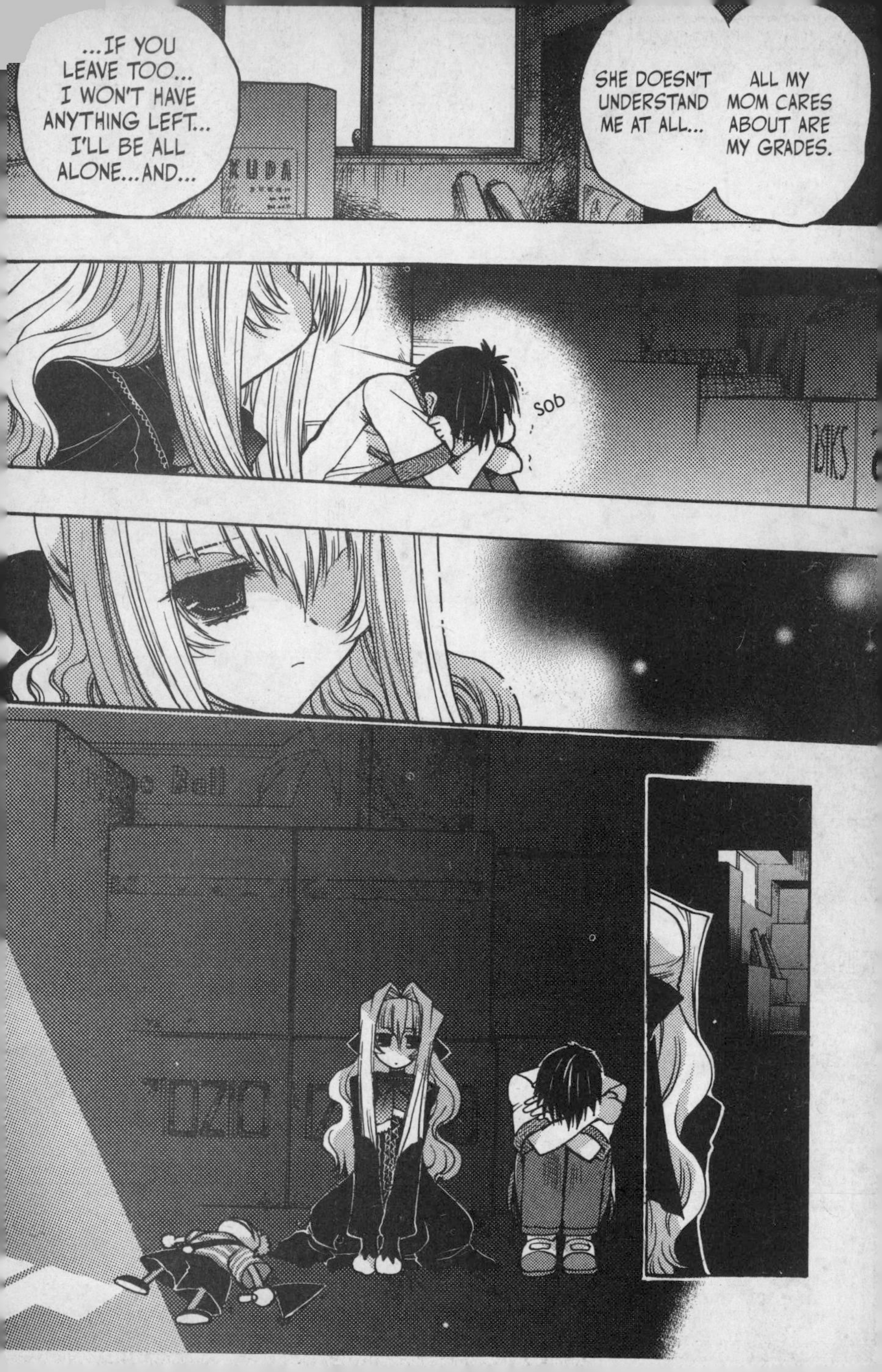
ALL MY MOM CARES ABOUT ARE MY GRADES.
SHE DOESN'T UNDERSTAND ME AT ALL...
...IF YOU LEAVE TOO... I WON'T HAVE ANYTHING LEFT... I'LL BE ALL ALONE...AND...
SOB

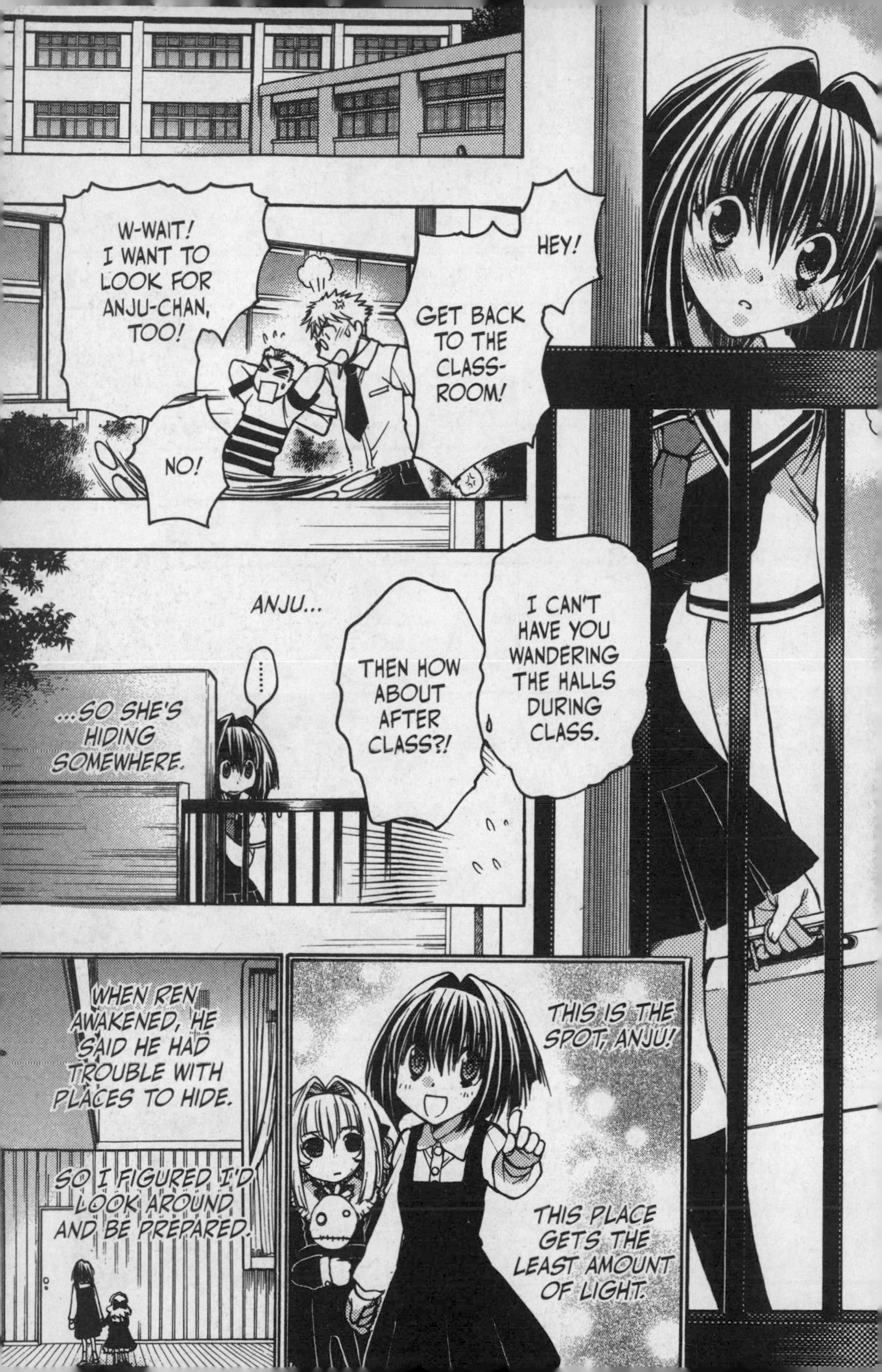
HEY!
GET BACK TO THE CLASSROOM!
W-WAIT! I WANT TO LOOK FOR ANJU-CHAN, TOO!
NO!
I CAN'T HAVE YOU WANDERING THE HALLS DURING CLASS.
THEN HOW ABOUT AFTER CLASS?!
ANJU...
......
...SO SHE'S HIDING SOMEWHERE.
THIS IS THE SPOT, ANJU!
THIS PLACE GETS THE LEAST AMOUNT OF LIGHT.
WHEN REN AWAKENED, HE SAID HE HAD TROUBLE WITH PLACES TO HIDE.
SO I FIGURED I'D LOOK AROUND AND BE PREPARED.

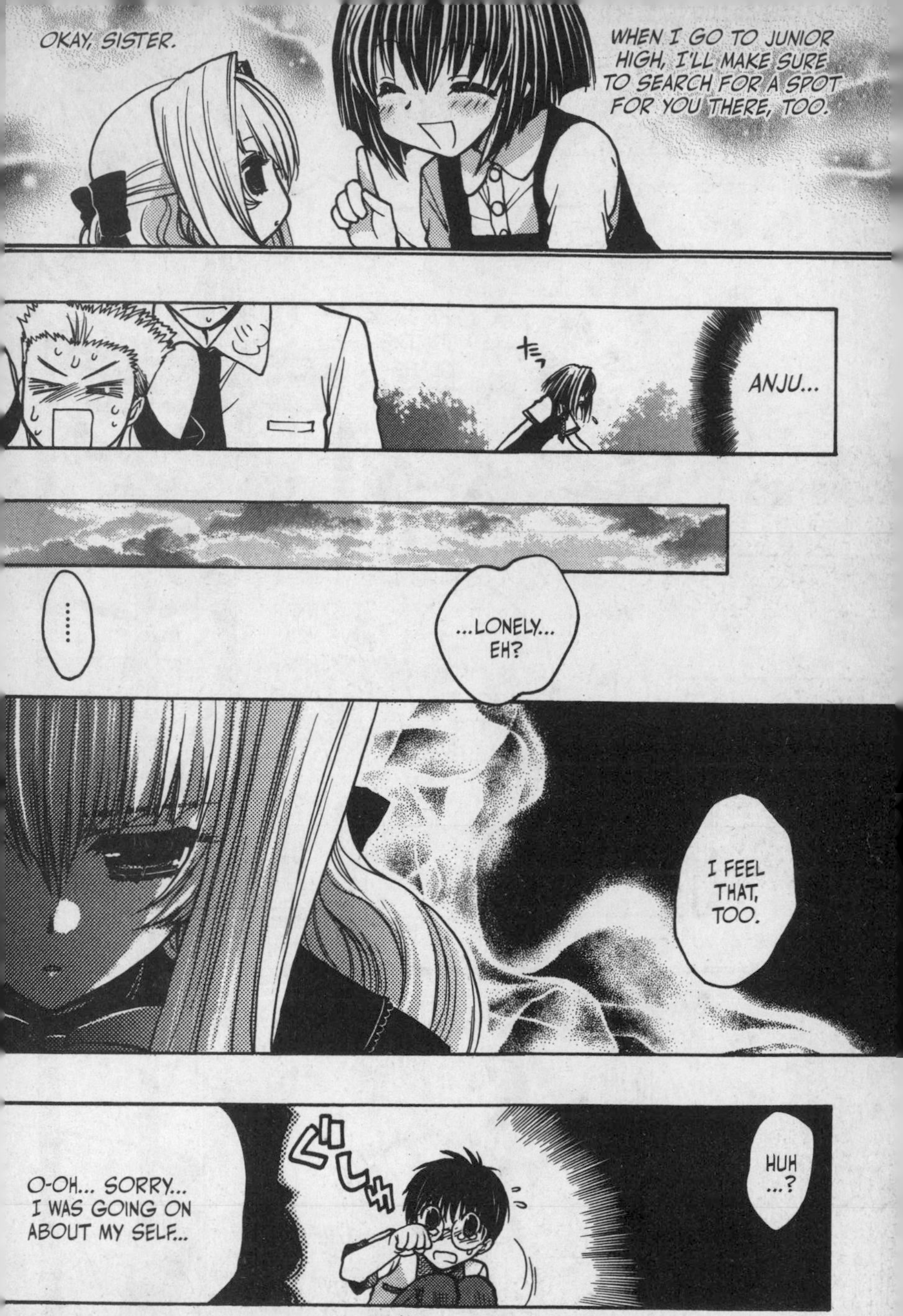
WHEN I GO TO JUNIOR HIGH, I'LL MAKE SURE TO SEARCH FOR A SPOT FOR YOU THERE, TOO.
OKAY, SISTER.
ANJU...
...LONELY... EH?
......
I FEEL THAT, TOO.
HUH ...?
O-OH... SORRY... I WAS GOING ON ABOUT MY SELF...

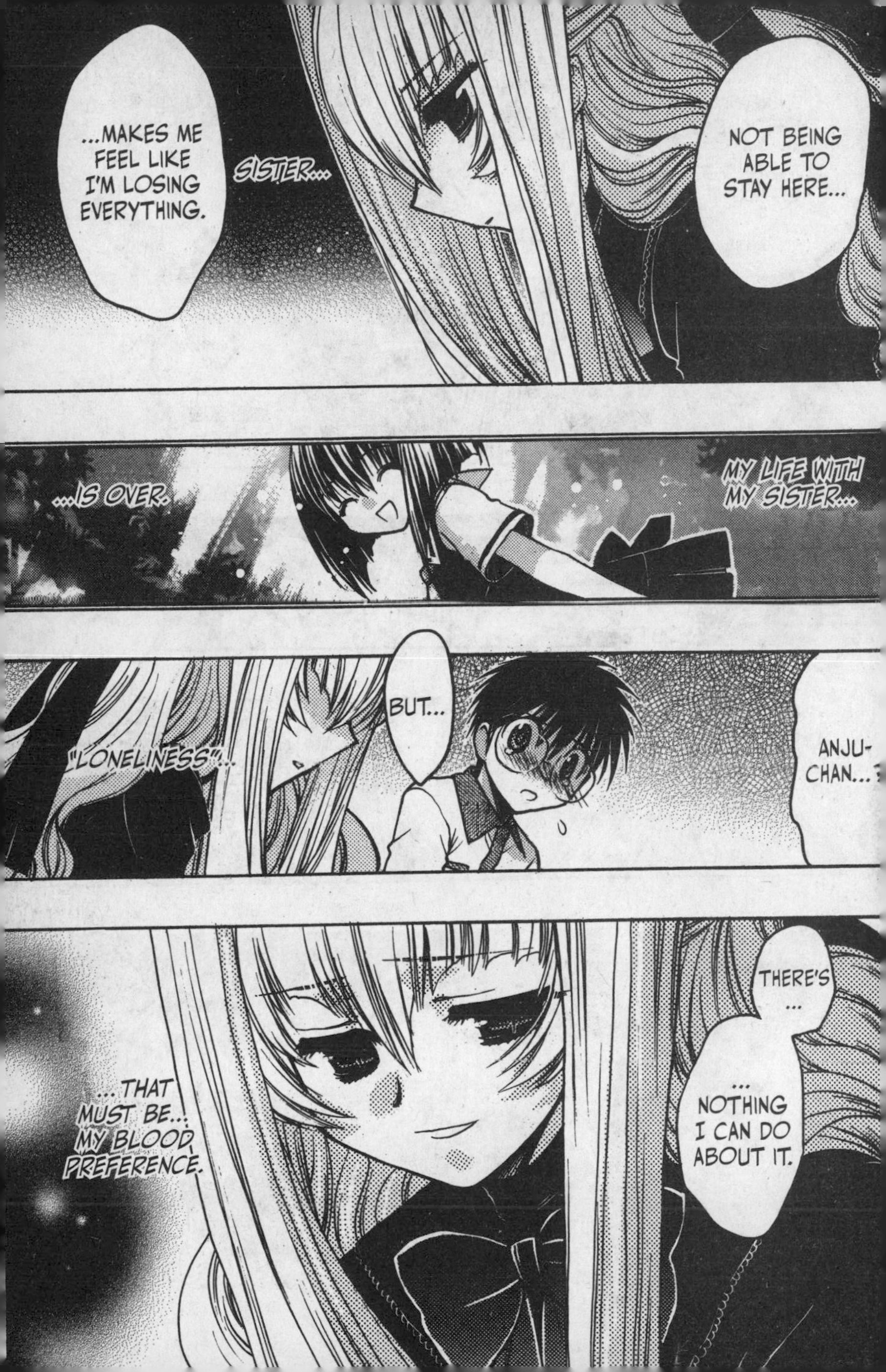
NOT BEING ABLE TO STAY HERE...
SISTER...
...MAKES ME FEEL LIKE I'M LOSING EVERYTHING.
MY LIFE WITH MY SISTER...
...IS OVER.
ANJU-CHAN...?
BUT...
"LONELINESS"...
THERE'S ...
... NOTHING I CAN DO ABOUT IT.
...THAT MUST BE... MY BLOOD PREFERENCE.

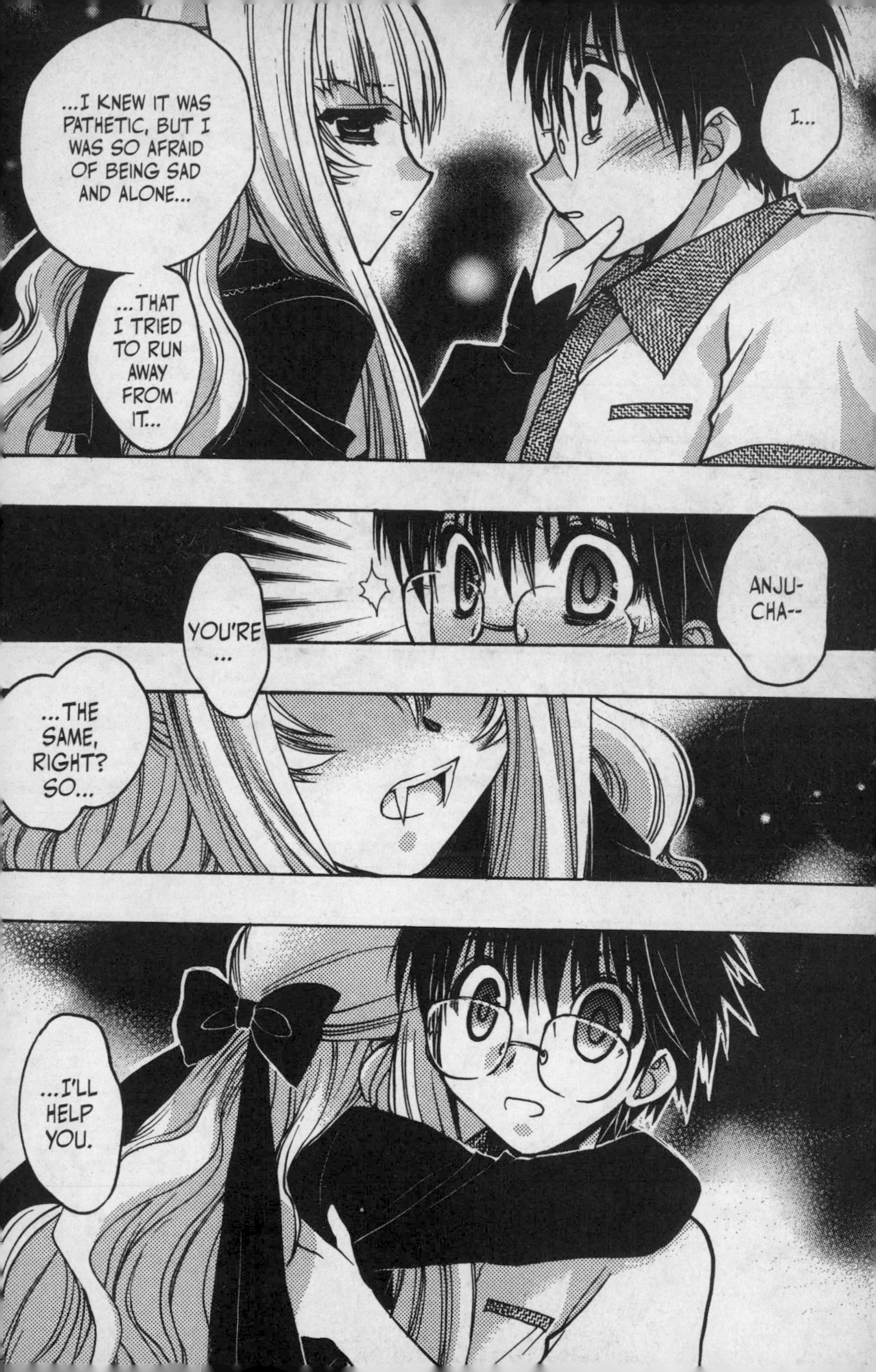
I...
...I KNEW IT WAS PATHETIC, BUT I WAS SO AFRAID OF BEING SAD AND ALONE...
...THAT I TRIED TO RUN AWAY FROM IT...
ANJU-CHA--
YOU'RE ...
...THE SAME, RIGHT? SO...
...I'LL HELP YOU.

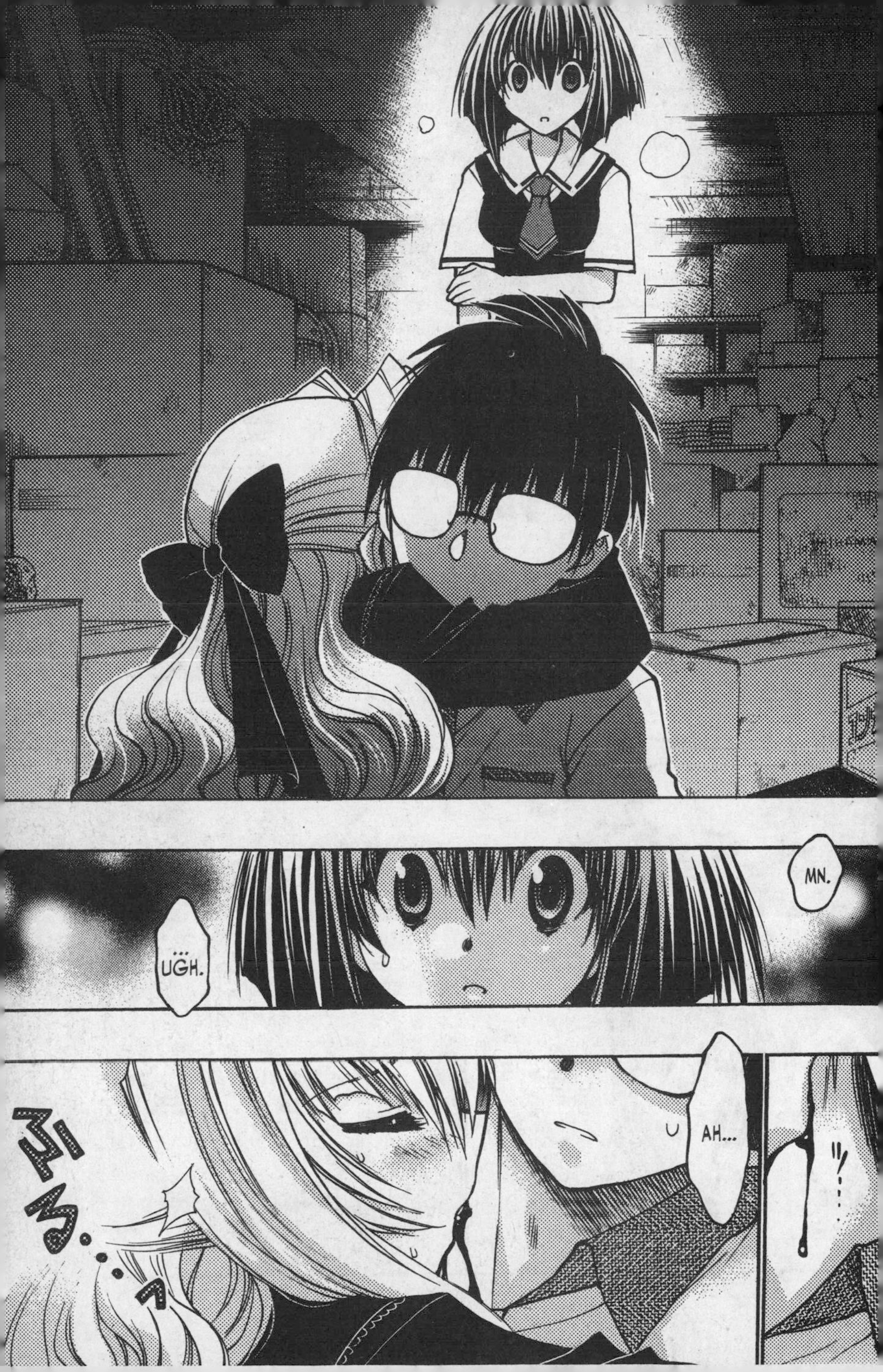
MN.
...UGH.
AH...
ぷつ…っ

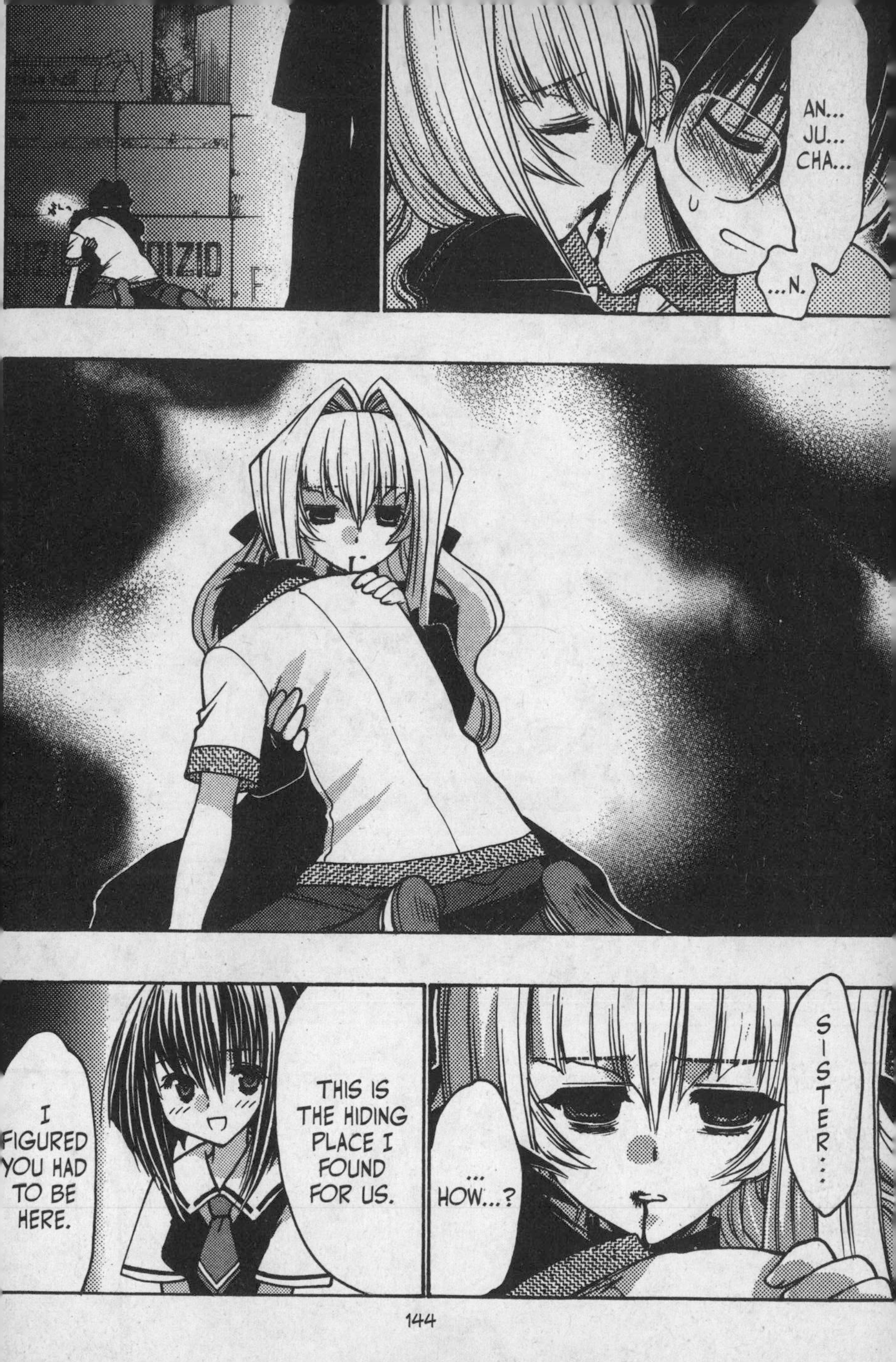

AN... JU... CHA...
...N.
SISTER...
... HOW...?
THIS IS THE HIDING PLACE I FOUND FOR US.
I FIGURED YOU HAD TO BE HERE.

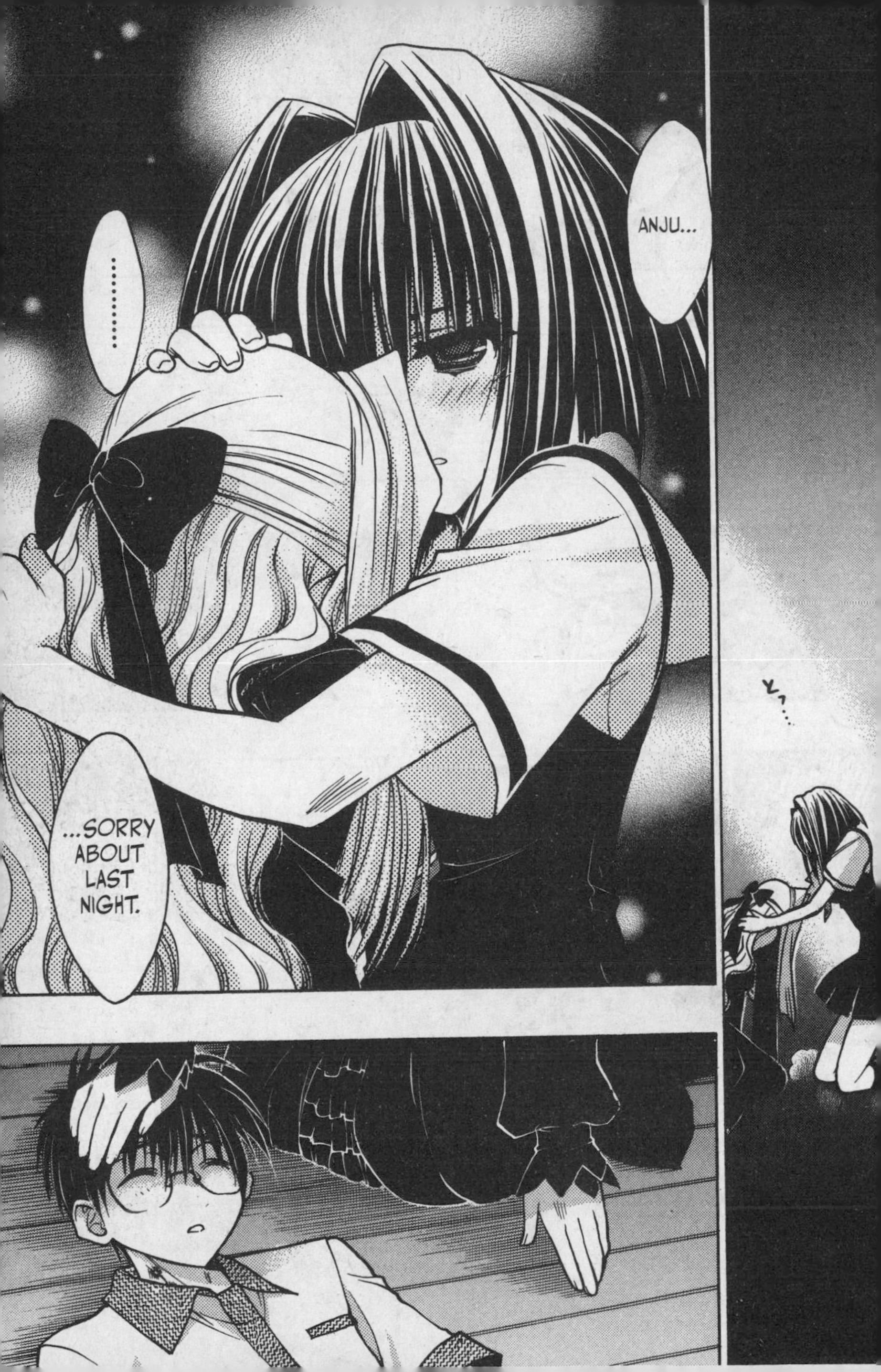
ANJU...
......
...SORRY ABOUT LAST NIGHT.

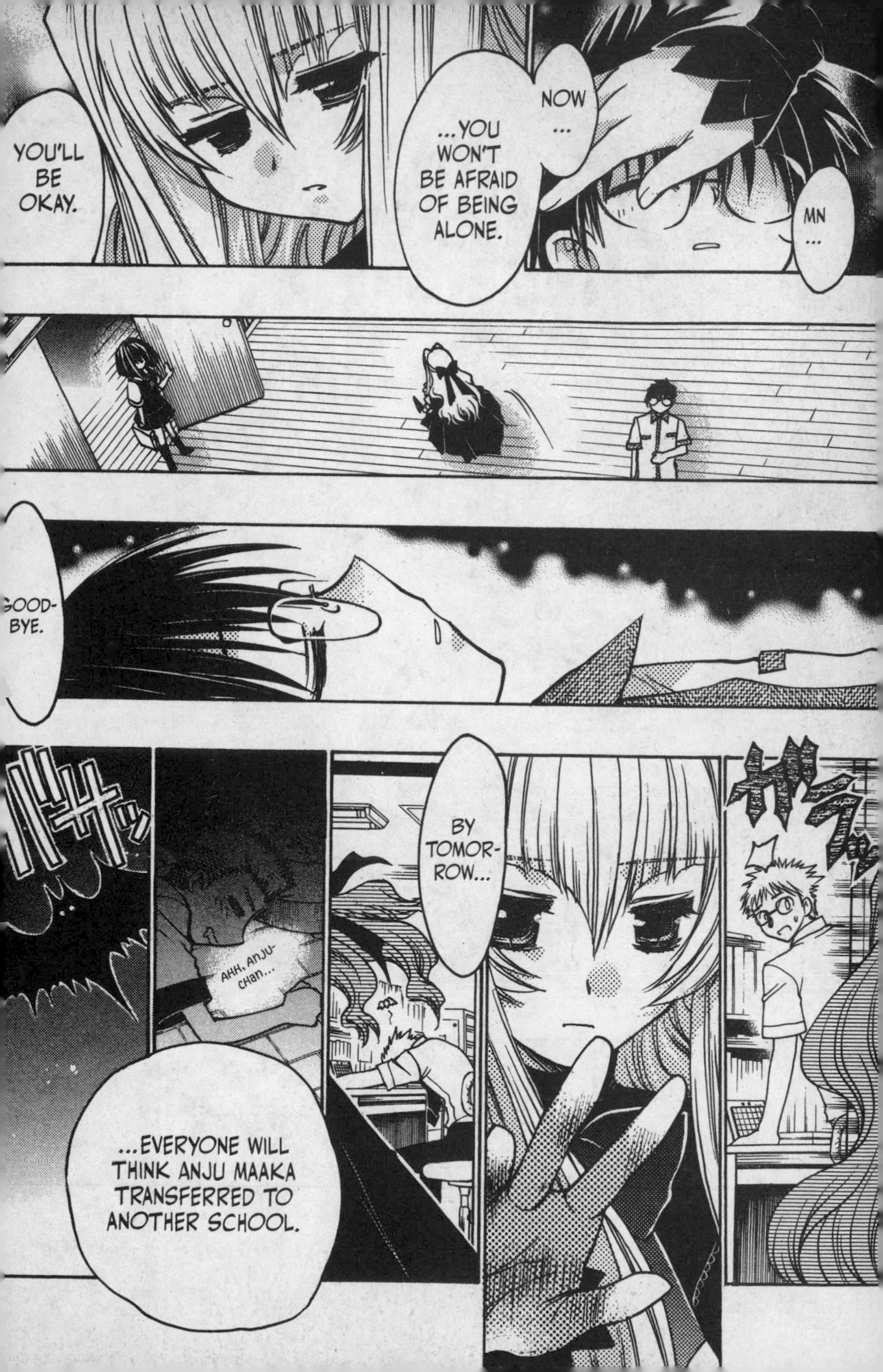
NOW ...
...YOU WON'T BE AFRAID OF BEING ALONE.
MN ...
YOU'LL BE OKAY.
GOOD-BYE.
BY TOMORROW...
...EVERYONE WILL THINK ANJU MAAKA TRANSFERRED TO ANOTHER SCHOOL.
AHH, ANJU-CHAN...

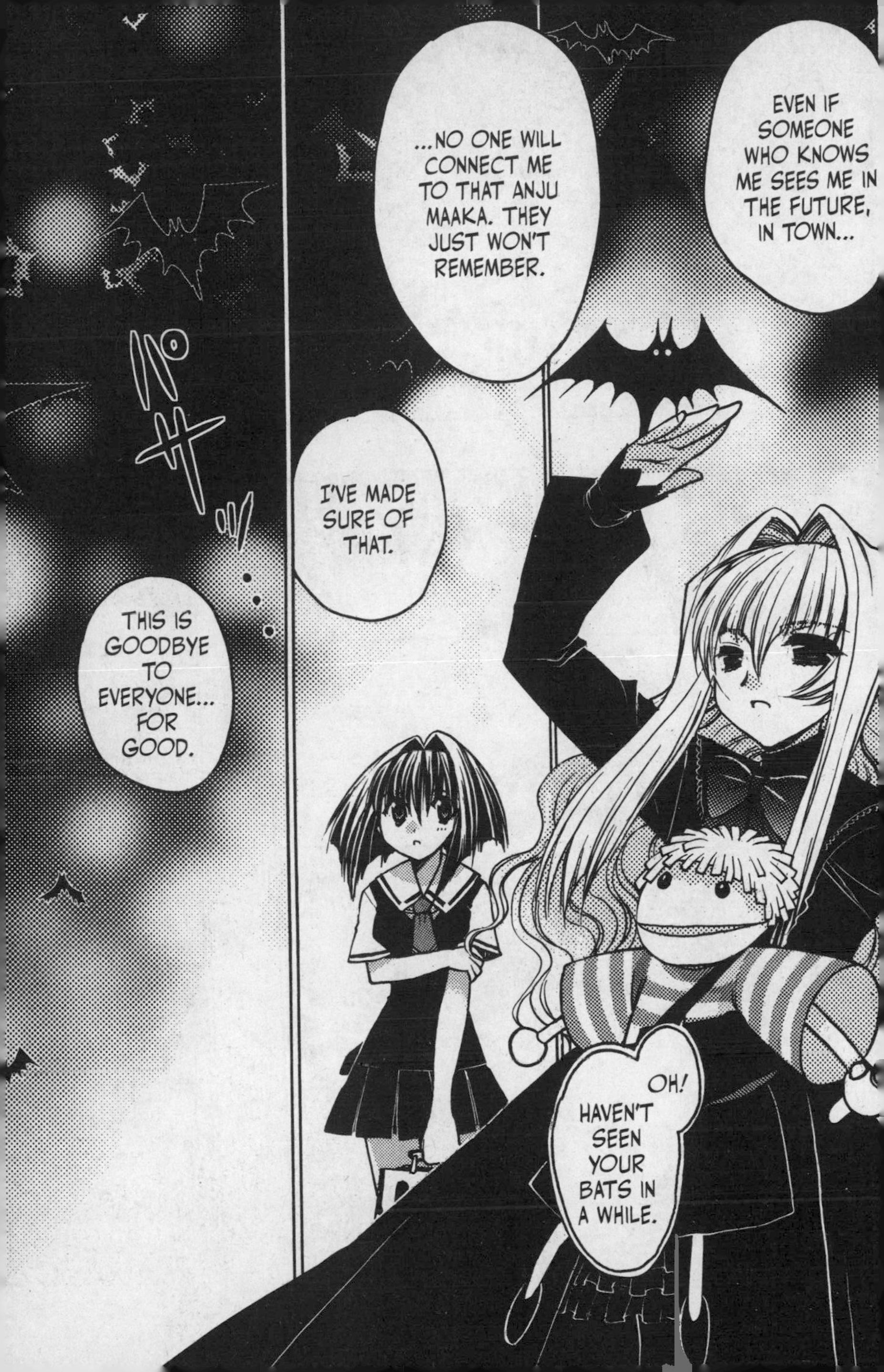
EVEN IF SOMEONE WHO KNOWS ME SEES ME IN THE FUTURE, IN TOWN...
...NO ONE WILL CONNECT ME TO THAT ANJU MAAKA. THEY JUST WON'T REMEMBER.
I'VE MADE SURE OF THAT.
OH! HAVEN'T SEEN YOUR BATS IN A WHILE.
THIS IS GOODBYE TO EVERYONE... FOR GOOD.

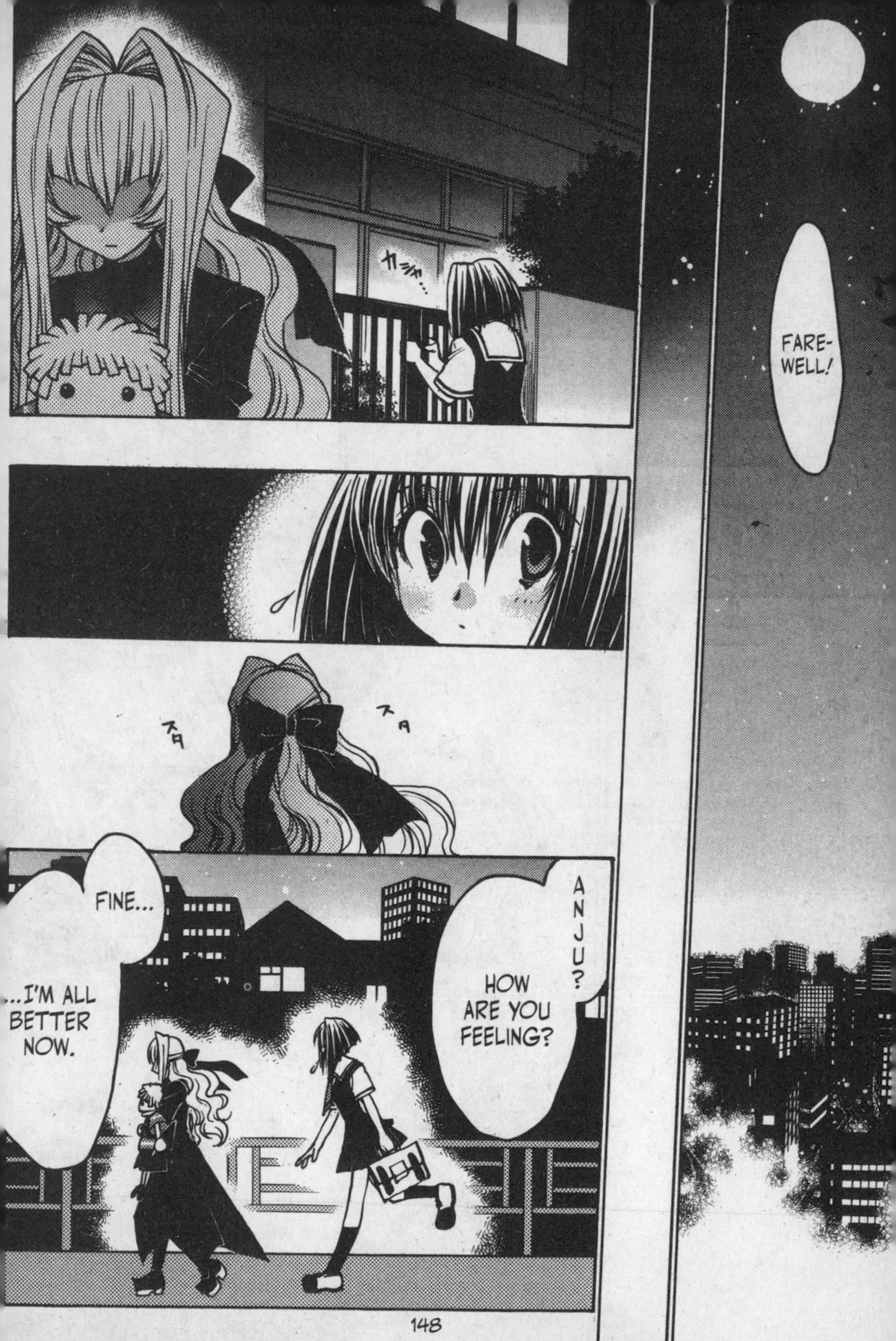
FARE-WELL!
カシャ…
スタ
スタ
ANJU?
HOW ARE YOU FEELING?
FINE...
...I'M ALL BETTER NOW.

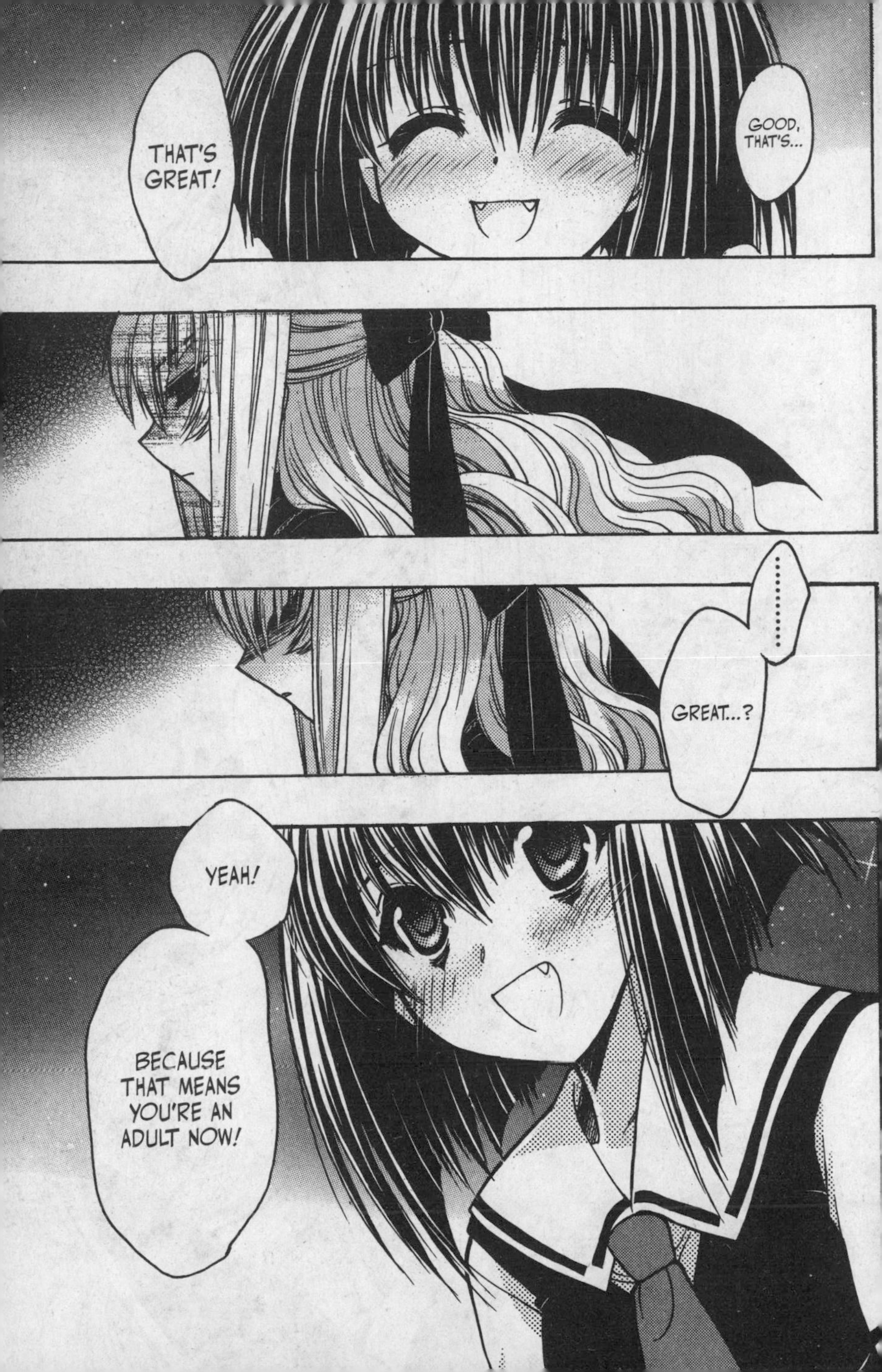
GOOD, THAT'S...
THAT'S GREAT!
......
GREAT...?
YEAH!
BECAUSE THAT MEANS YOU'RE AN ADULT NOW!

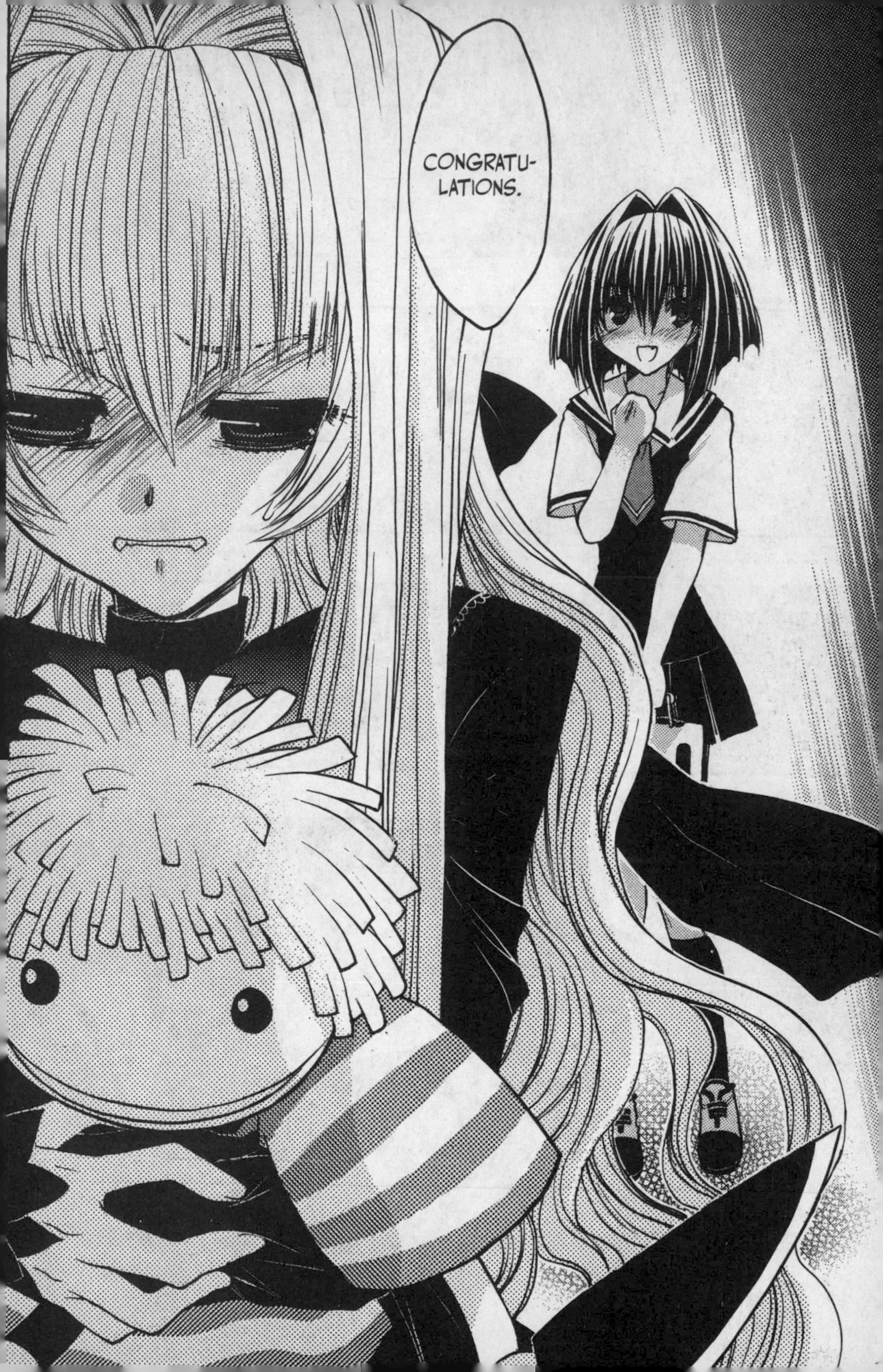
CONGRATU-LATIONS.

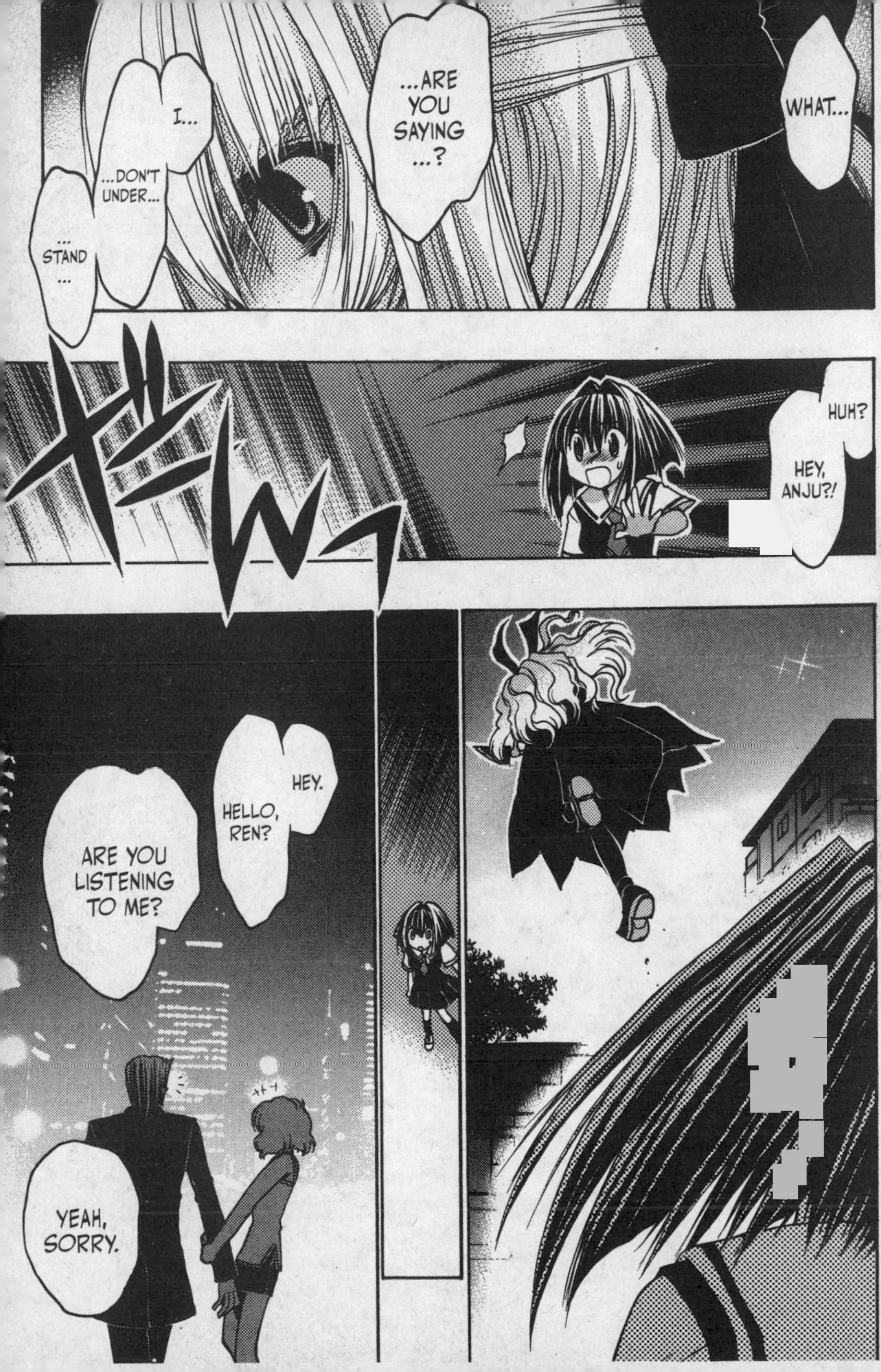
WHAT...
...ARE YOU SAYING ...?
I...
...DON'T UNDER...
... STAND ...
HUH?
HEY, ANJU?!
HEY.
HELLO, REN?
ARE YOU LISTENING TO ME?
YEAH, SORRY.

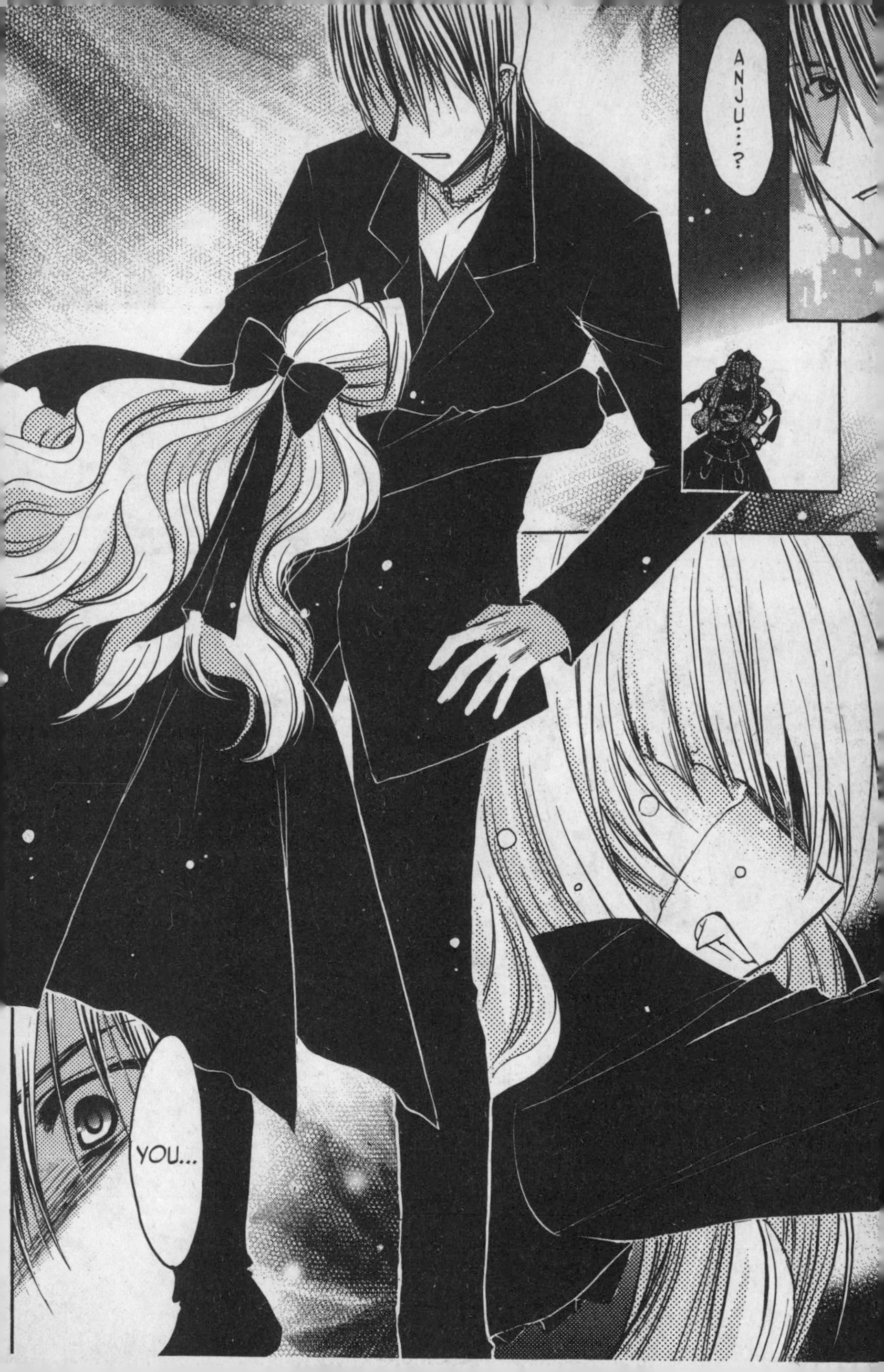
ANJU...?
YOU...

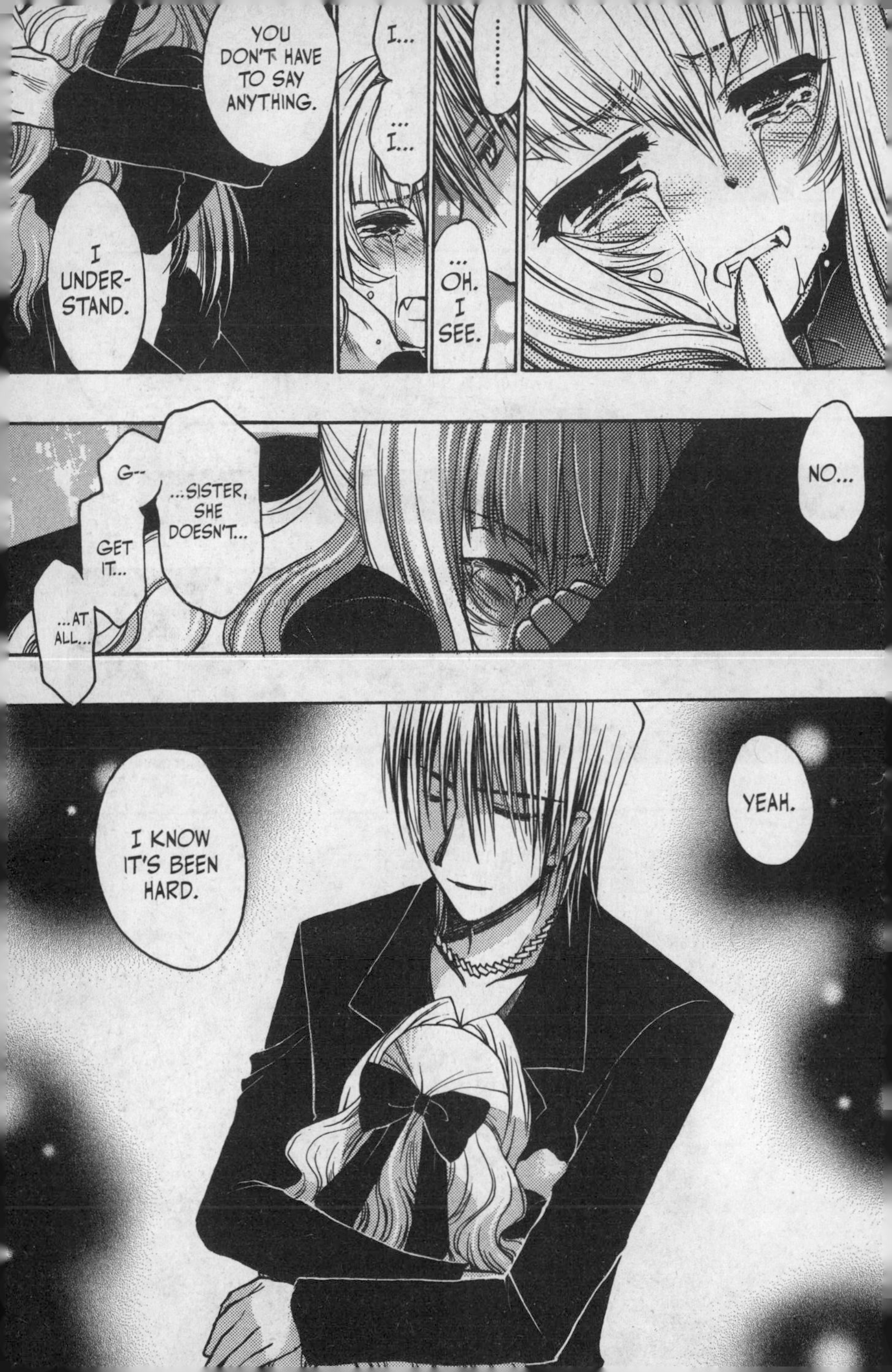
......
...OH. I SEE.
I...
...I...
YOU DON'T HAVE TO SAY ANYTHING.
I UNDERSTAND.
NO...
...SISTER, SHE DOESN'T...
G--
GET IT...
...AT ALL...
YEAH.
I KNOW IT'S BEEN HARD.

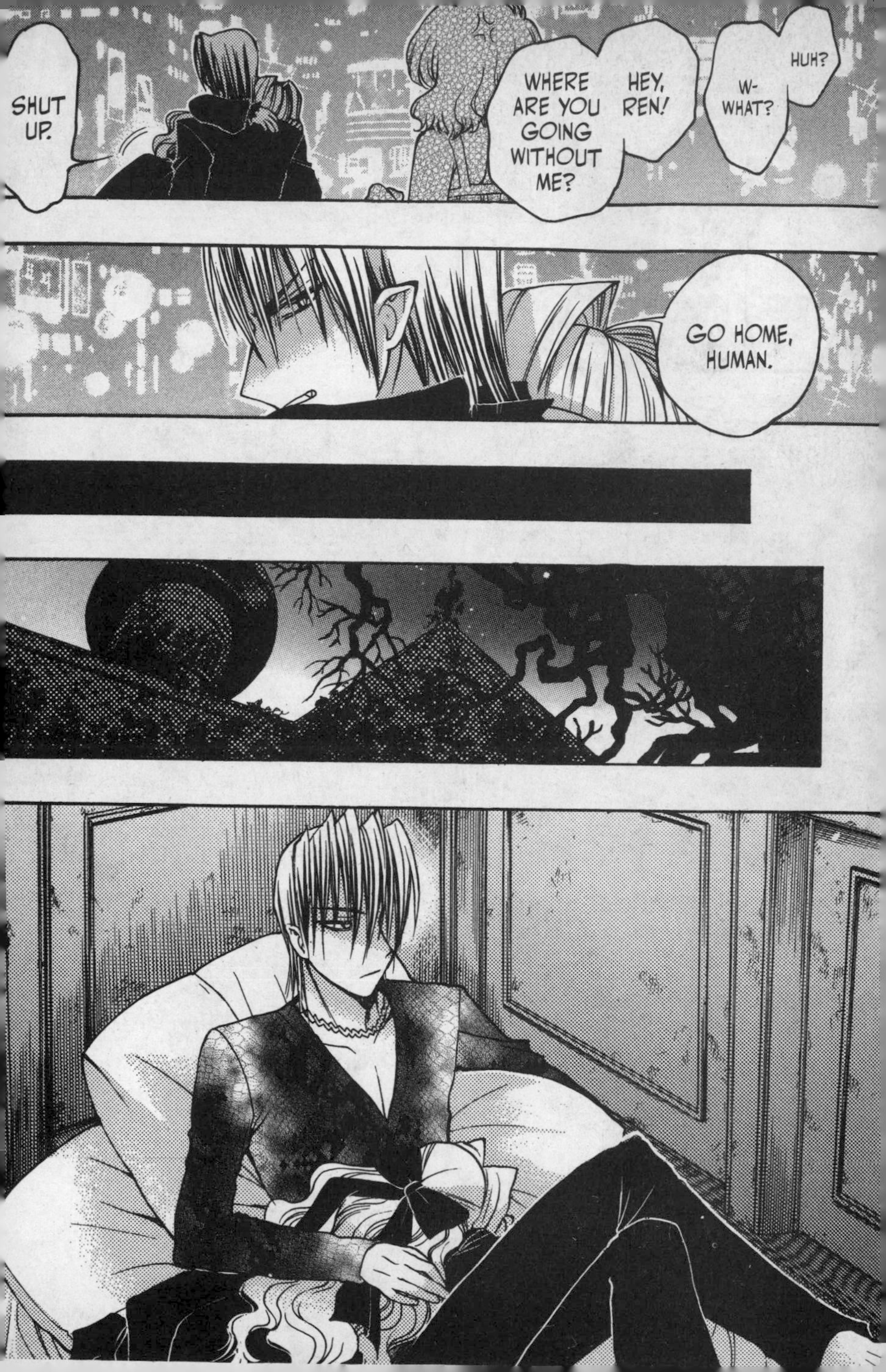
HUH?
W-WHAT?
HEY, REN!
WHERE ARE YOU GOING WITHOUT ME?
SHUT UP.
GO HOME, HUMAN.

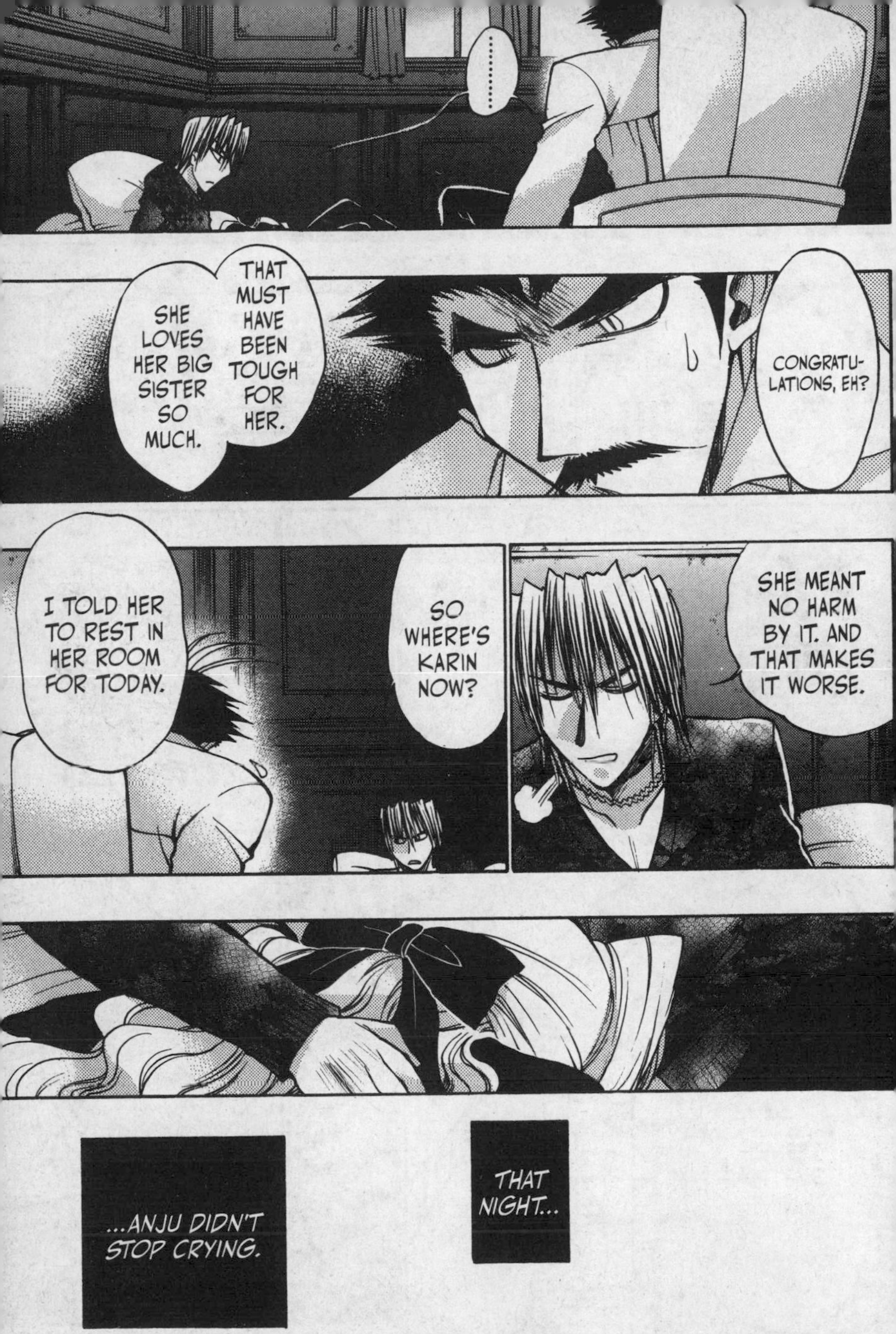
......
CONGRATU-LATIONS, EH?
THAT MUST HAVE BEEN TOUGH FOR HER.
SHE LOVES HER BIG SISTER SO MUCH.
SHE MEANT NO HARM BY IT. AND THAT MAKES IT WORSE.
SO WHERE'S KARIN NOW?
I TOLD HER TO REST IN HER ROOM FOR TODAY.
THAT NIGHT...
...ANJU DIDN'T STOP CRYING.

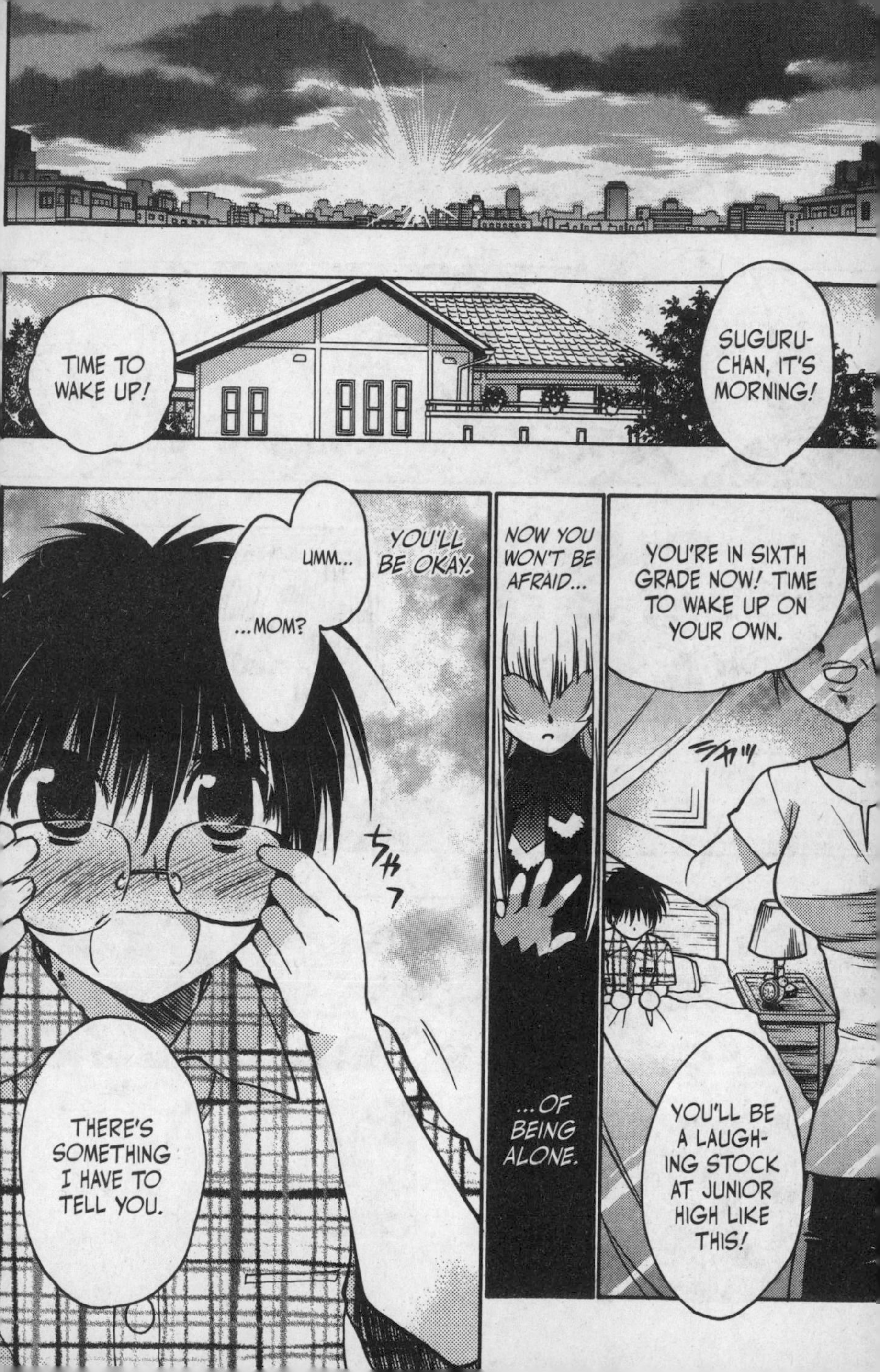
SUGURU-CHAN, IT'S MORNING!
TIME TO WAKE UP!
YOU'RE IN SIXTH GRADE NOW! TIME TO WAKE UP ON YOUR OWN.
YOU'LL BE A LAUGHING-STOCK AT JUNIOR HIGH LIKE THIS!
NOW YOU WON'T BE AFRAID...
...OF BEING ALONE.
YOU'LL BE OKAY.
UMM... ...MOM?
THERE'S SOMETHING I HAVE TO TELL YOU.

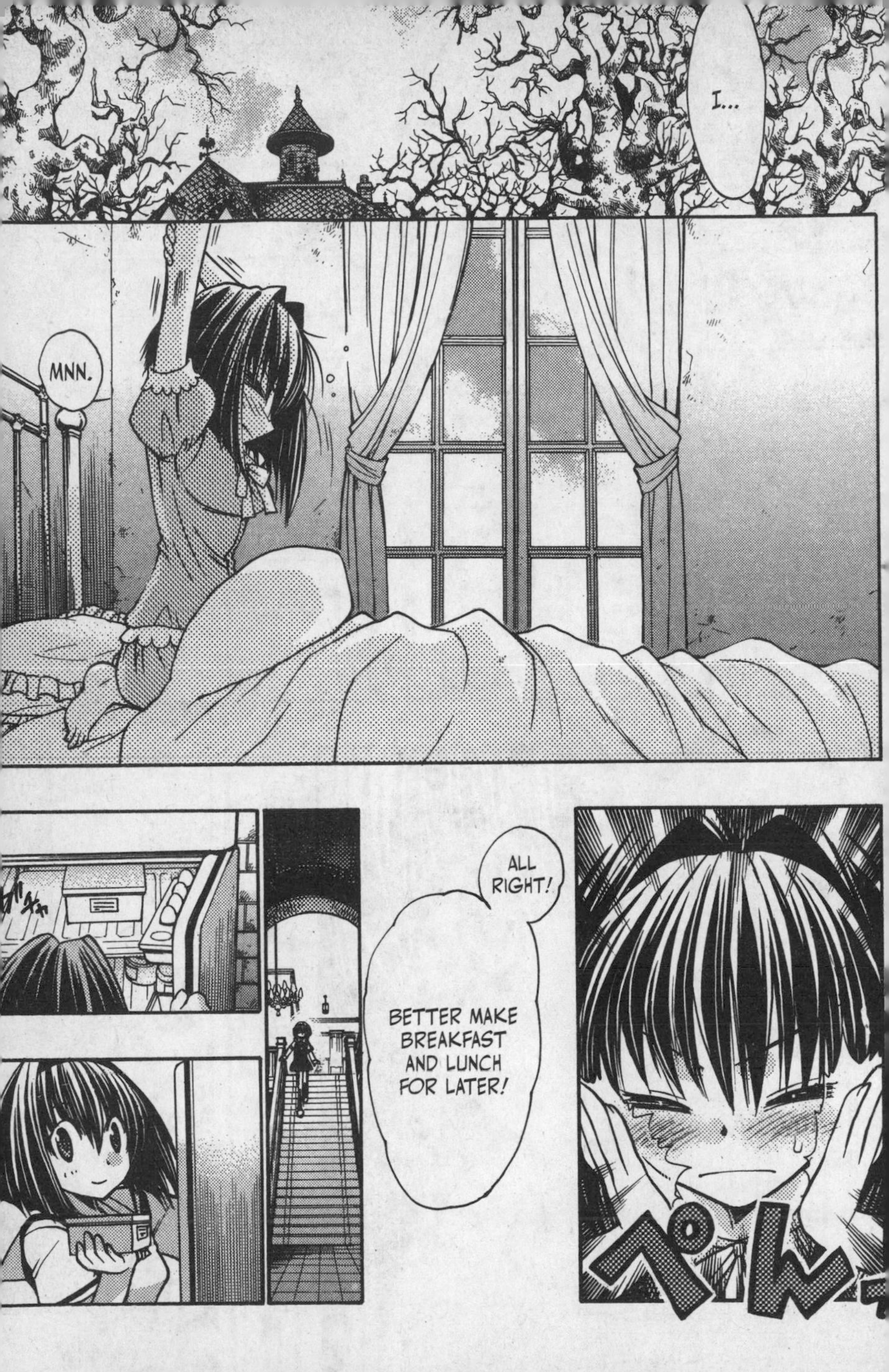
I...
MNN.
ALL RIGHT!
BETTER MAKE BREAKFAST AND LUNCH FOR LATER!

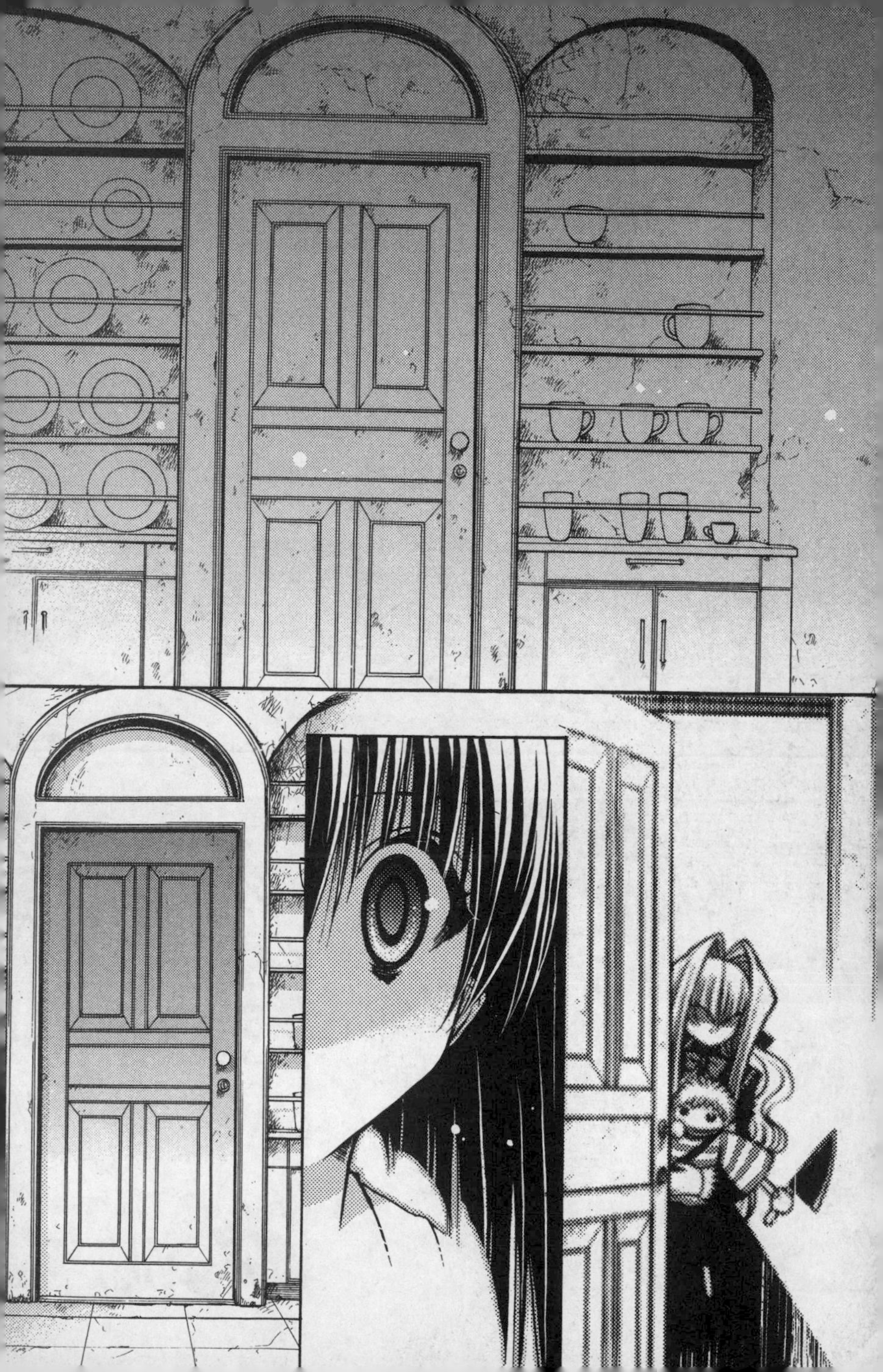

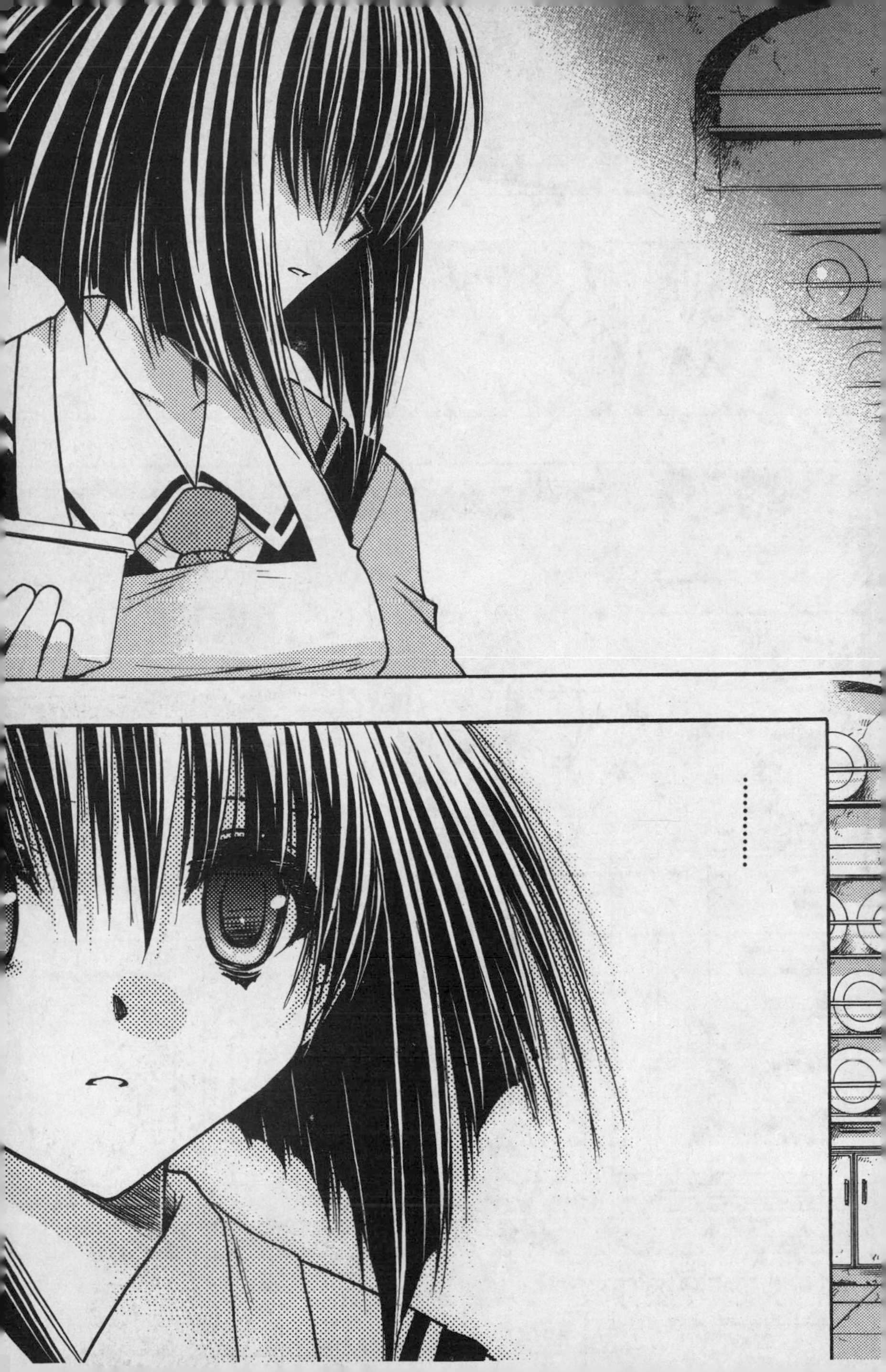
……

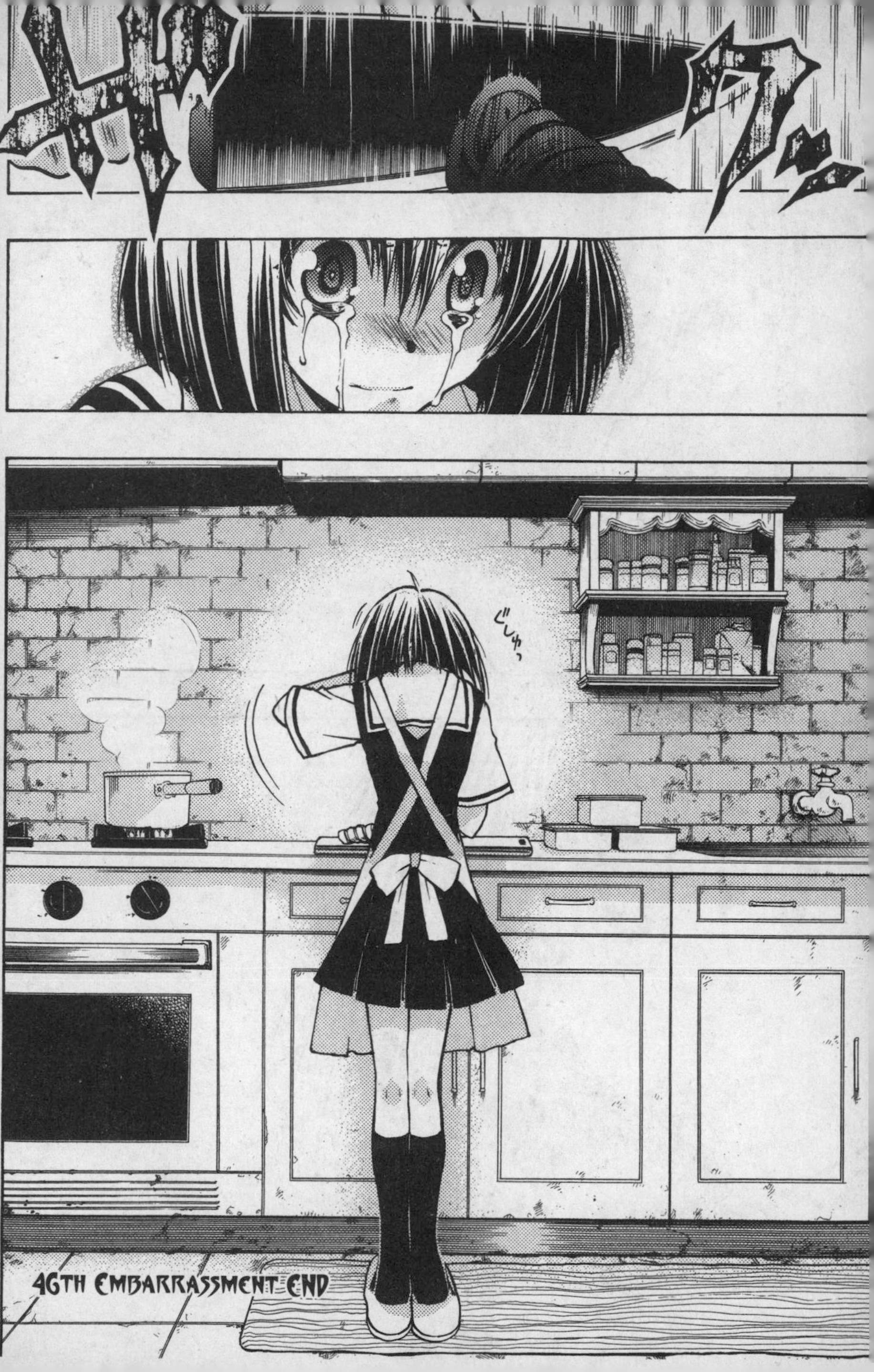
46TH EMBARRASSMENT END

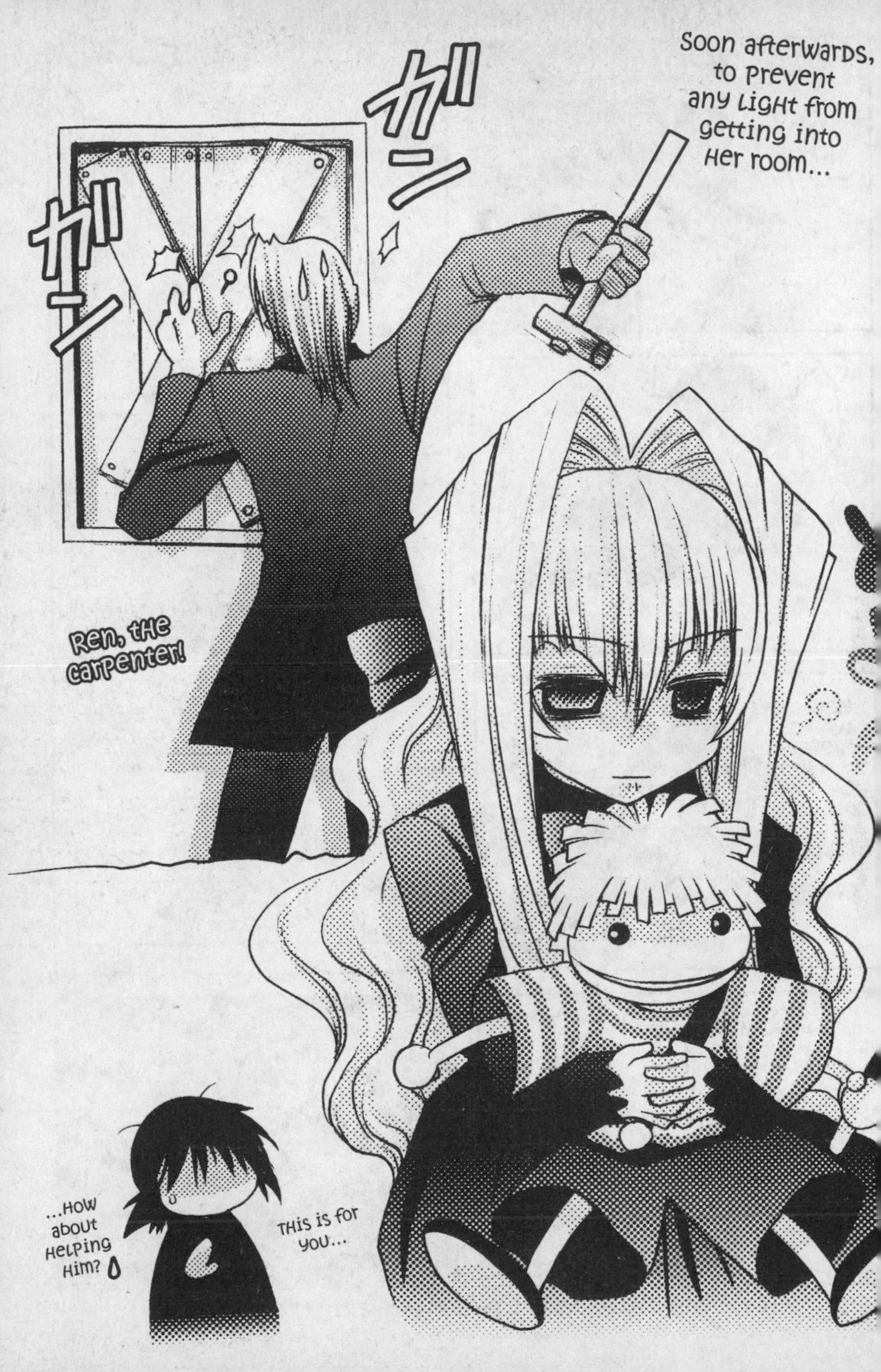
Soon afterwards, to prevent any light from getting into her room...
Ren, the carpenter!
This is for you...
...How about helping him?

AS I WAS FINISHING THIS VOLUME...

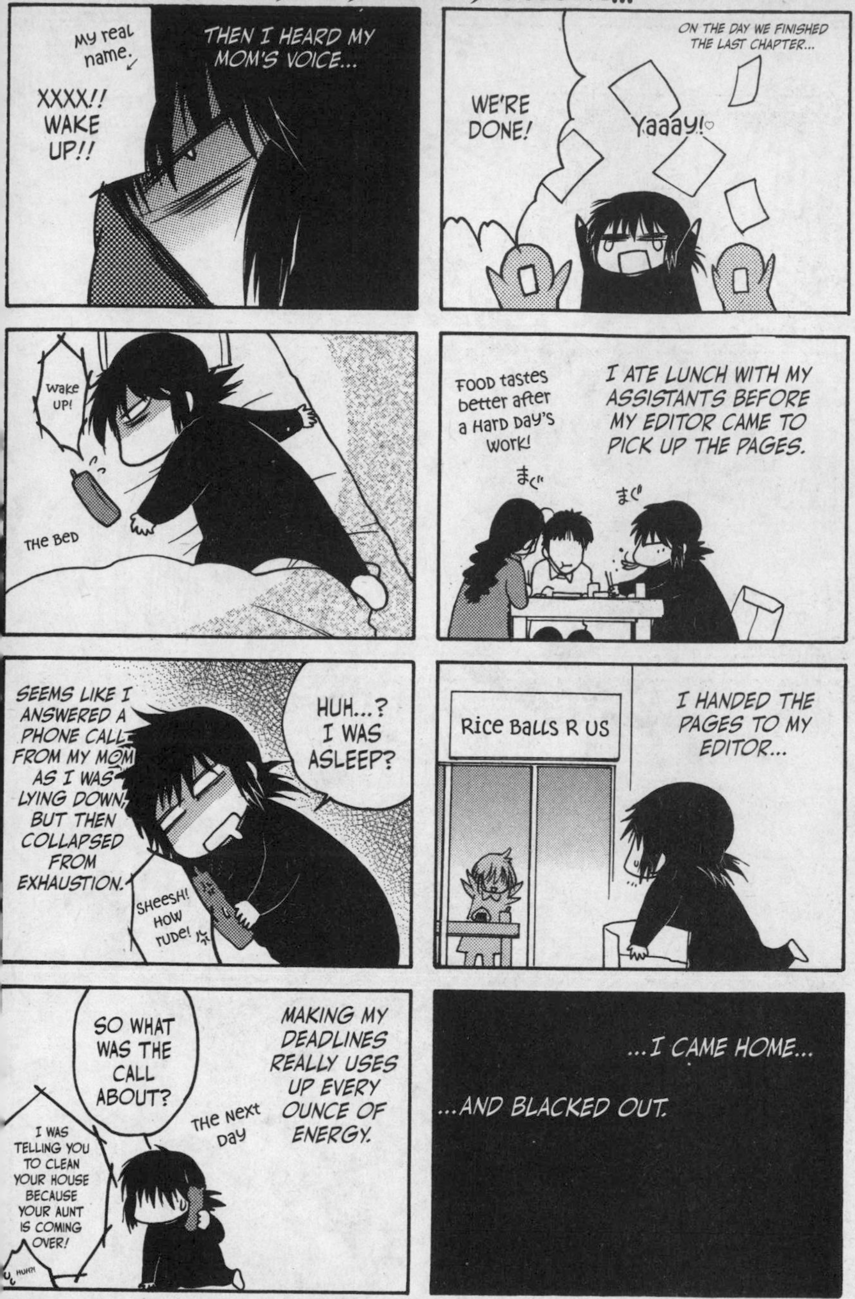
ON THE DAY WE FINISHED THE LAST CHAPTER...
WE'RE DONE!
Yaaay!♡
I ATE LUNCH WITH MY ASSISTANTS BEFORE MY EDITOR CAME TO PICK UP THE PAGES.
Food tastes better after a Hard Day's work!
まぐ
まぐ
I HANDED THE PAGES TO MY EDITOR...
Rice Balls R US
...I CAME HOME...
...AND BLACKED OUT.
THEN I HEARD MY MOM'S VOICE...
My real name.
XXXX!! WAKE UP!!
Wake up!
The Bed
SEEMS LIKE I ANSWERED A PHONE CALL FROM MY MOM AS I WAS LYING DOWN, BUT THEN COLLAPSED FROM EXHAUSTION.
HUH...? I WAS ASLEEP?
SHEESH! HOW rude!
MAKING MY DEADLINES REALLY USES UP EVERY OUNCE OF ENERGY.
The Next Day
SO WHAT WAS THE CALL ABOUT?
I WAS TELLING YOU TO CLEAN YOUR HOUSE BECAUSE YOUR AUNT IS COMING OVER!
HUH?!

Fainting WHILE on THE PHONE was a first for me!

CLUMSY VS. CLUMSY

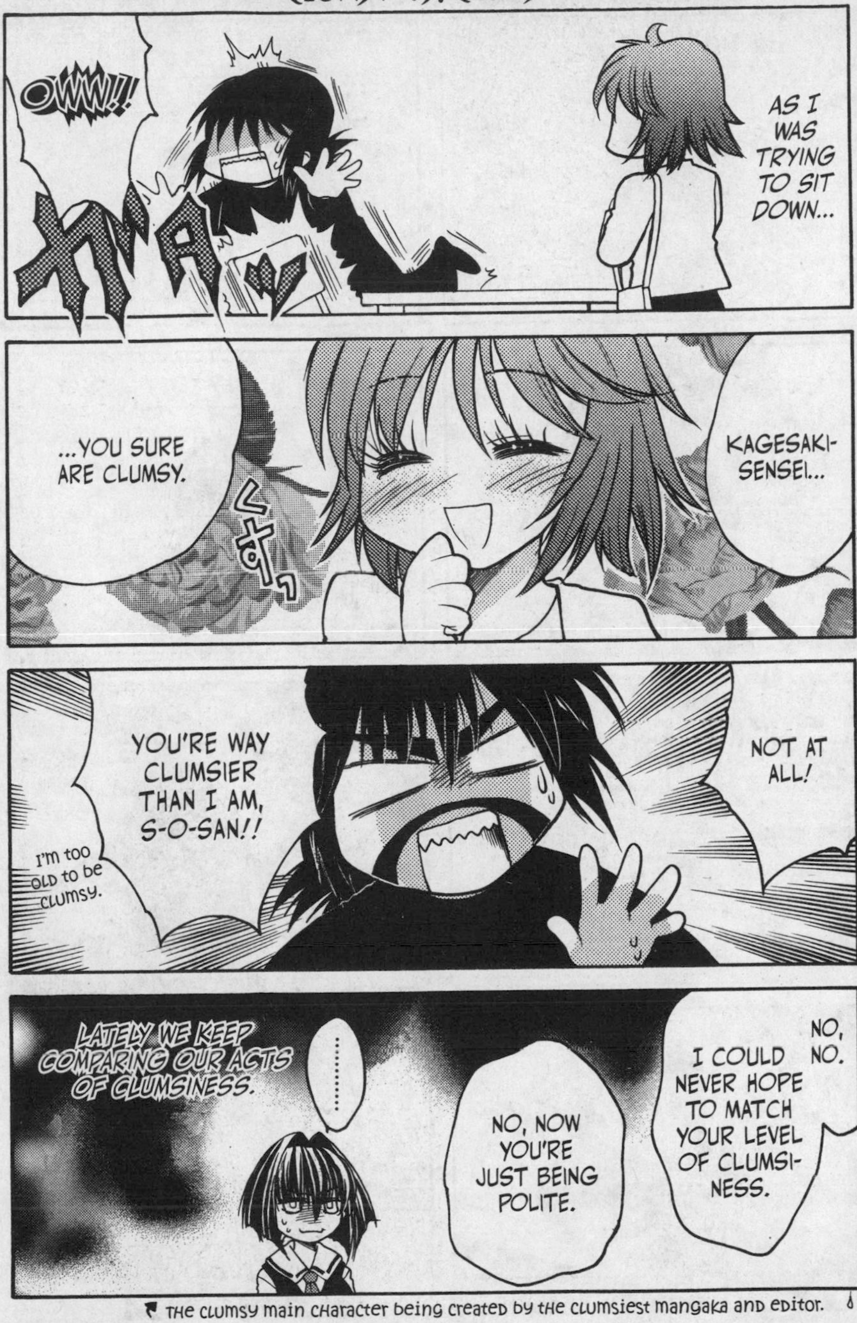
AS I WAS TRYING TO SIT DOWN...
OWW!!
KAGESAKI-SENSEI...
...YOU SURE ARE CLUMSY.
くすっ
NOT AT ALL!
YOU'RE WAY CLUMSIER THAN I AM, S-O-SAN!!
I'm too old to be clumsy.
NO, NO.
I COULD NEVER HOPE TO MATCH YOUR LEVEL OF CLUMSI-NESS.
NO, NOW YOU'RE JUST BEING POLITE.
......
LATELY WE KEEP COMPARING OUR ACTS OF CLUMSINESS.

↖ The clumsy main character being created by the clumsiest mangaka and editor.

HARD WORK DOESN'T ALWAYS PAY OFF

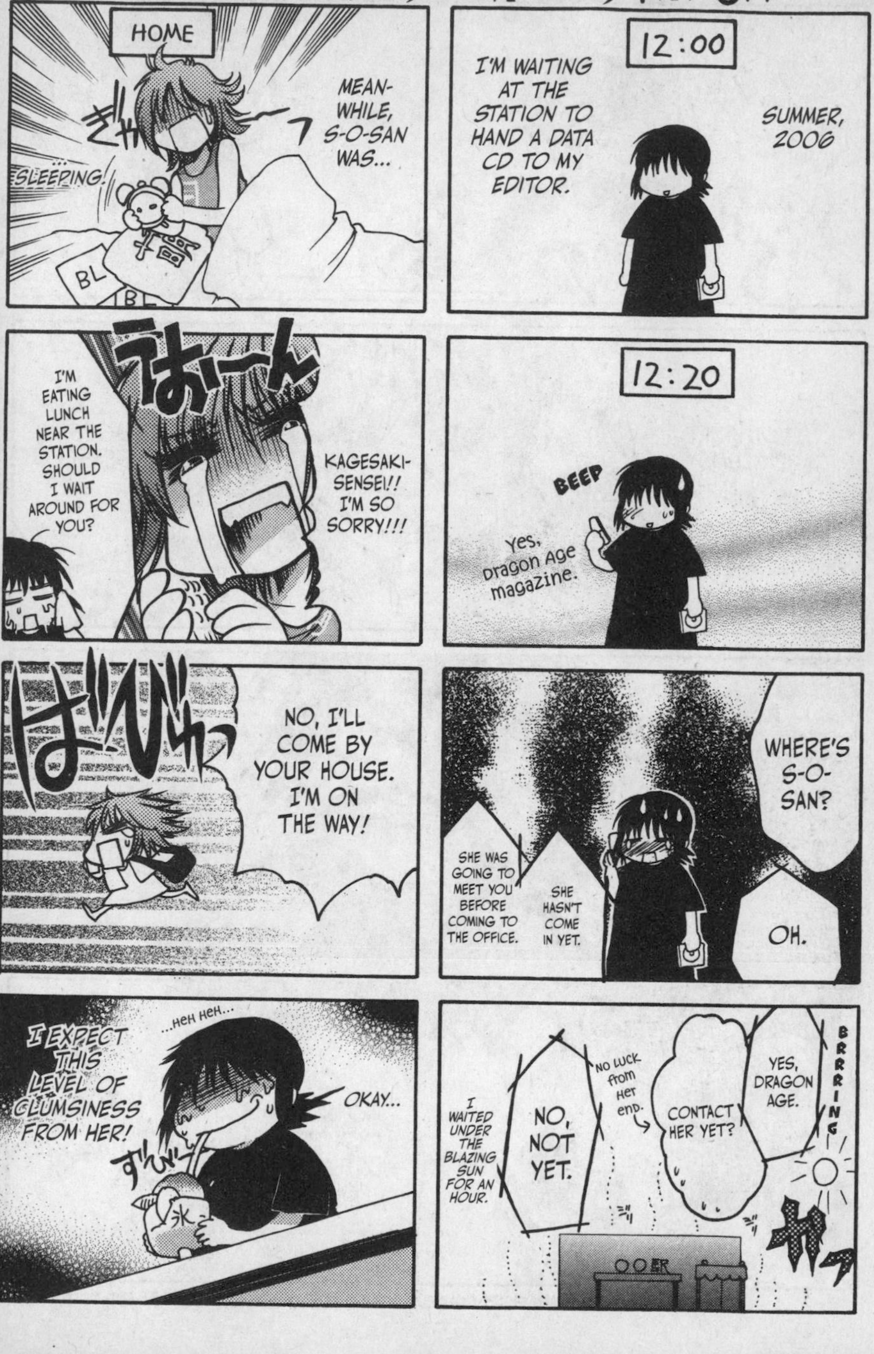
12:00
SUMMER, 2006
I'M WAITING AT THE STATION TO HAND A DATA CD TO MY EDITOR.
HOME
MEAN-WHILE, S-O-SAN WAS...
...SLEEPING!
12:20
BEEP
Yes, Dragon Age magazine.
KAGESAKI-SENSEI!! I'M SO SORRY!!!
I'M EATING LUNCH NEAR THE STATION. SHOULD I WAIT AROUND FOR YOU?
WHERE'S S-O-SAN?
OH.
SHE HASN'T COME IN YET.
SHE WAS GOING TO MEET YOU BEFORE COMING TO THE OFFICE.
NO, I'LL COME BY YOUR HOUSE. I'M ON THE WAY!
BRRRING
YES, DRAGON AGE.
CONTACT HER YET?
No luck from her end.
NO, NOT YET.
I WAITED UNDER THE BLAZING SUN FOR AN HOUR.
OKAY...
...HEH HEH...
I EXPECT THIS LEVEL OF CLUMSINESS FROM HER!

MAKE UP WITH MELON

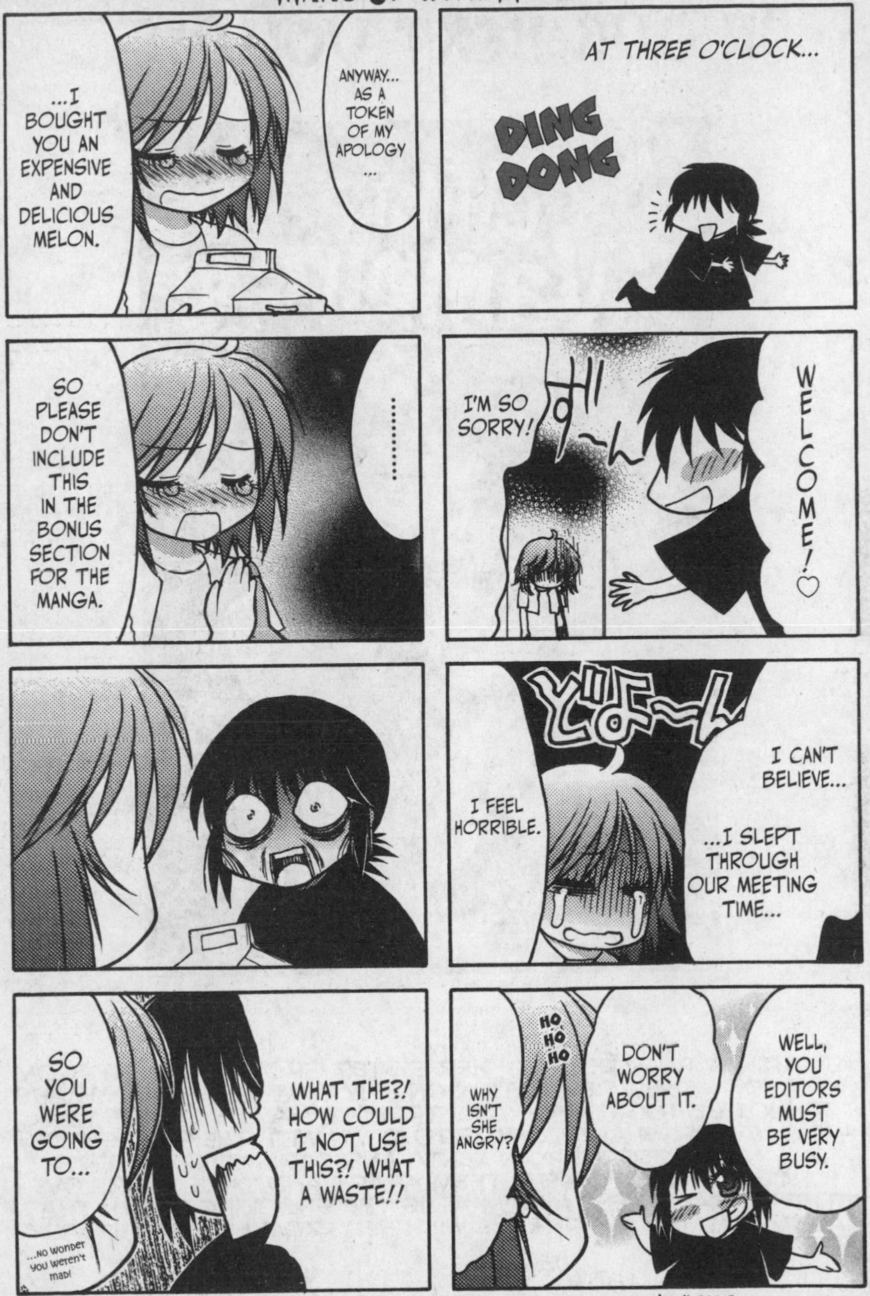
AT THREE O'CLOCK...
DING DONG
ANYWAY... AS A TOKEN OF MY APOLOGY...
...I BOUGHT YOU AN EXPENSIVE AND DELICIOUS MELON.
WELCOME! ♡
I'M SO SORRY!
....
SO PLEASE DON'T INCLUDE THIS IN THE BONUS SECTION FOR THE MANGA.
I CAN'T BELIEVE...
...I SLEPT THROUGH OUR MEETING TIME...
I FEEL HORRIBLE.
WELL, YOU EDITORS MUST BE VERY BUSY.
DON'T WORRY ABOUT IT.
HO HO HO
WHY ISN'T SHE ANGRY?
WHAT THE?! HOW COULD I NOT USE THIS?! WHAT A WASTE!!
SO YOU WERE GOING TO...
...NO WONDER YOU WEREN'T MAD!

"Lies, all lies... Err, I'm really sorry. It won't happen again." BY S-O

IN OUR NEXT VOLUME...

chibi Vampire
TOKYOPOP
Created By:
Yuna Kagesaki
12

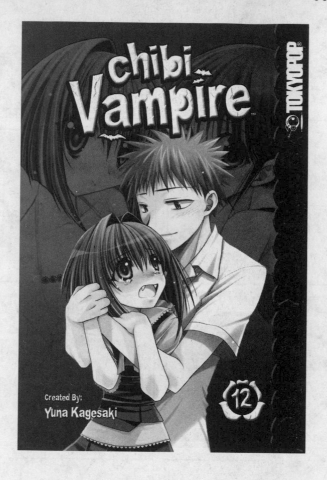

AS KARIN STRUGGLES WITH HER SISTER GROWING APART FROM HER AND THE NEW REVELATION ON WHY VAMPIRES AND HUMANS CANNOT BE TOGETHER, MORE TROUBLE MAY BE ON THE WAY. NEW VAMPIRES ARE COMING TO TOWN WITH THEIR EYES SET ON KARIN'S SECRET. CAN KENTA AND KARIN OVERCOME THE FORCES TRYING TO KEEP THEM APART AND TAKE THEIR LOVE TO THE NEXT LEVEL? AND WHAT IS THE SHOCKING TRUTH THAT CALERA HAS BROUGHT HOME WITH HER FROM HER BIRTHPLACE?

ANJU ALLIANCE

Sorry for being so cold to you...
...I was just... embarrassed.
The truth is...
...I love you.
かぁぁ…っ
AND THAT'S WHEN I WOKE UP FROM THE DREAM! HAH HAH HAH!
MAN, SO THAT'S HOW ANJU-CHAN REALLY IS!
So cute!!
AM2:00
UMM, SERA-KUN... YOU CAN TELL ME ABOUT YOUR DREAM AT SCHOOL TOMORROW... I'M HANGING UP NOW.
HONESTLY, I'M JEALOUS OF HIS TWISTED FANTASIES!

I want to Dream about Anju-Chan, too!! YeaH!

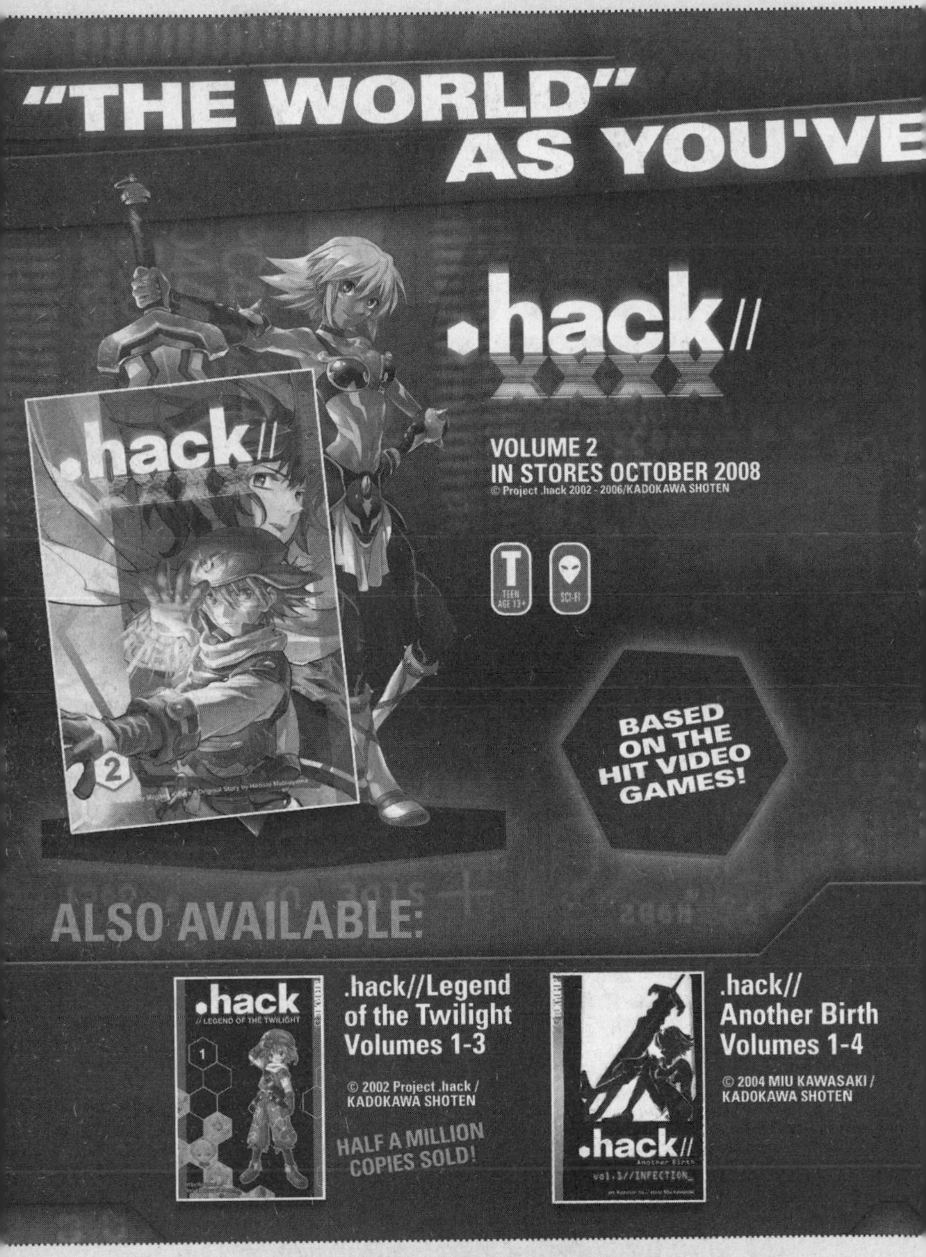
"THE WORLD" AS YOU'VE
.hack//XXXX
VOLUME 2
IN STORES OCTOBER 2008
© Project .hack 2002 - 2006/KADOKAWA SHOTEN
T TEEN AGE 13+
SCI-FI
.hack//
2
BASED ON THE HIT VIDEO GAMES!
ALSO AVAILABLE:
.hack // LEGEND OF THE TWILIGHT
1
.hack//Legend of the Twilight Volumes 1-3
© 2002 Project .hack / KADOKAWA SHOTEN
HALF A MILLION COPIES SOLD!
.hack//
Another Birth
vol.1//INFECTION_
.hack// Another Birth Volumes 1-4
© 2004 MIU KAWASAKI / KADOKAWA SHOTEN

FOR MORE INFORMATION VISIT:

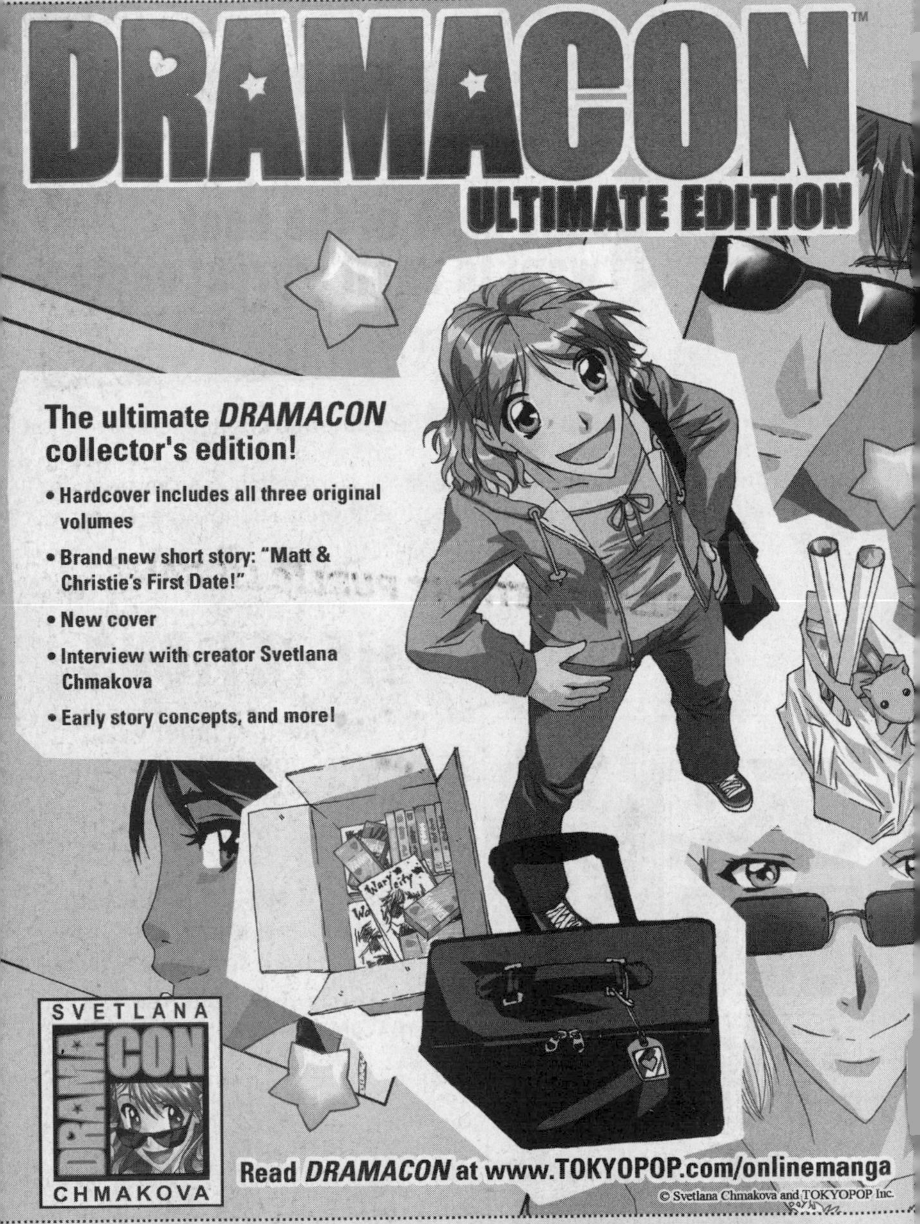
DRAMACON™
ULTIMATE EDITION
The ultimate DRAMACON collector's edition!
• Hardcover includes all three original volumes
• Brand new short story: "Matt & Christie's First Date!"
• New cover
• Interview with creator Svetlana Chmakova
• Early story concepts, and more!
SVETLANA
DRAMACON
CHMAKOVA
Read DRAMACON at www.TOKYOPOP.com/onlinemanga
© Svetlana Chmakova and TOKYOPOP Inc.

STOP!

This i
You wouldn't !

This book is printed "manga-style," in the authentic Japanese right-to-left format. Since none of the artwork has been flipped or altered, readers get to experience the story just as the creator intended. You've been asking for it, so TOKYOPOP® delivered: authentic, hot-off-the-press, and far more fun!

DIRECTIONS

1
2
3
4
5
6
7
8
9
10

If this is your first time reading manga-style, here's a quick guide to help you understand how it works.

It's easy... just start in the top right panel and follow the numbers. Have fun, and look for more 100% authentic manga from TOKYOPOP®!

THE MANGA REVOLUTION · LEADING 漫画革命